## About th

*New York Times* and *USA Today* bestselling a
**B.J. Daniels** lives in Montana with her husband, Parker,
and two springer spaniels. When not writing, she quilts,
boats and always has a book or two to read. Contact her
at bjdaniels.com, on Facebook or X @bjdanielsauthor

**Rosanna Battigelli** loved reading Mills & Boon novels
as a teenager and dreamed of writing them one day.
Rosanna is the author of: a Gold IPPY Award winning
historical novel, *La Brigantessa*; a fiction collection,
*Pigeon Soup & Other Stories* (a 2021 Finalist, American
BookFest Best Book Awards); and two children's books.
Rosanna is thrilled that her early dream has come true,
with five Mills & Boon romances published so far.

**Maureen Child** is the author of more than 130 romance
novels and novellas that routinely appear on bestseller lists
and have won numerous awards, including the National
Readers' Choice Award. A seven-time nominee for the
prestigious RITA award from Romance Writers of America,
one of her books has been made into a CBS-TV movie
called *The Soul Collector*. Maureen recently moved from
California to the mountains of Utah and is trying to get
used to snow.

# In The Spotlight

# In The Spotlight:
# Written in Passion

B.J. DANIELS

ROSANNA BATTIGELLI

MAUREEN CHILD

MILLS & BOON

All rights reserved including the right of reproduction in whole or in part in any form. This edition is published by arrangement with Harlequin Enterprises ULC.

This is a work of fiction. Names, characters, places, locations and incidents are purely fictional and bear no relationship to any real life individuals, living or dead, or to any actual places, business establishments, locations, events or incidents. Any resemblance is entirely coincidental.

Without limiting the exclusive rights of any author, contributor or the publisher of this publication, any unauthorised use of this publication to train generative artificial intelligence (AI) technologies is expressly prohibited. HarperCollins also exercise their rights under Article 4(3) of the Digital Single Market Directive 2019/790 and expressly reserve this publication from the text and data mining exception.

® and ™ are trademarks owned and used by the trademark owner and/or its licensee. Trademarks marked with ® are registered with the United Kingdom Patent Office and/or the Office for Harmonisation in the Internal Market and in other countries.

First Published in Great Britain 2025
by Mills & Boon, an imprint of HarperCollins*Publishers* Ltd
1 London Bridge Street, London, SE1 9GF

www.harpercollins.co.uk

HarperCollins*Publishers*
Macken House, 39/40 Mayor Street Upper,
Dublin 1, D01 C9W8, Ireland

In The Spotlight: Written in Passion © 2026 Harlequin Enterprises ULC.

*Rogue Gunslinger* © 2018 Barbara Heinlein
*Captivated by Her Italian Boss* © 2018 Rosanna Battigelli
*Fiancé in Name Only* © 2017 Maureen Child

ISBN: 978-0-263-42104-0

MIX
Paper | Supporting
responsible forestry
FSC™ C007454

This book contains FSC™ certified paper and other controlled sources to ensure responsible forest management.

For more information visit: www.harpercollins.co.uk/green

Printed and Bound in the UK using 100% Renewable Electricity at CPI Group (UK) Ltd, Croydon, CR0 4YY

# ROGUE GUNSLINGER

## B.J. DANIELS

This book is for Gale Simonson, part of the Simonson duo, who keeps our lives interesting in the Quilting by the Border group. You are always like a breath of fresh air. Thanks for keeping me smiling.

## Chapter One

The old antique Royal typewriter clacked with each angry stroke of the keys. Shaking fingers pounded out livid words onto the old discolored paper. As the fury built, the fingers moved faster and faster until the keys all tangled together in a metal knot that lay suspended over the paper.

With a curse of frustration, the metal arms were tugged apart and the sound of the typewriter resumed in the small room. Angry words burst across the page, some letters darker than others as the keystrokes hit like a hammer. Other letters appeared lighter, some dropping down a half line as the fingers slipped from the worn keys. A bell sounded at the end of each line as the carriage was returned with a clang, until the paper was ripped from the typewriter.

Read in a cold, dark rage, the paper was folded hurriedly, the edges uneven, and stuffed into the envelope already addressed in the black typewritten letters:

Author TJ St. Clair
Whitehorse, Montana

The stamp slapped on, the envelope sealed, the fingers still shaking with expectation for when the novelist opened it. The fan rose and smiled. Wouldn't Ms. St. Clair, aka Tessa Jane Clementine, love this one.

TJ St. Clair hated conference calls. Especially this conference call.

"I know it's tough with your book coming out before Christmas," said Rachel, the marketing coordinator, the woman's voice sounding hollow on speakerphone in TJ's small New York City apartment.

"But I don't have to tell you how important it is to do as much promo as you can this week to get those sales where you want them," Sherry from Publicity and Events added.

TJ held her head and said nothing for a moment. "I'm going home for the holidays to be with my sisters, who I haven't seen in months." She started to say she knew how important promoting her book was, but in truth she often questioned if a lot of the events really made that much difference—let alone all the social media. If readers spent as much time as TJ had to on social media, she questioned how they could have time to read books.

"It's the threatening letters you've been getting, isn't it?" her agent Clara said.

She glanced toward the window, hating to admit that the letters had more than spooked her. "That is definitely part of it. They have been getting more… detailed and more threatening."

"I'm so sorry, TJ," Clara said and everyone added in words of sympathy.

"You've spoken to the police?" her editor, Dan French, asked.

"There is nothing they can do until…until the fan acts on the threats. That's another reason I want to go to Montana."

For a few beats there was silence. "All right. I can speak to Marketing," Dan said. "We'll do what we can from this end."

"I hate to request this, but is there any chance you could do a couple of book signings while you're at home before Christmas, right before the book comes out?" Rachel asked. "I wouldn't push, but TJ, we hate to see you lose the momentum you've picked up with your last book."

"That would be at least something," Dan agreed.

"If you don't make the list, it won't be the end of the world," her editor added. "But we'd hoped to see you advance up the list with this one. I love this book. I think it's the best one you've ever written."

The first week a book came out was the most important and they all knew it. If she didn't make the list—the *New York Times* list—it would mean losing the bonus she usually got for ranking in the top ten. It would also hurt her on her next contract, not to mention the publisher might back off on promotional money for her.

"We don't mean to pressure you," Dan said. "But I'm sure if the police thought this fan was really dangerous—"

"I think going to Montana is smart," her agent cut in. "You'll be safe there with your family over the holidays. We can regroup when you get back."

She rubbed her temples. "I could do one book signing in my hometown since there is only one bookstore there. Whitehorse is tiny and in the middle of nowhere. The roads can be closed off and on this time of year, so there won't be much of a turnout though."

"Isn't the *Billings Gazette* doing a story on you as well?" Trish from Marketing asked.

"Yes." She groaned inwardly, having forgotten she'd agreed to that months ago.

"That will have to do, then," her agent said, coming to her defense. "Her next book will be out in the spring. Let's plan on doing something special for that."

"We have ads coming out in six major magazines as well as a social media blitz for this one," Rachel said. "You should be fine. You have a lot of loyal fans who've been waiting patiently for this book. Your presales are good."

"Are you all right with this?" her agent asked.

She nodded and then realized she had to speak. Her throat was dry, her stomach roiling. Just the thought of any kind of public event had her terrified. But before she could answer, the call was over. Everyone wished each other a happy and safe holiday and hung up, except for her agent.

"Are you sure you're okay?"

"I will be once I get home," she told her and herself. She couldn't wait to get on the plane. She hadn't been back to Montana for years except for her grandmother's funeral.

"Keep in touch. And if you need anything…"

TJ smiled. She loved her agent. "I know. Thank you." She disconnected. Every book release she worried it wouldn't make the list or wouldn't be high enough on the list—which meant better than the last book had done. Not this time.

"You have bigger things to worry about at the moment," she said to herself as she walked to her apartment window and looked out.

*I know where you live. You think you can sit in your big-city apartment and ignore me? Think again.*

That ominous threat was added at the bottom of the last written attack she'd received from True Fan. What was different this time was that her fan had included a photograph taken from the outside of her New York City apartment. She'd recognized the curtains covering the window of her third-floor unit. There'd been a light behind them, which meant she'd been home when her "fan" had taken the photo from the sidewalk outside.

It was recent too. One of the wings of Mrs. Gunderson's Christmas angel was in the photograph. Her elderly neighbor had put it up only two days ago. TJ had helped her.

Just the thought of how recent the photo had been taken made her shudder. She glanced at her phone. Her flight was still hours away but she preferred sitting at the airport surrounded by security screened people to staying another minute in this apartment.

Sticking her phone into a side pocket of her purse, she grabbed the handle of her suitcase and headed for the door.

Nowadays she always checked the hallway before she left her apartment. She did this time as well. It was empty. She could hear holiday music playing in one of the apartments down the hall. The song brought tears to her eyes. She was a mess, way too emotional to spend the holidays with her sisters—especially since the three of them had been estranged for months.

She hesitated. Maybe she should change her flight. Go to some warm resort. But just the thought turned her stomach. She was going back to Whitehorse. Going home for Christmas.

She rolled her suitcase down to the elevator and pushed the button.

When it clanged its way up from what sounded like the basement, she waited for the door to open. If anyone she didn't recognize happened to be on the elevator, she would make an excuse about forgetting something she needed in her apartment and turn back until the elevator left again.

She knew it was silly, but she couldn't help it. No one was taking the threats seriously. But she had watched the tone of the letters degenerate into angry, hateful words that were more than threatening. This person wasn't done with her. Far from it. She couldn't shake the feeling that her "True Fan" was coming for her.

The elevator stopped and the door began to open. Empty. She let out the breath she'd been holding. Stepping in, she pulled her suitcase close and pushed the button for the ground floor.

The fan writing her the threatening letters could be anyone. That was what was so frightening. It could even be someone who lived in this apartment complex. Or someone she'd met at a conference. She met so many fans, she couldn't possibly remember them all. It embarrassed her when they complimented her books. She wanted to hug them all. She doubted she would ever get used to this. Writing had been her dream since she was a girl. Getting published? Well, that was like a miracle to her. She couldn't believe her good luck.

Until she'd begun getting the letters from her True Fan.

Outside the apartment building, the sidewalk was filled with people hurrying past. Shoppers laden with packages, others rushing off to work… The city was bustling more than usual. She glanced at the faces of people as they passed, not sure what she was looking for. Would she recognize her rabid fan if she saw him or her?

She couldn't help studying their faces, looking for one that might be familiar. She didn't even know if her "fan" was male or female. She also didn't know if the person was watching her right now.

After a while, everyone began to look familiar to her. If anyone made eye contact, she quickly dropped her gaze as she made her way to the curb to signal for a cab. She wrote about crazed homicidal people. Wouldn't she recognize something in True Fan's eyes that would give the person away?

With a screech of brakes, a yellow cab came to a stop on the other side of the street. The driver motioned for her to hurry. But a large delivery truck was coming too fast for her to cross before it passed.

She felt something hit her in the back. Letting out a cry, she found herself falling into the street in front of the large speeding truck.

## Chapter Two

It happened so fast. One minute she was standing on the curb waiting for the large delivery truck to pass before crossing the street to the waiting taxi.

The next she was falling forward into the street and the truck bearing down on her. Her arms windmilled as she tried to catch herself, but there was nothing to grab. She could hear the deafening roar of the truck's engine, smelled diesel fuel turning the air gray and closed her eyes as she realized she was about to die.

The hand that closed over her arm was large and viselike. One minute she was falling headlong into the street in front of the truck and the next she was snatched from the crushing metal bumper as the truck roared on past.

Pulled by the hand gripping her arm, her body whipped back. She slammed into something so solid it could have been a lamppost. She turned just quickly enough that her face came in contact with the chest of a large male body as she tried to get her feet under her. He steadied her for a moment before the fingers on her arm released.

She looked up in time to see the man who'd saved her turn and walk away as if rescuing women was something he did every day. Trembling all over, she was still reeling from her near death.

"Wait!" she called after him. He'd just saved her life. But if he'd heard her, he didn't turn. All she got was a brief glimpse of granite features, collar-length dark, curly hair beneath a baseball cap above wide shoulders clad in a tan suede sheepskin coat before he disappeared into the crowd.

She turned to find her suitcase and purse had fallen to the ground at the edge of the curb. Still shaken, she reached for them. The taxi that had stopped for her was long gone. No one seemed to have noticed what had almost happened to her.

Why had the man taken off the way he had? A Good Samaritan who didn't like taking credit for his deeds? Or, she thought with a shudder, the person who'd pushed her in front of the speeding truck—and then saved her.

Was it possible the man had been her True Fan?

She remembered being hit from behind and then the viselike grip of his large hand as his fingers bit into her arm. He hadn't even taken the time to see if she was all right. A shudder rattled through her. Had this been a warning?

A cab pulled to a stop in front of her. Tears burned her eyes as she stepped toward it. After all this time of being away, she couldn't wait to go home to White-horse.

SILAS WALKER SWORE. He'd lost the man he'd been fol-lowing in the crowd of Christmas shoppers. Now he leaned against the front of a building, watching the street. His leg hurt like hell. He realized he was limping badly and cursed. If it wasn't for his injury, he wouldn't have lost the man.

Or if he hadn't stopped just long enough to grab that woman who'd been jostled by the crowd and almost fallen in front of a delivery truck. He shook his head. She should have known better than to stand that close to the street, especially with the sidewalk this crowded. He hated to think what could have happened if he hadn't been right behind her.

His cell phone vibrated. He checked the screen. A text from his boss that he wanted to see him ASAP. That couldn't be good. He quickly texted back that he was on his way.

One look at the way he was limping and he knew exactly what his boss was going to say. He'd come back to work too soon. That he knew his boss was right didn't make it any easier to accept.

But after today, after messing up an easy tail, Silas had to accept that he wasn't up to the job yet. That alone would force him to lay off his leg for a while. Just over the holidays, not that he was happy about it.

A taxi pulled past. He spotted the woman in the back seat. She wore a bright red long coat with a multicolored scarf—the same woman he'd grabbed out of the way of the truck.

But that wasn't the surprising part. He recognized her. He'd studied that face on the back cover of her book more times than he wanted to admit. He couldn't believe his luck. TJ St. Clair. The thriller writer. Her photo hadn't done her justice.

As the taxi drove on past, he realized she was probably headed for the airport given that he now recalled seeing a suitcase next to her. Somewhere for the holidays?

Smiling, he told himself she might be headed home to Montana. If he was right... Well, what were the chances they might cross paths again?

TJ HAD WONDERED what it would be like seeing her sisters again. The last time they'd been together they'd argued. Well, that is, she and Chloe had argued with their younger sister Annabelle over their grandmother's house.

Grandmother Frannie Clementine had died a few months ago. In her will, she'd left everything she had—basically her house in Whitehorse—to Annabelle.

"Did you know she was going to do that?" they'd demanded.

"No, I swear I didn't," Annabelle had said on the phone since she hadn't attended the funeral or seen the will.

"Why would she do that?" Chloe had demanded.

"I have no idea," their sister had said. "Except... well, I always got the impression that she liked me the best." She'd tried to pass that off as a joke, but they'd all hung up angry.

Now as TJ stepped off the plane, she felt bad about the argument. The house had turned out to be a whole lot of work—and had held some surprises that neither TJ nor Chloe would have wanted to handle. It had been clear why Grandma Frannie had left the house to Annabelle, who they all agreed was more like Frannie than either TJ or Chloe.

The Billings, Montana, airport was small by most airport standards and sat on rimrocks overlooking the state's largest city. She hadn't gone far when she saw her sisters waving at her from the bottom of the escalator.

TJ couldn't help but grin. They were both wearing elf hats. She groaned. "This has to have been Annabelle's idea," she said under her breath. But the sight of them in those hats had definitely broken the ice.

She laughed as she reached them, hugging one and then the other. As she pulled back, she felt such a surge of love for her sisters that it brought tears to her eyes.

"We didn't want you to feel left out," Annabelle said, and whipped an elf hat from her bag and settled it on TJ's blonde head. She grinned and put her arm around them. "We look like triplets."

"Heaven forbid," Chloe said.

"I'm starving," Annabelle said, surprising no one. Since she'd quit modeling for a living, she was always hungry. "Ray J's barbecue when we get home, eat here or just get snacks like we used to for the ride home?"

"Snacks!" TJ and Chloe said together.

"Did I mention I bought your favorite bottles of wine?" Annabelle asked. "Or we can go out and party tonight."

TJ and Chloe groaned in unison and then laughed. It felt good being around them again, TJ thought, and felt her eyes burn again with tears. Coming home for the holidays had been the right choice. She realized this was the best she'd felt in a very long time.

Annabelle chattered as they walked through the terminal toward the exit. TJ half listened, thankful that the trouble between them had blown over. They were all three back in Montana just like when they were growing up. They were sisters and she couldn't have been more delighted to be with them, even though people stared.

She laughed. She'd forgotten they were all now

wearing elf hats. For a few minutes, she'd completely forgotten her near-death experience this morning in the city and True Fan's threats.

But as she and her sisters passed a group waiting in one of the departure lines, she saw a woman raise her phone and take a photo of the three of them. Glancing back, TJ saw the woman quickly begin texting someone.

## Chapter Three

"Wow," Chloe cried from the front seat of the SUV as she showed TJ her phone. "It's already all over social media." There was the photograph of the three of them in their elf hats. Just as she'd feared, the woman had recognized her, tagging the photo with her pen name. "Ah the life of the rich and famous."

TJ groaned. "Now everyone will know that I've come home to Whitehorse for Christmas."

"It isn't like it was a secret, right?" Annabelle asked as she drove. "Everyone knows you're from Whitehorse, Montana. Not much of a leap that you would be going home for Christmas." She glanced in the rearview mirror. "Seriously, is it a problem?"

"No," TJ lied. "It's fine. Sometimes it would be nice to be anonymous though, but I don't have to tell you about that."

Annabelle sighed. "Yep, but when now faced with being anonymous the rest of my life… Well, it's an adjustment. I have to admit, it was fun seeing my photo on the front of magazines—even if it was a doctored photo of me. Nothing is all that real with modeling."

"So you're not going back to it?" Chloe asked their

baby sister. "You're just going to marry Dawson Rogers, become a ranchwoman—"

"And live happily ever after," Annabelle said with a giggle. "Yep, that's the plan."

They began discussing people they knew in Whitehorse and how things had or hadn't changed.

TJ only half listened to their conversation. She hadn't told either sister about the threatening letters—let alone what had happened in the city only hours ago. The more she'd thought about it on the plane ride back to Montana, the more unsure she was that she'd been pushed in front of that truck. Could it have been an accident? Or had it been deliberate? Either way, if that man hadn't grabbed her…

She shivered and looked out at the snowy landscape. If that man was her True Fan, he'd been watching her apartment. When the light had gone off in her living room, he would have known she would be coming downstairs. Or he might have been a stranger passing by.

TJ shook her head, determined not to think about it. She was safe now. At least for a while.

"So we're talking wedding bells," Chloe was saying.

"Wait, I must have missed something," TJ said, sitting forward to hear. "You and Dawson? When?"

"We haven't set a date yet. I know it's quick, but I would love a Christmas wedding, something small and intimate," Annabelle said, sounding dreamy. Both Chloe and TJ groaned and then laughed.

"Love," Chloe said with a shake of her head.

"Actually," TJ said, settling back into her seat, "I always thought you and Dawson were a good match."

They talked about weddings, growing up in Whitehorse, people they knew who'd left—and those who had stayed. The time passed quickly on the drive to their hometown.

As they pulled up in front of the house they'd grown up in after their parents had died, Annabelle cut the engine. Conversation died. They all looked in the direction of Grandmother Frannie's house. Even though Frannie had left the house to Annabelle, TJ would always think of it as their grandmother's. None of them spoke. The only sound was the tick, tick, tick as the motor cooled.

"Are you two all right?" Annabelle asked.

TJ hadn't realized it when they'd met her at the airport, but Chloe had flown in only thirty minutes before she had. Which meant that like her, she hadn't been to the house where they were raised since the funeral.

"It's like it was when we were kids," Annabelle said, as if trying to reassure them.

From the back seat, TJ glanced at her sister in the rearview mirror. All three of them knew the house would never be like that again. Not after their grandmother's secrets had been unearthed, so to speak.

"If you don't want to stay here, we can go out to Dawson's ranch," Annabelle said. "We have a standing invitation."

TJ smiled at that, seeing how happy her sister was to be back together with her high school sweetheart. "I'm good with staying in the house."

"Of course you are," Chloe said. "You write murder mysteries." She sighed. "I am good with staying here too. I think it's what Grandmother would have wanted. But it's still weird. I can't believe the secrets our grandmother kept from us."

TJ chuckled. Frannie had been a tiny, sweet little woman who everyone said wouldn't hurt a fly. "Seems all those wild stories we thought she made up to entertain us had some truth in them."

"Imagine if she hadn't toned them down to PG," Annabelle said.

They all laughed and opened their car doors, the earlier tension gone. Getting the luggage out, they made their way up the shoveled path through the deep snow. *Christmas in Whitehorse*, TJ thought. The last time she'd left here, she'd been pretty sure she'd never be back. But as she breathed in the icy evening air, she knew she was exactly where she wanted to be right now.

Annabelle scooped up a handful of snow in her mitten and tossed it into the air over them before running toward the door, fearing payback. Both TJ and Chloe let out cries as ice crystals glittered in the silver evening before covering them from head to toe.

TJ shook the light snow from her long blond hair and laughed. It was good to see Annabelle like this. It had been a long time. Now, she was again that adventurous young girl who'd gotten stuck in the neighbor boy's tree house.

"I thought you'd want your old rooms," Annabelle was saying as they crossed the porch and she unlocked the door.

TJ hadn't known what to expect as the door swung open. Her grandmother had been a hoarder in her old age. The last time she'd seen this place—when she and Chloe had come up for the funeral—it had been so full of newspapers, magazines, knickknacks, old furniture and so much junk there were only paths through the house. Little had they known what was buried in there.

She stopped in the doorway, dumbstruck. The junk was gone. The walls were painted a nice pale gray, and the place looked warm and welcoming, complete with new furniture.

"Annabelle, you shouldn't have gone to so much trouble. We aren't staying that long," TJ said, shocked.

"It wasn't all me. Willie insisted on helping and I wasn't about to say no," Annabelle said. "You remember Dawson's mom. When she takes on a project… You have to see the kitchen. Dawson completely remodeled it."

TJ could only nod and follow her sister into the kitchen where their grandmother used to attempt to cook. She stopped in the doorway. This was the room where Annabelle had discovered her grandmother's biggest secret. It looked like any other kitchen in an older remodeled house.

"Remember the cookie jar where Frannie kept her grocery money?" her sister was saying. "I saved it."

Chloe had stepped in and was looking around, wide-eyed. "It's amazing." She met TJ's gaze. "Ghosts?"

"Gone," Annabelle said, and crossed her heart with her index finger. "No ghosts."

TJ thought ghosts were the least of her problems. "Did Willie help you with our rooms as well?"

"She did. Come on, I'll show you." Annabelle ran up the stairs. TJ and Chloe followed, whispering among themselves.

"She did a great job," Chloe was saying. "Remember what it was like?"

"Unfortunately, I do," TJ said. "Like a horror story."

"Or a thriller," Chloe whispered back. "Like the kind you write."

TJ didn't need the reminder.

Annabelle had stopped at Chloe's old room. They joined her. The room had been painted her favorite color, pale purple, and decorated to fit their investigative reporter sister's style.

"You do realize that this visit is temporary, right?" TJ asked. Annabelle didn't seem to hear her. Stepping down the hall, TJ stopped at a room she knew at once was hers. It was painted a pale yellow. A quilt of yellow-and-blue fabric lay on the antique white iron bed. There was a small white desk and chair to one side of the bed with a lamp and spot for her laptop. On the wall above it was a framed collage of her book covers.

"Do you like it?" Annabelle said behind her, sounding anxious.

"Oh, Annabelle." She turned to hug her sister, hoping to hide her discomfort. The last thing she wanted to see were her book covers right now. They reminded her of the threats from her True Fan, who had found fault with all of her latest plots—and even her covers.

"It's perfect."

Her sister seemed to relax. "Is this going to be all right?" she asked.

"It is, Belle," she said using a nickname for her littlest sister that she hadn't used in years. "I'm glad you kept Frannie's house."

"It was Dawson's idea. He bought it for a rental but he thought it would be nice for us to have it for when the two of you visit. After we're married, we'll build a house with guest rooms for you and Chloe when you come home. Then we'll either rent this house or sell it. But I like the idea of keeping it. At least for a while."

She loved her sister's enthusiasm, but she couldn't imagine visiting Whitehorse often. So she said nothing, just smiled and hugged her again.

Chloe came out of her room holding a framed photo of the three of them.

"Check this out," she said, wiping tears as she showed TJ a photo of the them when they were girls. "We were so cute."

"We are still cute," Annabelle said. "Let's go to Ray J's and get some barbecue. Then I'm thinking we should go to the Mint and celebrate."

"Whoa," Chloe said. "Barbecue, yes. Our old bar, no." She looked to TJ to back her up.

"How about we come back here, open the wine and make it a fairly early night," TJ said. "At least for today. It's been kind of a long day. But could we stop by the bookstore before it closes on the way to supper? I need to see if they have everything they need for my book signing."

"You're doing a book signing this close to Christmas?" Chloe said.

"Don't ask."

THE BOOKSTORE WAS actually a gift shop that carried her books because she was considered a local author. TJ stopped inside the door. It had been so long since she'd had her very first signing here. She remembered her excitement from the acceptance of her book to actually seeing her words in print. She'd been over the moon. She hadn't been able to quit staring at her book. The memory made her smile. Her dream had come true.

Her first book signing under this roof had been good. She'd known most everyone who'd waited in line to talk to her, wish her well, say they knew her when, and then get their book signed.

TJ hung on to that feeling for a moment before stepping in to look for the owner. Her sisters scattered throughout the store, oohing and aahing over this or that as she made her way to the books.

There were a dozen piled up next to an older image of her along with some articles about her on poster board. She'd been interviewed so many times and freely told stories about her life, her dreams, her process.

She couldn't help but grimace at the memory of the tongue-lashing the New York City police officer had given her when she'd taken the threatening letters in to him.

*"Look, there's nothing we can do," the cop said. "These aren't the first threats you've gotten, nor will they be the last. You writers," he said with a shake of his head. "I checked out your web page, your social media. Your whole life, everything about you from what you ate for dinner last night to your favorite color, is out there for public consumption. You put your life out there to promote yourself and your books. So..." He shrugged. "What do you expect?"*

Not seeing the owner, TJ stepped away from the book display and the poster of her as she heard more people come into the store on a gust of cold air. She hadn't gone far when she heard a deep male voice ask if they had TJ St. Clair's latest book.

She turned and froze. The man was a good six foot five, shoulders as wide as an ax handle and arms bulging with muscle. But it was the dark curly hair at his collar, the baseball cap and the sheepskin coat that sliced into her heart like a knife.

The owner of the store was telling him about the book signing the following day and how TJ had grown up right here in Whitehorse. "Here, you'll want a bookmark. The signing is at 10 a.m. Best come early because it will fill up fast. Tessa Jane hasn't done a signing here in years so we're all very excited."

"Yes, I don't want to miss that," he said, his voice a low rumble.

TJ felt glued to the floor. This was the man who'd pulled her back from the speeding truck—and possibly pushed her to start with—early this morning in New York City and was now here in Whitehorse? Even as she told herself it couldn't possibly be the same man, she knew in her heart it was. The only way he could have gotten here this quickly was if he'd already had a flight out of the city. As if he'd already known where she was going.

Just then he turned and she saw the dark beard on his granite jaw. A pair of piercing blue eyes pinned her to the spot. What she saw, what she felt, it came in a jumble of emotions so strong and unsettling that she turned and ran.

## Chapter Four

TJ stumbled blindly out the door and around the corner. She leaned against the brick wall and tried to catch her breath. Her life felt out of control. *She* felt out of control. She'd never had a reaction like that and now, shivering out in the cold, she wondered what had possessed her.

She couldn't even explain her response to the man. What had she sensed that had her running out into the cold? She shivered, hugging herself as she thought of those blue eyes and the look in them. It was as if he could see into her soul. She knew that was pure foolishness, but how else could she explain her reaction?

"What in the world!" cried her sister Annabelle as she found her leaning against the outside of the building. Chloe came running up a moment later. "What happened?"

TJ couldn't speak. She shook her head and fought tears. But it was useless. She began to cry, letting out all the frustration and fear that she'd been holding in the past six months.

Her sisters rushed to her, drawing her to them as they exchanged looks of concern. "Let's get her over to the coffee shop," she heard Annabelle say.

TJ tried to pull herself together. At the sound of a truck engine, she looked up. To her horror, she saw that it was the man she'd just seen in the gift store driving by slowly. She couldn't see those blue eyes, but she could feel them on her.

"Who is that man?" TJ asked on a ragged breath before the truck disappeared down the street.

Her sisters turned to look.

"I saw him in the gift shop." Chloe shook her head. "I have never seen him before that," she said with a shrug.

TJ had expected Annabelle to say the same thing and was surprised when her sister said, "The mountain man?"

"You know him?" TJ asked as the pickup continued down the street. The truck, she saw with surprise, had a local license plate on it. How was that possible? It was the same man she'd seen in New York City earlier today. But how could that be? She was losing her mind.

"His name is Silas Walker. He moved here about six months ago," Annabelle was saying. *He'd moved here six months ago?* That was about the time TJ started getting the letters from True Fan. "He keeps to himself. Has a place in the Little Rockies."

"You can bet he's running from something," Chloe said. "Probably has a rap sheet as long as his muscled arm."

"Do you always have to be so suspicious?" Annabelle said with a sigh.

"Seriously, he's either a criminal or an ex-cop."

"One extreme or the other?" Annabelle grumbled. "Sweetie," she said, turning back to TJ. "You're shivering. Let's get you into the coffee shop."

It wasn't until they were seated, cups of hot coffee in their hands, that her sisters asked what was going on.

She wished she knew. Fearing that she was letting her paranoia get to her, she didn't know what to say.

"TJ?" Chloe prompted.

"She's finally getting some color back into her face," Annabelle said. "Just give her a minute."

She took a sip of the hot coffee. It burned all the way down, but began to warm her ice-cold center.

"Tell us what's going on," Chloe said. "Tessa Jane, you looked like you saw a ghost back there. Do you know that man?"

Looking up at them, she knew she couldn't keep it from them any longer.

It all came pouring out about the fan that at first was so complimentary but soon became more critical, making suggestions that when she didn't take them became angry.

"Who do you think it is? Probably some aspiring writer with too many rejections who's angry at you because you got published and she didn't?" Annabelle asked.

"Or maybe another writer who's jealous of your success?" Chloe added.

TJ shook her head. "That's just it. I have no idea. It could be just a reader who doesn't like the direction my books have taken. I'm not even sure if it is a man or a woman. I'm not the first writer to run into this problem. Readers bond with an author. They have expectations when they pick up one of your books. If you don't meet those expectations…"

"What? They threaten to kill you?" Chloe cried. "Have you gone to the police?"

She told them what had happened. "The officer was right. My entire life is out there in the cloud. When I was starting out, I hadn't realized that everything I said to the press or online would be available online forever. At first I was just so excited to be published. I never dreamed…" She shook her head.

"I can't believe the police blame you," Chloe said.

Annabelle agreed. "Though I have to admit, it goes with the business. I ran into this with modeling. Once you're out there, you become public property."

"That's ridiculous," Chloe said.

"Don't tell me that you haven't run into this as a reporter," TJ said.

"People storming in angry about something I've written? Of course," Chloe said. "It's part of the job. You can't please everyone. But if you're being threatened…"

"What are you going to do?" Annabelle asked.

She shook her head. "The police officer I talked to said I should ride it out. That the fan would get tired of harassing me. But I'm worried with this new book that True Fan isn't going to like it at all. After seeing that man…"

"You think it's him, your True Fan," Chloe said. "The one who looks like a mountain man?"

TJ sighed and told them what had happened only that morning on the street in front of her apartment. "He saved me, but did he? I felt someone push me in front of that truck. If he hadn't grabbed me…" She saw her sisters exchange a doubtful look. "I know it doesn't seem likely that they are the same person, but…" She halted for a moment. "I swear it's the same man. I… feel it."

"Okay, it's a stretch," Chloe said. "But I suppose it's possible. You were in New York this morning and now you're here. Why couldn't it be the same for him?"

"He could have even been on the same flight," Annabelle said. "You flew first class, right? He probably flew coach. And since you didn't have any luggage to claim…"

"Okay, it's not that much of a coincidence if he is the same man," Chloe said. "It doesn't make him True Fan though."

"Right, it isn't like he followed you here," Annabelle said. "He's been living here for the past six months."

"Six months," TJ said in a whisper. "That's how long I've been getting the letters from True Fan."

SILAS DROVE TOWARD the Little Rockies, anxious to get to his cabin. As he drove, he contemplated what had happened back at the gift shop. It didn't make a lot of sense and he was a man who prided himself on making sense out of situations.

At least he'd been right about one thing. TJ St. Clair had been headed home for the holidays. When he'd realized that, he'd been looking forward to meeting her. But after what had happened back there…

She'd run out of the shop in tears. Because of him? Or someone else she saw in the store? Odd behavior. He considered that it might have something to do with what had happened this morning in New York. A scare like that would make anyone jumpy. He frowned to himself, wondering again about her near accident this morning.

Was she merely jostled? Had someone purposely pushed her?

He shook his head, reprimanding himself for not leaving his job behind along with the suspicions that went with it. He was in Montana now. He'd bought this place outside of Whitehorse in the Little Rockies so he could get away from his stressful, dangerous, always unpredictable job.

Here, he did so much physical labor that all of that ugliness was forgotten—at least for a while. Here, he'd put that world as far away from him as he could.

*And yet you still read thrillers. Not just anyone's. You read her books.*

He laughed as he drove toward the mountains. That's because she was the reason he'd moved here. After reading TJ's books, he'd been curious about Montana, curious about the wild prairie, the endless sky, the wide-open places that she talked about in her books. Once he saw the area, he was hooked. She had always mentioned the Little Rockies so of course that's where he went when he was looking for land. While he loved the prairie, he also wanted a hideaway like the lawless days when Kid Curry and Butch Cassidy and the Sundance Kid roamed this area.

He'd bought into the mystique because of TJ St. Clair and because of her books, but he'd never dreamed he'd get a chance to meet her here in her home state. Which was why he couldn't miss her book signing tomorrow. He knew even before he turned onto the snow-packed road that led up into the mountains to his cabin that nothing was going to keep him away. He realized that he'd been wanting to meet her for far too long.

TJ LISTENED TO her sisters chatting, knowing they were trying to get her mind off True Fan and her book signing tomorrow. She smiled and nodded and added a word or two when required as she tried to enjoy her barbecued pulled pork. It was delicious and she was hungry after a long day with little real food.

But she couldn't keep her mind off the man she'd seen at the gift shop. The mountain man. Her True Fan?

She thought back to the first letter. It had been so complimentary. The writer had loved the book, sounding surprised as if not a thriller reader. She tried to reconcile that first letter with the more recent bitter, hateful ones she'd been getting. She couldn't square them anymore than she could the man she'd seen first in New York and now in her local gift shop asking about her book.

The first letter had been like so many of the others that she had hardly noticed it.

"You really need to hire someone to answer these," her friend Mica had said when she'd seen the stack TJ had been working her way through on that day six months ago.

"I've thought about it, but I'd rather not answer them than have someone else do it for me. I know that sounds crazy."

"No, I get it." Mica had opened a couple of the letters and begun to read them. "Aww, these are so sweet. They love you. This one is from a woman who is almost ninety. She wants you to write faster." Her friend had laughed. "Oh and this one is long." She'd watched Mica skim it. "Good heavens, do people often tell you their entire life histories?"

TJ had nodded. "They want to share their lives with me because they feel they know me from my books.

You can see why I try to answer as many of the fan letters as I can. Unfortunately I can't answer them all. I just hope they understand."

After her friend left, TJ had answered as many of the letters as she'd had time for since she had a book deadline looming. She *always* had a deadline looming.

That part she didn't mind. She loved writing the stories. It was the other things that ate up her time that she hated. There were always art forms that needed to be filled out describing her story, her characters, suggesting scenes for the cover.

Then there were the many edits and proposals that needed to be written. Add to that the blogs and promotion requests. It was a wonder she ever had time to write the books.

She had been thinking about that when she'd picked up one more fan letter to possibly answer. The first thing she had noticed was that there was no return address on the envelope. She hadn't thought too much about it since often the readers would put their addresses inside their letters.

Slicing open the envelope, she'd pulled out the folded unlined discolored paper. She remembered holding it up to the light, wondering how old it was to have turned this color. The letter had been typed on what appeared to be a manual typewriter. TJ had an old heavy Royal she'd picked up and kept in her office only as decoration. She'd always been impressed that Ernest Hemingway had written on a manual typewriter, since she doubted she would be writing books if it weren't for the ease of computers.

Dear Ms. St. Clair

I've never written an author before. I guess there is a first time for everything.

I recently checked out your first book from the local library. It was quite pleasurable to read. You clearly have talent. I was surprised when I started reading and couldn't put it down. I definitely enjoyed your descriptions of Montana and the country around your "fictitious" small town.

I'm actually looking forward to your next book,
Your True Fan so far


TJ had laughed. The reader certainly hadn't thought he or she was going to like it. It had pleased her that her True Fan had been surprised and willing to try another one of her books. Maybe next time the person would purchase one rather than wait to get it at the library.

She had looked to see if there was a name or an address. Apparently the reader didn't require an answer. She'd tossed the letter in the trash since long ago she'd given up keeping all the fan mail. She'd thought nothing more of it.

That, she realized now, had been her first mistake. There might have been fingerprints on that first letter before things went south.

## *Chapter Five*

"I want to read the letters you got from this so-called fan of yours," Chloe said once they were back at the house and alone. Their sister had gone to see her fiancé, Dawson Rogers, promising to come back before all the wine was gone. "Something tells me they are much more threatening than what you told Annabelle."

"I didn't bring them with me," TJ said. "I didn't even save the first few." But she remembered them and often saw them in her sleep, waking in a cold sweat, her heart pounding.

Dear Ms. St. Clair

I was so disappointed with your last book. To think a tree was killed to make the paper that book was printed on… You should be ashamed.

I expect each book to be better than the last. I don't think that's unreasonable. In my last letter, I made some suggestions as far as the plot and character development.

Clearly, you dismissed those suggestions. Maybe you think you know more about writing than I do. Since my opinion doesn't count, you

won't be surprised to hear that I don't trust you
as a narrator.

I'm your only honest fan. If this is the way
you treat a true fan, I hate to think how you treat
your other readers.

You have really let me down. We might have
to do something about that, don't you think?
Your only True Fan

She'd thought that would be the last time she'd hear
from that reader. She didn't remember a suggestion
for a book that True Fan had claimed to have sent her.
Readers often thought she should do books about various secondary characters from her novels. One even
suggested getting a woman out of the criminally insane
ward of a hospital so she could find her true love. What
readers didn't seem to realize was that those decisions
weren't always up to her—even if she was inclined to
do a certain character's story.

She'd thrown True Fan's letter away—just as she had
the first one—and moved on to a letter by a woman
who would love a signed book sent to her sister for her
birthday. Her sister loved TJ's books and was laid up
after a car wreck. The sister's name was Rickey. The
reader had said that the sister was a huge fan.

TJ had picked up one of her books and signed it:
*Rickey, Happy Birthday. Hope you're well soon, Best,
TJ St. Clair.*

She put it with the letter in the pile to be mailed,
only vaguely remembering that it went to a post office
box in Laramie, Wyoming.

After that, she'd gone back to writing her book and
forgotten both letters.

That had been her second mistake, though she'd had no way of knowing it at the time. It wasn't until she received the next letter from True Fan:

Dear TJ St. Clair

You really aren't as bright or as talented as I first thought. Actually, I'm amazed you make any money at this. A person you don't know from Adam tells you a hard-luck story and you send them a book? You are so gullible. But "Rickey" thanks you. Tee Hee. I'm feeling so much better and I like having a book that you touched.

Unfortunately, your books are getting worse. I didn't think that was possible. I told you what to do, but you just keep ignoring me. Because you think you're so much smarter than me, more talented? You keep making this mistake and we'll see who is smarter.

Your True Fan until The End

"Believe me," TJ told her sister now. "I've read them numerous times. I can't tell if they are from a man or a woman. They could be from *anyone*. Anyone who owns an old manual typewriter."

"Well, they have you running scared, so you must believe the threats are real," her sister said.

"The last one promised that True Fan would be seeing me soon and unless I apologized for ignoring the advice the person had been giving me, I was going to die like one of the characters in my book," TJ said. "True Fan said I could pick which character and which death and kill myself because it would be less pain-

ful than if a fan had to stop me from writing by killing me."

Chloe shivered. "That sounds like more than a
threat. The police didn't take that seriously?"

TJ poured herself a glass of wine, her hands shaking. "Even if True Fan had said he or she was going
to kill me, there is no return address. The postmarks
have been from all over the country. Where would
they begin looking for this person? We don't know if
it's a man or woman. So until True Fan actually makes
good on these threats…" She got to her feet. "I hate
talking about this."

"This man we saw earlier, you realize it's a long
shot that he's the same one from New York, but I could
do some checking. Annabelle said his name is Silas
Walker." She ran upstairs, returned with her laptop
and began to tap on the keys.

TJ was thinking how nice it was to have an investigative reporter in the family when Chloe let out a sharp
breath and looked up. "What?"

"He was one of New York's finest, but left a year
ago after being caught in some kind of internal sting
investigation."

"What kind of investigation?" TJ asked around the
lump in her throat.

Chloe shook her head. "Dirty cops. He apparently
was never arrested. All they said was misconduct that
betrayed the public's trust. That could be anything from
lying to cheating on overtime or much worse. Here's
the kicker: he was rehired a month later but then quit."
She looked up from her computer. "This guy could be
dangerous."

"What guy could be dangerous?" Annabelle asked

as she came through the front door on a gust of winter wind. TJ and Chloe shared a look. "Are you talking about the Mountain Man?"

"He's an ex-cop who was fired at one point," Chloe said. "I was saying he could be dangerous."

"Why was he fired?" their sister asked as she shrugged out of her coat, hung it up and joined them. She poured herself a glass of wine. Her cheeks were already flushed. From the cold? Or from her visit with Dawson Rogers?

"Let's not talk about this," TJ said. "Tell us about you and Dawson."

Annabelle shook her head. "If you really think this man is dangerous then you need to cancel your book signing tomorrow."

"Bad idea," Chloe said. "She'll be perfectly safe at the gift shop with us and half the town there. This is her chance to find out if he's this True Fan who's been sending her the threatening letters."

"You really think it's him?" Annabelle asked.

"First I'm shoved from behind in front of a speeding delivery truck, he saves me, then shows up in White-horse and I find out that he moved here six months ago—about the same time I started getting the threatening letters. What are the chances that he's *not* True Fan?" She shuddered at the memory of those blue eyes. She'd felt strangely drawn to him at the same time she'd felt afraid.

"What does she do if he *does* show up at the book signing tomorrow?" Annabelle demanded of Chloe. "Just ask him if he's her True Fan?"

Chloe groaned. "She'll play it cool. We'll be there. If he is this crazed fan, he won't do anything at the signing, but he might say something that gives him away. Once we know for sure then we go to the sheriff."

"TJ play it cool?" her youngest sister said with a laugh. "No offense, but if today was any indication—"

"I can do it." TJ nodded with more enthusiasm than she felt. She had to. This had to end because she couldn't take anymore. If it didn't, she feared True Fan would end it the way the letters had promised. "Maybe he won't even show."

"I wouldn't hold my breath," Chloe said. "If it's him, he'll want to get as close to you as he can. He's been taunting you. Now he'll want you to know just how close he is."

As if TJ didn't already know the psychology behind a person like this. She wrote about them all the time. If this man was her True Fan, he didn't just want her to know how close he was. He wanted her to know how easy it would be for him to get to her. For the past six months, this had been leading up to the moment when she faced her killer—just like in one of her books.

## Chapter Six

When TJ woke the next morning, she was shocked to see how late it was. She hurriedly showered and dressed. When she came downstairs, dressed for her signing, Annabelle handed her a cup of coffee and a donut.

She took the coffee, declined the donut and watched as Annabelle ate it.

"I love not being a model anymore," her sister said, smiling with a little sugar glaze on her lips before she licked it away.

TJ couldn't help smiling as well. Her sister looked great, not skinny and pale like she had when she'd been a top model. "I need to get to my signing."

"We're going with you," Chloe said, coming out of the kitchen. "Are you nervous?"

What did she think? She'd never been good at book signings. Probably because she'd never wanted the attention. She'd only wanted to write the stories that were in her head. Little had she known the rest that was required of a published author. TJ knew she was naive to think that she could simply lock herself away in a room somewhere and do what she loved.

When her editor had told her that she needed to

be more of a presence on social media, she'd actually thought about quitting the publishing business.

But she couldn't quit writing. When she'd take a break, the longest she could go was three days before she started writing in her sleep. The characters would start talking and she'd have to get their stories out. She loved that part.

TJ remembered how surprised she'd been when she found out that not everyone had stories going in their heads. She'd asked the person, "Well, then what do you think about when you're in the shower or driving?" The answer had been, "I've never thought about it. Something I'm sure, but not stories."

It had also surprised her when other writers had told her that their characters didn't talk to them. Well, hers certainly did. Soon the ones from her next book would be nagging at her to begin writing again.

"Come on," Chloe said, "or we're going to be late."

TJ wished they could just get into Annabelle's SUV—she'd traded her sports car for something more practical for Montana—and hit the road. She thought she could and not look back at this point in her life.

There was already a line at the gift shop when they arrived. TJ couldn't help looking for the mountain man, but with a sigh of relief, she didn't see him. Maybe after yesterday, he wouldn't show up.

"Park in the back," she'd instructed her sister.

"You aren't getting cold feet, are you?" Chloe asked.

"I always do but nothing like I have right now." They entered the back door. TJ dropped off her coat and purse in the stockroom and took a moment to compose herself. *You've done this dozens of other times. You can do this.*

But none of the other times were like this.

Stepping out of the back, she headed for the table that had been set up for her along with a chair and a huge stack of her books. The owner hustled over to see if she needed water, coffee, anything at all.

"A bottle of water would be wonderful," TJ said, her throat already dry as she felt eyes on her from the line of people waiting a few yards away. She tried to smile as she slid into the chair and picked up one of the pens the store owner had thoughtfully left for her.

"Here's your water," said a familiar voice.

TJ turned to see a dark-haired woman her age. "Joyce?" She couldn't help her surprise. She hadn't seen Joyce Mason since high school. Joyce had been voted the girl most likely to end up behind bars. It had been a play on words, since Joyce had been wild—and also a drinker who was known to make out with guys in the alley behind the Mint Bar.

"You work here now?" TJ asked, feeling the need to say something into the silence. Joyce was thinner than in high school, but wore the same shag hairdo and pretty much the same expression, one of boredom. The only thing different was that she sported a few more tattoos.

"Does it surprise you that I read?" Joyce asked.

"No." She let out a nervous laugh. "As a writer, I'm delighted."

"Yes, we all know you're a writer." Joyce put down the bottle of water and walked off.

TJ was still reeling a little from Joyce's attitude when she heard a squeal and looked up to see another familiar face. Dorothy "Dot" Crest came running up to her all smiles.

"I can't believe it!" Dot cried. "I just had to say hi. I'll get in line," she assured the waiting crowd. "I definitely want one of your books. I've read them all." She leaned closer. "They are so scary and yet I can't put them down." She laughed. "This is so exciting."

With that she rushed back toward the end of the line. As she did, she said hello to people she knew. Dot knew almost everyone it seemed.

"Ready?" the owner asked, coming up to tell her again how delighted they were to have her here.

Was she ready? She felt off-balance and the signing hadn't even begun. Normally, TJ was more organized. She'd barely remembered to grab a few bookmarks as they'd left the house. She hadn't even thought about a pen. That showed just how nervous she was.

She smiled up at the first woman in line. She looked familiar, but for a moment TJ couldn't come up with her name. That was the problem at book signings. The names of people she knew even really well would slip her mind.

"Just sign it to me," a person would say.

She often used the trick, "Would you mind spelling your name for me?"

That didn't always work. One woman who was so excited, telling everyone how long she'd known TJ, made her draw a blank. When she'd asked her to spell her name, the woman recoiled and said, "It's Pat."

TJ had been so embarrassed, but there hadn't been time to explain how often her mind went blank at these events, even with the names of her closest friends. So she never saw Pat again.

Now the older woman with the dyed-brown hair

standing in front of the desk said, "You probably don't remember me."

For a moment, TJ didn't. She looked familiar. Really familiar, but...

"I'm not surprised given how much you didn't pay attention in class."

Bingo. "Of course I remember you, Mrs. Brown. I had you for English in high school." Annabelle had told her that the woman had only recently retired after having a minor stroke. "Would you like me to sign this to you?" she asked her former teacher.

"Of course. But you probably don't know my first name. It's Ester."

She signed the book, stuck in a bookmark and handed it to the older woman.

Ester Brown hesitated. "Just the other day I told my husband I wasn't the least bit surprised when I heard you were writing books." She hugged the book to her. "You were never at a loss for words in my class." With that she turned and walked away.

TJ frowned. Hadn't Annabelle told her that Mrs. Brown's husband had died?

One after another new and old readers stepped up and TJ signed their books, visited and moved on to the next one. She was surprised how many people had turned out. But the last time she had signed a book in her hometown had been her first one years ago.

"Hi, TJ," said one of the men from the line. She'd seen him, but hadn't paid much attention. She was looking for the mountain man. But if Silas Walker was planning to attend the signing, he hadn't shown so far, and another five minutes and she would be done. The line had dwindled, she realized with relief.

Her hand hurt from signing books and smiling and trying to remember faces she hadn't seen in years.

Now as she looked at this man, his name suddenly came to her. "Tommy Harwood."

"Tom," he corrected. He seemed surprised that she remembered him. He'd been one of those on the fringe. He'd been an average student, an outsider. He'd been invisible—just like TJ. While her sisters had been popular, TJ was a dreamer who preferred to be off by herself with her head in a book.

Now Tommy was getting a little bald. From the jacket he was wearing, she saw that he worked at the local auto shop.

"Do you want it signed to you?" she asked as she opened a book and lifted her pen expectantly.

"Sure, as long as it's to Tom."

She nodded and signed *To Tom, Enjoy, TJ St. Clair*. It was the best she could do given that she didn't think she'd spoken more than a dozen words to Tommy over the years. No matter what Mrs. Brown said, she wasn't the talkative one in English class. TJ realized she must have her confused with Annabelle. Great.

"Are you in town long?" Tommy asked quietly.

"Just for the holidays." She handed him the book.

He continued to stare at her. "You're probably busy, but if you ever want to get a cup of coffee…"

"Thank you. That's sounds nice. I'll let you know."

He nodded. "I should let you get to your other fans."

She watched him walk away for a moment, trying to shake off the odd feeling he'd given her.

"I love your books," a woman said as she quickly took Tommy's place and it continued.

As the line dwindled, she began to relax. She loved

her readers and was reminded of the time before her first sale. She'd been writing short stories. That's when she'd gotten her very first fan letter. The magazine reader had said she should be writing books. She'd framed that first letter and put in on her wall. It had given her hope each time she looked at it during the writing of her first book.

She could smile at the memory. There'd been so many days when she didn't think she could finish an entire book. It had felt overwhelming. Add to that the fear that it wasn't good enough, that everyone would hate it, that it would be rejected.

And it was. Her first book was still in the bottom of her closet where it would remain, never to be published. But that first book had given her hope not only that she could finish a book, but also that she could write a better one.

And she had. A book a year for the past seven years, all of them published, each doing better than the last. She remembered the thrill of her fourth book making the *New York Times* list.

She'd heard of authors who'd treated themselves with trips to Europe or purchased new cars after making the list. She'd gone for a walk, grinning the whole way, and on impulse had treated herself to a hot fudge sundae. It was as decadent as she ever got. Restraint in everything, that was TJ St. Clair, aka Tessa Jane Clementine. Those words could have been stitched and hung on her wall.

She'd always been like that. Holding back, never letting herself go. It drove her sister Annabelle crazy.

"Don't you ever just want to let loose? Do something crazy? Take a chance?"

"I might want to, but I don't," had been her answer. The truth was she'd never been brave or daring. That huge hot fudge sundae? It had made her sick and had been a good reminder of why she used restraint in all things.

No, her heroine in her books, Constance Ryan, was the one who did crazy, brave and daring things. Constance loved defying the odds. And for so long, TJ had loved writing about her—living through her.

As she finished signing a young woman's book, TJ saw him. The mountain man, Silas Walker, had just come in the door and was headed her way.

## Chapter Seven

Silas was a little concerned about what kind of reception he might get. Because of his size and the way he looked, especially during his time in Montana when he was "roughin' it," he tended to scare little children. Lately he'd been working undercover, so his beard was longer than usual. He'd let his hair grow as well.

But the woman who wrote these murder mysteries? Come on, TJ didn't scare that easily, did she?

He guessed he was about to find out as he headed for the table where she had just finished signing a book. There were still several books left, he noticed with relief. He'd run late today because of the snowstorm in the mountains last night. He'd barely been able to get his pickup out. But he wasn't about to miss purchasing a signed book from TJ St. Clair today.

When she spotted him approaching, he had to admit, she looked like a deer in headlights. It perplexed him. She couldn't possibly have thought that he was the one who pushed her into the street yesterday. He'd been the one who'd saved her.

"Hello," he said as he reached the table. "I can't tell you how excited I am that I didn't miss your signing." His gaze locked with hers and he was shocked to see that her eyes weren't blue, but a languid sea green that took his breath away for a moment. Her blond hair framed a face that he'd memorized, since he'd looked at the black-and-white photograph on the cover jacket so many times.

She'd intrigued him from the first time he'd picked up one of her books. He normally didn't read thrillers. Hell, his life was one. No, he couldn't remember what had possessed him.

He'd opened one of her books to the first page and started reading. Before he knew it, he was on page 30. By then, he was hooked and knew he wasn't walking out of that bookstore without that book.

It wasn't until he'd finished it that he saw TJ's photo. He'd actually thought the book had been written by a man. He remembered smiling. He liked surprises and this woman had surprised him and intrigued him.

Now he watched her pick up one of the hardcover books at her elbow and open it with trembling fingers. That he made her nervous surprised him even given the way she'd acted yesterday. In her books, the characters were so gutsy. He liked to believe that TJ possessed—if not all of her character Constance's gutsiness—then at least some of it. The last thing he'd expected to see in her eyes was fear.

"Who would you like me to sign it to?" she asked, her voice breaking.

He knelt down, realizing he was towering over her, although he suspected that wasn't the problem. "Silas." He spelled his name and watched her write it out in her neat penmanship. "I can't tell you what a thrill this is. From the first time I picked up one of your books, I wanted to meet the woman behind them."

He saw her pen falter on the page. Those sea green eyes came up to meet his. He smiled and saw her shiver. She quickly looked down and hurriedly signed "Enjoy" and her name. Well, not her name exactly. TJ St. Clair he'd learned was her pen name. Her legal name was Tessa Jane Clementine.

She handed him the book. "I hope you like it." Her voice was throaty, almost a whisper.

He saw that there was no one behind him since he'd caught her at the end of the signing. "I have enjoyed your books so much. I just had to tell you that." He started to rise, but stopped. "I know this is probably out of line, but is there some reason I make you so nervous?"

She parted her lips as if to speak. She had a great mouth, he noticed. She quickly closed it for a moment before she spoke. "Is there a reason you should make me nervous?"

"Not that I know of," he said. "When I saw that you were going to be signing books here, I had hoped…" He shook his head. "You probably don't accept dates from your readers. I don't blame you. It's just that reading your books…well, I feel I know you. That must sound crazy. But you're why I ended up building a cabin here." He shrugged. "I'm sorry, you're probably anxious to leave." He smiled as he rose. "Maybe we'll see each other around town. Thank you so much for this," he said, looking down at the book in his hands. "I'll treasure it." He met her gaze. "It was wonderful meeting you."

TJ SAT STUNNED as she watched Silas Walker stride over to the checkout counter and pay for his book.

She kept thinking about his intense blue eyes and his disarming smile. He knew that he made her nervous. Had he been enjoying that, or was he trying to make her less nervous?

"Well," Chloe whispered as she rushed over to her. "Is it him?"

For a moment she couldn't speak. "I have no idea. Apparently, he was going to ask me out but changed his mind."

Annabelle appeared to hear the last part. She let out a laugh. *"So he just wanted a date?"*

"He gave you no indication that he might be True Fan?" Chloe demanded.

"None." And yet... She remembered the way he'd looked into her eyes. What had he been looking for? She shuddered and let out a sigh. "I am so glad this book signing is over."

"He was at your table for quite a while," Chloe said, not letting it go. "What else did he say?"

"I don't know," TJ said. "My brain was on spin cycle. He said he felt as if he knew me from my books and that was probably crazy. Oh, and that I was the reason he built a cabin here. That is, my books were."

Annabelle's eyes went wide. "That doesn't sound good, but you don't live here anymore. You live in New York City, so..."

"He didn't mention saving your life in the city yesterday morning?" Chloe asked.

"No," TJ said with a shake of her head. "I should have asked him but my suspicions all seemed so ludicrous at the time. He kept looking at me as if..." She shook her head. As if he really just wanted to ask her out? Or something else? She had no idea.

"You knew your True Fan could be charming, right?" Chloe asked. "Maybe you should have accepted the date."

"No!" Annabelle cried. "What if he is… True Fan?"

"Well, he changed his mind about asking me out, so the point is moot," she pointed out. "Tommy Harwood asked me out though." Her sisters gave her a blank look, which confirmed that Tommy had gone through high school as invisible as she had been.

When she described him, Chloe said, "I do remember him vaguely."

"Kind of getting bald guy with the little potbelly?" Annabelle asked.

"That's him. He works at the auto shop."

They both quickly lost interest in him.

"I saw Dot. She hasn't changed a bit," Chloe said.

"Joyce Mason apparently works here," TJ said, keeping her voice down. She thought Joyce might be hiding nearby listening. "She was a little strange."

Chloe put an arm around her as she got to her feet to leave. "You survived it."

She smiled. She had. But she was no closer to finding out if one of the people who'd come through the line was True Fan.

"I say we go have some lunch," Annabelle said.

"It's that or head straight to the Mint Bar," Chloe said. "Up to you, Tessa Jane."

"Didn't someone say food?" Annabelle asked innocently. "I'm starved."

Chloe looked to TJ and said, "Food. I've never seen you this thin."

"Yes, we'll get you some good Montana eats and

fatten you right up," Annabelle agreed. "How about some chicken-fried steak?"

TJ felt her stomach roil at the thought. "Yum."

Her sisters laughed as they headed out the door. It was a wonderful sound that felt like a much-needed salve. She told herself that her True Fan hadn't been in Whitehorse today, hadn't come through the line, hadn't gone home with her latest book.

And yet she couldn't help but think about each and every one of the people who'd come through the line, including the young woman who'd been right before Silas Walker. TJ had been distracted, but now that she remembered...

"I signed a book for Nellie Doll," she said as they started up the street.

Chloe stopped, coming up short. "Lanell? I didn't see her in the line."

"She sent her niece to get it for her," TJ said. "The niece had me sign it 'to Nellie, just like old times.'"

"That is kind of creepy, isn't it?" Chloe said. "You and Nellie weren't friends."

"No," TJ said. "Far from it." She tried to shake off the memory.

"You aren't thinking that Nellie..." Annabelle was walking backward in front of them, looking from TJ to Chloe and back again.

"That she's True Fan?" Chloe shook her head. "Anyway, didn't you say that the letters had been sent from all over the country? I'm betting Nellie's never been out of the county."

TJ nodded, remembering the girl Nellie had been in high school. She couldn't imagine that she'd want to drop so much money on a hardcover book, especially TJ's.

She tried not to think about True Fan. She had so many amazing readers. Why did one fan have to spoil it? What bothered her was that she really didn't know whether True Fan was a man or a woman. She'd had several women murderers in her books. In fact, in the book she'd just signed, the antagonist was a woman.

# Chapter Eight

TJ woke with a headache after a night of weird dreams. She took a couple of OTC painkiller tablets after her shower. She was not looking forward to her interview with a reporter from the *Billings Gazette* later this morning.

As she dressed, she could hear her sisters already downstairs in the kitchen. Opening her bedroom door, she followed the rich, wonderful scent of coffee down the stairs.

She couldn't help smiling to herself. There was something so comforting about being back in this house with her sisters. Just the sound of them lightened her step as well as her heart. As she walked into the kitchen, she headed straight for the cupboard where she knew she would find a mug.

"Good morning!" Annabelle called from the table, where she and Chloe were already sitting with their coffee. "It's a beautiful day."

TJ blinked as she looked outside to see the sun shining on the new snow, making it glitter blindingly. "Were you always this cheerful in the morning?" she asked her as she took a seat at the table.

"Don't you hate morning people?" Chloe said, and grinned, since she was one as well.

"I thought we'd get a Christmas tree today," Annabelle said with unusual jubilance. "Willie saved some of Grandma Frannie's ornaments from the trip to the dump. We could decorate the tree later, and I need to do some Christmas shopping."

TJ could see what her sister was trying to do—get her mind off True Fan and yesterday's book signing.

"Is there a place to buy a tree in town?" Chloe asked.

"Don't be silly," Annabelle said with a laugh. "We're going to take a picnic lunch and go up into the mountains and cut one. I found an ax in the garage."

"Ax?" Chloe cried.

"The Little Rockies?" TJ said, and both sisters turned to look at her.

"Why do I detect a strange excitement in those three words?" Chloe asked. "You aren't thinking what I think you're thinking."

"Of course not," TJ said. "It's just been so long since I've been up there." Both sisters were studying her. "Come on, he isn't True Fan."

"He said you were the reason he moved here," Chloe reminded her.

"Yes, but a lot of my readers say they feel as if they're in Montana when they read one of my books and they can't wait to visit," she pointed out. "It's not that unusual."

"This one *moved* here," Chloe said.

"So you really don't think he's the one?" Annabelle asked suspiciously.

"He did nothing to indicate that he was anything more than a normal fan," TJ said truthfully. "So," she said, getting to her feet. "I'll pack the lunch. Let's go to the mountains and get a tree." She started at the knock on the door.

"I wonder who that is," Annabelle said as she went to answer.

TJ heard her laugh. "You're delivering mail door-to-door now?"

As she stepped out of the kitchen, TJ saw the woman hand her sister a letter. "You got mail," the woman said with a laugh as she looked past Annabelle to TJ. "Fan mail. Our own famous author. I tell people I know you—well, know that you used to live here—and they don't believe me."

All TJ could do was nod and smile as her heart sank. She felt all the color leave her face as Annabelle thanked the woman and closed the door.

"Carol from the post office," her sister was saying. "She said this came for you yesterday and since you don't have a post office box, she decided to drop it by. How's that for service? TJ?" Annabelle had seen that she'd gone pale.

Chloe took the envelope from Annabelle by the corner. "I'm sure there aren't any prints, but…" She held it out to TJ.

She didn't reach for it. Even from where she stood, she could see the typewritten address. Any other city and the letter would have ended up in a dead file because it had no return address and was addressed only to TJ St. Clair, Whitehorse, Montana. Another joy of living in a small Montana town.

"Aren't you going to open it?" Annabelle asked.

TJ couldn't find the words to speak.

"I'll open it," Chloe said, and walked into the

kitchen to get a sharp knife. She carefully opened the letter, using the point of the knife to unfold the discolored paper.

How had the fan known she would be here? TJ groaned inwardly. Her fan knew she was in Whitehorse. Of course her fan knew; she'd just had a book signing. Not to mention she'd been recognized at the airport. That person had put it up on social media. Everyone in the world with a smartphone knew she was in Whitehorse—especially True Fan.

"The writer mailed it to you in Whitehorse, Montana," Chloe said. "So True Fan knew you were here. Only in a small town like this would you have gotten it," she said, voicing what TJ had just been thinking.

"Remember when we first came to live with Grandma Frannie?" Annabelle asked. "Frannie said Whitehorse wasn't the end of the earth, but it was damned close. She said on a dark night you could see the fires of hell." She laughed but quickly stopped when she saw that she wasn't helping lighten the mood.

"Wait a minute," Chloe said. "This letter was mailed *before* you got here. Whoever sent it knew you were coming here. Either that or figured it would be forwarded to you."

TJ couldn't wrap her head around that. She felt as if someone was always watching her, trying to figure out what she would do next. "How bad is it?" she asked from the kitchen doorway.

Chloe turned to look at her. Annabelle was standing off to the side, hugging herself as if she didn't want to know what the letter said any more than TJ did.

"Read it to me," she said, not wanting to touch it.

Dear Tessa Jane,

I would love to see the expression on your face right now. You really think you can get away from me? I told you, I'm your True Fan until the end. Now that I have your latest book, I hope you won't disappoint me again. I'm not sure I can take any more disappointment from you. I'm not sure what I'll do.

I thought I could help you, make you a better writer. But you've continued to ignore me as if you think I have no value. That hurts me deeply. I'm not sure I can let you go on writing these books.

The only way you can save yourself is if you made up for it in this recent book. Let's both hope that you do.

Still your True Fan until The End

"What is this person talking about?" Chloe asked as she finished reading.

TJ couldn't speak for a moment. The letters had started out being addressed to Ms. St. Clair. Then TJ. Now Tessa Jane. Each growing more familiar.

"TJ, what is it this person wants you to do?" Annabelle asked, worry in her voice.

She sighed. "One of the main characters told a lie but went unpunished."

"So punish the character," Annabelle said. "It's got to be more than that."

"True Fan also wants the lead character to fall for—"

"Durango," Chloe said with a curse.

She looked at her sister. "You read my books?" This day was just filled with surprises.

"Guilty. I hate to ask since it's going to spoil your latest book for me, but Constance doesn't end up with Durango?"

TJ shook her head. "Durango dies in this book."

SILAS HAD WOOD to chop and bring into the cabin. On the way home from town he'd heard that another storm was coming in. He'd bought groceries before leaving Whitehorse since he could be snowed in for a few days with the blizzard that was reportedly coming. As long as he had plenty of firewood, he would be fine.

But when he'd reached home, the one thing he wanted to do more than anything else was start TJ's book. Her books aside, he now couldn't get the woman herself off his mind. When he'd looked into those amazing sea green eyes... He'd started to ask her out even though it was clear that he made her nervous. But just the thought of having a chance to talk to her about books, writing... Not that he hadn't noticed how attractive she was. He shook himself. He had wood to chop.

After unloading everything from town, he made short work of getting enough wood in for the next few days. The first few snowflakes drifted down as he started to carry in the last load of split logs. He stopped for a moment to look up at the heavens. Snowflakes whirled down from a white, low sky. The air was cold and crisp and smelled of the tall pines that surrounded him and his cabin.

But it was the utter silence that captivated him. He'd never known such quiet after living in the city all his life except for his stint in the army overseas. His close friends thought he was crazy for coming here.

"Why the middle of nowhere in Montana?" one friend had asked.

"It's because of that writer he likes," another friend joked. "TJ St. Clair. How'd this guy talk you into something so crazy?"

Silas had let his friends think that the books were written by a man. He'd thought so himself at first, so why not? "I liked the way the writer described the area. It's exactly like in the books."

"Just be glad he's not doing this because of some woman," his friend said.

"That's the worst," the other agreed. "We'd know for sure that he's lost his mind."

They'd all laughed, Silas the heartiest.

TJ MET THE reporter at the Great Northern. She'd suggested it because she knew they would be able to find a quiet corner in the dining room to talk. After ordering coffee, the reporter began to ask her questions.

She'd done dozens of interviews since publishing her first book. Reporters asked many of the same questions. Where do you get your ideas? Everywhere. She'd spent years being a wallflower and watching people. She was fascinated by what made each one tick. The good, the bad, the truly ugly all made for great characters.

What inspired you to write this book? She'd seen a news story on television and while her story had taken a different twist, it had been the starting point.

TJ answered one question after another, adding examples and little asides, all the time her mind on the mountain man, Silas Walker.

Finally the reporter asked her what she knew now that she wished she'd known when she started. How hard it is.

"This is the hardest work I've ever done," TJ said truthfully. "It isn't an eight-to-five job where you go home at night and forget it until the next day. There's no Thank God It's Friday. No paid vacation and sick leave. Once I start a book, those characters are with me until I finish their story. They wake me up in the middle of the night. They nag me until I finish the book."

"So one of the fallacies is that you have all this time on your hands because you don't have to punch a time clock," the reporter said.

TJ laughed and nodded. "Everyone dreams of staying home, working in their pajamas, not having a boss looking over your shoulder. It's a little more complicated than that. It's a lot of long hours at a computer."

She was glad when the interview was over and she could walk back to the house where her sisters were eagerly waiting. By then, snow had begun to fall. The flakes were huge and drifted on the breeze.

"Did you know it was supposed to snow?" Chloe asked later as Annabelle slowed the SUV to make the turn at the tiny town of Zortman stuck in the side of the Little Rockies. Zortman had a bar-café, post office, church and a small building used as a jail.

Huge flakes drifted down from the dull white sky to stick on the windshield. The SUV's wipers were having a hard time keeping up. Several inches of snow had already fallen on the road. Their tracks were the only ones so far on the road south.

TJ could see patches of dark green through the falling snow as they approached the Little Rockies. The mountains rose from the prairie in steep rock cliffs and pine-covered slopes.

Before the town of Zortman, set back against the cliffs, Annabelle turned off on a road that passed the cemetery and some summer campsites. As the road climbed deeper into the mountains, the snow seemed to fall harder.

They had gotten bundled up, determined to get rid of the pall that had fallen over them after the latest letter from True Fan. Annabelle had thrown the ax into the back of the SUV along with some rope to tie the tree on the top—once they found it.

"I'll park up here and then we can get out and walk," Annabelle announced. "I'm sure we'll find the perfect tree."

Chloe groaned as she looked out the window. "I know it's beautiful, but I don't like this. What if we get stuck?"

"It's not that far of a walk into Zortman," Annabelle said as she kept driving up the narrow, snowy road through the dense pines. "Also there are cabins up here. I'm sure we can find someone to help us."

Chloe made a skeptical sound and turned up the radio as a Christmas song came on. She began to sing along, with Annabelle joining in. TJ didn't feel like singing. She'd seen a newer mailbox back on the county road. S. Walker. Silas Walker's cabin must be up this way.

She hadn't wanted to worry her sisters, but there was something about the man. So much so that she had to know if he was True Fan. This latest letter made her even more suspicious that it had to be him. The post-mark on the letter had been Whitehorse.

"So True Fan knows someone in all these places where the letters have been mailed," Chloe had said back at the house before they'd left. "She or he gets friends to mail them, saying it's a game she/he is playing with you."

"You're saying True Fan knows someone in Whitehorse who mailed the letter?" Annabelle had said. "But wouldn't that person know TJ?"

"Not necessarily," Chloe had said, and had shot her sister a look.

"Stop trying to make me feel better," TJ had said. The owner of the gift shop had called her Tessa Jane, the name everyone in Whitehorse had known her by. And now her True Fan was also calling her by that name after meeting her at the book signing? Or had True Fan known her real name all along since it was right at the front of the book under copyright?

She knew he could have found out her name in any number of places, but that True Fan was now using it...

Annabelle pulled out in a wide spot and cut the engine and radio. The silence was as deep as the snow around them. "Ready?"

They tugged on coats, snow-pants, boots, hats and mittens and disembarked with Annabelle toting the ax. At first they walked up the road but quickly realized they would have to separate and go into the woods to find a tree.

"Remember no taller than eight feet," Annabelle warned them. "Trees always look smaller out here."

"You'd think she'd been doing this her whole life," Chloe commented to TJ before they split up. "One trip to get a tree with Dawson and now she's an expert." Growing up, their grandmother had had a fake tree, one of the first ones they'd come out with.

TJ stepped off the road into the trees and then waited until her sisters disappeared into the woods before she dropped back down on the snow-covered dirt road. She could see older tire tracks now filling with snow from where someone had driven in here earlier. She followed the tire tracks in the deep snow, determined to find Silas Walker's cabin.

Walking through the falling snow had a dizzying effect on her after a while. It was like being inside a snow globe. She stopped to look back and saw how quickly her tracks were filling in.

TJ had no idea how far she'd gone when she noticed fresh tracks had turned up an even more narrow snowy road that led up the mountain. There were no new tire tracks on the road she'd been following. If Silas Walker had driven back in to his cabin after the signing then there was a good chance these tracks were his.

She decided to follow the tracks in the hope of coming across his cabin. Following the tire tracks, she hadn't gone far when she caught the smell of wood smoke on the air. She kept going through the falling snow, losing track of time and distance.

After continuing to climb up the road deeper into the mountains, she stopped to catch her breath and considered turning back. But she'd gone too far to do that. She told herself that if she didn't come across the cabin soon, she would.

She wasn't worried, but when she looked back, she saw that her boot tracks had filled in. All around her was nothing but white. The snowflakes were falling much harder now. She could barely see the road ahead through the snow. She felt a chill and realized how crazy this had been.

Just a little farther, she told herself, and was almost ready to give up when she spotted smoke rising up out of the trees in the distance. Hurrying now, she headed toward it. Annabelle had said that there were several cabins up here. She told herself that this one had be Silas Walker's. There'd only been one set of tracks this far into the mountains and most of the cabins up here only were used in the summer.

As she drew closer, she saw the truck he'd been driving parked next to the small log cabin. Wet and cold, she hesitated. She knew she should get back to her sisters. They would be worried about her.

From the side of the cabin Silas Walker stepped out carrying a huge armload of firewood, startling her. As if sensing her, he looked up. Surprise registered on his face, then another emotion.

TJ spun around and tried to run back the way she'd come. Her boots slipped on the icy road beneath the snow. She went down hard. Her left leg twisted under her as her boot heel caught on the ice. She let out a cry of pain. Struggling to get up in the deep snow, she realized her ankle was hurt badly. She dropped back to the ground, grimacing in pain, suddenly terrified because she wasn't going far on this ankle.

When she was suddenly lifted off the ground, she screamed. She struggled, but Silas had her in a bear hug and this man was way too large and strong for her to overpower him. Her scream was suddenly cut off by a large gloved hand over her mouth.

"Stop struggling, you're only going to hurt yourself

worse," he said next to her ear. "I'm going to set you down on your good leg. Okay?"

She sucked in air through her nose and stopped fighting him to nod.

The moment he set her down, she slugged him in the stomach. It was like hitting a block wall and turning, she tried to run and immediately collapsed on her bad ankle.

He was on her again, covering her mouth as she began screaming in both pain and terror. "One of us is crazy. Since it's not me," he said, "we're taking this inside the cabin where it's warm." He tossed her over one broad shoulder and turned them both toward the cabin.

She screamed and pounded his back, but it had no effect as he strode up the porch steps of the cabin, shoved open the door and stepped inside. Swinging her off his shoulder, he dropped her unceremoniously into a large overstuffed chair.

Immediately she tried to get up, letting out a cry as she put pressure on her hurt ankle. Not that she was going anywhere even if she hadn't twisted it. He dropped a hand to her shoulder and held her in place as he kicked the door shut. It was warm inside the cabin and at the smell of something cooking her stomach growled, although she hardly noticed.

"What are you doing out in a blizzard?" he demanded, towering over her. He smelled of freshly cut pine. There was a maleness about him that was intimidating and at the same time intoxicating, even if he was her demented True Fan. She thought of a mountain lion on the prowl and felt like a small rabbit wanting to run for its life.

"You have to let me go!"

He held up his hands. "Not until you tell me what's going on. What are you doing here, TJ?"

So he had recognized her, even bundled up with her hat covering half of her face.

"I was out looking for a Christmas tree. I got turned around." She started to push out of the chair but he held up his hand.

"Hold on. Looking for a Christmas tree? And you just happened to stumble onto my cabin? Tell me you didn't come up here by yourself."

"I didn't. I came with my sisters. They'll be looking for me. That's why I have to go. They'll be worried."

But even as she said it, she knew they wouldn't be able to find her. They thought she'd come up here to find a Christmas tree. They would be looking for her closer to where Annabelle had parked the SUV. By now they could have a tree and be loading it.

She imagined them calling her name, joking around until they started to get worried when she hadn't appeared. Would they try to track her? As hard as it was snowing right now, her tracks would have filled in. They'd never be able to find her.

What had she been thinking? She hadn't. She'd acted on instinct and this is where it had led her.

She tried to get up again. He didn't push her back down, but he did move to crouch down in front of her. "TJ, you're a terrible liar, no offense. What are you really doing here?"

If only she knew. It wasn't as if she'd had a plan. She'd wanted to find his cabin. She'd wanted to spy on him. She'd wanted to learn more about him because she believed he was True Fan? Or because of that exhilbarating and yet confusing mixture of strong feelings she'd had the first time she'd laid eyes on him?

What she hadn't wanted to do was get caught and end up trapped in his cabin with him. It galled her what she'd done, since there was no way she would have let the heroine in her books do something this stupid.

Past him, she could see just how small the cabin was. It was only one room with a fireplace, a very small kitchen area, the chair she was sitting in and a bed. Next to the bed was a makeshift desk. It was what she saw on it that stopped her heart.

Sitting on the desk was a large old manual typewriter.

## Chapter Nine

TJ felt her eyes widen in alarm. Silas had seen her look in the direction of the typewriter. Now he was frowning at her in a way that turned her blood to slush.

She thought of all the books she'd written where the heroine escaped by hitting the villain with a makeshift weapon. Or catching him off guard and kicking him in his private parts before bolting for the door.

While there was a floor lamp next to the chair, she couldn't imagine how she could grab it, swing it and hit him hard enough to get away. That was if she could walk on her ankle—let alone run.

But given no other option—she sat up a little. He was crouched directly in front of her. She'd barely kicked out with her good leg when he grabbed it, stopping her foot before it could reach its mark.

"That only works in your books," he said, his voice deep and rough. "Most of the time, it only makes the bad guy more angry. Let's quit playing around. Tell me what's going on."

"I know who you are." She hated that she sounded near tears. "You're my True Fan."

He frowned again. "Yes, I'm a fan of your books but…"

She felt fear give away to anger. "You've been send-ing me the letters!"

"Letters?" he repeated.

"Don't deny it. I know it was you who pushed me in front of the truck in New York yesterday morning."

He rocked back on his haunches. "Whoa. Yes, I was there, luckily for you. I didn't realize that you even saw me. Only I didn't push you," he said, enunciating each word. "I was the one who *saved* you before you became roadkill."

"Right, you just *happened* to be walking past."

"No, as a matter of fact, I was following someone." He made a face as if he saw what she was thinking. "It wasn't *you*. I was on a stakeout."

"I know you're not a cop anymore because you got fired."

"Did some research on me, did you?" He grinned. "I'm flattered. But don't believe everything you read in the paper. Anyway, I work for a private investigative business now. Or I did. I just took a leave of absence. Or did you already know that as well? And, sorry, but I haven't been writing you any letters."

"You've been taunting me for months. Admit it. I just got your latest threatening letter today."

"You've got the wrong guy."

"Really? Next you're going to tell me that you just happen to have a manual typewriter like the letters have all been written on," she said, jabbing a finger in its direction. She saw his sheepish look. "That's what I thought."

"You have it all wrong," he said, getting to his feet. "If you must know, I've been trying to write a book." He shrugged, looking embarrassed. "I use a manual up here because the power goes out more than it's on this time of year. I read that you write every day so I've been trying to do that." He moved to the woodstove. "You inspired me to at least try. Unfortunately, I don't have your talent."

She watched him throw another log into the woodstove. Did he really think she believed him? "I need to go. My sisters will be looking for me."

He turned to look at her. "Have you checked out the weather outside?"

She hadn't, but she did so now. The wind had picked up, whirling snow in a blinding white that covered everything. Worse, the visibility was only a few yards. She'd grown up in this county. She knew how easy it was to get lost. Ranchers often tied a rope from the house to the barn so they didn't wander off track and freeze to death.

"Once the storm stops, I can try to get us out of here in my pickup," he was saying. "But the truth is, I barely made it back earlier with a load of wood I cut from that beetle kill area by the road. I shouldn't have to tell you how slick that road into the cabin is. By the way, how is your ankle?"

"It's fine." She started to get up. He didn't move to stop her. But as she put pressure on her twisted ankle, she winced in pain. Who was she kidding? She wasn't going anywhere on that leg even if she could find her way back. She dropped into the chair and dug out her cell phone.

"Good luck with that," he said as he watched her. "I've never been able to get much coverage in a storm. Sometimes a text will go through."

TJ saw that he was right. She only had two bars. She

bit her lower lip, fighting back tears as her call didn't go through. Her sisters would be frantic.

She sent a text. At Walker's cabin until storm lets up. It was the best she could do since the text appeared to have gone through.

Raising her gaze, she realized that at least Annabelle and Chloe were together. While she was the one in real trouble.

"LOOK, MAYBE WE could start over," Silas said, seeing how upset she was. "We're stuck here until the storm stops. By then, your sisters will have Search and Rescue looking for you. In the meantime, I've got some beef stew and some homemade bread I baked in the woodstove yesterday. It was my first attempt so I'm not making any promises."

She swallowed and looked out at the storm before turning back to him.

"Are you all right?" he asked quietly.

"I shouldn't have come here."

No, she shouldn't have. "Hey, you thought I was this person who's been writing you threatening letters. Actually, I'm relieved. I couldn't understand your reaction to me at the gift shop or at your signing. I didn't think I was that scary." Still she said nothing. "You really think someone pushed you yesterday in New York."

"I know someone did. I was shoved in front of that truck."

She was looking at him as if she wasn't convinced it hadn't been him. He could see now where she might have gotten that idea. He should have stuck around and talked to her. But he would have lost the person he was tailing. As it was, he did anyway.

"That was pretty gutsy of you to come looking for me the way you did. Given you thought I was the person who was writing you threatening letters let alone suspecting I pushed you in front of a truck. Probably not your best plan. Good thing I'm not that person."

"Good thing," she said, a little sarcastically. "Otherwise I would be trapped here with someone who wants to hurt me."

He rubbed his whiskered jaw. "How can I prove to you that I'm not this fan you say has been taunting you?" He stepped over to the typewriter. "Truth is, I admire the devil out of you. You're why I wanted to write my own book. I thought it would be easy." He laughed, picked up a handful of typewritten pages and came back over to where she was sitting.

To his surprise, she seemed to flinch at the sight of the paper. "Don't worry, I wasn't going to ask you to read it." He realized that she was staring at the paper as if…as if what?

She snatched a sheet from his hand. "Where did you get this?" she said, holding up the paper. His expression must have conveyed his total confusion. "Copy paper is usually white or some color. This is discolored. There even appear to be watermarks on some of it as if—"

"As if it was stored in a basement for years?" he asked. "I bought it at a garage sale in town last summer."

"*Whose* garage sale?" She sounded as if she didn't believe him. But then again, she hadn't believed anything he'd said.

"How should I know whose garage sale? Remember? I'm new here." He could see that she was still expecting more of an answer. "It was some elderly woman. Her house was for sale. Apparently she'd had boxes of the stuff in her basement for a while. She was practically giving it away."

"Why would she have boxes of it in her basement?"

"I have no idea. Wait. I might have overheard someone say she used to have a business in town that sold office products. Is it really that important to you? I bought one of the boxes filled with reams of paper. You're welcome to—"

"The person who has been sending me the threatening letters typed them on a manual typewriter like the one you have on paper exactly like this." She held up the sheet, her eyes glittering with tears. "Still going to tell me that you aren't True Fan?"

SILAS HELD UP both hands. "Maybe, since we have a little time now that we're snowed in, I can convince you of my innocence. In the meantime, why don't you get out of those wet outer clothes?" he suggested. "By the way, if you have to use the facilities, there's only an outhouse in the back. It's a short walk, but if you can't make it out there with your ankle, I'll be happy to help you."

TJ wished he hadn't mentioned it because now she felt the need to go. She pushed to her feet, grimacing as she put weight on her ankle. Silas was at her side in two long strides.

"Lean on me," he suggested as he walked her to the back door off the kitchen. As he opened the door, a gust of wind showered them both with snow crystals. They stepped out into winter, Silas closing the door behind them.

He was right. It was a short walk and he'd shoveled

earlier. But the snow had filled in the path. Tucking their heads into their coats they made their way to the outhouse.

"Sorry. It's pretty primitive. No hurry," he said as he opened the door and let her limp inside. "I'll wait at the back door of the cabin. I'll come help when I see you."

She closed the door. It was freezing in the one-hole outhouse. She couldn't remember the last time she'd used one. Drawing down her pants was no easy job as bundled up as she was. As she lowered herself to the wood seat she was sure her behind would freeze to it.

No hurry, Silas had said, but she hurried, anxious to get her pants pulled back up to get heat to return to her backside. Shivering, she opened the outhouse door. Good to his word, he came charging out.

As they made their way to the back door of the cabin, TJ saw that the storm had only worsened. She thought of her sisters and felt horrible for taking off the way she had. She just hoped they were smart enough not to be out looking for her in this. Hopefully Chloe had gotten the message she'd sent.

Back inside, Silas led her to the sink and provided her with soap and warm water that he'd heated on the woodstove in a large kettle. She washed her hands, dried them on the towel he handed her and let him lead her over to the chair again. While he busied himself at the stove, she got out of her wet boots, coat and ski pants. Down to a sweater and jeans and socks, she shivered in the chair until Silas brought her over a quilt to wrap up in. She watched him take her wet things and hang them up on hooks by the door, telling herself he had to be True Fan, and yet…

As she watched him, she told herself that a man

who was this thoughtful couldn't possibly have written those vile things about her. But like her other readers, he probably thought he knew her, thought he knew what was best for her.

The man unsettled her no matter who he was. She reconciled that strange feeling she'd had at the gift shop when their gazes had met. She'd seen…darkness. Something dangerous. Something violent. She tried to shake off the memory. Where had those feelings come from? Worse, because she still felt them, why were they so strong?

She tried not to flinch as Silas pulled up a stool that had been by the fire and sat down in front of her, his expression somber. "How serious were these threats against you?"

TJ debated how much to tell him. If he was True Fan, then he already knew, so what was his game? And if he wasn't? "One of them suggested I should kill myself and do the reading world a favor. Another said I should die like one of my villains in my books. The latest one just indicated that the letter writer couldn't let me keep writing these books, that this would have to end."

He shook his head. "How did this all get started?"

"Why the interest?"

He smiled. "Believe it or not, I'm still a lawman at heart. I like catching the bad guys. But I also admire you and enjoy your books. Since we're going to be here until the storm passes… Maybe I can be of assistance."

TJ couldn't help being skeptical. It came with her personality. Maybe that was why she wrote what she did. She didn't trust what was behind a smile or kind words. Grandma Frannie used to tell her to lighten up. Like that was possible.

More to the point, she wasn't sure what to make of Silas Walker. All the evidence pointed to him being True Fan. So was this just him still taunting her?

Looking into his blue eyes, she thought she saw genuine concern. She felt confused, thrown off balance by the man. She remembered how easily he had thrown her over his shoulder and carried her into the house. If he was True Fan...

"It started like any other letter from a fan," she told him, gauging his expression as she talked. She told him about the first few letters from the person who called him or herself True Fan's being complimentary, all the time studying his face, looking for...looking for a lie in all that blue. But she saw nothing but sympathy and a growing anger at True Fan.

When she finished he got up from the stool without a word and moved to the woodstove. He seemed to be thinking as he stirred the stew.

She studied his broad back, wondering why he'd been fired from the police department. "Well?" she prodded.

He stirred the stew for a minute or two before he turned back to her. "If you really were purposely pushed into the traffic yesterday, then we would have to assume your True Fan either lived in New York or just happened to be there yesterday. But if you're right about the paper True Fan is using to write the letters on coming from the same place as I got mine, then..."

She nodded, her heart pounding. Was this where he told her it had been him all along? "True Fan had to have gone to the same garage sale you did. Someone

with connections to both New York City and Whitehorse since True Fan also took a photograph of my
apartment," she reminded him.

He raised his gaze to hers. "A fan anywhere in the
country could have had a friend in New York snap a
photo of your apartment. Also, your near accident yesterday could have been just that. I think your True Fan
is right here in Montana."

"Right where you just happened to be. Right where
you just happened to be passing by yesterday."

He mugged a face at her. "The reason it's called a
coincidence is because they do exist. I had no idea the
woman I grabbed to keep her from falling in front of
a delivery truck yesterday was you." He crossed his
heart with the index finger of his left hand.

"You're left-handed." The words were out before
she could stop them.

He looked confused again for a moment before he
smiled. "I forgot. Your heroine Constance Ryan always falls for left-handed men. I'm betting there were
a couple of left-handed boyfriends in your past." He
turned back to the stove.

He'd be wrong about that. There had been one
though—Marc. He'd been left-handed and one of the
mistakes she'd made when she'd first started writing
was that she'd made her heroine in her ongoing series
too much like herself. *Write what you know*, she'd always been told. She didn't know anyone as well as she
knew herself.

But while Constance Ryan always fell for left-
handed men, she was the woman TJ wished she was.
Unfortunately the similarities were obvious to anyone
who knew her. Constance was a blonde with aqua-

marine-blue eyes, five foot six, curvy. A woman who loved spicy food and drank her coffee black and by the gallon.

But that was where the similarities stopped. Constance was daring. As a private investigator, she took on cases that others had turned down. She was smart and determined. Even after almost getting killed in every book, she still came back for more.

Constance also loved men—and men loved her. She always ended up curled up in bed with some handsome man. She wasn't one to stay long with any of them. Constance Ryan lived her life the way TJ wished she could.

But TJ was too much of a prude who'd hardly dated, even at college. Also she believed in happy-ever-after—even if her alter ego didn't. She didn't want a string of men. She just wanted that one man who would make her heart pound.

Like this man was doing right now. Only was it fear? Or something just as dangerous, given the two of them were alone, snowed-in deep in the mountains?

"I CAN SEE why you thought I was writing the threatening letters to you," Silas said after dishing them both up bowls of hot beef stew with a side of his homemade bread slathered in butter.

He'd pushed his stool over against the wall and leaned against it as he ate. He was glad to see that TJ seemed to have relaxed a little. Outside, the blizzard was still raging. He'd built the cabin to withstand the winter cold so it was cozy inside, but he could hear the wind and see snow piling up at the windows. He wondered if the snow would be too deep to drive out once the storm stopped.

"I've been thinking how to go about finding this fan of yours," he said between bites. Because he'd realized he had to help her whether she wanted it or not. The only way to prove to her that he wasn't True Fan was to find the culprit. Also, finding the nasty letter writer with TJ definitely had its appeal. He'd never dreamed he would get a chance to even have a cup of coffee with her—let alone spend time in his cabin with her.

"I can't wait to hear your plan." She'd stopped, her spoon in midair, to look at him. He could see she was still suspicious. He didn't blame her. Given the evidence against him, he would have thought the same thing she did.

"It seems simple to me. It all comes down to the old discolored copy paper. Anyone can shoot a photograph of the outside of your apartment—"

"How would they know where I lived unless they had contacts…say, inside the police department?"

He smiled at that as he watched her take a bite of the stew. He could see that she liked it, which made him a lot happier than it should have. Pride cometh before the fall, his father used to say. "You like the bread?"

"You really baked this in that woodstove?" she asked skeptically.

"I did. See that iron box on the top? It's an oven. This is my first attempt. I'll get better."

"It's very good. I've never attempted bread—even in a real oven."

He smiled, warmed by her compliment more than by the stew. He took a couple more bites before he said, "As to the question of how to find out where you lived…all anyone had to do was follow you home from a book signing. How many have you done in New York and gone straight home afterward?"

She didn't answer, his point taken.

"As for the push, there were so many people rushing around with Christmas shopping. I got jostled myself just moments before that. I didn't see anyone push you but I was in a tight crowd of people who were forced to the curb. I just caught you falling out of the corner of my eye, but there were people in front of me, including a woman with a huge shopping bag who could have hit you."

He watched her lick her lips after taking a bite of the bread covered with real butter. No butter substitute in his kitchen, ever. He could tell she was considering his theory.

"So let's say True Fan knows someone in New York who could have followed me from a book signing and taken a photo of my apartment from the street."

"Or she could have even hired someone to do it," he added, thinking about the private investigative business he'd been working for since leaving the police department. It was amazing to him what people would pay to learn.

TJ nodded, no doubt thinking of Constance, the heroine in her books. "So then it would just come down to the copy paper you both purchased at a garage sale last summer in Whitehorse?"

"August. I also bought this stool there."

Her gaze darkened to deep sea green. "So it's someone who lives in Whitehorse." She shivered and for the first time, he thought she might actually be considering that it wasn't him.

"I'd suspect it's someone who knows you and has reason to be jealous of your success," he said. "Maybe an old rival? An old boyfriend? Maybe even a former friend."

## Chapter Ten

"I still can't believe you really made this bread," TJ said as she accepted another piece. Her walk to find his cabin had left her famished.

He grinned, obviously pleased. "For my first time, I think I got lucky, huh."

"It's delicious and so is the stew," TJ said, feeling conflicted. Could she trust this man? Sometimes the way he looked at her with those potent blue eyes, it made her squirm uncomfortably. It was when she glimpsed a dangerous edge to him that she had her doubts. She tried not to think about the predicament she was in—trapped in a cabin in a blizzard in the mountains with a man she didn't trust.

Common sense told her he had to be True Fan.

But after seven books, she knew from experience that the villain often proved to be the person you least expected—not the obvious one. Of course, that was fiction and this felt more like any real life she'd lived so far.

There was something so charming about Silas because of his easygoing manner. And that he was a little domesticated made him even more appealing. He seemed almost shy around her. She saw none of the anger that had practically dripped from True Fan's threatening letters.

After months of running scared she wasn't sure she could trust her instincts, though. Look where they'd brought her.

As she finished her stew and bread she noticed it had gotten dark, although it was hard to tell how late it was since the thick-falling snow still made it fairly light out. She pulled out her phone, hoping for a response from one of her sisters, but there was nothing. She looked at the time and realized with a start that she would be spending the night in this cabin with this man. Her heart began to pound a little harder.

Silas rose to his feet, stepping to her to take her bowl and spoon. "Don't worry," he said as if reading her mind. "You can have the bed when you get tired. I have a sleeping bag I'll drag out. I've curled up in front of the fire on the rug more times than I can remember when I was building this place. The bed came later."

He moved to the makeshift kitchen. Earlier, he'd refilled the kettle on the stove. Now she watched him wash up their dishes in a pan in the sink. He was so self-sufficient. Handsome too in a rough, untamed way that both intrigued her and scared her.

"Don't you get lonely out here?" she asked, wondering if there was a woman in his life back in New York.

"Just the opposite," he said without turning around. "I come here for the peace and quiet. Listen." He stopped what he was doing to half turn to look at her.

She heard nothing but the pop and hiss of the fire in the woodstove.

"Not one siren to be heard. No traffic. No honking taxis. No loud music from the apartment next door."

He let out a sigh. "This is why I love this place. Sometimes I just have to get away from all the racket. Here I get up when I feel like it, I go to bed when I'm tired. I spend my days working on the cabin, cutting wood for the stove, cooking my own meals. When I'm not working, I'm reading. Or attempting to write," he said with a chuckle as he went back to his dishes.

"I had forgotten what it was like living in Montana," TJ had to admit.

"That's right, you grew up in Whitehorse."

She nodded, remembering sledding and ice-skating in the winter, tubing the river in the summer. She'd forgotten what small-town living was like, the slower pace, the unlimited space, the quiet. "I hadn't realized that I missed it."

He turned then to look at her as he dried his big hands on a dish towel. "You must enjoy the glamour and excitement of New York City though. Isn't that why you live there? You can write anywhere."

"I did enjoy the city, especially at first. It felt as if it was where I needed to be to have the career I wanted."

"But now?"

She shook her head. "I hate it. True Fan has ruined the city for me. I don't feel safe there anymore." She let out a bitter laugh. "I don't feel safe anywhere."

He put down the dish towel carefully and turned to lean back against the kitchen counter. "I'm so sorry about that. It's another reason we have to find this person and put a stop to it. I would imagine it's also been hard for you to write."

She looked away. "You have no idea. Or maybe you do."

Silas cocked his head. "I know you still don't trust

that I'm not this person. That's okay. You have to be skeptical to write the books you do—and to be safe. But I promise you I'm going to find True Fan even if you don't want to help me." He pushed off the counter. "Hot chocolate or tea?"

"Tea."

TJ watched him put a smaller kettle on the stove and prepare two cups with tea bags. "I'd like to read some of your book."

He froze for a moment before turning. "You're going to laugh, but right now I'm more terrified than when I'm facing down a junkie with a gun."

"If you don't want me to…"

"Oh, that's just it. The thought of you reading anything I've written both excites and terrifies me. Didn't you feel that way?"

She smiled, nodding. "I remember the first time I took a writing class. I just wanted the instructor to tell me I could do this."

"Did the instructor?"

"No. Looking back, the woman didn't know anything more than I did about how to have a writing career, even though she'd sold a couple of books. I don't think she wanted to get my hopes up since by then she knew how hard it was."

"Well, you don't have to worry about that with me. I enjoy writing, so I'll keep at it hoping I get better no matter what you say. But I really would appreciate your opinion."

Crossing to the typewriter, he reached beside it and picked up a few pages.

"Give me the first chapter," she said. Aspiring writers always wanted to show her their favorite chapter in the middle, not realizing an editor would never read that chapter if they couldn't get past the first one.

He brought over a dozen sheets of paper. She noticed the way he held them in those large hands, like he was carrying a bird with a broken wing.

"You don't have to read the whole chapter," he said, carefully handing her the pages.

The first thing she noticed was that the pages had been typed with a new ribbon. There were none of the light and dark letters like on True Fan's.

Silas stood over her for a moment, then quickly moved away to take his coat from the hook by the door. "I'm going to bring more wood in from the porch," he said. "I suspect the temperature is going to drop tonight. I'll have to keep the stove going." With that, he went out the door on a gust of cold, snowy wind.

For a moment, TJ watched the snowflakes that had swept in melt on the wood floor. Then she turned to the pages of his book and began to read.

SILAS STOOD OUT on the porch in the blizzard smiling like a fool. TJ St. Clair was reading his book. He felt his stomach roil. What if it stunk as badly as he feared it did? What if she told him to use it to start his next woodstove fire? Or maybe worse, he thought, what if she told him it wasn't bad? That it was good enough that he should keep at it? That he had promise?

He wasn't sure which was his greatest fear—fear of failure or of success. They scared him in ways his job never had—even when he'd recently been shot. He rubbed his thigh unconsciously, realizing that his limp had been hardly noticeable. Or maybe he'd tried harder for it not to show around TJ.

Silas felt a shudder when he thought of her True Fan. How dangerous was this person? Would they really go through with their threats if pushed too far? More than ever, he was determined to find the person and put an end to all this.

The wind whipped snow into his face and down his neck. He shivered and hurriedly grabbed an armload of split firewood to take back inside. By now, TJ would have read far enough that she'd have an opinion. Feeling as if he was about to step in front of a firing squad, he told himself he could take whatever she had to offer, and pushed open the door to the cabin.

At first he didn't see her. The chair was empty and for one heart-stopping moment, he thought she had taken off out the back door. But as his gaze shifted, he saw her standing on one foot by the woodstove. She had the small kettle handle in one hand and was pouring boiling water in each of his mismatched mugs.

He dropped the load of wood in the bin near the stove and tried to slow his pulse. "You shouldn't be on your ankle."

"I hopped over. The kettle was boiling." She studied him. "You thought I'd left."

"I thought I was going to have to try to find you out in that storm. I wasn't looking forward to it."

She nodded. "That's the only reason?"

"Maybe I like your company." He could tell that wasn't what she meant at all. She thought he'd lured her here and that he was never going to let her leave. "Here, let me finish the tea." He helped her over to the chair and she dropped into it. "Are you warm enough?"

She nodded and seemed to watch him as he went back to the stove, returning with her cup of tea.

"I'd ask if you want sugar…"

"Constance Ryan takes sugar in her coffee, not me," she said, taking the mug of tea. "We aren't our characters."

"Aren't we? I knew you took your coffee black. Wasn't sure about tea." He thought of his own protagonist in the book he'd started. It was him and it wasn't. But still there was so much of him in his words that he felt vulnerable, something he'd seldom felt even on duty as a cop.

TJ sipped her tea as he hung up his coat and walked back to the counter to pick up his mug.

"I hate to even ask," he said, seeing his chapter lying on the footstool near the chair. He couldn't tell if she'd read any of it, let alone the whole chapter.

TJ NOTICED THE way the large mug disappeared in his hands. Silas seemed so gentle and yet she'd seen the way his muscles had bulged when he'd carried in the wood. For a man his size, he moved with a grace that again reminded her of a mountain lion.

"You have talent, but I don't have to tell you that," she said as she picked up the chapter from the stool and he moved to it to sit down. "I was drawn right into your story. I wanted to read more." He was eyeing her as if he was waiting for a "but." "You've had other people read some of your book, right? I'm sure they've told you…"

He shook his head. "You're the first and only."

She couldn't help being surprised. "Then you really didn't know."

"I'm trying to decide if you're just being nice."

"I'm not. The one thing I learned a long time ago

was that people who tell you you're better than you are are of no help. You need real criticism if you're going to get better, and I believe we have to continue to strive to do so."

He seemed to let out a breath before taking a sip of his tea. "Like I said, I enjoy writing so I'll keep going, but I'm overjoyed to hear it's okay."

"It's more than okay," she said. "I won't promise you that you can have a career writing. Just being good isn't enough. It takes determination and some luck."

"I have the determination. I'm not so sure about the luck." He smiled. "But I feel lucky right now. It's nice to have company."

They drank their tea in the comfort of the cabin as the storm raged on outside. The stove popped and crackled. Silas got up to throw more wood on the fire, then turned and looked at her shyly. "You wouldn't be interested in playing some cards, would you?"

She laughed. "What did you have in mind?"

"I don't even care. Crazy eights. Old maid. Five-card stud. I love to play cards and I'm sick of solitaire."

"My sisters and I used to play all the time. Do people still play with actual cards now that they have virtual games?"

"I have no idea," he said as he brought over a deck of worn cards. From a space behind her chair, he pulled out a small folding table. "You can even beat me. That's how desperate I am," he said with a laugh.

TJ snuggled into the chair. She hadn't played cards in years. She watched Silas shuffle the deck and realized she was beginning to trust him. She hoped that wouldn't be her last mistake.

## Chapter Eleven

They played cards until after midnight. Silas couldn't recall a time he'd had more fun. TJ was an excellent player no matter what game they played. She challenged him. He couldn't remember the last woman who'd done that. She'd relaxed during their games and he'd gotten to see the woman behind the best seller.

She was fun and funny, sharp-witted. He liked her, and not just because she thought he had talent.

It wasn't until the last game that she began to look nervous again. He put the cards away and went to the built-in drawers on the other side of the bed. Pulling out one of his T-shirts, he held it up.

"I think this will cover everything but your toes if you're interested in wearing it to sleep in," he said. "I'll go out and get some more wood and give you a chance to change. Or you can sleep in your clothes. Whatever you prefer." He put the T-shirt down on the bed. "You need to go out back first?"

She shook her head. They'd made several trips out to the bathroom earlier during their card games.

"Sorry, I don't have a spare toothbrush. Wasn't expecting company, but there is toothpaste and water by the sink. Let me know if there is anything else you need." He headed for his coat by the door.

Once outside, he killed time thinking about True Fan. If it hadn't been for this crazed reader, he might never have gotten this close to TJ. That was a thought he wasn't about to share. He also tried not imagining her in his T-shirt. The thought made him grin and ache at the same time.

It had been so long since he'd been truly interested in a woman. He blamed it on everything that had been going on in his life. But he knew that had only been part of it. He'd missed the companionship. Hell, he'd missed the sex. And just thinking of TJ wearing his T-shirt... He shook off the thought.

If he wanted this to go any further, he'd best take it slow. The woman was beyond skittish. She was running scared. Not just that. She still didn't trust him. He hoped to fix that.

He warned himself that she'd be gone as soon as the storm quit. That's if her sisters didn't show up with the National Guard and probably half the county's lawmen before the night was over. Otherwise, he would get her out of the mountains in the morning one way or another.

The thought that he might not see her again was almost physically painful. He'd been captivated by her since her first book. Now that he'd gotten to spend this time with her, well, he didn't want it to end.

That alone surprised him. He dated in New York, but usually he was fine only seeing a woman a time or two. He didn't feel that way about TJ—even if he hadn't been worried about her.

Loading up another armful of wood, he tapped at the

door. Hearing nothing, he stepped in. She was tucked in bed, the down comforter up to her chin. She looked so damned cute in his bed. He quickly closed the door on a blast of snow and wind and, turning his back to her, dumped the wood and took off his coat.

Seeing her in his bed made him ache. It also threw him a little off-balance. He felt both protective and attracted to this woman. Just the thought of kissing her… "Have everything you need?" he asked, his voice sounded strange to his ears.

She nodded and watched him with just her eyes as he went to the area by the bed, opened a cabinet and pulled out his sleeping bag.

Rolling it out on the rug in front of the fire, he turned out the lights and lay down on top of it. A moment later, she tossed him a pillow from the bed.

"Thanks," he said into the quiet darkness. The storm had let up a little. He felt like he did when he was a kid at a sleepover. He didn't want to sleep. He wanted to talk about all the things that interested him, from life on other planets, to Big Foot's possible existence, to what TJ's favorite Christmas gift of all time was.

"Do you remember lying in bed waiting for Santa?" she asked from the darkness.

He chuckled. "I do. I never wanted to close my eyes. I was afraid I'd miss it."

"I hated it when I found out he wasn't real."

"He's not?" The fire crackled and after a few moments, he realized that she'd gone to sleep.

TJ WOKE TO find the cabin empty. The bedroll and pillow were no longer on the floor in front of the wood-stove. And while a fire was going, Silas was nowhere to be seen. Sitting up, she saw that the pillow she'd tossed him was lying next to her on the bed. His bedroll had apparently been put away.

Had he only gone to the outhouse and would be back any minute?

She heard something outside. For a moment she thought it was his heavy tread on the porch, but soon realized it was him trying to start his pickup. She threw back the covers and got up. Her ankle was better, only tender to the touch and black and blue along one side.

Silas had been right about his T-shirt. It fell to her ankles. As she slipped it off, she sniffed it as if she thought it might contain his scent. She held it for a moment, feeling like a teenage girl again, before tossing it on the bed and quickly pulling on the clothes she'd worn. She'd moved to the chair and was putting on her socks when she heard him come up the porch stairs and into the cabin.

"Good morning!" he greeted her, brushing snow off his coat and stomping it from his boots before stepping in on the rug. "Truck's cleared off and the motor turned right over after a few tries. If I have to, I can chain up all four tires to get us out of here. I wasn't sure how much of a hurry you're in to get home."

Last night she'd been champing at the bit. This morning, she hated to leave this cabin. Hated to leave Silas. Which was why she needed to, even if she wasn't worried that her sisters would be frantic.

She glanced around the cabin. "I can go whenever you're ready. I appreciate your taking me back to town."

"Not a problem. I've enjoyed having you here. But

I'm not much of a host if I don't offer you breakfast," he said.

She was tempted. The warmth of this cabin, the scent of homemade bread, the good-natured, handsome man standing in the doorway. At that moment, she desperately wanted Silas Walker to be anything but True Fan.

"Thank you, but I really should get back. My sisters will be worried even after the text." Actually, more worried after the text.

He nodded, not looking any more anxious to leave than she was. "I'll be in the pickup. Come out when you're ready." He turned then and disappeared back outside.

TJ stepped to the hooks by the door, pulled down her coat, tugged on her snow-pants and boots. She took one last look around the cabin, thinking she might never see it again. Out of the corner of her eye she saw the typewriter. Curiosity killed the cat and every B movie heroine who decided to see what the noise was in the basement. Still, she moved to the typewriter and shuffled through the papers. Just pages of his book. She checked the trash can next to it. No partial letters written in too much haste.

Silas Walker wasn't True Fan. But Silas wouldn't be living out here in the woods unless he was running from something. She hated that she was thinking like her sister Chloe, the investigative reporter. But something had to explain those glimpses of darkness she'd seen in his blue eyes.

Walking out of the cabin, she limped her way through the deep snow to the pickup, where he was waiting behind the wheel. He leaned over the seat, pushed open the passenger side door and held it for her to get in.

"Shoot, I forgot about your ankle," he said. "I should have offered to help you."

"It's better, but thank you. Are you always so cheerful in the morning?" she asked.

"Do I detect that you aren't?" he asked with a laugh as he shifted the pickup into low gear. "Cross your fingers."

They chugged up the hill, the back of the pickup sliding a few times before they reached the road she'd come down earlier. There was no sign that anyone had been down the road last night.

"Okay," Silas said with a sigh of relief. "That was the worst of it. At least I hope so."

The sun topped the pines, making the fresh snow sparkle so bright that it was blinding. "It's so beautiful," she breathed. "I'd forgotten days like this."

He glanced over at her, but said nothing as he quickly turned back to his driving. The pickup bucked and slid and chugged until they reached an even wider snowy dirt road and finally the plowed, though snow-packed highway.

Silas patted the dash and said, "I knew you could do it, Gertrude."

"Gertrude?" she asked with a laugh. She was relieved they'd gotten out of the mountains without any trouble. She was also relieved that the easiness between them had returned.

"Be careful," Silas joked. "Don't insult her."

"I wouldn't dream of it," TJ said.

"Old Gert here reminds me of Constance."

She lifted a brow as she looked over at him. "Your

truck reminds you of the heroine in my books?" She couldn't help feeling a little offended, since she and Constance had a lot in common. No man had ever compared her to a pickup.

"Both Gert and Connie are dependable. They're up for anything when you need them. They both have their own kind of charm."

TJ smiled. "Well, when you put it that way…"

He chuckled and drove, looking comfortable behind the wheel even though the highway was slick and the landscape so white that it was hard to tell where the two-lane began and ended.

Normally, TJ would have been nervous about going off the road and ending up in a snowbank. But there was something about Silas that was a lot like his truck.

# Chapter Twelve

"I don't know how to thank you," TJ said when Silas pulled up in front of the house. "It was interesting and…fun."

He grinned. "Glad to hear it. I was delighted for the company. It was nice visiting with you. But I hope we see each other soon." He jumped out to open her door. "I meant what I said about helping find that fan of yours. If I can figure out which house I went to for that garage sale and what happened to the woman who sold me the paper, do you want to go with me to talk to her?"

She couldn't help her smile. "I do."

He nodded, his smile broadening. "Then I'll let you know."

"Thank you." She gave him a nod and a wave as she started for the house. She heard him close her door, go around and climb behind the wheel. As he pulled away behind her, she hoped she wasn't wrong about the man. His words had made her all warm inside. Not to mention what happened when she'd looked into those blue eyes.

He was the kind of man a woman could fall hard for. Which made her all the more leery. There was a reason Constance never gave away her heart in the books. Her creator had given her heart away once, only to have it broken badly. To say they were both gun-shy was to put it mildly.

She'd barely reached the porch when her sisters came rushing out, both talking at once.

As Silas drove away, a sheriff's patrol car pulled up out front. TJ and her sisters turned to see Sheriff McCall Crawford climb out.

"Are you all right?" Annabelle whispered.

"I'm fine. What is the sheriff doing here?" she whispered back.

"Chloe called her."

Of course she did. TJ sighed under her breath. "Did you get a tree?"

Annabelle smiled. "Of course. We're putting it up later."

The three waited until Sheriff Crawford joined them before going inside. Chloe, who clearly had taken charge, ushered them all into the kitchen.

"I see you made it home safe and sound," the sheriff said to TJ.

"I'm sorry my sister got you over here," she said. "I'm fine."

"She was trapped in the woods in a blizzard with Silas Walker," Chloe said, as if TJ had to be reminded. "I asked the sheriff here because I want to know more about this man who had my sister, especially since he'd been fired from the police force."

McCall smiled and declined the coffee Annabelle offered her. The two were on a first name basis after what Annabelle had found in the house last month.

"I could use a cup," TJ said as they all sat down.

"Silas bought some land in the Little Rockies about six months ago," the sheriff said once they were settled in. "I believe he built a cabin." McCall looked to TJ, who nodded. "Yes, he was fired from the New York City police force as part of an internal sting operation." Chloe looked at TJ as if to say "See?"

"But Silas was innocent. He was working undercover on behalf of the department to root out the dirty cops."

"That sounds dangerous," Chloe said.

All TJ could think about was the man who'd served her homemade bread and stew he'd made himself. The man who wrote beautiful words, deep with meaning. A man with many talents.

McCall continued. "He was offered his job back, but he declined because a cop who testifies against his own isn't necessarily welcomed back with open arms. There was an attempt on his life. He was shot. He is now employed part-time by another former police officer who started his own private investigative business."

TJ realized that she hadn't been the only one limping. But Silas had been trying hard not to show it.

"Have you met him?" Chloe asked McCall, clearly still skeptical.

"I have," the sheriff said. "I found him to be quite delightful." She looked to TJ, who nodded before picking up her coffee cup. She could feel both of her sisters watching her intently.

"I hope that answers any concerns you have about the man. But your sister told me that you've been getting threatening letters from one of your fans," the sheriff said, meeting TJ's gaze.

She nodded. "I was worried Silas might be the fan."

"But you're not now?" McCall asked.

"No, I'm not." After hearing what the sheriff had to say, she realized she could trust her instincts about Silas. Her new instincts that told her he wasn't True Fan. Not that he wasn't dangerous to her. Just the thought of him made her heart beat a little faster.

"Well if you need anything, you know where my office is," McCall said as she got to her feet.

TJ said she did and was glad when Chloe walked the sheriff to the door.

"Well?" Annabelle said the moment their older sister was out of earshot. "What happened?"

"Nothing happened."

Annabelle rolled her eyes. "How did you end up at his cabin?"

Chloe had returned after seeing the sheriff out. "Yes, how did that happen?"

TJ recounted seeing the mailbox by the road and wandering back into the woods, curious about him. "I didn't realize how far I'd gone and the blizzard was getting worse. I fell and twisted my ankle. Fortunately, he helped me into this cabin. By then it was snowing too hard to drive out so he suggested I stay the night."

"Why do I suspect there is more to the story?" Annabelle asked.

"He was very nice, charming actually, and he fed me homemade stew and bread that he'd made and we played cards until it got late."

Her sisters exchanged a look. "Have you forgotten that you thought he was True Fan?" Chloe demanded.

"No," TJ said. "And at first I thought he was. But none of that matters now. You heard the sheriff. There is nothing to worry about with him." They both looked at her as if they weren't convinced. "Isn't it possible that he's just a nice man who still wants to help me?"

"What does that mean?" Chloe asked.

"He's determined to help me find True Fan," she said with a shrug.

"Seriously?" Annabelle asked, eyes widening. "He is awfully good-looking if you like that big, muscled, chisel-jaw kind of man."

"I would be very careful," Chloe said. "Even if he isn't True Fan, this man could still be dangerous."

"You mean dangerous to someone as naive as me?" TJ said, bristling because she'd figured that out all on her own—but wasn't about to admit it.

Her sister seemed to take her time answering as if taking care with her words. "You haven't dated since Marc. That's all I'm saying."

She wanted to argue that Chloe had no idea how many men she'd dated, since they didn't live in the same city. But she saved her breath. Her sister was right. She hadn't dated since Marc. He'd been her college boyfriend. Her first. Her last. Their senior year at university, he'd gotten a job with a defense contractor working in high-risk countries.

The plan had been that she would kick-start her writing career and they would get married after he had an adventure and made a lot of money. She hadn't liked the plan, but Marc had been so excited, saying he needed to live a little dangerously before he could settle down. He'd been killed in Iraq when the company office where he worked was bombed.

"I'm only saying that I don't think you want another man who lives that close to the edge," Chloe said quietly.

TJ felt tears burn her eyes. Her sister was right. Silas Walker had gone into a dangerous profession and even volunteered to go undercover to weed out dirty cops. Just as Marc had felt the need for adventure in danger zones in the world.

"Don't worry," she said, more to herself than to her sisters. "I won't make the same mistake again."

A knock at the door relieved the tension in the kitchen. "I'll get it," Annabelle said, jumping to her feet.

TJ stayed where she was. She couldn't help thinking about how gentle and caring Silas had been. And yet from the first she'd sensed that darkness, that violence, that menace. Was she doomed to be attracted to men who liked to risk their lives?

Annabelle returned on a gust of cold air. TJ had her back to the door but she saw from Chloe's expression that something was wrong.

"Who was that at the door?" Chloe asked.

"It was Carol again from the post office," Annabelle said.

TJ didn't need to turn around. She knew without seeing the letter in her sister's hand. True Fan had sent her another threat.

SILAS DROVE AROUND Whitehorse street by street, looking for the house where he'd picked up the reams of paper at the garage sale. Whitehorse was only ten blocks square so it didn't take long to find the house where he remembered stopping at the garage sale.

He pulled up out front, got out and started toward the front door. As he did, he saw a front curtain twitch.

A moment later, he knocked at the door and waited. He knocked again.

A small elderly woman opened the door a crack. "Yes?" she asked.

"Hello." He smiled, but she still looked wary. He couldn't remember the woman who had sold him the reams of papers, but he was pretty sure it wasn't this one. The house had been for sale because the owner was moving into the rest home as he recalled.

"Who is it, Mother?" said a younger voice from behind the woman.

"I don't know."

The door opened wider as another hand appeared on the edge of it.

"Can I help you?" asked a woman a good thirty years younger.

"I was looking for the woman who used to live in this house," Silas said. "She had a garage sale here last summer?"

The younger of the two nodded. "Melinda Holmes. She moved into the rest home." She pointed down the street.

"Thank you." He started to turn away.

"You bought something at her garage sale?" the woman asked, clearly curious why he would be looking for Melinda Holmes about dealing with an item from last summer's garage sale.

"Reams of paper," he said, turning back.

"Oh." She looked disappointed. Had she been hoping for a chest with a secret in it? Or something of more value that he might have wanted to return? Whatever she'd been hoping for, those hopes dashed, she closed the door.

Glancing at his cell phone, he saw that it was still early. He drove over to the house where he'd dropped off TJ earlier. Getting out, he walked to the door, wondering what kind of reception he would get not only from her, but also from her sisters.

He climbed the stairs to the porch and knocked. The young woman who opened the door was blonde and blue-eyed. There was just enough resemblance that he knew she was one of TJ's sisters.

"Hi," he said, and smiled. "I was hoping to see—" Just then another sister appeared, followed by the one he'd come for. His smile broadened as TJ came into view.

"Silas," she said, sounding a little breathless as if she'd just raced down from upstairs. There was an awkward moment where they all stood there looking at him. The sisters were definitely giving him the once-over.

"Please, come in," TJ said, shooing her sisters aside. He wiped his feet and, removing his Stetson, stepped into the house. "I don't think you've met my sisters. This is Chloe, who's an investigative reporter, and Annabelle, who is—"

"Just Annabelle now," the young woman said.

"I was going to say, just nosy," TJ finished.

All three were beautiful alone, but together they made quite a sight.

"This is Silas Walker," TJ said almost shyly.

He nodded to the other two women. "Nice to meet you."

"Can we offer you some coffee?" Annabelle asked.

"Thanks, but I'm fine. I just came by to tell your

sister…" his gaze went to TJ "…that I found that house we talked about. The owner is in the local rest home. Melinda Holmes. Do you know her?"

"She should, since you used to steal the apples out of her tree on the way home from school," Annabelle said with a laugh. "I wonder if she'll remember you."

"Isn't that the woman who beat you with the broom as you were climbing her fence?" Chloe asked.

"Ah, the memories," TJ said as she reached for her coat. "I'd love to stay and reminisce but I have to find True Fan."

"If you haven't already found him," Chloe said under her breath.

Silas merely smiled, said how nice it was to meet them and TJ closed the door behind them. He saw that she'd showered and changed into jeans, boots and a sweater under her coat. Her blond hair was brushed and now floated like a golden cloud around her shoulders.

"I apologize for my sisters," she said. "They're… protective."

He chuckled. "You should be thankful for that." Glancing over at her, he grinned. "You really did steal apples from this woman we're going to see?"

"Let's hope the reason she's in the rest home is because she has forgotten the past," TJ joked.

"Not too far into the past though," he said as he opened the passenger side of his pickup. "We need to know who all she sold paper to."

THE REST HOME sat on a hill overlooking Whitehorse and the Milk River drainage. The valley was covered in trees that seems to follow the river northward. Silas parked and started to get out, when she stopped him.

"I got another letter."

"Let's see it." He heard the fear in her voice, but when he turned to look at her, she looked deceptively calm. However, as she opened her purse and removed the envelope, he saw that her fingers were trembling.

Silas carefully opened the envelope and pulled out the letter, trying not to touch it more than necessary. He wondered if TJ had taken the same precautions or if all three of the sisters had manhandled it. Not that he thought there would be fingerprints on it. With all the crime shows on television now, only a fool would send an anonymous threatening letter and leave behind evidence of the sender.

Tessa Jane,

I had such expectations for you and your books. I am sick over what has become of you—let alone what you have dragged your characters through. I knew you would corrupt Constance. For a while, she was the best of you.

Not anymore. That she could kill Durango… That YOU could kill him. He was the good in Constance. How could you not see that? You took a beautiful thing and ruined it.

I told you I was your only True Fan until the end. Well, I'm afraid this has to end. I can't let you write another book. I'm sorry, but you've abused your talent, and for what? Fame? Fortune?

You've been playing God with your characters—and your readers.

It's time to pay the piper.

SILAS FELT FURY roiling up deep inside him. Who was this crazy person? And more important, just how dangerous was True Fan?

He looked over at TJ. She'd gone pale, as if remembering each word of the letter as he was reading it. He told himself it didn't matter how crazy this person was or if they were serious about their threats of violence; they had to be stopped. He could tell that TJ was terrified. He couldn't imagine what it must be like for her to try to write another book with this hanging over her.

"All right if I keep this for now?" he asked as he carefully put the letter back into the envelope. She nodded as if she wanted nothing to do with it. "When is your next book due?"

"Four months from now. And no, I have nothing done on it," she said. "I might have to buy back the contract—if my publisher will let me."

He swore under his breath. "Let's hope Melinda Holmes has some answers for us," he said as he opened his door.

TJ HAD FELT sick to her stomach since opening the letter from True Fan. But having Silas helping her made her feel stronger as they entered the rest home. She'd been surprised that he'd moved so quickly on this. She hadn't expected him to go in search of the garage sale house so fast.

But she was thankful that he had and that he was taking the threats seriously. Once inside the rest home they were directed to Melinda Holmes's room. Unfortunately it was empty. A passing nurse told them to try the dining room.

They found her sitting by the window staring out

at the winter day. TJ barely remembered her from the broom-swinging woman who'd pounded her backside as she scrambled over the wooden fence behind the Holmeses' house.

"Mrs. Holmes?" Silas asked. No reaction. "Mrs. Holmes?" he said a little louder.

The elderly gray-haired woman turned from the window. "I'm not deaf," she snapped, her narrowed gaze going from Silas to TJ. "I know you," she said in a hoarse voice as her gaze bored into TJ. "You're one of those wild Clementine girls. You've been in my apples again, haven't you?"

"You grow the best apples in the valley," she said as she took a seat next to her. "This is my friend Silas."

Melinda's gaze shifted to him. "You stealing my apples too?"

"No, ma'am. I wouldn't do that."

His answer seemed to satisfy her. "So what do you want, then?"

"You're the woman who used to own the store here in town that sold paper supplies, right?" Silas said.

"That was years ago."

"I bought some reams of paper from you at your garage sale last summer."

She looked from him to TJ as if to say, "So?"

"Do you remember who all you sold the paper to?" he finished.

She looked suspicious. "Why? There wasn't a thing wrong with that paper. Might have been a little discolored, that's all. Some of it got wet, but it dried out just fine."

"It was great paper. In fact," Silas continued, "I'd

like to see if I can find more of it. I thought some of the people who bought it might make me a deal."

Melinda Holmes seemed to appreciate a man who liked a good deal. "A lot of people were at that garage sale. You expect me to remember after all this time?" She huffed at that. "There was that one woman from the school. She bought a few reams. Probably all gone now since she said she was going to give it to the school district to use."

"You don't remember her name?" TJ asked.

"Never knew it," she snapped without looking at her. Her face was set in a grim line and for a moment TJ thought that was all they were going to get.

"Then there was Nellie," the elderly woman said as if there hadn't been a break in the conversation. "She bought my bowl set. It had belonged to my mother." The woman bit her lower lip for a moment looking as if she might cry, before she said, "And there was that maddening Dot." She shook her head. "That woman has always annoyed me since she was a child. And that one fella… Sulky and kind of creepy as a boy— you know who I'm talking about," she said, turning to TJ. "He used to follow you girls home every day from school. He seemed to favor you."

"Tommy Harwood." TJ had known who she was referring to right away even though she hadn't realized that he'd followed them every day from school. She'd only caught him at it a few times.

"That's all I can remember," Melinda said, clearly finished with them. She turned back to the window.

TJ and Silas rose and left. "For someone with a bad memory she did well, I'd say," he said with a laugh. "You know these people she was talking about?" She nodded as they climbed into the pickup. "Could one of them be True Fan? Maybe this creepy kid who used to follow you home?"

"Maybe. I think I heard he lives by the railroad tracks on the way out of town," she said. "But he wouldn't be home now. He works at the auto shop. But Nellie should be home. Do you want to try her?"

Lanell "Nellie" Doll answered the door, opening it only a few inches. Still TJ saw enough of the inside to see that the woman's mother, who she lived with, was much like TJ's own grandmother—a hoarder.

"What are you doing here?" Nellie asked suspiciously.

"I stopped by to make sure you got the book I signed for you," TJ said.

"I did." She looked at Silas, clearly still waiting for an explanation.

"That wasn't the only reason we stopped by," Silas said. "Last summer I bought some paper at a garage sale from Mrs. Holmes. She thought you might have bought some as well and might have some extra still."

*"Paper?"*

"Mrs. Holmes sold it by the ream."

"If I bought some, I can't remember," Nellie said. "I probably used it up by now."

"I'm sorry, I should have introduced my friend," TJ said. "This is Silas Walker. He's a writer. Along with inexpensive paper, he was looking for a good manual typewriter."

"And Mrs. Holmes thought I might have that as well?" Nellie asked, sounding indignant. "That old woman should mind her own business."

"If you do have either, I would be happy to buy them," Silas put in.

Nellie was shaking her head. "I don't have any paper or a typewriter to sell. I'm busy so if that's all…"

"Have you started reading my book?" TJ asked before Nellie could close the door in her face. She was odd and secretive enough that she could definitely be True Fan. Not to mention unfriendly.

Nellie rolled her eyes with an impatient sigh. "If you must know, I don't care for your books. But my niece knows that we went to school together. Yesterday was my birthday so she thought it would make a nice gift to have you sign it for me."

"I see," TJ said, trying not to laugh. This was too funny. She loved the woman's honesty. "So you didn't read at least the first one I wrote, out of curiosity?"

"I couldn't get through it. But I never was much of a reader."

TJ could hear the drone of the television in the background and recognized the sound of a daytime drama. They were keeping Nellie from her "soaps."

"We're sorry to have bothered you," TJ said and Nellie quickly closed the door.

"Well, that was fun," Silas said as they climbed into the pickup.

TJ chuckled. "Wasn't it though."

"You went to school with her?"

"We weren't friends," she said unnecessarily.

He laughed. "I would have never guessed."

"I think we can scratch her off our list,' she said.

"I don't know about that. She definitely has some hostility issues."

TJ looked out the window at the town where she'd

grown up. "Some of the people I went to school with thought I was stuck-up. Annabelle was stuck-up, but me?" She shook her head. "I was shy. Introverted. I've always had stories going in my head, which were more interesting to me than school. I remember being called on by the teacher and not having a clue what she'd been talking about. I'm sure the teacher and the other students thought I was slow if not stupid. My teachers used to tell my grandmother that I didn't apply myself."

"Me, I actually didn't apply myself." He shrugged and started the pickup. "Dot next?"

"Dorothy Crest? It seems unlikely that it would be her, but I guess that's the point. Whoever True Fan is, it's someone who is hiding behind anonymity."

"True Fan is probably capable of putting on a good front to your face. The fact that he or she doesn't sign his or her name makes me think that True Fan is a coward and probably not dangerous—at least face-to-face. But if they undermine your writing then they have to be dealt with."

She smiled over at him. "Then by all means let's go see Dot." She put in a call to Annabelle, who informed her that Dot had bought her parents' house and now lived in it with her husband, Roger. With Roger at work, TJ figured they would find her alone. She was right.

Dot came to the door in an apron, throwing it open, all smiles when she saw them. "Come in! This is such a treat. A real live famous author in my home."

TJ introduced Silas.

"You write as well? Wonderful. You'll have to tell me the title of your latest book so I can pick it up. I love to read when I have time, which isn't often keeping up this house, you know."

She led them through the living room, pointing out that she had all of TJ's books on a special shelf of their own. The house was immaculate even though Dot kept apologizing for the mess.

In the roomy farm-style kitchen, she offered them cookies straight from the oven and coffee, saying that the coffee was always on at her house.

TJ took a warm chocolate chip cookie and listened while Silas visited with Dot. He asked about the paper she'd bought at the garage sale last summer, adding, "I think that's where I saw you before." He told her he'd been using his to write a novel on.

"I gave mine to the grandchildren. They love to draw and go through so much paper."

TJ was glancing around the kitchen when Dot said, "You've never seen my house. Would you like a tour?"

"I'd love one," she said, and got to her feet. The rest of the house was just as spotless as what TJ had already seen. In what appeared to be a den, she saw a laptop, but no typewriter.

"I'm halfway through your new book. I had to quit because I wasn't going to get my work done." Dot shook her head. "But I didn't want to put it down. I'm in awe of the way you make our little town come alive."

"You do know that the books aren't about Whitehorse," TJ said.

"Of course." She gave TJ a wink.

"They're supposed to be any small town in Montana."

Dot either ignored her or didn't hear her. "I'm so

glad you stopped by with your friend. I'd seen him around but I had no idea he was a writer."

TJ found it amusing that when locals called him a mountain man they were a little leery of him. But now that they would soon know he was a writer, his mountain man appearance would be accepted as just the way writers were.

They found Silas sitting where they'd left him in the kitchen, but TJ had the feeling that he'd looked around the lower floor while they'd been gone.

They thanked Dot and left, but only at her insistence that Silas take a few cookies for later.

"It's her," he joked as they drove away. "All that cheerfulness has got to be hiding something."

TJ chuckled. "I had the same thought," she said as she settled back against the seat. The sun shone in the pickup's side window. She felt warm and content and realized she hadn't felt like this in months—except in this man's presence.

"Any other leads we should follow up, or should we have lunch?" he asked.

"You probably have other things you need to do," TJ said.

"The sooner we find this creep, the better," he said.

But as he drove down the main drag of Whitehorse, she saw him suddenly look in the direction of a man crossing the street ahead of them—and freeze for a moment.

"Silas?"

He didn't answer.

"Is everything all right?" she asked, fearing what now had him looking like a man who'd seen a ghost.

He seemed to come out of his fugue state as the

vehicle in front of them that had been waiting to turn finally moved. The man who'd crossed the street was now nowhere to be seen. He appeared to have stepped into the Mint Bar. "Sorry, I just thought I saw… Never mind. It wasn't who I thought it was."

But she caught him looking back at the bar and later watching his rearview mirror as if he thought they might have been followed. Whoever he'd thought the man was, his reaction had been powerful. Silas was still spooked and she had a feeling he didn't scare easily.

## Chapter Thirteen

Silas glanced at his phone and groaned inwardly. He was still shaken. The last thing he wanted to do was cancel out on TJ. But right now he had to take care of some business—and quickly.

"I'm sorry. There's something I need to see about right away," he said to her. "Can I take a rain check on lunch? I'll call you later."

"You don't need to go see this Tom Harwood with me. I appreciate you finding the house where you got the paper. I can take it from here."

That's what worried him. "I don't like you doing this on your own. I'll take care of my business, then check with you later, if that's okay."

"Of course. But are you sure everything is all right?" she asked, looking worried. She'd seen his reaction to the man crossing the street. He felt bad enough that the man might have seen him—and TJ. He didn't want her dragged into his dirty business.

"I'm fine. We'll talk later," he said, smiling over at her. He must not have been as convincing as he'd hoped, because she still looked worried.

"I need to go Christmas shopping with my sisters,

so please, take care of whatever you need to, and don't worry about me."

He glanced over at her, his heart breaking a little with worry over her. "I can't help but be concerned. That last letter…" What he wanted to say was, "We have to find True Fan before True Fan finds you," but he held his tongue. She was already scared enough. She didn't need him sharing his instincts or experience with her.

Unfortunately, those instincts and his experience on the job told him that True Fan would be making good on those threats—and soon.

As he pulled up in front of her house, he turned to her and reached for her hand. "Do me a favor, okay?" She nodded, seeming surprised by how serious he'd become. "Don't go anywhere alone. Take one of your sisters if you insist on going out. Especially don't go chasing True Fan. Wait for me. I'm not sure how long my business is going to take me but—"

"You don't have to worry about me. I'll be fine."

How many times had he heard those words? "That's what they all say." He felt her shudder. "Just do it for me."

TJ FELT HER throat constrict. Silas was so worried about her that it gave her a chill. "I will. But promise me something," she heard herself say. "Be careful. I don't know what this business is you have to take care of, but I'm betting it's dangerous from your reaction back there."

He said nothing for a moment, just squeezed her hand. "I'll call you later."

She nodded as he let go of her hand. For a moment

she was afraid to leave him. But he reached over and opened her door and all she could do was look at him for a moment before climbing out. It felt so strange to feel this close to someone she'd met only hours before. She was making her way toward the house when she heard him drive away. There was an urgency about his leaving that made it all the more frightening.

What kind of trouble was Silas in? Something to do with his former job? Or something to do with his more recent one as a private investigator? She knew so little about him and yet she felt she knew him. Just the first chapter of his novel had made her feel closer to him. She could understand why readers thought they knew her and feared some of them did.

Her heart ached as she turned to watch his pickup disappear around a corner.

"Well?" Chloe said from the open doorway.

"Is that what you're going to say to me every time I return to the house?" TJ demanded as she stepped past her and into the warmth of the living room.

"It is if every time you leave it's with that man," her sister said.

Annabelle called from the kitchen that she'd made sloppy joes for lunch and TJ was just in time. Taking off her coat and dropping it on a chair in the living room, she followed the sweet, temping scent into the kitchen.

"I haven't had sloppy joes since I left Whitehorse," TJ said as she helped set the table. Chloe was standing in the doorway, arms crossed, looking upset. That was the problem with mystery writers and investigative reporters, TJ thought. *We see things other people miss.* Chloe knew there was more to Silas. She'd seen the darkness, the danger.

"Silas found the house where he bought reams of paper last summer at a garage sale," she said as she took a seat at the table. Annabelle brought over the dish of sloppy joes and put it on the table before taking a seat. Chloe joined them, though with some reluctance.

"The paper is the same paper True Fan uses to write me letters," TJ said. "Or at least it looks to be the same. So we asked who'd bought some of it at the garage sale last summer."

"And?" Chloe said. She hadn't touched her lunch yet.

"She gave us a few names. Dot, Nellie Doll, someone from the school and Tommy Harwood were the ones she could remember. She said Tommy used to follow us home from school all the time." She turned to Chloe. "Do you remember that?"

Her sister nodded. "He had a crush on you." She frowned. "Wasn't he at the signing?"

"He was." TJ took a bite of her lunch. "Annabelle, this is delicious. I didn't realize how hungry I was."

"So did you talk to the others?" Chloe asked.

"We didn't get a chance to talk to more than Nellie and Dot," she said, not looking up from her meal. "Silas had some business he had to take care of. He's going to call later." She lifted her gaze to meet Chloe's dark blue one. "He isn't True Fan."

"No, but he certainly has taken an interest in finding this person, hasn't he?"

TJ shrugged. "Maybe he's more interested in me."

Annabelle's eyes went wide. "So something *did* happen at the cabin. Did he…kiss you?"

TJ laughed. "No, and nothing else happened either. He was a perfect gentleman." She saw that Chloe felt that proved her point that Silas was in this just for the excitement. For the possible danger. That he was like Marc.

"So are we going Christmas shopping this afternoon?" she asked, hoping to change the subject.

"I thought we'd walk since it is such a nice day," Annabelle said. "I want to find something for Dawson. I need your opinion. I found a shirt down at Family Matters. But is a shirt too unexciting for our first Christmas together—well, first this time around?" she added with a giggle.

It was impossible not to smile at their sister's happiness. Even Chloe, whose brow had been knitted with worry, broke into a smile.

"I'll have to see this shirt," Chloe said, and finally began to eat her lunch.

TJ tried to relax. She hadn't told them about Silas's reaction earlier or her fears. She'd gotten close to this man so quickly. That alone should have been a red flag. That Silas was in some sort of trouble seemed more than likely. He'd tried to play it down, but she'd seen how scared he'd been. What did it take to scare a man like him?

She tried to put him out of her mind. It hadn't been that hard with other men she'd met and even dated. But Silas… There was something special about him. And yet, Chloe's fear that he was too much like Marc kept nagging at her. She couldn't go through that again. Her heart couldn't take it.

"You're sure it was him?"

Silas held the phone more tightly in his hand. "Not positive. I only got a glimpse of him."

"Okay," said his friend and employer at the PI agency Cal Barnum. "First things first, I'll see if he's still out here in New York. This town you're in, it's small, right?"

"It doesn't even have a stoplight."

"So there is little chance he just happens to be there?"

"None. If he's here, then he's come for me."

"Maybe you should make yourself scarce," Cal suggested.

Any other time, Silas would have taken that advice. "It isn't that simple right now. I'm helping a friend with a problem she has."

"A friend? A new *female* friend, I take it?"

"She's in trouble. I can't just drop it."

"Okay, so how long before DeAngelo finds you?"

Silas pulled off his Stetson and raked a hand through his hair. He'd figured out how small towns worked pretty quickly after moving here. People weren't suspicious. They were annoyingly helpful. Looking for someone? Hell, they'd draw DeAngelo a map to his cabin.

"I'm going to have to find *him*," he said.

Cal swore. "I'm sorry. You knew it was just a matter of time. From the start, you'd been suspicious of that crazy bastard Nathan DeAngelo."

Silas and Nathan had been thrown together as partners when Silas had started with the force. Nathan had been there for a while and had promised to teach him the ropes. It hadn't taken any time at all to see that his partner liked cutting corners.

"I'd hoped he'd have the sense to let it go," Cal was saying.

"That isn't his way." He put his hat back on, his mind already working. He had little choice. He'd have to run DeAngelo to ground—or wait at the cabin for the man to come gunning for him. Silas had never been good at waiting.

"Let me know if you hear anything I should know," he said to Cal.

"Keep in touch and…good luck."

It was going to take more than luck. He knew DeAngelo well. He'd helped bring the man down for his crimes. But when it came to hard time, the man had slipped the noose. Too many friends in high places. Too much dirt out there that DeAngelo was holding over even those in the judicial system.

So where to begin looking for the man? Although that wasn't the main question on his mind. *What are you going to do when you find him?*

TJ TRIED NOT to worry about Silas as she and her sisters walked uptown. Annabelle was right. It was a beautiful December day, the sun shining, the new snow so pure white and sparkling. Christmas decorations adorned all the houses they passed and each of the stores along the main drag of Whitehorse.

"We should drive down to Billings," Chloe said, not as enamored with the small Western town as her sisters.

"This is so much better than the rat race in the largest city in Montana," Annabelle said, and laughed because all three of them lived in cities that made Billings seem small.

"Okay, come see this shirt I found for Dawson," she said, dragging them into the clothing store.

TJ spotted her former high school English teacher looking at scarves and quickly stepped behind the racks of clothing to escape. By now Ester would have finished the book. TJ didn't want to discuss the theme or her mistakes in grammar. Ester was one of those teachers who couldn't help wanting to continue to teach even in retirement.

Annabelle held up the shirt she'd picked out. "What do you think?"

It was a blue checked Western shirt. "It looks just like him," TJ said.

"I'd just buy him a rope. He's going to need it, married to you," Chloe joked. TJ was glad to see that her older sister had quit worrying about her for the moment.

"What does that mean?" Annabelle demanded. "That he'll want to hang himself or that he'll have to hog-tie me to keep me on the ranch?"

"I hadn't thought of either of those, but you have a point," Chloe said. "Buy the shirt. He won't care. He adores you and anything you give him, he'll love it."

Annabelle still looked skeptical. She shifted her gaze to TJ who smiled and nodded. "What he really wants for Christmas is you."

"I need to go down to the gift shop," Chloe said after Annabelle bought the shirt and had it wrapped and they exited the store. Annabelle said she wanted to look in the gift shop as well.

TJ had no desire to go into a place that sold her

books for fear of running into someone who wanted to talk about the latest one. She knew killing off Durango was going to cause some readers to be upset. But she had to take the books where they led her.

Also, she had no desire to see Joyce Mason again. She considered her for a moment as True Fan and couldn't imagine the woman going to the trouble to write her the threatening letters. Joyce was more of an in-your-face kind of person.

"I'm going to duck into the coffee shop," TJ said. "Why don't you meet me there when you're through?" They agreed and parted. She breathed in the winter day, her thoughts instantly returning to Silas. Worrying about him, she didn't even notice a figure step out of the alley until she was grabbed.

A hoarse voice whispered, "Don't scream. It's just me, your biggest fan."

# Chapter Fourteen

Silas drove down the main drag, parking next to the city park. Whitehorse had been one of those spots along the railroad that had grown into a town. Because of that the unmanned depot sat beyond the small park on the other side of the tracks.

His senses were on alert as he got out of his truck and checked the street. With all the shoppers, the small town was bustling. DeAngelo couldn't have picked a better time. The rest of the year a large, dark-haired burly man wearing city clothes would have stood out from the locals and been easier to spot.

DeAngelo always wore expensive slacks and polished black shoes. He was obsessed with shoes and many times couldn't stop himself from stopping in the middle of the sidewalk to wipe away a spot on the leather.

Silas had been expecting him to show up for over a year. He'd thought it would be outside his apartment in New York City. Or maybe even *inside* his apartment. He'd been rigging his doors all these months, so sure that it was only a matter of time before they came face-to-face.

When that happened, he'd always told himself that

he would have only a matter of seconds to make his move. In truth, he would probably not have any time at all. DeAngelo knew him too well. Also there was nothing to say that hadn't already been said in court. From the witness stand, DeAngelo had mouthed "You're a dead man" the last time he'd seen him.

But after a year had passed with DeAngelo back on the streets, Silas had thought maybe the man had wised up. Maybe even a little time behind bars had taught him that he didn't want a repeat appearance.

Silas should have known better.

And now DeAngelo had not only shown up in Montana, but also at the worst possible time. Now Silas had met TJ and promised to help her. Lately, he'd even let himself think he might have a chance at settling down, having a home, a family. He desperately wanted this chance to get to know Tessa Jane. He'd actually been thinking that he might have a future.

Now those thoughts mocked him. As long as there were DeAngelos in the world, he would never find peace, let alone chance falling for someone and starting a family.

He waited for a car to pass, then ran across the street to the last place he'd seen his former partner. Pushing open the door to the Mint Bar, he stepped into the warm beer-scented darkness.

TJ SCREAMED AND kicked as she tried to free herself from the person who'd grabbed her. The toe of her boot came in contact with bone.

"Damn, you didn't have to kick me."

She spun around to come face-to-face with Tommy

Harwood. The scream died in her throat as she saw him rubbing at his shin as if she'd nearly broken his leg.

"You can't just grab someone like that," she said, furious with him for scaring her the way he had.

"I just wanted to get your attention."

Well, he'd done that.

He quit rubbing his leg and looked embarrassed. "I thought… I thought you might want to have a cup of coffee with me."

She'd been headed for the coffee shop, she reminded herself. Also, hadn't she wanted to quiz Tommy about the ream of paper he'd bought? "I'll buy," she said. "For kicking you."

Grudgingly he agreed.

"You're not working today?" she asked after they'd ordered two black coffees and taken them to a table by the window.

"Got off early."

She realized that this could be the longest coffee date she'd ever had if the conversation was anything like this. She decided to get right to it. "I meant to ask you about some paper you bought last summer at a garage sale."

He seemed surprised by the question, but answered anyway. "At Melinda Holmes's house."

"So you remember." When he said no more and looked away, she said, "Do you own an old manual typewriter?"

He looked up then, his dark eyes boring into her. "Is that really what you want to talk about?"

"I'm looking for one to buy," she said.

"And you thought I'd have one?" He shook his head. "Why wouldn't you go out with me in high school?"

Seriously? "High school? Is that what you want to talk about?"

"Yes. You knew I had a crush on you. You weren't even famous then. You weren't even *popular.* So why not go out with me?"

He wanted to be honest? Fine. "Since apparently you followed me home every day after school you would know that I didn't date much. Also it was creepy, you always looking at me the way you did, not to mention the only time you asked me out was in the middle of Biology class. You expected me to say yes in front of everyone?"

"That wasn't my best moment, I'll admit, but you still could have said something after that."

"I wasn't interested. But I wasn't interested in anyone else either."

"You went out with Darwin."

"That was his junior prom. I double-dated with my sister Chloe. She forced me to go." TJ remembered the scratchy dress, the uncomfortable high heels, the whole awkward night right up and through Darwin's sloppy kiss. The memory made her shudder. "It was a mistake. One I wasn't about to repeat."

"So you were shy and awkward. So was I. You didn't even give me a chance."

"Tommy—"

"Tom."

"That is all history. I can't undo any of it. If I could, I would never have gone out with Darwin, all right?"

"But you might have gone out with me?"

She picked up her coffee cup. "So you don't have an old manual typewriter?"

"What if I do?" he asked challengingly.

"Then I'd like to see it."

THE BAR WAS dim enough that he had to walk half-way in to see everyone inside. He told himself that he'd recognize DeAngelo without any trouble. He was wrong. The man who turned around on his bar stool had changed. His dark hair had receded. His face was gaunt and pale, and he'd clearly lost weight. He didn't look healthy, let alone strong and dangerous.

"Took you long enough," DeAngelo said. "I see you got rid of your date," he said, looking past him. "So have a seat. You can buy," he said, patting the empty bar stool next to him. "We need to talk."

The last thing Silas wanted to do was have a drink with his former NYPD partner. From the beginning they were too different. Silas went by the book. DeAngelo never met a rule he didn't want to break. But even so, Silas had never dreamed just how crooked the man had become before it was over.

"We have something to discuss?" he asked without moving.

His former partner chuckled. "You were always as stubborn as a brick. Sit down. If I was here to…" he lowered his voice even though there was no one sitting close by "…kill you, you'd already be dead and we both know it."

That, Silas thought with a grimace, was true. He knew firsthand how dangerous this man was. A part of him was thankful that DeAngelo wanted only to talk. Silas had become complacent. Up here away from the city, he'd become too comfortable. He'd let his guard down. Given that DeAngelo was here, Silas knew he should be dead. So why hadn't his former partner made his move?

Sliding onto the bar stool, he nodded to the bartender that he'd take the same thing his "friend" was having. A few minutes later, two beers were plunked down in front of them.

"I've never seen you drink beer," Silas commented. "You always went for the hard stuff."

"Maybe I've changed."

He wouldn't bet the farm on that, but he said nothing as he took a swig of his beer from the bottle. "What are you doing here, Nathan?"

TOMMY HAD WANTED her to ride in his car with him, but TJ had insisted on meeting him at his house. She let him think she had her own car. She also let him know that she had to tell her sisters where she was going since she was supposed to be shopping with them.

"Whatever," was all he said as he headed for his pickup parked across the street.

TJ waited until he drove away before she started to go down to the gift shop to tell her sisters where she was going. It was the smart thing to do. If Tommy was True Fan, she had no business being alone with him, period—let alone being with him alone and with no one knowing where she'd gone. So she was glad when the first sister she came across was Annabelle.

"I'm running over to Tommy Harwood's," she said, making it sound casual. "I'll be back soon. Shall we meet up before supper, maybe go have a steak or something?"

"Dawson's mom invited us out, remember?" Annabelle said. "You remember Willie and she wanted to see you."

"Okay. I won't be long. I have my cell." With that

she left Annabelle looking at jewelry, knowing she could be there for a while.

The walk to Tommy's house was only four blocks down the side road that followed the tracks out of town toward Glasgow. Back when the towns along this stretch of new rails were being named, whoever was in charge got tired of coming up with ideas and simply spun a globe and randomly picked. It was why there were towns with names like Malta, Zurich, Havre and Glasgow.

Tommy's car was parked in front of a small neat white house. She tapped at the front door and it opened almost as if he'd been watching out the window for her.

"You *walked*?" He sounded appalled that she'd done that after turning down a ride with him.

"I decided to leave the car for my sisters. Anyway, it's such a nice day, I wanted to walk."

He shook his head and turned back into the house. She followed. The place was as neat inside as it had been outside. She wondered if there'd been a woman in his life at some point. Hadn't Annabelle told her that he'd lived with his mother for years until her death?

"Can I get you something to drink or eat?" he asked as she closed the door behind her.

She turned and seeing how nervous he was, instantly became more nervous herself. Coming here had probably been a mistake. Knowing Annabelle she might not even remember where her sister said she was going.

"I just came to see the typewriter," she said, trying not to be rude, but not wanting him to get the wrong impression. "It's a gift for my sister Chloe."

"Yes, the typewriter," he said glumly. "It's in here."

He led the way through the house. She found herself looking for possible weapons she could use against the man if needed. Tommy wasn't large but he looked strong. Definitely stronger than she was.

He'd reached the kitchen. She saw stairs that went down into the basement but had already decided she wasn't going down there. He could bring the typewriter up if that's where he kept it. She was beginning to doubt he even owned one and was beginning to suspect this had been a ruse to get her into his house. But if that was the case, then at least he wasn't True Fan.

"There it is," he said, not going near the basement stairs.

She looked to where he was pointing and saw an old manual Royal sitting on the floor in front of a door to the screened-in back porch.

"I use it for a doorstop. It weighs a ton," he said.

She stepped over to gaze down at the machine. It had an old, worn-out ribbon in it, but from the dust on the key arms it appeared it hadn't been used in years. "This is the only one you have?"

He gave her a disbelieving look. "You didn't come here to buy a typewriter. I know. I read your book."

That stopped her cold. She held her breath, always wary when this was the way someone began a conversation with her. *I read your book.* Sometimes that was all they said. But she had a feeling Tommy had a lot more to say.

## Chapter Fifteen

"Look," Nathan DeAngelo said after taking a long gulp of his beer. Silas could tell it wasn't his first. "I don't blame you for what you did. I knew the kind of guy you were from the start. A Goody Two-shoes." He held up his hand before Silas could say what he was thinking. "Don't get me wrong. You did what you thought you had to do bringing us all down. But some of the guys aren't as...forgiving."

"This isn't news," Silas said, already bored with this conversation. He took a drink of his beer, wondering what had really brought his old partner all the way to Montana. Not to tell him something he already knew.

"I've moved on," DeAngelo continued. "I've got a pretty good gig going with a security company." He shrugged. "Keeps me out of trouble. The thing is, you taught us all an important lesson. We're not going to make the same mistakes again. We're not going to get our hands caught in the cookie jar again. That's why the guys all chipped in to hire a hit man to take you out. No way to trace it back to them."

Silas looked over at him and saw that he was serious. "And you came all this way to warn me."

"Like I said, I'm more forgiving." His gaze softened. "You and I were partners. The others can't believe you'd turn in your own partner. But I knew you would. I even suspected you were coming after us."

He shook his head. "I don't get it."

DeAngelo shrugged and drained his beer before pushing to his feet. "I can't explain it myself. Maybe I'm getting soft." He did look like he was. The security job obviously wasn't keeping him in as good of shape as the police department had. Or maybe he couldn't get his hands on the kind of drugs he'd had on the streets.

"Like you said, you could have killed me yourself and been on the next plane out of here. Why hire someone?"

"A professional seemed the way to go. Also we have something on the assassin so less chance of any blowback, you know what I mean?"

He did. "When?"

His former partner laughed. "Now what would be the fun of me telling you that?" He patted Silas on the shoulder. "Thanks for the beer. Almost like old times."

"One more thing," he said. "Did you chip in for the hit man as well?"

DeAngelo laughed and raked a hand through his thinning hair. "You know I did. Don't want them gunning for me next. It's bad enough that I didn't get the amount of time a lot of them did. And before you ask, no. No one knows I came up here to warn you. I know it's crazy, but I guess it's my way of saying I'm sorry. If you hadn't been so damned straitlaced we could have been great friends."

"I wasn't straitlaced. I just wasn't a dirty cop."

DeAngelo's smile blinked out, just like the light

in his dark eyes. "See, you have to go and ruin a nice moment. Good luck." With that the man turned and walked away.

"I'm sorry, but I don't have any idea what you're referring to," TJ said, just wanting to leave this house and Tommy. "You read my book and you know what?"

"Durango. I know why you killed him."

She hated to ask, but saw no way not to. "Why?"

"Because he wasn't the kind of man you wanted anymore."

"Tommy—"

"Tom."

"I'm not Constance. Durango died because he got cocky. He felt invincible. He forgot he was mortal." Also because Constance needed to move on from him. She needed another hero, maybe one not as flawed as Durango. Or maybe more flawed. She wouldn't know until she wrote the book.

"He was Marc, the guy you were engaged to in college," Tommy said.

She felt her face burn with irritation and embarrassment. That was one of the problems with a small town. People knew way too much of your business even after you left. Anger overtook her embarrassment. She didn't have to explain her actions to anyone, especially Tommy.

"I really don't want to talk to you about this," she said, and looked at her watch. Her sisters should be through shopping by now, or at least interested in eating.

"It's fine if you don't want to admit it," he said. "But if you ever quit making the same mistakes with men…"

She stared at him. True Fan told her how to write. Tommy was telling her how to run her love life? "Who are you to tell me who I should be with?" she demanded angrily.

"Just the man who's watched you make the same mistakes since you were a girl," he said, apparently unperturbed by her angry outburst.

"I can see myself out," she said, and spun on her heel, stomping out of the house. The walk back into town did her good, even though the temperature had dropped. The air smelled as if snow was imminent. She'd heard that yet another storm was coming in. Winter in Montana, she thought, and pulled her coat tighter around her.

She was almost back when a horn honked right behind her. She jumped, having not heard a vehicle approach. Turning, she told herself that if it was Tommy she would kick in one of his door panels.

But as the car pulled alongside, she saw it was her former English teacher Ester Brown. Great, she thought, as Ester whirred down her passenger side window.

"Why don't you get in," she said in a tone that made it clear it wasn't a question but an order. "It's too dangerous to walk along this road."

TJ bristled. A few too many people had been telling her what to do. She wasn't one of this woman's students anymore.

"Thanks, but no thanks. I want to walk so I'll take my chances getting run down on the road." She turned and stalked off, keeping to the edge of the road facing traffic so the elderly woman didn't mow her down on principle.

She heard Ester mumble, "Always was too stubborn for her own good," before she hit the gas and took off with the chirp of the tires.

Fortunately, town was only a short walk. She found her sisters coming out of the drugstore, both carrying an assortment of packages. They really had been Christmas shopping. She realized that she should be doing some of her own. But she couldn't get into a holiday mood—not with True Fan so close by.

"Where have you been?" Chloe asked with her usual suspicion.

"Didn't Annabelle tell you?"

Annabelle, who had been looking into one of her bags she was carrying, looked up at the sound of her name.

"You didn't tell Chloe where I'd gone?" TJ chastised. What if Tommy had been True Fan? What if she was bound and gagged in his basement?

"Oops, sorry." Annabelle turned to Chloe. "She went to Tommy Harwood's house."

"Not all that helpful now, sis," TJ said.

"Why in the world would you do that?" Chloe cried.

"I thought he might be True Fan," she said, suddenly tired. She watched Ester Brown drive by, glaring at her as she passed and turned away from the street. She was reminded of all the reasons she'd left here, threatening never to come back. "Tommy gave me a lecture on my mistakes when it comes to the men I choose."

Both of her sisters lifted brows at that.

"I'm starved," Annabelle said quickly to change the subject before they got into an argument on the street. "Let's go to the Great Northern and have some lunch."

TJ looked up the street and saw Silas coming out of

the Mint Bar. He spotted her and stopped. He'd been headed toward his pickup parked across the street when he saw her. Now he stood as if unsure what to do.

"You guys go on ahead. I'm tired and not hungry right now. I think I'm going to walk home." She headed toward Silas, ignoring Chloe's comment that for the first time Tommy Harwood might actually know what he was talking about.

JUST THE SIGHT of TJ stopped Silas in his tracks. His spirits instantly lifted and just as quickly dropped. Nathan DeAngelo was a lot of things, a liar among them. But this time, Silas believed the man. He'd found over the years that there really was often some misguided honor among thieves. He also knew how much Nathan had hoped that Silas would adopt his way of thinking when it came to following the letter of the law.

"Hi," TJ said as she approached. She was frowning.

He realized that she'd seen him come out of the bar. She'd also seen his reaction earlier when he'd spotted DeAngelo crossing the street to the bar. She was too sharp not to have put it together.

As he looked into her beautiful face, he knew he had to keep his distance from her. It was bad enough that Nathan had seen him with TJ. He couldn't have his enemies using her against him. And at the same time, he couldn't just dump her unceremoniously.

The thought surprised him since it wasn't like they were a couple. But he'd promised to help her find True Fan and the one thing he'd lived by all his life was making good on his promises. He also couldn't put her in any more danger than he had and yet, seeing her, all he wanted to do was take her somewhere, just the two of them. He felt torn. While he shouldn't be with her right now, he also couldn't explain himself on the busy street.

A snowflake drifted down, followed by another large lacy one. His breath came out frosty white as he stepped to her. "Is there somewhere we can go and talk?" he asked. "Alone?"

She nodded and let him take her arm as they crossed the street to his pickup. Once inside, he started the engine, waiting for the heater to warm up enough to chase off the frosty chill in the cab. TJ hadn't said anything since climbing into the passenger seat. Outside, snow began to fall in a blur of white.

"I could take you to one of my favorite places outside of town," she said, breaking the quiet.

He looked over at her, telling himself all the reasons this was a bad idea and yet unable to simply walk away from her. The heater began to warm, clearing off the frost on the windshield enough that he would be able to see to drive.

Shifting the pickup into gear, he pulled out and followed her directions as they left town and headed northeast. Neither of them spoke as he drove. Snow blew across the highway. He recalled someone telling him they were called snow-snakes. It had a hypnotizing effect. He had to concentrate to keep the pickup on the highway as both the snow on the ground and the now falling snowflakes whipped around the truck.

They'd gone out of town some miles before she told him to turn. He checked his rearview mirror, not for the first time. He didn't believe they'd been followed.

That was the problem with a small town. There was no reason to follow them. All the killer had to do was wait. It would be easy to find Silas's cabin. This was the kind of job even an amateur should be able to handle.

The road TJ had him turn onto went from snow-packed pavement to deeper snow-covered gravel before she told him to turn once more. He could see an expanse of flat white through the falling snow. As they neared it, he realized it was a frozen-over lake. He saw picnic tables covered with snow under the trees along the edge of the lake and pulled down into one of the campsites.

This one was somewhat sheltered by the trees. He left the engine running, knowing how quickly the cab would get cold without the heater, and watched the snow whirling around them. He liked the intimate feeling. He could almost pretend that they were the only two people on earth in the warm cocoon of the pickup's cab.

"You're in some kind of trouble, aren't you?" TJ said after a few moments.

He glanced over at her and simply nodded. "I can't let you get dragged into it so I'm going to have to stay away from you for a while."

"What if that isn't what I want?" she asked, her voice breaking.

He met her gaze. His blue eyes shone. "It is the last thing I want. I know I promised to help you find True Fan—"

"Is that the only reason?"

"I think you know better than that." He let out a frustrated sigh and reached over to brush a lock of her hair back from her face.

TJ closed her eyes at the warm caress of his finger-tips on her cheek.

"Tessa Jane." He said her name like a curse, his voice thick with emotion. "All I can think about is you. You've completely captivated me."

She opened her eyes and met his blue gaze. Without another word, he reached for her, drawing her across the bench seat of the pickup. She felt a burst of pleasure expand inside her as he wrapped her in his strong arms and kissed her. His mouth was warm and sweet on hers.

"I've been wanting to do that since the first time I saw you," he said pulling back to look into her face.

She kissed him in response, weaving her fingers through the curls at his nape, breathing in the male scent of him. Desire sparked into a blaze inside her. She didn't care what Tommy or her sisters said. Silas was all man and more enticing than any she'd ever met. She felt safe in his strong arms and desperately wanted to lose herself in him.

He kissed her again, this time slowly, expertly. He deepened the kiss as he slid out from under the steering wheel to pull her onto his lap. She pushed aside his coat and opened the buttons on his shirt until she could press her palms to his rock-solid chest. She felt him shudder, desire a blowtorch in all that blue. Heat pulsed through her to her center.

Silas unzipped her coat and found his way to her bare breast. She arched against him as he thumbed the already hard nipple to an aching point. His hand slipped into her jeans and panties. He found the spot and she knew this had been building for some time because she cried out as the release came almost immediately.

He drew her to him, holding her as she felt the waves of release ebb through her, leaving her feeling weak. She started to reach for him, but he stopped her and kissed her tenderly. "I hadn't meant for it to go this far. The first time I make love to you, I don't want it to be in the front seat of my pickup. I want to take this up sometime soon." He touched her cheek, his fingertips warm, his gaze filled with desire. He groaned and pulled back his hand. "We should get going."

She fixed her clothing, zipping her coat. Even with the heater going, the windows had fogged over. This was so not like her. She barely knew this man. This was the kind of thing that Constance would do. For some reason that made her smile to herself.

Silas slid back over under the wheel and turned up the heat. "I'm not going to be able to see you for a while." He glanced over at her.

"You're not going to tell me what kind of trouble you're in."

He shook his head as he reached over and caressed her shoulder for a moment. "I can't tell you how much I hate this. But while I'm worried about you and True Fan, being around me right now is more dangerous."

"I'm getting it narrowed down. I talked to Tommy Harwood today." She shook her head at the memory. Wouldn't Tommy love to know about this? She felt her face heat and looked out at the lake for a moment. "It's not him. I've reached a dead end."

"I thought by following the paper trail we might find this creep. I'm sorry. The paper didn't lead us anywhere."

She agreed. "Too many people could have gotten some of that paper even if they hadn't bought it at the garage sale. But I think you're right. True Fan is a coward." She turned toward Silas. "So take care of your trouble and don't worry about me."

"That won't be easy," he said as he removed his hand from her shoulder and got the truck going. She heard the worry in his voice and knew that whatever trouble he was in, it was serious.

## Chapter Sixteen

Silas dropped her off at her house after another kiss. TJ could tell that he hadn't wanted to let her go any more than she had wanted to leave him. Their feelings for each other had happened so quickly, it scared her. But it also excited her. For the first time in her life, she was being adventurous. It felt good.

She thought about his kisses. It felt wonderful.

"I don't know when I'll see you again," he said, his voice rough with emotion. "But know that you won't be far from my mind."

She'd wanted to ask him how dangerous this trouble was, but in her heart she knew. She'd seen how scared he'd been when he'd recognized the man crossing the street earlier. Someone from his past? Someone he'd helped put in jail? Whoever it was, the man was dangerous.

Her heart ached. She and Silas had just found each other and now... Both of them had someone who was clearly threatening to hurt them and it had thrown them together. Earlier, at the lake, that feeling of impending doom had pushed them together faster than either of them had wanted.

But there was no denying the chemistry between

them. They'd bonded at the cabin. She thought of their card games late at night with a blizzard howling outside the cabin and hugged that memory to her, afraid she might never see Silas alive again.

"This is about those cops you put in prison, isn't it?" she asked.

He looked at her. She could see him fighting not telling her the truth. "Was that man in town to kill you?"

"No. Warn me."

Her chest felt as if an elephant had settled on it. "Can you go to the sheriff?"

He shook his head. "I have to take care of it myself."

"Oh, Silas."

He touched her cheek again. "I need you to be careful."

"You too." They locked gazes for a long moment before he reached over and opened her door. There was nothing more either of them could say.

She watched him drive away before making her way up the porch steps and into the house. Her sisters were in the living room. They'd opened a bottle of wine. Both looked up expectantly at her as she came in and hung up her coat.

"Oh no, you didn't," Chloe said.

TJ turned, feeling her face heat even as she denied it. "We kissed and made out some…"

Her sister groaned.

"Oh let her have some fun," Annabelle said.

As TJ joined them and poured herself a glass of wine, she found herself near tears with worry. "I like him."

"We can see that," Chloe said.

"You should invite him to the Christmas dance at

the old gym," Annabelle suggested. "Everyone in town will be there. Dawson and I are going." She grinned, hugging herself.

"The two of you are killing me," Chloe said.

"Isn't there someone you were interested in at the newspaper?" Annabelle asked.

Their sister shrugged. "I dated some, but no, I've never met The One."

"How do you know?" Annabelle said, turning in her chair as she warmed to the subject. "Look at Dawson and me. I left him even when he bought a ring and asked me to marry him. I thought he'd never forgive me. He said I broke his heart." Her voice cracked with emotion and tears flooded her blue eyes. "But we found our way back to each other. What about your old boyfriend, Justin Calhoun?"

Chloe shifted uncomfortably in her seat. "He wasn't my boyfriend exactly. Anyway, that ship sailed a long time ago. Didn't he marry…what was her name?"

"Nicole Kent," Annabelle said. "But he didn't marry her. They were engaged—at least according to Nici—but they broke up. She married someone else, got divorced. She lives here with a couple of her sisters and their kids."

"You've certainly gotten caught up on local gossip," TJ said, and took a sip of her wine. "Didn't Tommy live with his mother for a long time?"

Annabelle laughed. "As a matter of fact, he did. She died a few years ago and he sold her house and bought that one out by the tracks."

TJ looked over at Chloe. She seemed to be lost in thought. Justin? The two of them had seemed perfect for each other but Chloe had been on her way to college so nothing had come of it. But TJ had always wondered if Nicole Kent hadn't been the reason the two hadn't seen each other after that. She remembered the girl and felt a shiver. That one had always been trouble.

They all jumped at a knock on the door. Exchanging looks, TJ got up this time to answer it.

"You really should get a post office box," Carol said as she handed her the letter that had come for her. "You're going to get me fired."

"Thanks for bringing it by, but if anymore come—"

"Don't worry. I'll see that you get them." Carol turned on the step and, the bells she was wearing jingling, took off toward her vehicle. Carol always wore bells at work this time of year.

TJ looked down at the letter in her hand and realized her hand was shaking.

"Here, let me open that," Chloe said, taking the letter from her as TJ stepped back inside. She tore it open and pulled out the sheet, discolored like all the others.

This time True Fan didn't even bother with her name.

I told myself not to take it personally. But you have ignored everything I've told you. You seem to think you're so much smarter than me. You don't need my help. You never have.

All my attempts to make your books better have been ignored. You find me to be nothing more than a pest you can't seem to get rid of. Well, that will soon be over. I've tried to let it go. But in good conscience I can't let you go on the way you are.

I don't think of myself as a violent person.

But someone needs to stop you. This time you've gone too far. I guess I'm going to have to do it myself since you didn't take my advice. You could have done the world a favor by taking your own life, but why would you listen to me now? I'm going to have to take care of this myself. There is apparently no one else.

There was no True Fan to the end. The letter just ended.

Chloe threw it down in disgust. "This person is crazy. I think it's time to take it to the sheriff." She got to her feet. "Do you have the other letters that have come since we've been here?"

TJ nodded. There was a chilling violence to the letter, as if the person had reached some breaking point. She hugged herself as her big sister made the call.

Annabelle took the empty wine bottle and glasses into the kitchen. She'd finished washing the glasses when there was a knock at the door.

THERE'D BEEN FEW times in Silas Walker's life that he hadn't known what to do. He prided himself on making quick decisions, the kind that had saved his life more than once. But right now he felt adrift. He had no idea who had been sent to kill him—not that it would make much of a difference if he did.

He'd like to think that DeAngelo had exaggerated about just how professional this hit man was. He hoped for an amateur. Or at least someone who would give him a fighting chance by being just bumbling enough to give him a slight edge.

As he drove through the falling snow back toward

the cabin, he considered his options. He could return to New York City. Or he could take his chances at the cabin. He couldn't get TJ off his mind. Right now, the last thing he needed was his mind on anything but staying alive.

Earlier, he and TJ had come close to making love in his pickup. He'd wanted her more than he'd wanted to stay alive at that moment. To find someone like her now, now when his life was on the line, seemed too cruel a cosmic joke. It made him more determined to come out of this kickin'.

He stopped at the turnoff where he still had good cell phone coverage and called his friend and boss. "I just had a visit from my former NYPD partner. My buddies hired a hit man to take me out."

Cal swore. "How can I help?"

"I thought there might be something on the street. I'd like to know who this guy is and if he's already in Montana."

"I'll put my ear to the ground and see what I can find out. Aren't most of these old buddies still locked up?" his friend asked.

"A couple of them skated, but most of them are still behind bars, why?"

"You're talking cold-blooded murder. They knew some lowlifes on the street, but not hit men. I'd say they met someone while in the pen and contracted him. Let me see who recently got released and call you back."

Rather than hope for service at the cabin, Silas drove on into Zortman to the bar. He braved the storm and climbed out to go inside even though the last thing he wanted was alcohol. The place was packed with the approaching holiday and the weather. He found a small empty table near the door and sat down where he could see anyone who entered. When the waitress came over he ordered a beer and a burger, realizing he hadn't eaten all day.

He'd finished the burger and half of the beer when Cal called back. A boot-stompin' song was playing on the jukebox so he tossed down some money for the waitress and took the call down the hallway toward the men's restroom.

"I'm good friends with the warden at the local penitentiary," Cal said without preamble. "He says the dirty cops are in a wing by themselves fearing for their lives so they didn't have much contact with inmates. However, there was one they were seen talking to in the yard a few times. He recently got out. He's called Little Huey, a mean son of a bee who's done a lot of time for everything *but* murder. Real name's Herbert Jones. Caucasian, five foot nine, doesn't weigh a hundred and fifty pounds soaking wet, but rotten to the core."

"Might explain why he's so mean. Probably had to be at that size on the streets," Silas said. "If it's him he'll try to shoot me in the back, blindsiding me rather than come right at me."

"That would be my guess. You won't see him coming."

Sheriff McCall Crawford read the letters twice before folding them and putting them back in their envelopes. "You say there have been others?"

TJ nodded. "A dozen or so over the past six months."

"More threatening than these?" the sheriff asked.

"Some. At first True Fan was complimentary, but

then that began to change. I didn't listen to the advice the reader was offering."

"Your fan suggested suicide?" McCall asked.

"Highly suggested it so I didn't write any more books that I would be embarrassed by," TJ said.

"And what makes you believe this individual might be in this area other than the postmark on the letter?"

TJ told her about the reams of paper that Melinda Holmes had sold after it had been stored for years in her basement. She told her about Nellie, Dot and Tommy, the people who had bought the paper that Melinda remembered. "It's a rather distinct color that would be hard to match."

The sheriff agreed. "Man or woman?"

"Sometimes I think man. Other times, woman. I have no idea."

"You had a book signing the other day. Anyone come through who made you suspicious?"

TJ laughed. "Everyone makes me suspicious. But I suspect it is someone with a connection to New York City since True Fan sent me a photo taken from the sidewalk outside my apartment. The person wanted me to know how close they were." She thought about mentioning being pushed into traffic but tended to agree with Silas that it might have been accidental.

"There are people in town with connections to New York," McCall said thoughtfully. "Others who have visited. Would be interesting to find out who might have asked one of them to take a photograph of her favorite author's apartment. Or if they did it themselves. Is that information public knowledge?"

"No, but Silas suggested that someone could have followed me from one of my book signings. I've done signings only blocks from my apartment and walked home afterward. I wasn't paying attention. Anyone could have followed me without my knowledge, waited on the street and seen me close my curtain before turning on a light on the third floor."

The sheriff nodded. "I noticed in one of your social media photos there is a pretty good view of the interior of your apartment. The curtains were open and I could see not only their design—but the building across the street. Probably wouldn't take anyone with a knowledge of the area long to find you."

TJ shivered. While she was writing about stalkers and killers and how they found their victims, there was one stalking her—and she'd probably made it easy for True Fan. She could have even given her stalker ideas on how to find her in her books.

"Mind if I take these with me?" McCall asked as she got to her feet, still holding the letters.

"Please take them," TJ said, and watched the sheriff pocket the envelopes. "You agree that it's someone here in Whitehorse?"

"It would certainly appear that way. Let me see what I can find out. If you get any more or you think of anything else, please contact me at once," the sheriff said.

"I will." TJ walked her to the door and stood on the porch hugging herself against the storm as the sheriff drove away.

As she started to turn back inside the house, she looked out at the neighborhood wondering if she was being watched at this moment by True Fan.

Silas finished his call and rather than walk back through the bar, decided to exit through the back. He circled around to his pickup. He'd already checked out the clientele enjoying themselves in the bar and hadn't seen anyone suspicious, let alone Little Huey. He had looked for the man who would be sitting alone. Even if Little Huey tried to blend in, he would stick out like a sore thumb in Montana.

He'd been aware of that very thing when he'd first moved here. It hadn't mattered how he'd dressed; it wasn't as if he could just put on a Stetson, jeans and boots and no one would know he wasn't from here.

That's why he knew his would-be killer would be sitting alone nursing a drink. That's if he'd already gotten this far.

Now as he walked out into the cold snow, Silas tried to think like a killer. If he was after a man like him in a state he didn't know, where would he start?

He'd fly in, rent an SUV or a pickup. A town like Whitehorse had a ten trucks to one car ratio. Then he would drive up the three hours from the airport to the western town.

Then what? If he asked a lot of questions, people would notice and say something about it. So he'd come armed with not just weapons. He'd know as much of his victim's backstory as he could get out of the men who'd hired him.

So he'd know about the cabin outside of Zortman. Silas thought of his mailbox down by the road. He couldn't have made it easier for someone to find him. Look how TJ had found him in a blizzard.

Climbing into his pickup, he started the engine and let it run. Snow had piled up on the windshield and now frozen down. His wipers were covered with ice. He let the defrost run while he thought it out.

His would-be killer would have to come prepared for the weather. That might be tougher. Unless he'd been in a Montana blizzard he would have no idea how hard it was to see—let alone get around—in the deep snow. He would have had to have purchased good boots, snow gear, a hat, goggles. Even that might not save him if he got turned around in the storm or stuck on the road.

Most people, with towns so far apart, carried food, water, blankets and matches. Silas had taken to carrying a sleeping bag behind the seat of his pickup. He never knew when he might need it. Which was also why he carried the shotgun on the rack behind his head—and the pistol under his seat.

But neither would protect him if Little Huey shot him in the back.

He saw that some of the snow had melted on the windshield, but the wipers would have to be cleaned off. He started to climb out when through the small defrosted spot on his windshield, he saw a man exit an SUV and head toward the front of the bar.

Silas felt his heart drop like a stone. His buddies hadn't sent Little Huey.

## Chapter Seventeen

Kenny "Mad Dog" Harrington. Silas thought about ending this right here and now as he watched the man go into the bar. Kenny hadn't seen him with the windshield still mostly covered with snow and ice.

Silas stayed where he was for a moment and then hit his wipers. Enough snow and ice came off that he could see well enough to drive. Eventually the falling snow would cake on the wipers and he'd have a blurry mess on his windshield, but right now that was the least of his worries.

He drove out of town, watching his rearview mirror. Had Mad Dog already been out to his cabin? He would know soon enough. On the way, he tried to think. Little Huey would have been waiting in the trees to ambush him. Mad Dog was a whole other breed of violent criminal. He'd come head-on. It would take a cannon to stop the crazy bastard.

Turning on to the road into his cabin, he saw that there were two sets of tracks. Someone had gone in—and come back out. Mad Dog had been to his cabin. Which meant he would be back. Silas had no idea how much time he had to get ready for the killer.

His mind raced as he drove, all the time keeping an

eye on the rearview mirror. No Mad Dog yet. Maybe he would have a few drinks, snort some coke or take some uppers. Silas knew how hard it was to stop a junkie. A junkie with Mad Dog's size and determination would be almost impossible to stop even filled with lead shot. But Silas had no choice unless…

He was almost to the cabin when a plan began to crystallize. It would be damned risky. Crazy under other circumstances. But worth a shot, he told himself as he pulled in front of the cabin and cut the engine. He would have to move fast. He had one thing going for him: Mad Dog wasn't smart. Also it was snowing so hard, his tracks would be covered quickly.

TJ's CONCERN FOR Silas had been growing by the hour. The thought of him alone at the cabin was driving her crazy. She kept telling herself that he was an ex-cop; he could handle himself. But she'd seen his reaction to the man.

"Can you sit still for five minutes?" her sister Chloe snapped. "This is about Silas Walker, isn't it? What has you so worked up?"

She wasn't about to tell Chloe. Her sister already thought that he was the wrong man for her. If she knew the danger he was in right now… "We left things a little…up in the air," she said truthfully.

Chloe shook her head.

"He isn't anything like Marc," TJ said in her defense.

"Nothing at all," her sister repeated sarcastically.

"What are you two arguing about?" Annabelle asked as she came into the living room with a plate of cookies. "Who wants milk?"

"Leave it for Santa," Chloe joked as she took a cookie. "We were arguing about men."

"So who's the right one for you?" Annabelle asked Chloe as she curled up in a chair and took a warm cookie.

"Justin," TJ said. "Is he still in town?" she asked Annabelle.

"Sorry, he moved away after he married some rich movie star." Annabelle almost choked on her cookie at her joke, before she said, "No, seriously, after Nici married, he was single for a long time. About five years ago, he married Margie Taylor and they moved to Bismarck, North Dakota, to farm her father's place. The marriage didn't last."

TJ raised a brow. "I'm amazed after being in town for such a short period of time how quickly you got caught up on all the local news."

Chloe groaned. "Excuse me, but we weren't talking about my lack of love life. We were talking about Silas Walker."

Her cell phone rang and she sprang to her feet. "Saved by the bell." She headed for her bedroom as she took the call from her agent.

"How are you doing?" Clara asked.

"Okay. I did the signing."

"I heard. Nice turnout?"

"Not bad."

"You made *The New York Times* Best Seller list," her agent said.

TJ knew she should be more excited about that. "That's wonderful."

"Not as high as last time, but it's early. Let's see if it stays where it is or goes even higher."

She was amazed how little any of this mattered right now.

"Have you heard from your True Fan?"

"A few letters, but I'm fine."

"Okay, but you don't sound fine. Maybe True Fan will give you a break over the holidays. When are you coming back?"

That was the question, wasn't it? "Not sure yet." She hadn't booked round-trip. Getting a flight could be difficult. But that didn't worry her either.

"Okay, I'll let you go. If you need anything…"

"I'll call. Have a wonderful holiday." She disconnected. She hadn't even asked where her book had hit on the *Times* list. Lower than last time. That was enough to know. She wasn't even tempted to check online. Normally, she watched closely the first few weeks of a release.

When she came back downstairs, Annabelle's fiancé Dawson Rogers was sitting in the living room. He got to his feet when he saw her, hugged her, wished her a Merry Christmas, then announced that he'd come to get them all for dinner out at the ranch.

"I decided to drive in for you since the visibility is poor and the roads are a little slick," he said.

She glanced out the window and realized he was downplaying how bad it was. "I hate to be a party pooper, as Grandma Frannie used to say, but I'm going to have to pass. Please give my best to your mother. I'm sure I'll see her over the holidays."

Her sisters started to put up an argument, but gave up quickly when they realized she had dug her feet in and wasn't going to change her mind. She wasn't in the mood for dinner and polite conversation. She had a terrible feeling about Silas that she couldn't shake.

As they all departed, she noticed that Annabelle had left the keys to her SUV on the hook by the door. She told herself that going out in this storm was more than risky. It might prove to be suicidal. Worse might be going to Silas's cabin when from what she could gather, there was a killer after him.

She thought about calling the sheriff. And telling her what? That Silas's former cop friends wanted to kill him? McCall couldn't do anything more than TJ could. That's when she knew that if she really wasn't going to do this, then she had not only to dress for the winter storm, but also to go armed.

"You're acting as if you think you really are Constance Ryan from one of your books," she said to herself as she went around the property getting things she thought she might need.

Silas worked as quickly as he could, given the weather. Another storm had blown in. Snow whirled around him, the cold wind biting at any exposed skin. When he'd first bought the land and begun to build on this spot, he'd thought about booby-trapping the area around it.

That was back when he'd been more worried about his former cops' plotting vengeance. He'd ditched the idea, fearful that he'd catch hikers or hunters in his traps and find himself in a lawsuit—if not worse. Also he hadn't wanted to live like that—fearing for his life every day.

Instead, he'd told himself that if they came for him, he'd deal with it then. As time went on, he'd begun to relax. Montana had that effect on him. He had liked feeling safe here, even knowing that it could change at any point.

Now as he finished loading the last booby trap, he stopped to listen. It was hard to hear anything over the wind whipping the pines and howling off the eaves of the cabin. He stared out into the storm, unable to see more than ten feet through the whirling snow.

Mad Dog would have the same problem.

Silas had worked hard since returning to the cabin. He'd known he didn't have much time. From the tracks around the cabin, he'd been able to surmise that Mad Dog had looked around, probably deciding how to come at him.

Now all he could do was wait. The question was where? Inside the cabin would make it too easy for his would-be killer. He couldn't depend on his booby traps stopping Mad Dog. All he could hope for is that one of them would delay the man long enough to give him the upper hand.

TJ STARTED THE SUV, then remembered something she'd forgotten in the house and, leaving the motor running, had run back inside.

Her heart was pounding. Common sense argued that she was doing a foolish thing. But that ache in her stomach, the feeling that Silas needed her, wouldn't let her turn back.

Inside the house, she found the flashlight she'd forgotten. It would be dark by the time she reached the cabin. She thought about texting Silas to tell him she was coming but he would just try to talk her out of it and right now she feared any reasonable argument would be all she needed to change her mind.

Back at the SUV, she was delighted to see that part of the windshield had cleared off. She used her gloved hand to take care of the rest. The snow was still falling so hard that it would cover it again if she didn't jump inside and use the wipers.

She climbed in, cranked up the heater even higher and turned on the wipers. To the steady clack, clack, clack, she shifted into Reverse and backed out.

It wasn't that far to the cabin. Once she was sure that Silas was all right… Text him, the voice in her head said. Text him. Don't make this drive in this kind of weather. Not to mention the fact that he wants you to stay away while he handles this.

She thought of Marc. She'd begged him to come home, but he was having too much fun. He loved the danger. He loved telling her about the close calls he'd had. She'd heard it in his voice. He thrived on the near misses.

Silas was different. He didn't want this. She remembered seeing both fear and dread on his face. *He knows he's mortal,* she thought. *He's strong, courageous, but only when it is demanded of him. He doesn't go looking for trouble.*

She was almost to the Zortman turnoff. She began to slow when she heard a sound in the seat behind her. Her gaze shot to the rearview mirror, her pulse taking off like a rocket as a face appeared a second before Tommy dove over the seat and dropped in beside her.

TJ screamed. The SUV swerved.

"Don't do anything stupid," he cried. "Keep driving or you're going to kill us both.

"Don't hit the brakes," he yelled as she hit the brakes.

The SUV went into another skid, but straightened as she jerked her foot from the pedal. Fortunately, there weren't any other vehicles on the road.

"What are you doing?" she demanded of him. "How long have you been back there?"

"I climbed in when you went back inside the house for your flashlight." He sounded so reasonable. "I couldn't leave things the way we did earlier."

"You were back there all this time and didn't say anything?" she demanded, furious with him.

"I wanted to see where you were going," Tommy said. "I had a pretty good idea. Nice to see that I was right."

"What do you want?"

He looked over at her in that irritatingly calm way he had about him. "Why would you drive up here in this storm? You're worried about him. You think he might have another woman in his cabin?"

"No!" She slammed her palm on the steering wheel. "I think he's in trouble. That's why you shouldn't have gotten into this vehicle. You're messing up everything."

"Wait a minute. You think this ex-cop is in trouble and you've come to save him?" Tommy reached down to look into the bag she'd brought. His gaze shifted to her at the sight of the makeshift weapons. He shook his head. "It's a good thing I came along."

"How do you figure that?" She didn't want him here, nor did she like him knowing the impulsive and no doubt foolish thing she'd done. Because seeing it through his eyes, she knew that's exactly what it had been.

The realization moved her to tears. She wiped angrily at them.

"What are you doing?" Tommy asked.

"Turning around and taking you back to town."

He stopped her with a hand on her arm. "I can help."

She looked over at him. Her skepticism must have showed.

"I have a little training for this sort of thing."

She continued to look at him.

"In the service. You do know that I was in the military, right?"

Did she know that?

"Just tell me one thing. Who wants him dead? The cops he put in prison?"

It surprised her that he knew so much about Silas. It made her wonder if his interest was before she came back to Whitehorse or if it was more about her.

"That's my guess. There's a man in town who wants him dead I'm afraid," she said.

Tommy nodded. "I wish I'd known that before we got here, but not to worry. Turn around and go into Zortman. I have a friend I can borrow a few real weapons from. Do you know how to shoot a gun?"

She shook her head as she turned around. That Tommy was taking this seriously made her feel less foolish about driving here, but just as ill-prepared.

Tommy told her where to turn once they drove into the tiny town. "Stop here." The moment she cut the engine, he grabbed the keys. "No offense," he said, and jumped out.

She waited, wondering what she'd gotten herself into. If Silas wasn't in trouble… Or even if he was, what would he think of her showing up with Tommy?

She didn't have long to consider that before he was back with two handguns and a rifle and who knew what other weapons he had under his coat. He tossed them into the SUV and then slid into the passenger side again.

"Let's go," Tommy said as he handed her the keys. "I know a back road."

She stared at him for a moment, realizing she'd never seen this Tommy, before she started the SUV.

# Chapter Eighteen

Mad Dog came out of the trees and rushed the cabin like the wild man he was. He was almost to the door when he hit the first trip wire. The hatchet struck him in the thigh, falling short of the chest where it had originally been aimed.

The hit man let out a shriek of pain. The blade had left a nasty bleeding gash but did little to stop Kenny. He roared and charged the porch. The second booby trap sprung, this time working better than the first. Mad Dog was caught by his ankle and jerked off his feet.

He was hanging upside down from a tree limb five feet off the ground when Silas came around from the back of the cabin. He had only a second, not long enough to raise his rifle and shoot before Mad Dog fired.

The bullet grazed the size of his head. He rocked back, connecting with the corner of the cabin as he got off a shot. It went wild. He pumped another cartridge in and fired. Mad Dog howled with pain, swung around and let loose a barrage of bullets.

As Silas was diving behind the corner of the cabin, he caught another one; this one grazed his shoulder.

He fired another three shots, all of them hitting their mark, but Mad Dog showed no sign that any of them had done mortal damage.

Silas's head wound was losing blood fast. He could see that Mad Dog was also bleeding, but not bleeding out fast enough. Mad Dog tossed a handgun away and pulled another. Even hanging upside down, the man didn't stop.

Silas ducked back as bullets pelted the corner of the cabin. He wiped at his temple and felt the darkness wanting to close in. He felt himself getting lightheaded. He had to finish this one way or another.

Firing around the edge of the cabin, he heard his bullets hit their mark but Mad Dog's only reaction was a roar of anger. Another barrage of bullets pelted the ground and the corner of the cabin as Silas ducked back again. Even upside down, Kenny was still a damned good shot.

He heard a loud crash and the splinter of wood and knew that Mad Dog had cut the rope he'd been dangling from and had crashed down on the bottom steps of the porch. He also knew that the man would be coming for him. There was a reason Kenny had been tagged Mad Dog Harrington.

With so many bullets pumped into the man, Kenny should be down for the count. But given the drugs he'd no doubt taken, Silas was wondering if he would be able to kill him before Mad Dog killed him.

Darkness faded in and out at the side of his vision. He blinked, trying to stay on his feet but feeling the effects of his blood loss. If he didn't finish this, and soon…

TOMMY INSTRUCTED TJ to kill the engine. "This is where we get out."

She looked into the storm raging around the vehicle and could see nothing but snow and the blur of the green pines beyond it.

"You might want to stay here," he said. "I'll come back and let you know what's happening."

TJ shook her head. She'd come this far. Now she had Tom involved in this. She had begun thinking of him as Tom—not Tommy anymore. He offered her a gun. She shook her head. "I'd probably shoot myself." Instead she grabbed one of her simple-to-operate weapons, ready to brave the storm and whatever else was waiting for them.

They exited the vehicle and Tom led the way through the woods as they dropped down the mountain. He motioned for her to be as quiet as possible. She could hear nothing but the wind high in the pines and the pounding of her heart as she tried to see through the snowstorm. All her instincts were still telling her that Silas needed help. But what if she was wrong? What if it was too late?

Snow whipped in her face and down her neck. She pulled her hat lower and coat tighter around her. They hadn't gone far when she spotted part of the cabin's roof through the trees. Tom motioned for her to stay back as he moved forward toward the back of the house.

They reached the outhouse. Tom stepped around it, TJ right behind him. She saw Silas first. He lay against the side of the cabin at its corner as if he'd just decided to sit down there. She couldn't tell if he was dead or alive, but the snow was red around him. She started to run to him, but Tom held her back.

A huge man came around the corner of the cabin holding a gun. He stopped to look down at Silas. As the man raised his weapon to finish the job he'd started, Tom lifted his rifle and fired. He kept firing as he charged forward until the big man returned fire.

Tom stumbled and went down. The big man limped over to him. She could see that the man was wounded and bleeding badly, but he was still on his feet—and still about to kill both men.

As the man raised his gun, TJ did something that even her heroine Constance wouldn't have done. She charged the man.

SILAS KNEW HE must have blacked out because when he came to, he was sitting in the snow. Confused for a moment, he saw his rifle in the snow next to him and wasn't sure if it was still loaded or not. Snowflakes drifted around the corner of the cabin to melt on his face. He turned his head, not sure what he was seeing.

Mad Dog stood over someone lying in the snow a few yards from him. As the hit man raised his rifle to shoot the person, a figure came screaming out of the storm. With a jolt, Silas saw that it was TJ. She had a baseball bat in her hands.

Turning slowly as if not so steady on his feet, Mad Dog looked over at her as if he didn't believe what he was seeing. Silas felt the same way. She was so small compared to him. Mad Dog looked almost amused.

Silas tried to sit up, but felt his head swim again so he laid back. Just the act of pulling his handgun from his shoulder holster, almost made him black out again.

He finally managed to get it loose just as TJ, still charging the man, swung the bat. The sound reminded him of a pumpkin left by kids in the street being crushed by a car tire. Blood shot out of Mad Dog's mouth and flew over the snow, leaving a bright red trail. Silas fired the handgun, emptying it into the crazed man.

For too many seconds, Mad Dog didn't move. Silas could see that TJ was ready to swing the bat again if need be. As Mad Dog started to lift his weapon in her direction, Silas yelled his name and tried to get up. The darkness closed in.

TJ SAW WHAT the big man planned to do. Silas sat bleeding by the corner of the cabin. Tom was down in the snow just feet away. She looked into the big man's eyes and knew she was about to die as he raised the gun in his hand and pulled the trigger.

There was a click, then another one, followed by two more, but no gunshot. The man looked down at the gun in his hand, as confused as TJ for a moment. Her heart pounded so hard her chest ached. Her throat had gone dry. She'd looked death in the face.

She swung the bat. It caught him completely off guard. This time, his head snapped back as the bat connected with his temple. He dropped like a sack of potatoes. She stood there, the bat ready to hit him again if need be, trembling so hard she could hardly hold on to the weapon, terrified that he would get up again.

But he lay in the snow, his eyes open and blank, and after a few moments she dropped the bat and fumbled out her phone. As she did, she heard the sirens. How was that possible? She rushed to Tom. He was still breathing. Then she went to Silas. He too was breathing. He smiled up at her, then closed his eyes and dropped off into unconsciousness.

From behind her, she heard movement and swung around. Tom was on his feet. "I called the sheriff when I went in to get the guns," he said as he approached her. Then he smiled. "You really are Constance."

## Chapter Nineteen

TJ had plenty of time to think about Tom's words as she waited at the hospital for word on him and Silas. She still couldn't believe what she'd done. She'd acted on instinct and it had almost gotten her killed. If the crazy big man hadn't run out of ammunition in his gun...

Her sisters spotted her and came running down the hall, only to be reprimanded by the head nurse. They pulled her into the waiting room, both talking at once. She held up her hand and realized it was still covered with blood.

Both of her sisters saw it, their eyes widening. Chloe dropped into a chair. Annabelle just stood there, mouth open for a moment.

"It's kind of a long story," TJ said. She told them what Silas had told her about the police officers sending someone to kill him and how she'd had this bad feeling that he needed her, so she'd decided to drive up to his cabin.

Chloe looked at her as if she'd lost her mind.

"I had just turned onto the road to Zortman when Tom popped up from the back of the SUV. He'd been hiding there waiting to see where I was going."

"Tom?" Chloe repeated, having noticed that she was no longer calling him Tommy.

"He told me he had experience in the military and wasn't letting me go alone after I told him why I was determined to check on Silas." Her breath caught in her throat at the memory of the crazed big man standing over Silas about to kill him when Tom starting firing at him.

"If Tom hadn't been there, Silas would be dead. You can't believe this hit man. The EMTs said when they're high on all these drugs these kind of men are nearly impossible to kill. I don't know how many times the man had been shot…" Her voice broke. "Tom was shot. He's in surgery."

"What about you?" Chloe asked as she reached over and took TJ's trembling hands in hers. "The sheriff mentioned something about a baseball bat?"

TJ nodded. Looking back it was as if it had been Constance Ryan who'd leaped out of her books to swing that bat. "He would have killed us all but he'd run out of ammunition in his gun. He pointed it right at me. The look in his eyes…" She shuddered at the memory. "I watched him pull the trigger again and again, but there was only this loud *click, click, click*."

"What did you do?" Annabelle asked, on the edge of her seat.

"I'd already hit him with the baseball bat once and it barely fazed him. But I swung it again and that time…" She shook her head. "That time he went down and he didn't get up. Tom had called the sheriff when he went into a friend's house in Zortman to get guns. I've never seen him like that."

"And Silas?" Chloe asked.

"He's going to make it. He's lost a lot of blood and has a concussion, but he's going to be fine, the doctor said. Now I'm just worried about Tom. If he hadn't come along with me…"

Her sisters got up to come over and hug her as the doctor appeared at the door to tell them that Tom Harwood had come out of surgery and was doing fine.

SILAS OPENED HIS EYES. The room seemed too white. Was he dead? He blinked and brought everything into focus. A hospital room. For a moment, he couldn't remember what had happened. He touched his head. Bandaged and hurting like hell. Something shifted on his bed. He looked down to see TJ. She'd pushed her chair over so she was right next to his bed. Then she'd apparently fallen asleep with her head on the edge of his mattress.

He stared down at her, enough of last night coming back to him to make him scared for her all over again. She'd been at the cabin carrying a baseball bat? Or had he only dreamt it? He touched his bandage again and this time TJ stirred awake.

She blinked at him and brushed some stray locks from her face. "You're awake. How are you?"

"Alive. I think I have you to thank for that."

"Actually, it was more Tom Harwood. I'm sure you'll hear all about it. Right now, the doctor said you just need to rest."

"There is something about a baseball bat," he said.

"Don't concern yourself with that right now," she said, avoiding his gaze.

He wanted to throttle her. "I should turn you over my knee…"

She shifted her gaze to him and smiled. "There's time for that when you get out of here."

He laughed, even though it hurt his head. "You saved my life. I owe you."

"We can discuss that too," she said, still smiling as she took his hand and brought it to her lips.

TJ COULDN'T REMEMBER the last time she'd decorated a Christmas tree. She'd done little to her apartment during the holidays. From the back of her closet she would pull out a small fake tree that was already decorated and plug it in.

She had found herself dreaming sometimes of Christmas back in Whitehorse. Sledding and snowball fights with the boys in the neighborhood, hot chocolate back in the kitchen with their grandmother before decorating her truly ugly fake tree.

Today though, their grandmother's house smelled of pine and gingersnap cookies. Annabelle couldn't seem to quit baking. Her sisters had dragged in the tree they'd cut up in the Little Rockies and they'd stood it up. Instantly, it was like being in the woods again. Being at Silas's cabin, TJ thought.

"Is this practice for marriage?" Chloe had wanted to know when they'd found Annabelle in the kitchen early that morning baking. The house smelled of ginger and cinnamon, and TJ breathed it in as if it was her last breath. Her apartment never smelled like this, not that she baked. In the city, it was too easy to run down and pick up anything you wanted to eat.

This morning, the three of them had sat around the kitchen table reminiscing about Christmases past. They'd eaten warm cookies and milk for breakfast, laughing about some of their Grandma Frannie memories before deciding it was time to tackle the tree.

TJ had been the first one up, long before Annabelle began baking. Even before the sun was up, she'd gone to the hospital to see how Tom was doing. He was sitting up and had more color than the first time she'd seen him right after surgery.

"How are you feeling?" she'd asked.

"Not bad." He'd smiled. "You were amazing."

She'd laughed. "I could say the same about you. You saved my life and Silas's."

He'd given her an embarrassed shrug.

"Thank you, Tom."

"Tom," he'd said and grinned. "Does this mean that Tommy is behind us?"

She'd nodded.

"I'd ask if you've fallen for this ex-cop, but it's clear you have. Does this mean you'll be staying in Whitehorse? I'd like it if we could be friends. Just friends."

"Truthfully, the future is a bit blurry right now. But we can definitely be friends."

Now, she stood back for a moment to look at the beautiful tree her sisters had found and cut down all on their own in the mountains. It was a fir and smelled wonderful. The branches were thick and already naturally decorated with tiny pinecones.

"I'm so glad you saved Grandmother's ornaments," TJ said as she dug in the last of three boxes that had been full. She held up a paper angel. "Remember this one?"

The whole morning had been like that. Each ornament had a memory for one of them. That's why it was taking so long for the tree to get decorated. All those trips down memory lane had derailed them multiple times.

At the sound of someone at the door, they all turned and then shared a troubled look.

"I'll get it," TJ said and hurried to the door, expecting to see Carol from the post office standing outside. But it wasn't Carol. "Silas? I thought you weren't being released until tomorrow."

"I talked the doctor into letting me out. I had to see you."

TJ ushered him inside. He was limping badly, he had a smaller bandage on his temple, but he was alive and smiling. Her sisters said hello, asked about his health and then discreetly left them alone.

"The sheriff filled me in on everything that happened," Silas said after she'd offered him a seat. He leaned toward her. "TJ, you could have been killed!" He shook his head. "What were you thinking?"

"That you were in trouble. The feeling was so strong I couldn't ignore it."

His gaze softened. "I don't know how to thank you and at the same time, never do anything like that again."

She smiled. "I can't promise that. If I feel like you need me…"

He rose and pulled her to her feet and into his arms. "I do need you. But what am I going to do with you?"

"I bet you'll think of something," she said and he kissed her, pulling her into him as if he needed to feel her body against his as much as she did.

"Go to the Christmas dance with me?"

She laughed. "I haven't danced in years."

"Me either. But I heard there will be mistletoe." He grinned.

"Are you sure you're up to dancing? You just got out of the hospital."

His grin broadened. "Oh, I'm up for a lot more than dancing."

Just then Annabelle came careening down the stairs to race into the kitchen. Smoke billowed up from the oven. "I forgot my last batch of cookies," she cried, making them both laugh.

Silas pulled TJ to him and kissed her, backing her up against the wall. His gaze locked with hers. Then something crashed in the kitchen and they heard footfalls on the stairs and moved apart, laughing as Chloe appeared.

TJ couldn't remember being so happy. She wanted to pinch herself. When Silas looked at her like he was right now, she almost forgot about True Fan.

THE OLD GYM was rocking with the sound of loud music and the roar of voices as the Christmas dance kicked off for the season. It was a huge yearly event. Some listen to the music and watch from the bleachers as others danced. It appeared that the whole town had turned out.

The old gym had been decorated with lots of sparkly lights. It reminded TJ for a moment of the only prom she'd attended, which made her grimace. Then Silas had put his arm around her, bringing her back to the wonderful, amazing present.

Chloe hadn't wanted to come. "You both have dates."

"You're going," Annabelle had told her. "I promise you'll have fun."

Chloe had made a face but had finally agreed to come at least for a little while. TJ had seen her talking to three cowboys they had gone to school with and later dancing.

As Silas pulled her out onto the dance floor, TJ put her head on his shoulder and closed her eyes. She loved the smell of him, fresh from the shower and yet so male. He pulled her closer as they swayed with the music. She felt so safe in his arms. But it was so much more than that. That feeling of being complete, being content, being happy filled her.

She never thought she'd ever experience this. She'd been such a loner all of her life. All she'd ever wanted was to write. That had been her driving force for so long. Silas made her want more. Opening her eyes, she looked around the room and felt such a sense of community. She'd forgotten what it felt like being part of a small town.

As the song ended, she was shoved hard against Silas. She turned to see Joyce stumbling away. It appeared she'd been drinking because she turned to sneer at TJ and kept going.

"You know her?" Silas asked.

"Went to school with her."

He chuckled. "What did you do to her?"

"That's just it. Nothing that I can recall. Sometimes I think I get blamed for things I didn't do."

As they both watched Joyce weave unsteadily through the crowd and disappear out the door, TJ wondered if Joyce could be the one writing her the threatening letters. The woman seemed so angry, she could be True Fan.

"Can I get you a drink?" Silas asked as they stepped

off the dance floor. She could tell his leg was bothering him and said as much. He denied it.

"Fine," she said. "But let's sit out a few dances."

He smiled at her, cupping her cheek, his gaze locking with hers. "After this is over, I was hoping to get you alone."

Her heart hammered in her chest. Heat rushed through her, colliding at her center to make her cheeks flush. Pulse pounding at the thought of being alone with him, all she could do was nod. She watched him walk away and could tell that he was trying not to limp. She headed over to where her sisters had gathered.

"Who was that I saw you dancing with?" she asked Chloe.

"Cooper Lawson."

"Justin's best friend from high school," Annabelle said.

"Don't read anything into it, all right?"

TJ laughed. "So you didn't ask him anything about Justin?" Chloe shot her a warning look, but TJ noticed that her sister looked happier than she'd been for some time.

"Where's Dawson?" she asked Annabelle.

"Drink line."

TJ looked in that direction but she didn't see Silas. "Oh, no, there's Mrs. Brown."

Annabelle looked toward the door where Ester had just come in and now stood brushing snow from her sleeve. "I heard she had a series of ministrokes and it's changed her personality."

"Maybe she isn't as grumpy as she used to be," Chloe said, and laughed.

"Or worse," Annabelle said.

"I just remember how upset she used to get with me in her advanced English class," Chloe said. "She would go to write something on the board and actually break the chalk in her fury. She once threw the chalk at me, missed, but almost hit Kirt, who was behind me. Later I saw her in the teachers' lounge crying. I know I was terrible. But she was always singling me out, especially when she knew I hadn't been paying attention."

"No wonder she is always glaring at *me*," TJ said with a groan. "I swear she's mad at me because she has me confused with the two of you. I was the good sister." She was distracted for a moment as she noticed Joyce standing by the entrance. The woman was looking right at her before she pushed out the door. The look gave her a shiver.

SILAS INSISTED ON a last dance since it was a slow one. "I like holding you," he said as he drew her to him. "The problem is that I don't like letting you go and the holiday will be over before we know it." He drew back to look at her. "I was wondering if you'd like to come up to the cabin for a few days after Christmas. I know you'll want to be with your sisters for the holiday—"

"I would love to."

He smiled and let out a breath as if he'd been holding it. "I might even decorate the cabin."

"There's no need. The cabin is perfect just like it is."

"You really do like it," he said, sounding a little surprised.

She frowned. "Of course. I have such good memories…" Her voice trailed off. "I know it was only one night, but I felt as if—"

"As if we'd known each other a lot longer." His smile

broadened. "I felt the same way. I've never had that happen before. Dates are always so—"

"Awkward, and you promise never to go through it again," she said with a laugh.

"Exactly." His blue eyes sparkled in the twinkling Christmas lights. "But with you, it was different. With you—"

"It was nice."

He nodded and leaned down to kiss her as the song ended. They stood on the dance floor as people began to leave. He kissed her again, then stepped back as if just then realizing the dance was over. "I'll get our coats," he said, his voice sounding rough with no doubt the same desire she was feeling.

Her legs felt a little wobbly as she made her way toward the bleachers where her sisters had gathered along with Dawson and some other friends. She heard them discussing going down to one of the local bars for a nightcap or two.

She'd almost reached them when someone grabbed her arm.

"Dear, would you mind walking me out to my car," Ester Brown said as she latched on to TJ's arm with shaking bony fingers. "I think I might have overdone it."

TJ looked toward the cloakroom and the huge line. It would be a while before Silas could get their coats. Ester apparently had never taken hers off.

"It's just right outside," Ester said, as if seeing her hesitation. "It won't take you a minute." She tugged on TJ's arm and the two of them headed for the door.

TJ shot a look over her shoulder at her sisters. She

got Annabelle's attention and called, "Tell Silas I'll be right back."

"Silas," Ester said as they reached the side door. "Is he your beau now?"

Was he? She supposed so. At least until the holiday ended. "He's just a friend."

"Sure he is," the woman said under her breath. "My car's right over there." They walked through the freezing night air. Unlike Ester, who was all bundled up and in snow boots, TJ wore only a party dress and high heels.

As they stepped outside, TJ saw Joyce standing in the shadow of the building having a cigarette. She could feel her dark eyes on them as they crossed the parking lot.

"That woman doesn't like you," Ester said, following her gaze. She still had a bony-fingered grip on TJ's arm.

"I can't understand why."

Ester chuckled. "Maybe she's read one of your books."

TJ glanced over at her. Mrs. Brown had a sense of humor? She was still chuckling as they crossed the parking lot.

Fortunately, Ester didn't seem to have the breath for walking—and talking. She'd thought her former teacher might want to bend her ear about her books, but that didn't seem to be the case. While in apparently good shape other than those minor strokes she'd had, Ester appeared to be winded by the time they reached her car.

"You know, I'm not really feeling up to driving," the elderly woman said. "I hate to impose, but would you mind, dear? My house is so close by. You're welcome to bring my car back."

"I can walk. It's no problem." She was already freezing, but she couldn't say no. Ester seemed to be breathing hard. What if she was about to have another stroke? TJ definitely didn't want her driving.

"You are such a dear," Ester said as TJ helped her into the passenger side, then, taking the keys the woman handed her, climbed behind the wheel.

Ester's home was only three blocks from the old gym where the Christmas festivities had been held. Snow crystals hung in the air as she drove, the night clear and cold. All TJ could think about was getting Ester home and then returning to the old gym—and Silas. Right now, in his warm, strong arms was the only place she wanted to be.

She started to park the car in the driveway, but Mrs. Brown had already hit the garage door opener.

"I prefer to keep my car in the garage," she said as the door yawned open.

TJ pulled the car in and had barely stopped before Ester had the garage door closing behind them. She turned off the motor and started to turn to the elderly woman when she saw what Ester was holding. Her heart slammed against the walls of her ribs. "What?" The word came out on a surprised and suddenly scared breath.

"Not very succinct for a woman who makes her living writing," her former English teacher said as she waved the gun at her. Ester was still breathing hard, but she didn't look at all incapable of pulling the trigger.

"In case you're wondering, I know how to use this," the woman said. "I'm an excellent shot. Get out of the car. I don't want to shoot you in my garage, but I will if you don't do exactly as I say. It will be a first for you."

"Why are you doing this?" TJ cried.

"Because I can't let you write another one of those awful books," Ester said. "You had so much promise." She shook her head. "Parents over the years have chastised me for being too blunt." She huffed at that. "Honesty, that's what kids need. Good, old-fashioned honesty. That's what I've tried to give you. But did you listen? Of course not."

TJ stared at her as realization froze her in place. "You're True Fan."

"Not anymore," the elderly woman said. "I said I would be until the end. Well, this is the end. Now get out of the car and don't test me, Tessa Jane. If you had listened to me back when you were in my classes… Well, it's too late, isn't it. You won't be embarrassing me any further."

Ester pressed the barrel end of the gun into her back and shoved her toward the door into the house. They moved through the kitchen and into the living room. TJ's mind raced. What was Ester planning to do? She'd said that she couldn't let her write another book. Was she going to shoot her?

As they moved through the house, she looked for something she could use as a weapon. But she saw nothing that would allow her to spin around and disarm the woman before Ester shot her.

She tried to calm down, telling herself that her sisters would realize she hadn't come back. They would look for her. Silas had gone to get their coats. When he returned and they told him where she'd gone he would eventually come looking for her. If Annabelle remembered to tell him. She had to believe that he would find her—that someone would find her—as Ester jabbed her with the gun and pointed toward a door ahead.

TJ heard the word "basement" and knew that she had to do something. Surreptitiously she slipped off her bracelet. Silas had commented on it earlier. It was silver with tiny silver trees on it. She'd bought it the day before because it had reminded her of his place in the woods.

"Mrs. Brown, you can't do this," she said rather loudly to cover the sound of her dropping the bracelet next to one of the chairs in the living room. If the woman didn't find it before someone came looking for her, they might see it; they might know that she was here.

"I've already done it," Ester snapped and, reaching around her, opened the basement door.

All TJ could see was darkness. Before she could react, Ester shoved her. She fell forward, screaming as she tumbled downward.

## Chapter Twenty

When Silas returned with their coats he looked around, but he didn't see TJ. Her sisters, though, were standing over by the bleachers. Most everyone had already cleared out. A few stragglers were standing around.

"We were just going uptown for an after-the-party drink," Annabelle announced when she saw him. "Do you and TJ want to come along?"

The last thing he wanted was a drink, and he was considering how to decline without hurting anyone's feelings when he asked, "Where is TJ?" He thought she might have gone to the women's room and looked in that direction.

"She just took our former English teacher out to her car," Chloe said. "It will give us a chance to talk."

He tried not to laugh as she drew him away from the others. He'd been expecting the third degree from TJ's older sister so he wasn't surprised. "I love TJ."

Chloe waved that off as if it wasn't important.

"I want to marry her. I was thinking of asking her on New Year's Eve," he said. "But I was worried that it's too early. I don't want to scare her off."

"You hardly know each other," Chloe said, sounding shocked.

"I know her. I knew her through her books before I met her."

She huffed at that. "You think she's Constance Ryan?" Chloe shook her head. "She's not. She's a prude. She's a chicken. She's—"

"She's braver than you know," he said, remembering the woman who'd saved his life. "She and Constance have a lot in common."

"She's been hurt by a dangerous man before."

He nodded. "She told me about Marc. I'm not him." He realized he was still holding their coats. He looked toward the door. "Shouldn't TJ be back by now?"

"Mrs. Brown is probably out there chastising her for some improper grammar she found in one of her books," Annabelle said, joining them. "Remember what a stickler the old bat was? All that stuff about participles and gerunds? It's a kick that Ester reads TJ's books. But then again, TJ was one of her best students. She should be proud that TJ has made a career as a writer."

Silas looked at Annabelle, hating the sudden worry that had begun roiling in his stomach. "How long have they been gone?"

"Quite a while," Chloe said, now frowning. "We'd better go save TJ from her."

Silas pulled on his coat and, taking TJ's with him, said over his shoulder, "I'll check on her. You guys go on to the bar." He headed for the door, but stopped before going out. "What kind of car does Ester drive?"

"An older model. As big as a tank," Annabelle said. "Blue, I think."

Silas told himself TJ was fine, but all his instincts told him otherwise. He thought about the boxes of old discolored paper. Mrs. Taylor had said she'd sold one of the boxes to someone from the school. A teacher? A former teacher?

Once outside he looked around. A few people were coming and going. He didn't see a big blue car. He didn't see TJ or Ester Brown. Maybe TJ had decided to drive her home. He ran back inside, asked for directions to the woman's house and then ran to his truck.

He told himself that TJ could hold her own with an elderly woman. But his fear was that she wouldn't see it coming.

TJ GASPED AS a glass of cold water was thrown in her face. She didn't know how long she'd been knocked out. After the shock of the cold water, she became aware of the pain. She hurt all over. Worse, she found herself bound with tape on the floor. In the dim overhead bulb Ester had turned on, she could see that her ankles were bound, along with her hands. Her arms and one knee were scraped and bleeding, and her head ached.

She looked up into Ester's weathered face, still feeling as if this couldn't be happening. Her former teacher had pushed her down the basement stairs. It was a wonder the fall hadn't killed her, and yet Ester didn't seem to be in the least bit concerned. *Probably because she plans to kill me anyway.*

She looked around the basement, still feeling as if her brain was fuzzy. She spotted a small desk with the old manual typewriter sitting on it. Next to it was an open ream of the discolored paper. The rest of the box sat on the floor next to the desk. She thought as her mind seemed to be clearing that this was the teacher who'd said she bought it to give to the school.

Ester had been down here secretly writing the letters? But not just those, she saw. The trash can next to the desk was filled with wadded-up paper. Even from where she was tied up TJ could see what appeared to be a stack of typed pages on the other side of the typewriter. A book Ester was working on? Why write down here and not upstairs? Why keep it a secret?

She saw that Ester was fiddling with something over by the stairs. TJ began working at the tape binding her wrists behind her. It felt a little loose. If she could get her finger under the last loop...

Ester, she realized, had been wiping TJ's blood off the basement stairs railing. The thought made her stomach drop. How long did she plan to keep her in this basement? Or was she going to kill her and maybe bury her down here? Ester knew that surely she'd never get away with this.

Unfortunately, as the woman turned toward her, TJ saw something in her eyes that told her Ester wasn't worried about getting away with it.

"Did you know that I used to do some writing myself?" Ester asked conversationally as she pulled up a chair in front of her.

TJ stared at her, wondering if she was hallucinating all of this. "I didn't know," she managed to say, since it appeared Ester was waiting for a response.

"Of course you didn't. I was talented, but I needed to make a living." At the edge of the bitterness was pain and regret. TJ had heard it before from aspiring writers. "I dreamed of writing books and being famous like you." Her voice broke.

TJ didn't know what to say. "Now that you're retired—"

Ester shook her head, the gun in her hand still pointed at TJ's heart even though she was bound to the chair. "It's too late."

She decided now wasn't the time to point out that Ester could have written in her spare time as a teacher. The woman had never married or had more to look after than a cat. Maybe she could have found time to write.

But it was clear Ester wanted to blame someone for the fact that she'd never written the books that she'd dreamed would have brought her fame and fortune.

TJ felt badly for her because there'd been a time when she'd had to work at an eight-to-five job. All she'd wanted to do was write. She remembered the frustration. She had the feeling that if she could just write full-time, she could get published. She could support herself on her writing.

It had been hard back then, but she'd gotten up early in the morning and written as much as she could before she had to go to work. Then she'd written late into the night. It hadn't been easy and what she'd written wasn't that great, but she wasn't the only writer who'd had to make a living as well as write starting out.

"That's why you're so angry with me," TJ said, realizing what this really was about. Tessa Jane had the audacity to become a writer while Ester felt she'd been kept from it by students like TJ and her sisters.

"I had talent," Ester said angrily. "I tried to share that talent as a teacher with students like you. But you never appreciated it. When I wrote you the letters, I knew you wouldn't take them seriously if they were from me. That's why I didn't sign them. I thought I could help you..." Her voice broke.

So instead of writing her own books, Ester had wanted to rewrite TJ's.

She didn't know what to say, but she knew she had to say something. Ester seemed confused, as if now that she'd taken TJ, she didn't seem to know what to do with her. Had she just wanted her to know the truth?

"Ester, I'm so glad you've finally told me that the letters were from you. I didn't realize that you were just trying to help me."

Ester stared at her. "How could you not realize it? I told you—"

"But how could I trust it not knowing who the advice was coming from?"

The older woman stared at her. "As if you would have listened even if you'd known. You were impossible in my class."

"I think that was my sister Chloe, or maybe Annabelle. Mrs. Brown—"

"You're just trying to confuse me. I need to think." Suddenly she seemed agitated. The hand holding the gun was shaking.

"You don't want to hurt me. You need to let me go. This is not the way you want to end your teaching career."

Ester huffed. "I didn't even get a gold watch. A luncheon and a pat on the head before I was replaced with a young teacher who doesn't know grammar and couldn't care less."

"I'm sorry," TJ said, not knowing what more there

was to say. Ester felt as if her life hadn't mattered. TJs heart went out to her.

"Actually, I owe you so much. I learned a lot in your class. I wouldn't have been as successful as I've been without you."

Ester cocked her head at her as if trying to judge if she was just saying this.

She rushed on, all the time still working at the tape around her wrists. "I loved the writing assignments you gave us," she said, trying to remember one of them that Ester might also recall. High school had been so long ago and yet for Ester it had been only months ago. It was no wonder the students had all run together in Ester's mind—at least TJ and her sisters.

She thought about what Annabelle had said about Ester having a series of ministrokes. That could account for some of this strange behaviour as well, especially if Ester had had them in the past six months.

"My favorite writing assignment was a character study. Do you remember that?"

"Of course I do," her former teacher snapped. "I used it in all my classes."

"I wrote mine about the hall bully. You liked it so much that you read it to all your classes. It was the first time I realized that I might actually be a writer. That I might actually succeed at it."

Ester got a faraway look in her eyes for a moment. "Rick. That was the boy's name."

TJ nodded and felt a ray of hope even though Ester was still holding the gun steady and pointed at her heart.

"I do remember that," Ester said, and looked confused again. Her gaze met TJ's. "Tessa Jane Clementine. Yes, that was one of my best." She frowned. "Your sister wrote about a character on television." She shook her head and sighed.

"You gave me hope that day. All I ever wanted to do was write."

Ester nodded, tears in her eyes. "That's all I wanted too."

"So you need to let me go. This is just a misunderstanding."

Unfortunately, the woman shook her head again. "I can't do that."

ESTER BROWN'S HOUSE was only a few blocks away. The moment Silas pulled up in front of the small white home, he saw that there were no lights on inside. Also there was no blue car parked outside. But there was a garage to one side.

Is it possible they would have gone somewhere else? He couldn't even be sure that TJ was with the older woman. But both Annabelle and Chloe had seen her leave with Ester. He told himself that TJ was so accommodating that she might have taken her by the gas station to fill up the car for her. Or even the grocery store for milk and bread.

But his gut told him that wasn't the case. Fear gripped him as he climbed out of the truck and ran up to the garage. He peered in. A big blue boat of a car filled the small space. He ran up the front steps, rang the doorbell and then hammered with his fist before trying the door. Locked.

Where the hell were they?

He tried to calm down. But he knew that something was terribly wrong.

He saw a loose brick in the planter that ran the full length of the house and jumped down to retrieve it. Back up on the porch, he threw the brick through the small window next to the door. The glass shattered. He knocked the lethal-looking shards aside and reached in to unlock the door.

AT THE SOUND of breaking glass upstairs, Ester jumped, and for a moment TJ flinched, fearing that she would accidently pull the trigger. They both froze, listening. Someone was breaking into the house.

TJ opened her mouth to scream only to have a balled-up sock stuffed down her throat. She gagged and tried to spit it out, but Ester held it in place with a strip of tape.

"Stay here," she ordered before taking the gun and starting for the stairs.

Like she was going anywhere bound like this. But she had managed to loosen the tape on her wrists. She waited until Ester's back was turned as she headed up the stairs before she worked frantically at the tape. Whoever had come to rescue her wouldn't be expecting Ester to be armed. That could be a fatal mistake.

SILAS HAD JUST gotten the door open when Ester Brown appeared. She still wore her coat as if she hadn't been home long. Her hands were in the pockets. She didn't look that surprised to see him or that upset that he'd just broken into her house.

"What do you think you're doing?" she demanded in a voice that reminded him of a teacher he'd had in middle school.

"Where's TJ?"

"TJ?" she asked, and frowned as if the name didn't ring a bell.

"Tessa Jane. She helped you out to your car, possibly drove you home?"

Ester frowned. "Well, yes, but the last I saw her was in the parking lot with Joyce Mason."

He thought of the woman who'd seemed to purposely bump into TJ at the dance. He'd seen Joyce's expression. It had been hateful. For a moment, he thought he'd broken into the wrong house. But then he saw something over by one of the chairs and recognized it at once as the bracelet TJ had been wearing at the dance tonight.

Ester had followed his gaze—and seen it as well. She stepped to the side as if to block his view, but then must have realized it was too late. Her face filled with anger.

"Ester, what have you done with TJ? TJ!" he called.

"She can't hear you."

He started to rush past her when she pulled the gun. It looked so incongruous that for a moment he thought it was a joke.

But one look in her eyes and he knew this was no joke. His heart dropped at the thought of what she could have already done.

"As I told Tessa Jane, don't try me," she said. "I know how to use it. I don't want to shoot you, but I will." Her voice was so calm he froze. He wasn't quite close enough to her to disarm her. Nor did he doubt she would shoot him. Something in her eyes.

"Where is TJ?"

"You'll see soon enough," Ester said. "Close the

door. You'll have to pay for that window you broke."
She leveled the gun at him. "Unless you're dead too."

TJ HAD HEARD Silas calling for her. Fear gripped her for
a moment as tears blurred her eyes. Ester had taken her
gun when she'd gone upstairs. The woman didn't look
like someone who would carry one—let alone use it.

And that could be Silas's fatal mistake. TJ had
certainly underestimated the woman. She wouldn't
make that mistake again, but Silas might not get a second chance. I might not either, she thought, her heart
pounding.

She heard nothing from upstairs. No gunshot. Ester
hadn't killed him. Yet. She waited a moment as if expecting to hear a gunshot and praying she wouldn't.

Then she went to work on the ropes on her wrists
again. Now she worked even more frantically, feeling
as if time was running out. As she worked, she listened.
Earlier, she'd heard someone ring the doorbell numerous times and then the loud knock; she should have
known it was Silas. Of course he would come looking
for her. The sound of breaking glass had startled her
as well as Ester.

What terrified her was that Ester seemed to know
that she would never get away with this. She didn't
seem to care. It was as if this was something she'd decided to do before she died. Ester was determined to
see this through even though it made little sense.

But TJ had seen the anger that had been apparent
in the letters. Ester was furious with herself, with the
world. And TJ had become the object of that anger.

The tape gave. She shoved it away, aware of the pain
in her shoulder. Her arms were scraped and bleeding,

her wrists aching from being taped up for so long behind her. But she barely noticed.

Tearing off the gag, she thought about calling to
Silas to warn him, but realized that might put him in
more jeopardy. But what if he believed Ester when she
said that she wasn't here? What if he left?

Instead, she hurriedly untied her ankles and got
to her feet, blood rushing into her extremities as she
looked around for a weapon before she started up the
stairs at a run.

SILAS COULD SEE that Ester seemed out of breath, but
she still held the gun in her hand plenty steady enough
to kill him. He'd complicated whatever plan she'd had
and he knew it. But he could see the wheels in her
head turning as she motioned for him to lead the way
down the hallway.

"Where are we headed?" he asked, walking slowly.
He could feel her behind him, intent on keeping that
gun leveled at the middle of him.

"Don't worry about it," she snapped. "Just keep
walking a little farther."

Ahead he could see a door on his left and an opening into the kitchen off to his right. The tension in the
air was thick as salami. Ester was in planning mode
and that was making him very nervous.

He was almost to the door on the left when he heard
footfalls. It dawned on him that someone was running
upstairs from the basement about the time the door was
flung open. TJ came bursting through it.

Silas only had a second to decide what to do. He
spun around, bringing up a foot. Ester had been distracted for only a moment, but it was long enough that

she hadn't gotten a shot off. He kicked at the gun in her hand, but the woman must have had a death grip on it. All he accomplished was shoving the gun off to the side.

The report of the shot was deafening in the small hallway. Sheetrock exploded on the wall to the right, sending a cloud of chalky dust into the air. Silas rushed Ester, but not before she fired again. She was already swinging the gun back in his and TJ's direction when it went off.

He grabbed the woman's arm, heard her cry out as he wrenched it hard enough to take the gun from her bony fingers. She attacked him with her hands, flying at him. For her age, she was much stronger than he'd expected. With the gun still in his hand it was hard to wrestle her into compliance. He finally shoved her face-first into the wall and held her there as he pocketed the gun.

He realized he hadn't heard a sound out of TJ. Turning to look, at first all he saw was the open basement door. Past it was a bare foot, the high heel shoe she'd been wearing lying next to it.

"TJ?"

No answer.

He fought to move the struggling Ester along the wall so he could see TJ. Reaching the door, he slammed it closed. Sitting in the hallway staring was the woman he'd fallen in love with even before he'd met her. She had a hand over her side, blood leaking from between her fingers.

"TJ!" he cried, giving up on trying to hold Ester. He opened the basement door and put her down on the first step before closing the door and locking it. Then he dropped beside TJ and tried to call 911 at the same time as he worked to stanch the bleeding. "You're going to be all right," he kept saying, praying it would be true. "You're going to be all right."

He held her as the sound of sirens filled the air.

# Chapter Twenty-One

TJ remembered little after she was shot other than being in Silas's arms and then holding his hand in the ambulance. It had all seemed like a bad dream. Or an ending to one of her books. The scream of the sirens. The blood. The feeling that it was over and yet not knowing if everyone would get out alive.

She vaguely remembered seeing her sisters as she was being wheeled down to surgery. They were both crying. Chloe telling her not to die. Annabelle saying something about Christmas. And Silas standing at the end of the hall, his face a mask of pain and worry. The rest was a blur of dreams and waking up in the middle of the night to see a nurse bending over her.

"It's all right," one nurse had said when TJ had been startled by her, making one of the machines go off. "You're safe here. It's all right."

She was in and out of consciousness so much that she hadn't known what was real and what wasn't. At one point there was a doctor standing over her. He was talking to someone. Silas. She'd felt his hand take hers and when she woke again it was still dark and she could hear Chloe arguing with the nurse outside her door.

Or maybe she'd dreamed it all. When she finally did

surface in the daylight, TJ thought all of it had been a bad dream. But she was groggy from the drugs, lying in a hospital bed, so she knew that at least getting shot had been real.

Silas sat beside her bed—just as she had sat beside his. He rose when he saw she was awake. "How are you?"

She tried to speak but her mouth was so dry. He poured her some water and helped her with the straw. The doctor came in then and told Silas he needed to check his patient.

"I'll be right outside in the hallway," Silas said, and left.

"You were lucky, young lady," the doctor said after checking her wound. "I was able to get the bullet out. No major organs were involved. It should heal nicely. Any questions?"

She shook her head because she had way too many questions. Some of her ordeal had come back, but the last part had happened so quickly...

The doctor hadn't been gone long when her sisters came in. She heard the nurse warn them that they couldn't stay long. One on each side of the bed, they looked at her with concern.

"I'm fine," she said, the words coming out in a hoarse whisper.

"That crazy old woman," Chloe said. "Who would have thought she was the one?"

"As mean as she was to me in English class?" Annabelle said. "I was scared of her."

"She was sick," TJ managed to say.

"Aren't they all," Chloe said. "She could have killed

you. Almost did. If Silas…" She seemed to catch herself. "But you're safe here and it's all behind you."

"The doctor said you might be out before Christmas," Annabelle said. "But if you aren't, we're going to hold Christmas until you are."

"She doesn't care about Christmas right now," Chloe scolded their youngest sister. "Look at her. She's drugged up and probably in pain. Are you in pain?"

TJ was, but she shook her head anyway.

"If you're in pain, you just push this button," Annabelle said. "They told you that, right?"

Maybe they had. TJ couldn't remember. She struggled to keep her eyes open.

"Okay, that's long enough," a female nurse said from the doorway, and her sisters were shooed out.

TJ closed her eyes. A few moments later she heard the door to her room open and close softly. She knew who it was before he took her hand. She kept her eyes closed, feeling herself drawn back into the darkness. With her hand in his, she slept.

THE DOCTOR FINALLY insisted Silas go home and get some sleep. He knew he needed a shower, a shave and clean clothes. He also needed sleep. He hadn't had much since the dance.

But when he closed his eyes, he kept reliving the scene at Ester Brown's house. The sound of the gunfire, seeing that one bare foot and high heel shoe lying next to it. The scene was the kind nightmares were made of.

Even when he told himself that she was going to be all right, he still couldn't sleep. He'd never been so afraid. Even Mad Dog hadn't terrified him the way Ester had because he'd looked into her eyes and he'd known that she had nothing to lose. She would have killed them both that night. As it was, she'd almost killed TJ.

"So you don't know when you're coming back to the city?" Cal had said when he'd called him.

"No. Honestly, I'm not sure I am. Things are too up in the air right now."

"Are you worried that the cops you fingered will hire someone else to come after you?" his friend had asked.

"No, Kenny 'Mad Dog' Harrington did me a favor," Silas had said with a chuckle. "He taped their conversations, including when my former NYPD partner paid him for his services. Mad Dog wasn't as stupid as they thought he was. He was worried that he'd take care of me and then they would turn on him to insure that he wouldn't rat them out some day when he got picked up for another crime. Mad Dog would have sold them out for a lesser sentence and they knew it. He was right. They would have had him killed to tie up the loose ends."

"Why haven't I heard about these tapes?" Cal asked.

"Could be because he made copies and made sure I had one. He left it for me in my cabin. I didn't see it until after he was dead. Apparently he wanted me to know who'd hired him before he killed me. So now, if they ever make a move on me, the tapes will surface."

"Tapes?"

"He made copies. Now the copies are being held in several safe places as…insurance. There's one on its way to you," Silas said. "My former…associates have been notified. They don't want any more years behind bars, or, in my ex-partner's case, he doesn't want to go straight to prison."

"So," Cal said. "This has to be about a woman."

Silas laughed. "Isn't it always? Only this woman, well, she's a keeper. That is if she'll have me."

THE NEXT TIME TJ WOKE, she found Sheriff McCall Crawford next to her bed. "The doctor said I could ask you some questions if you're up to it."

She nodded. "Ester?" The moment she saw McCall's expression she knew.

"Ester had another stroke," the sheriff said. "She didn't make it."

TJ felt a well of sadness. Yes, the woman had terrorized her and almost killed her, but she felt sorry for her too. "She felt she was never appreciated. She gave up her dream to be a teacher—at least that's the way she saw it."

The sheriff pulled out her notebook and recorder. "Why don't you tell me what happened."

She did, finishing with, "I don't remember all that much after I was shot."

McCall closed her notebook and shut off the recorder. "We found the typewriter and paper downstairs. She was definitely the person who'd been sending you the threatening letters."

TJ nodded. "There were other typewritten papers down there. Is there any chance I could have them?"

The sheriff hesitated. "It would be up to her relatives. I've been trying to find out if there are any. So far I've had no luck."

"What Ester wanted more than anything was to publish," TJ said. "I don't know if she even finished the book she was working on, but if there is any way it is publishable… I'd like to do that for her."

McCall smiled. "I'll make sure you get whatever there is."

## Chapter Twenty-Two

TJ made it home for Christmas. She was still sore and had been forced to assure the doctor that she would take it easy. But Christmas Eve she was with family. Annabelle had always been like a kid in a candy store at Christmas. She'd baked and her future mother-in-law had brought over more food than they could eat in a month.

"Willie's teaching me to cook," Annabelle had said. "But we both think I have a way to go before I serve it to humans. The pigs out at the ranch love my cooking though," she added, making them laugh.

"Wait," TJ said as she remembered. "Belle, you were going to get married on Christmas!"

Her sister shook her head. "It just didn't work out. I couldn't get married without you there."

"I don't want to be the reason you didn't get married," she said. "I know how anxious you and Dawson are to tie the knot."

"It's not that big of a deal. We're thinking New Year's Day. It's just going to be a few people, nothing extravagant. Willie is insistent that it be held at the ranch and we let her take care of everything. I have the coolest mother-in-law-to-be ever." They agreed she did.

They ate, opened presents and sat around talking. TJ hated the months they'd been estranged and swore she was never going to let it happen again. "I wish Grandmother was here."

"Me too. I would love to ask her some questions," Annabelle said.

Chloe got up to adjust one of the ornaments on the tree. "It just goes to show that you never really know a person. Grandmother. Ester. Who knows what secrets everyone in this town has?"

"You're talking about how I make a living," TJ said. "If you assume everyone has a secret, well, it makes a good story."

"Have you read Ester's novel?" Chloe asked.

She nodded. "The sheriff said that no relatives have come forward. Once Ester's estate is settled, I'm going to self-publish it under her name."

"Is it any good?" Annabelle asked.

TJ hesitated, making Chloe laugh.

"You can tell us if it's awful," her sister said.

"After all, she tried to kill you," Annabelle added, and was quickly chastised by Chloe for bringing that up on Christmas Eve. "Come on, it's like the elephant in the room. If it hadn't been for Silas, TJ would be—"

"The book isn't very good, but it was Ester's first," TJ interrupted.

"And last," Chloe said.

She nodded. "I know it probably seems silly to publish it."

"No," Annabelle said. "It's sweet and more than the old bat deserves." She mugged a face at Chloe.

"So does this mean you're ready to go back to writing soon?" Chloe asked her.

"In a while."

Annabelle grinned. "She has other things on her mind."

"Speaking of Silas," Chloe said. "I hope the two of you are going to give it some time before you do anything rash."

TJ laughed. "Anything rash?"

"Leave her alone," Annabelle said. "Let her do whatever she wants to. It's her life and Silas is…"

"At the door," TJ said after there was a knock and he put his head in.

"I don't want to interrupt."

"You're not," Annabelle said, getting to her feet and motioning for Chloe to do the same. "We were just leaving." She ushered Chloe up the stairs, the two arguing all the way.

"I didn't mean to run them off," Silas said.

"It's fine. We just finished opening our presents. The two of them were starting to argue over me."

"Good thing I showed up, then," he said with a grin. "How are you?"

"Still sore, but the doctor said I am healing well."

"What about mentally? You've been through some traumatic holidays," he reminded her.

As if she needed to be reminded. "It hasn't been dull, that's for sure. But there won't be any more True Fan letters. There's no reason I can't get back to work. I have a deadline looming… What about you?"

Silas sat down across from her and took both of her hands in his. "Are you well enough that you still want to come up to the cabin with me?"

She smiled. "It's just what I need. *You're* just what I need. That and your homemade bread."

"You've got it. I'll pick you up tomorrow. Say, nine? Will your sisters be all right with it?"

"I don't need their permission."

"How about their blessing?" he asked. "I want them to like me because if I have my way…" He shrugged.

"I'll see you in the morning."

She went to the window and waved as he drove away, wondering if she would be able to sleep tonight. She was excited about returning to the cabin, but even more about spending the next few days with him up in the mountains away from everyone.

"You can come back down now," she called up the stairs to her sisters. She knew they hadn't gone far and had been listening to everything she and Silas had said. Annabelle because she was nosy. Chloe because she was worried.

They both came down the stairs, Annabelle all starry-eyed. "He wants us to like him because he's going to ask you to marry him," she said in a sing-song fashion.

"And live in that one-room cabin?" Chloe demanded.

TJ shook her head. "You're both way ahead of yourselves. Slow the roll," she said, something she hadn't said since high school. Both sisters laughed.

"Then why are your cheeks flushed?" Annabelle asked. "You're in love with him and he's crazy about you. Just make sure that you're back for my wedding on New Year's Day."

"I wouldn't miss it for anything," TJ said.

# Chapter Twenty-Three

TJ almost didn't recognize Silas. He'd shaved off his beard and trimmed his hair. He no longer looked like a mountain man when he came to pick her up.

"Are you leaving?" she asked, thinking he'd done this because he had been called back to his job in New York City.

He shook his head. "I thought you might want to see what I really looked like."

She laughed, amazed that the man could be even more handsome without the full beard. She reached out and cupped his cheek, his strong jaw covered in designer stubble. "I'd take you either way."

He grinned as he stepped closer. "That's what I wanted to hear." He pulled her to him. "Ready to spend a few days at the cabin?"

TJ had never been more ready for anything. Silas drove through the snowy landscape toward the Little Rockies. It was one of those incredible winter days in Montana, not a cloud in a robin-egg blue sky, the sun making the new snow shine like fields of diamonds.

She felt herself relax. She'd come home to hide out from True Fan and make up with her sisters. Instead True Fan had been here waiting for her. The sheriff had told her that Ester used former students who'd moved away to mail the letters for her, including one now living in New York City.

"I suspect she was the one who took the photograph of your apartment," McCall had told her. "They just thought Ester was a fan."

She felt only sadness when she thought of Mrs. Brown. All those years when Ester was teaching, she had yearned to write, not realizing the only thing that had held her back was her own fear, her own misgivings about her talent.

"It is so heartbreaking," she'd said. "And yet what I told her was true. She helped me become a writer. She felt she'd wasted her life and it just wasn't true. I'm just sorry that I never thanked her for what she did do for me. Not until it was too late."

"But you got to tell her," McCall had said. "I'm thankful it ended without either of you being killed. The doctor said a lot of her behavior was due to the strokes she'd been having for some time. I don't think she realized what she was doing."

TJ looked out at the passing snowy foothills and reminded herself that it was over. She'd had a wonderful Christmas and felt closer to her sisters than she had in years. Glancing at Silas, she had to smile to herself. Annabelle was right. She was in love.

"I don't think I'm going back to New York," he said, and glanced over at her. "I don't need the job financially or emotionally or mentally. To tell you the truth I don't want to leave Montana."

She chuckled, as she'd been thinking the same thing since her return. "I love being here. And as you said, I can write anywhere. I was thinking earlier that I would let my New York apartment go. Chloe will be going back home to work and Annabelle will be getting married New Year's Day and moving in with Dawson, so the house will be empty. There's no reason I can't stay."

He grinned over at her. "I can't tell you how much I was hoping you would say that." He sounded relieved. "I want to spend as much time as I can at the cabin, but eventually either build a larger place or buy one."

"You wouldn't sell the cabin though, right?" she asked.

"No. Never. It's even more special to me since I got to share it with you."

As Silas pulled up in front of the cabin, she saw that the woodstove was going. Smoke curled up into the snow-filled pines. She couldn't wait to get inside, but he had other plans. As she started to open her pickup door, he stopped her.

"There's something I want to do first," he said, and reached into the pocket of his sheepskin coat to pull out a small jewelry box.

TJ felt her heart leap as she looked from it to his blue-eyed gaze.

"I know this is silly, but once we get into that cabin with that bed right at the center of the room, I'm going to want to make love to you. And maybe it's old-fashioned, but I want to do this right." He shifted in the seat and found a way even in the cab of the pickup to get down on one knee.

Sunlight poured through the window. Outside the fresh snow gleamed. In the warm cab of the pickup, Silas said, "Tessa Jane Clementine, will you marry me?"

She broke into a wide smile as tears filled her eyes. "Yes. Oh yes."

Silas slipped the ring on her finger. The pear-shaped diamond shone like the snow outside the windows. The ring fit perfectly.

TJ threw herself into his arms. The kiss was a promise of what was to come. Years cuddled up in that cabin. Late-night card games. Homemade baked bread. Best friends forever.

But for tonight, all TJ wanted was to spend it in this man's arms listening to the wind in the tall pines and the crackle of the fire in the woodstove. She was home.

SILAS FELT LIKE a man who'd won the lottery. He turned off the pickup engine, ran around and pulled TJ out and into his arms.

"I believe you're supposed to do this *after* we're married," she said, laughing as he carried her up the porch steps and over the threshold into the cabin.

"I feel as if our lives are starting now," he said as he put her down. He looked into her blue eyes. "Beautiful and smart and talented. How did I get so lucky?"

"You liked my books."

He laughed. "But nothing like I like their author." He kissed her, pulling her close. Outside, snow crystals danced in the air against the big sky. Inside, the woodstove crackled and popped invitingly. "How soon can we get married?"

She looked up at him in surprise. "As soon as we can find a preacher."

"I love you," he said, his gaze locked with hers. "I think I left that out earlier. Also I forgot to ask you how you feel about kids."

"I'm for them," she said. "Two, three…"

"Four, five…" He laughed, still feeling as if he needed to pinch himself. "Tell me this isn't a dream."

"If it is, I don't want to wake up," she said. "I love you, Silas Walker. I know this happened fast. But I know it's right."

"I've never been this sure of anything." He kissed her, determined to find a preacher soon and make her his wife.

\* \* \* \* \*

# CAPTIVATED BY HER ITALIAN BOSS

**ROSANNA BATTIGELLI**

To Calabria, a land of resilience and enchantment that continues to captivate me. And to all my Calabrese relatives and friends worldwide, starting with those in Camini, where my heart first began to beat.

# CHAPTER ONE

WHEN NEVE SPOTTED the ad in the Vancouver newspaper in the second to last week of June, she felt a shiver of excitement run through her. It was an ad requesting applications from Canadian nannies for a position for the summer. In Italy. And Southern Italy, at that. A place she had visited with her mother when she was eighteen. Her parents had traveled through Calabria and Sicily on their honeymoon, and her mother's nostalgia had drawn her back for what would have been their nineteenth anniversary.

Neve had loved the leisurely five-week tour through the seaside towns and mountain hamlets, culminating with the last week in Valdoro—Valley of Gold—on the southeast coast of Calabria. It was the town where Neve had been conceived. Neve could still envision the shimmering, color-changing waves of the Ionian Sea. And the dazzling sun that rose at dawn, its face an orange-gold orb that soon took dominion of the cerulean sky. By 8:00 a.m., the temperature would register over thirty degrees Celsius, and Neve couldn't wait to head to the beach.

Her imagination had gone wild as they explored the ancient places she had read about in the works of British authors who had traveled to the area over a century earlier. Because of Greek colonization a thousand or so years ago, the area had become known as Magna Grecia, or Great

Greece. Neve had read the books her parents had discovered about the South, including George Gissing's *By The Ionian Sea* and Norman Douglas's *Old Calabria*. She had particularly enjoyed Edward Lear's *Voyages in Southern Italy*. Lear had traveled to the South with another artist to paint landscapes. As he traveled from hamlet to hamlet, he had written about his experiences in a journal. His accounts of peculiar townsfolk and the places they had stayed had put Neve in stitches, like the story of a pig running out from under a table as they were feasting on a dinner of macaroni. As an adolescent, Neve had dreamed of returning to Italy one day to rediscover the places that had so enchanted her.

Reading the details in the ad, Neve's jaw dropped. What were the chances of coming across a job opportunity in Valdoro for the summer? And one that she could easily apply for, since her job as a kindergarten teacher meant she had summers free. The ad read:

*Canadian Nanny wanted to prepare child for Kindergarten.*
*Summer Position.*
*Only highly experienced applicants will be considered.*
*Skills in Behavioral Management and Modification a must.*
*Child has experienced trauma and requires a special caregiver.*
*Three nannies have been recently dismissed; please do not apply if you believe this will be a vacation.*
*Position is full-time, with one day off per week.*
*Send a letter including your CV to my assistant, Mrs. Lucia Michele, email address below.*
*Do not inquire as to the status of your application.*

*You will be contacted within one week for an interview if I am interested.*

Neve read the ad over several times. The prospective employer obviously wanted to make it quite clear to the applicant that this job was not going to be an easy one. She wondered at the trauma of the poor child. A death? Divorce? Abuse? Her stomach twisted. She had a special place in her heart for children; she always had, even as a teenager. She had babysat regularly in her neighborhood, and she had decided early on that teaching would be the career for her. She had been teaching now for three years, and maybe that didn't make her *highly experienced*, but she *had* dealt with a few difficult and sensitive situations, and as a result, had taken specialized courses to help children who had experienced trauma of some kind.

She herself had experienced the loss of her father as a child. He had succumbed to a sudden stroke when she was eight, and it still made her heart twinge when she remembered the day she had come home from school and had found her house filled with relatives and family friends, some gathered around her mother. Bewildered, she had run toward her mother, who had sobbed the news to her before collapsing. Sadly, over the years, her mother had been more preoccupied with *her* loss and less over Neve's trauma of losing her father.

Neve's eyes prickled. She squeezed them shut, then focused on the ad.

*Who was the sender?* The most logical answer was that it was a parent who couldn't stay at home and needed someone to help the child deal with the trauma and help prepare him or her for the challenge of another transition: school.

*A tall order.* Especially since progress so far had been

limited. At least that was what she had inferred from the terse statement: *three nannies have recently been dismissed.* She felt a twinge in her heart at what the child must be going through and the poor, desperate parent. A thousand thoughts swarmed her mind about the sad possibilities, and then one thought pushed the others away: *I'm going to apply.*

And why not? She had the sensitivity required for such a position, given her own personal history. And she had dealt with behavioral and trauma issues in her three years of teaching, everything from stubbornness and aggression to grief over the loss of a parent or pet.

Yes, she would have loved to return to a *vacation* in Valdoro, but just being there and knowing she would be helping a child in distress—or attempting to help—was enough to motivate her. She would be content with reacquainting herself with the area on her day off. Of course, that was *if* she was hired for the position.

Neve had been ready to go to bed when she had picked up the newspaper, but now she was too excited to sleep. She reached for her laptop and typed up a letter. She read it over twice, added a section, read it over again and then attached her most recent CV. Taking a deep breath, she typed in the email address and pressed Send before she could change her mind.

With a shiver of anticipation, Neve ran a bath, her imagination sparked. As she stepped into its bubbly warmth, her floral-scented body wash reminded her of the jasmine and other flowers blooming in the pots on the balconies at Villa Morgana, where she had stayed with her mother in Valdoro. She inhaled deeply and closed her eyes, her memories reactivated.

Visions of the villa came rushing back: the spacious, elegant rooms with their sparkling marble floors; the colorful glazed pots on the balcony, bursting with blooms of every color; and the scent of the nearby bakery wafting up to her when she stepped out on her balcony—

Neve's eyes flew open. She blinked. There was something wrong with this picture. *Well, not wrong, exactly.* It was just missing one thing. *One person. The guy walking down the road. The guy whose intense gaze had seemed to blaze across the street to connect with hers.*

She had been drying her hair outside after a cool shower, enjoying the balmy heat of the midday Calabrian sun. Her mother and their friends, the owners of the villa, had been taking their usual siesta after the sumptuous lunch they had all feasted on. The merchants had shut down their businesses for the afternoon, and would reopen in a few hours. Nobody strolled about in the scorching afternoon heat, which is why Neve had been taken aback to see him walking by. His stride seemed to have slowed down when he was directly across the road from her balcony. And although other boys in Valdoro had openly demonstrated curiosity about her with sly nudges and winks when she walked in and out of the ice cream shop or bakery down the street, they hadn't turned her knees to jelly, like this guy had just done.

He must have been working on a farm. His dark hair had been tousled and sweat-dampened, and his white T-shirt and jeans had been streaked with earth. He had been carrying a large burlap bag on his back, filled with greens and vegetables. But it had been his eyes that had galvanized her. Ebony eyes that had sent a shiver coursing through her veins. Eyes like river stones gleaming in the sun. And even with a coating of dust on his face, Neve had been able to make out his chiseled features, straight nose and sensual curve of his lips.

Suddenly flustered, Neve had shifted her gaze and in

mere seconds, had taken in his tanned arms—his biceps bulging from holding the burlap bag—and his well-fitting, straight-leg jeans. *He is not a boy*, she remembered thinking. She had guessed him to be in his early twenties. And she had been eighteen… For a few moments she had felt a strange weakness overcome her and had wondered if she was about to pass out.

*And then he had stopped.* She had felt him staring at her and had looked up. *Is he going to say something?* she had wondered. Their eyes had locked. And then he had given a slight nod and, readjusting his bag, had kept walking. The following day Neve had watched him from behind the wooden shutters, too shy to suddenly appear on the balcony. But when he had slowed down and looked up toward her balcony, her heart had fluttered. *He had been hoping to see her.*

Neve realized she was holding her breath and let it out in a rush. And then other memories of that summer eight years ago came tumbling out. The way he had started going by the villa several times a day, not just to and from his farm job, but also later in the evening. He had made evening trips to and from the bakery, the Pasticceria Michelina. Sometimes he had walked; other times he had rumbled by on a motor scooter. Neve had felt herself falling under the spell of the Southern ways, the age-old custom of locking gazes, communicating with eyes only, a slow dance of intuition and anticipation. Her heart had thrummed all evening and night after that first encounter, and over the next few days she had found she could concentrate on little else.

Her mother, Lois, had caught the exchange once. He had been walking by after his work on the farm, and Lois had come into Neve's room and walked toward the balcony at the same moment that he had paused to look up and smile at Neve, who had taken to sitting out on the balcony with a book every afternoon. Neve had returned the smile, and then had become aware of her mother's presence.

"What are you doing?" her mother had asked. "You don't pay attention to farmhands, Neve. That could get you into real trouble."

Neve had flushed, embarrassed to have been discovered flirting and even more embarrassed to think that *he* had heard or understood. But when she had looked back toward him, he had walked on and was almost out of sight. She had glanced at her mother, whose frown had deepened.

"I've read stories about how some men in the South used to kidnap young ladies, take them up to a mountain cave and compromise their honor so their family would have no choice but to let them get married."

"*Mom! Really?* Are we talking about the same century?" Neve couldn't believe what she had just heard. "I wasn't doing anything other than smiling back. And I didn't get the feeling he wanted to marry me," she had added flippantly. "I don't think you have to worry about him carrying me off."

Her mother's cheeks had reddened. "Neve, you are not to give him or anyone like him any attention. You're in Italy, remember. Men are more…*passionate* here. You came here a virgin. I don't want you to fall for the first Romeo that pays attention to you and let him—"

"*Mom! Oh, my God!*" Neve had jumped up, *her* face flaming. "Just *stop*! Give me some credit, would you?"

She had barricaded herself in her private bathroom, ignoring her mother's calls and halfhearted attempts to apologize. She had come out after her mother had gone, and wiping her tear-streaked eyes, she had walked to the balcony…

\* \* \*

For the next few days Neve had been too busy with her school obligations to think much about the ad. When an email from a Mrs. Lucia Michele arrived, informing her that she was one of the applicants who could proceed to be interviewed, Neve's heart had done a leap. She had thought it was a long shot, as there must have been hundreds of applicants, if not more, and her pulse had quickened at the thought that she might actually stand a chance of being hired.

Mrs. Michele's email had informed Neve of the interview details. It would be conducted by *her*. The employer would be watching the interview privately. Due to the sensitive nature regarding the child, she had been instructed to keep the employer's identity confidential until the chosen applicant actually arrived in person in Southern Italy.

And now here Neve was, communicating with Signora Lucia Michele, who was asking her in halting English about her philosophy of discipline. Neve felt a little self-conscious doing a Skype interview while her prospective employer watched from his computer.

Neve paused for a moment, wondering what stance "the boss" expected her to take. She looked beyond the woman, almost expecting that he—why she thought it would be a *he*, she didn't know—would appear, and took a deep breath. She could only answer truthfully.

"I believe that consistency is essential in discipline," she replied, her voice steady. "The child must know what you expect, and as a kindergarten teacher, I tell my children right at the beginning that I expect to be treated kindly, with respect, and that I will be treating them in the same manner. I make sure they know right away that A, their parents have trusted them to my care because I will keep them safe and take good care of them, and B, they will learn and have fun with me."

She couldn't help smiling, thinking of her school kids as they looked at her with wide eyes on the first day of school. "Those are the two main things they need to know. And then, day by day, they will learn how to interact, how to solve problems, how to be a good leader." She looked straight at the camera. "And they will learn about consequences when they do something inappropriate. I believe in positive discipline and fairness, and flexibility when it is required...without laying a hand on the child."

Signora Michele gave a curt nod. "And I see you have... ah...some *esperienza* with children who have suffered— how do you say?—oh, yes—loss?"

Neve tried to control her eyes from misting. Yes, she had experience, she replied, and bit her lip. She told the *signora* about the courses she had taken to help understand what children who had lost a parent through death or separation or divorce were going through. "You can't assume that every child who enters your classroom has had a happy, cheerful childhood," she said wistfully. "If only..." She blinked and thought of a frail-looking girl called Tessa, who had lost her mother to cancer a month before starting kindergarten.

*Don't cry*, she told herself. *Hold it together.*

And then Signora Michele turned slightly and touched her ear. Neve spotted the hearing device that was obviously the means of communication between her and the employer.

She nodded and turned back to Neve, her face expressionless. "Thank you for your time, Signorina Wilder. You will be contacted with an answer within a day or two. There are still a few other applicants to consider... *Grazie*."

Neve nodded and gave her a small smile before the

woman left. She looked again right into the camera at the top of her screen, knowing the employer would be watching until the last moment. Neve stared briefly, then nodded, her eyes never faltering.

*"Grazie,"* she addressed the unseen employer before shutting down her laptop.

Davide Cortese's pulse leaped. If he had entertained the smallest doubt when she had first appeared on his laptop screen in his study, after mere seconds he could no longer deny it. The interview had lasted twenty minutes or so between his assistant and the applicant, but it had taken him only a few stunned moments to realize the latter's identity.

*Neve Wilder.* He hadn't seen her name and the others in the file Lucia had prepared; he had wanted to see all the Skype interviews first. Neve was the thirteenth applicant to be interviewed by Lucia, and Davide had almost lost hope that a suitable nanny could be found for his five-year-old niece, Bianca.

His expression softened at the thought of his niece. She looked like the mirror image of her mother, his sister, Violetta. Her face still had the cherubic roundness of babyhood, but she had grown taller, even since the accident. *The accident.* Just those two words caused his body to freeze, just like the first time he was told by Violetta's friend Alba that Violetta and her husband, Tristan, had skidded on an icy mountain road after their skiing weekend in Banff and had died instantly when their vehicle hit a tree.

Alba, who had been babysitting Bianca, had delivered the news tearfully by phone, and all at once Davide had felt numb, devastated, angry, sad and desperate. His only sibling, *gone.* She was six years his senior, and he had always looked to her for guidance growing up, especially after both their parents had died. Their father had passed first when Davide was ten, and their mother, heartbroken, had succumbed to cancer a year later.

Life had been hard enough without his gentle father around, but losing his mother so soon after was a blow that had siphoned what remained of Davide's childhood spirit. Davide had lost his joy, his appetite, his interest in school. He had become frail, withdrawn and had often missed school.

He and Violetta had been looked after by their uncle, Zio Francesco, a priest in their town of Valdoro. Zio Francesco had told Davide when he was older about how he had begun to despair of reviving Davide's spirit and physical health. He had wondered if bringing him out to the farm and letting Davide occupy himself with planting jobs and the tending of the animals might restore him in some way.

His uncle had wept while reciting his rosary after noticing how several days on the land had brought a change in Davide's behavior and outlook. After a few weeks Davide had willingly returned to school, but had continued to work on the farm after school and on weekends, as well as throughout high school and in the summer when back from university.

Davide's heart tightened. He would never forget what Zio Francesco had done for him.

Davide's sister, Violetta, had been shaken but more stoic than he was after the deaths of their parents. She had overseen the household responsibilities that their mother had managed while still at school, but when Violetta was eighteen, she fell in love with a tourist from Canada and she married him at twenty and moved to his home in Steveston, about a half an hour from Vancouver. Tristan had worked as a tour guide at a whale-watching company, while Violetta had worked to develop a small home business with her sewing talents. She had been so happy that she could work from home once they had had their baby, which was five years ago. She had studied English and learned it quickly, and when Bianca was born, she had made sure to speak to her in both languages.

Davide's English was also fairly good. Violetta had encouraged him to study it with the possibility of moving to Vancouver one day, and he had, but destiny had had other plans for him and he had remained in Valdoro.

Valdoro was where he had first spotted Neve. *Neve*, pronounced *Neh-veh*, meaning *snow* in Italian. She had been standing on one of the balconies of Villa Morgana, owned by one of the wealthiest families in town, a family that derived their wealth from the bounty of the bergamot groves on their outlying properties. Their coral-colored villa was on the main street heading into Valdoro, with ornate wrought iron balconies and ceramic planters bursting with flowers. The entire roof of the villa was a terrace with bougainvillea spilling over the railing. Chairs with bright yellow and blue upholstery were scattered around a table protected by an *ombrellone*, a huge umbrella tilted to one side.

Davide had been returning from his uncle's small farm, which he tended to from before sunrise till late morning, as the scorching sun was too prohibitive past noon. He had been later than usual that day, having had to chase after a goat that had found an opening in the enclosure and had wandered off. Afterward, Davide had gathered some of the garden vegetables in a huge burlap bag, and as he had passed the Villa Morgana, he had spotted a girl on the balcony. He hadn't seen her in Valdoro before. Her hair was wet and she was air-drying it.

Davide's T-shirt had been sweat-soaked, his jeans earth-stained, and he could feel his face prickling with perspiration. As he had passed in front of the villa from the opposite side of the road, the girl had tossed her hair back and caught sight of him. She had cocked her head and Davide could feel his steps slowing. He had wanted to stop completely and just feast on the vision before him.

He had been mesmerized by her light skin, her strawberry-blond hair catching the rays of the sun and shimmering like spun gold, the white halter dress with big red polka dots, her lean legs. His heart had thumped erratically at her gaze, which couldn't have lasted more than a few seconds before she had started to blink, and he had noticed her eyes traveling past his eyes and down his body.

Davide remembered the embarrassment he had felt at his dusty and sweaty appearance, although she hadn't give him any sign of arrogance, and he had nodded slightly in the respectful way he had been taught when encountering girls or women, and had forced his cement-like shoes to keep walking.

Showering at the house he had shared with his zio, Francesco, his insides had quivered at the thought of the girl. She had looked to be around seventeen or eighteen. He had been twenty-two, home for the summer from university, and although some of the mothers in Valdoro had discreetly made it known that he was welcome to court their daughters, he had been more intent on his studies. He hadn't said so much to his uncle, but he was hoping to join his sister in Vancouver after university. His parents had left him and his sister with very little; what money they had was tied up in their small farm property, so his uncle had encouraged him to keep working the land, and he would support him with a modest salary.

That had been the plan.

*Until Neve Wilder's arrival in Valdoro.*

\* \* \*

Now, looking at her face on the screen, and knowing she couldn't see him or ever imagine his identity, Davide felt his gut tighten. He wasn't a love-struck young man anymore, and how and why fate had thrown Neve Wilder back into his life after eight years was a bizarre mystery to him. When he had tried to meet her back then, her message to him had been very clear. She had wanted nothing to do with him. He was below her and should remember his place.

She had crushed him then and Davide had spent the next few years trying to forget her and vowing to never be *below* anyone again. He would finish his university education and make something of himself. He didn't need *her* or anyone like her.

He had discovered that her family was visiting from Vancouver, where he had planned to go after his graduate studies. Overcome with bitterness, he had changed his mind immediately. He wouldn't move anywhere where there was even the *remotest* chance of bumping into her. No, he never wanted to see her face again.

This was a cruel twist of fate, watching an interview with the same girl who, eight years later, was applying for a job as a nanny for his niece. Only she wasn't a girl anymore. Her pretty looks as a teenager had blossomed into what he had to admit could only be called stunning.

Her fair skin was luminescent, with a faint smattering of freckles over her nose and peach-tinted cheeks, and that mane of hair, although restrained in a loose chignon, seemed even more burnished. Her eyes, never close enough for him to determine their exact color, were a dark bluish-green that reminded him of the sea in winter. *And that mouth.* Her lipstick was a luscious magenta pink, the same color as the delicious inner fruit of the cactus pear.

*She could be a sea witch*, he thought, a modern *Scylla*, the whirlpool in the waters off the coast that was personified in Greek mythology as a female monster impeding the way of the hero Odysseus...

Davide watched as Neve's eyes shifted to the camera. She leaned forward and her face filled the screen. He swallowed, his pulse drumming wildly as a corner of her mouth lifted and she nodded. And then said *"Grazie,"* her witch eyes never blinking once.

Twelve interviews, and none of the applicants had impressed him. *Until the thirteenth.* Thirteen was a lucky number for Italians. But the last thing he felt now was lucky. If it had been anybody but Neve, he'd have hired her on the spot. Her qualifications were spot-on; her answers had been genuine. She had seemed so humble, so *caring and devoted*. How could this be the same Neve who had arrogantly put him down and rejected him?

Bianca needed a competent nanny. She would be starting school in a couple of months, and the trauma of losing her parents had shattered her world. None of her previous nannies had worked out. The first hadn't been sensitive enough, the second had been caught snooping through his desk papers and the third had shown more interest in wanting to help *him* through his grief, using her physical allure...

Bianca's occasional tantrums and crying outbursts had increased. Davide's gut was telling him to offer Neve the job. *His bruised heart was pounding No!*

Davide watched as Neve shut down her laptop. He stared blindly at the screen and let the voices in his head battle it out. The memories of Neve in Valdoro eight years ago clashed with his fresh memories of the interview. Wearily, he finally stood up from his desk and drummed his fingers along the edge before buzzing for Lucia in the smaller office next to him.

"What did you think of the last applicant?" he said curtly in Italian.

"She was the best, Signor Cortese."

Davide trusted Lucia's opinion; she was his valued research assistant and friend, and genuinely cared for Bianca. When she addressed him in such a formal manner, he knew she was very serious.

"Yes…she *was*," he murmured, his fingers beginning to tap again.

He cleared his throat. This wasn't about *him*, he tried to convince himself. He had to do this for Bianca. What were the chances of finding someone as perfect as Neve Wilder for the position of nanny?

"Send her an email offering her the position. Sign it with your name, not mine. And tell her her flight and all travel costs will be covered. Rail, hotel, food, everything. I understand she's finished with her school year toward the end of June. I want her here for the first or second of July. Please and thank you."

"*Prego*, Davide. Let's hope for the best." She gave his hand a reassuring pat and left the room.

Davide sat back down at his massive sixteenth-century carved walnut desk. He opened a drawer, and then reached farther into a hidden back drawer and retrieved a folded note. His heart thudding, he gently opened it and read the message inside:

I will *not* meet you.
    Your bold request is inappropriate and offensive.
You would do well to remember your place.
Neve

Davide felt the heat rise from his chest to his neck and face. The silly note still got to him. His jaw clenched. Eight summers ago, Neve Wilder had succeeded in humiliating him and putting him in his place with her arrogant reply.

And now she'd be working for *him*. How could he not help feeling even the tiniest temptation to put *her* in her place?

# CHAPTER TWO

THIS NANNY JOB, if she got it, would be like winning the lottery, Neve thought wistfully. She wanted to get away. No, she needed to get away. Her mother, who was controlling at the best of times, had become especially clingy and obtrusive lately.

Neve sighed. She wished that some of the attention her mother was directing toward her nowadays had been given when her father had died and afterward. Neve could still remember feeling heartbroken and confused in her youth. Devastated that her dear father would no longer accompany her to any of her school events or swimming lessons, or read her any fairy tales at bedtime, and bewildered by her mother's emotional distance. While her mother had eased her grief with a drink while staring out a window, Neve had often cried herself to sleep hugging the plush dragon her father had bought her for her seventh birthday. Her eyes prickled at the memory of her dear father, always encouraging, never judgmental of her or others.

*Unlike her mother.*

It hadn't taken Neve long in her youth to recognize certain traits in her mother that made her feel uncomfortable, especially in public. Lois Wilder, who had enjoyed a wealthy lifestyle since she was young, expected and often demanded service from others. Saw herself as above certain people. Neve had become embarrassed more than once by her mother's arrogant demeanor, even with some of her school friends. Whenever she had brought a friend over, Lois had always asked them about their parents' jobs, scrutinized their clothing and ultimately tried to manipulate whom Neve should socialize with.

She had even tried to dissuade Neve from pursuing such a common profession as teaching. "Why don't you accept a position in your father's company?" She owned the company now and had pressed Neve constantly to get on board. "You could have it made, sweetheart, instead of trying to educate rug rats. And in kindergarten, how much teaching will you actually be doing? They're still babies. You'll be spending most of the time on your knees, cleaning up after their accidents, wiping snotty noses, dealing with tantrums. And you'll be making peanuts compared to what you'd be earning working in your dad's computer business."

"Mom, I have no interest in the world of computers. I want to make a difference with kids. Help them to love learning."

"Well, at least get your masters and doctorate, and then you'll be able to teach at the university level. *That* would give you some status."

"I'm not interested in status, Mom." *Like you*...

Neve had had to control herself from being rude, although sometimes she had come very close. By the time she had graduated with her teaching degree, she had been more than ready to leave home. Lois had tried to bribe her with a luxury car and promises of travel if she stayed put.

Neve was having none of it.

Her mother had been hinting about a new manager in one of the departments that she thought might be a good match for Neve. The last thing Neve wanted was a man her mother approved of. A man who had similar qualities as her mother. Rich and snooty. Controlling and manipulative.

No, Neve had started her search and had found herself a bachelor apartment in a section of a house owned by Italian immigrants, and her teacher's salary had covered her rent and expenses. The "allowance" her mother insisted on sending her, Neve had put in her savings and travel accounts. Lois had insisted that she wanted Neve to have her inheritance—or at least some of it—before she passed away. "That way I can see you enjoying the finer things in life, darling."

Neve was immersed in watching a recent YouTube video of Valdoro when her cell phone chimed. She glanced down on the counter where she had left it and felt a swirl of butterflies in her stomach at the sender and the subject.

Lucia Michele. Re: Your Application

She hadn't expected to hear back the same day, let alone after half an hour. It had to be a form letter, fired off that quickly. Her heart sank. What had she expected, anyway? There had obviously been other applicants with much more experience than she had…

Neve sat down at the kitchen island and opened up the message on her phone. Her heartbeat quickened at the first sentence.

Dear Miss Wilder,
You have been accepted for the position of nanny. I will be sending you another email with information about the child's situation as well as other pertinent details you should know. The child's name is Bianca. She is five years old and living with her uncle.

I trust that you will be satisfied with the proposed salary and conditions of employment. After you have read the email, please download the attached contract, sign it and either scan and resend, or take a photograph and email it to this address.

Once this is done I will book your flights and send you an email with itinerary details. On July second you will be met at Lamezia Airport and a driver will bring you to your employer's residence.

Cordially,

Lucia Michele

Neve blinked, stunned. *She had the job!* She read the email again. She couldn't exactly call it a *warm* letter; it was very matter-of-fact and to the point. There was no commentary on her qualifications, the interview itself or anything else. The employer had obviously been satisfied with her detailed CV and with how she had responded in the interview.

Neve thought about everything she needed to do in the next two weeks. *Less than two weeks*, actually. Finalize report cards. File. Clean up her classroom. Pack. No, shop first. She needed some light dresses and new shorts. And definitely a couple of new swimsuits. Her favorite one, a fuchsia one-piece, had faded from the chlorine at the local swimming pool. And not that she'd have much time to herself, but the ad did say there would be one day off. Well, she would most certainly be frequenting the nearest beach on that day.

Neve thought about the little girl she would soon meet. *Bianca.* Such a lovely name. What had occurred in Bianca's young life to cause her such distress? Why was she living with her uncle? Dozens of questions swarmed in Neve's mind... She would get the answers soon enough.

She opted for an early night after a quick shower. The school was having their end-of-year play the following day, and she needed to store up her energy for the scheduled activities that included her class of twenty-four kindergarten students. There would be fun and laughter, but Neve was prepared for the possible tears and other behaviors that some of her five-year-olds might display after a few hours in the sun.

Yawning, she changed into a light blue baby doll and snuggled under her covers. She thought about Bianca's uncle. It was hard to get any kind of impression of him from his assistant's email. Did he have a wife, and if so, she must be working, or else wouldn't she be taking care of Bianca? *Stop*, she told herself. She'd know more when she got Mrs. Michele's next email.

Neve felt her eyelids getting heavier. *What if Bianca's uncle is single?* And the sudden thought: *What if that guy from across the street is still in Valdoro?* He may very well have moved to work in a bigger city up north, like Rome or Milan, as many of the Southerners tended to do. But if he *was* still in Valdoro, would she recognize him? He'd be maybe twenty-eight or so, and he'd probably be married with a couple of kids... *Or maybe not...* The picture of him she had kept in her mind had faded and blurred a little, but even so, she felt her pulse quicken.

And the image of his intense black eyes was the last thing she saw before she drifted into sleep.

Davide shut down his laptop. He left his study and strode to his bedroom. He opened the shutters and stood for a while, gazing at the twinkling lights dotting the countryside, and the indigo streak beyond—the Ionian Sea. It had been another scorching day; the locals had said it was the hottest summer in history. A smile curved his lips. For as long as he could remember, Valdoro's residents had said the same thing every summer. And the people in neighboring hamlets and towns were no different.

He almost felt like driving down the mountain to have a swim in the refreshing depths of the sea. But Bianca was sleeping and Lucia had gone home. They had decided to carry out the interview in early afternoon Vancouver time, which was nine hours behind Italian time.

Davide peeled off his shirt and pants and tossed them over a chair. There was hardly a breeze, and the night air had dropped a dozen degrees, but it was still too warm. He didn't have to worry about his neighbors seeing him, though. Last year he had purchased this house on a steep mountain on the outskirts of Valdoro, a few kilometers away. There were no neighbors to look across from their windows or balconies to his.

He smiled wryly. It wasn't actually a *house*; it was an eighteenth-century castle that had been built by the Baron of Valdoro. Fortified castles had been built inland on impossibly high mountains throughout Calabria, and their lords or barons had employed the locals to work the land of their vast properties, or *latifundi*, as they had been known. The last descendant of the Baron of Valdoro had died childless a hundred or so years earlier, and the land around his castle had long been abandoned. Although the castle was within the boundaries of Valdoro, it had not been maintained; the town simply hadn't had the financial means to restore it.

Three years ago, when Davide's first novel had been awarded Italy's prestigious literary award—the *Premio Strega*—followed by international sales and a film and miniseries option that made him a multimillionaire in months, he had spent the first year swirling from interview to interview, in between countless literary readings and festivals all over Italy. His face had been on the cover of practically every newspaper and magazine.

He had been one of the youngest recipients of the *Strega*. His hometown had attracted tourists, which had boosted the economy and profile of Valdoro, pleasing both the town officials and the residents alike. Davide was given the ceremonial key to Valdoro, and he had celebrated with his uncle and neighbors in a day of festivities culminating in a spectacular show of fireworks.

He still couldn't believe that the words he had penned about a family during the unification of Italy in 1861 had garnered such fanfare. It had been compared in scope to *Il Gattopardo*, the famous novel written by Giuseppe Tomasi di Lampedusa. Davide had studied *The Leopard* in high school, had been riveted by its rich complexity, propelling him to pursue further studies in history and literature.

He had made a promise to himself the summer Neve Wilder had visited Valdoro with her mother. And that was to let Neve's harsh words on the note she sent him burn into his soul until he had accomplished one goal, and that was to elevate himself to the point where she, or anybody else, could not look down on him.

That meant continuing to further his education and to *make something of himself*. His uncle had lived very humbly as a priest, and had stretched himself to the limit to provide for him. Davide had been very appreciative, but he had realized that he had to push himself to go beyond his or his uncle's normal expectations.

In between his studies and work on the farm, Davide had taken to writing. Late at night and before dawn, he had let his knowledge of history, his culture and his imagination combine and transform into the fictional story of the daughter of a Bourbon lord, who had become captivated with the ideals of General Giuseppe Garibaldi in his quest

to oust the Spanish Bourbon regime and unify the South
with the rest of Italy. The girl had fallen in love with one
of Garibaldi's soldiers during the revolution and successful
ousting of the Bourbons, and had abandoned her family
and relinquished her status to elope with him in the mysterious Aspromonte mountain range in Calabria.

Writing this story had been bittersweet, and his hand
had sometimes trembled with emotion as he created the
scenes between the two lovers. His protagonist, Serena,
had turned out to be an Italian version of Neve, dark-haired
but with the same fair skin and blue-green eyes that were
not often seen in the South.

Davide had made Serena everything he had fantasized
about Neve before she had crushed his illusions…and Vittorio was the name he had called the man who had captured her heart.

Davide gave a harsh laugh. What a fool he had been
eight years ago. A romantic fool.

After first catching sight of Neve on that balcony, he
had used every excuse possible to walk by. He had had
asked his friend Agostino, whose mother had been working as a housekeeper at the Villa Morgana, to keep him
informed of any excursions Neve's family was planning,
and Davide would innocently show up around that time.
*Just to catch sight of Neve.*

When he had had the good fortune of first spotting her
on the balcony, he had dared to hold his gaze for longer
than a casual glance. And to his delight, after gazing away
shyly, she had returned it. But then, with each subsequent
walk-by, she had attempted a quirky smile, her face flush-
ing like a ripe peach.

After a couple of days Davide had made the bold move
of crossing the road to walk on the same side of the villa on
his way home from working on the farm. And then later,

once he had showered and changed, he had returned. The local bakery was just down the street from the villa, and this had become his excuse to walk by every day.

Zio Francesco had commented about Davide's sudden sweet tooth, for Davide was bringing home a bag of brioche filled with custard one day, or a few marzipan fruit cookies or hazelnut biscotti the next day. Davide couldn't very well reveal the real reason for his purchases to his uncle; he had shared his feelings only with Agostino, who had revealed the girl's name to him.

When Agostino had told him one evening that Neve's mother was planning an outing to the sea, Davide's stomach had churned with anticipation. *He would go, too!* He had convinced Agostino to join him, for it would have looked odd for him to show up alone on the beach used by the Valdoro locals. They had set out on Agostino's Vespa and had spent the morning alternately sunning and swimming, with Davide trying to keep his observations of Neve as unnoticeable as possible.

He and Agostino had laid out their beach towels a short distance from Neve and her mother, who had rented an umbrella and had brought a picnic basket. Davide's heart had started to pound when Neve, still unaware of his presence, had removed her beach wrap and started to apply sunscreen to her slender arms and legs. She was wearing a blue two-piece swimsuit with pink polka dots. He had smiled; she had had a thing for polka dots, obviously, and they had suited her something crazy.

He had felt the sun and the inner heat suddenly get to him, and slapping Agostino on the arm, he had challenged him to a race out to the third marker in the water, indicating one hundred meters.

"Race you there and back," he had urged. "I'm burning up."

They had splashed their way back to shore, with Davide winning by three meters. Laughing, they had dried off and collapsed on their beach towels. That was when Davide had looked across and realized Neve was watching him. Her mother had been busy laying out the picnic food. *Had Neve seen the whole race?* Self-consciously, he had given her a nod and after checking to make sure her mother was still occupied, he had waved.

She had waved back and seemed self-conscious herself, looking around as if to see if anyone had noticed her wave to Davide. Tossing her hair back, she had tiptoed quickly on the hot beach sand and had ventured a little way into the water before immersing herself completely in a graceful dive.

It had all happened in slow motion. The sights and sounds around Davide had blurred, and all he had been conscious of was Neve, her lithe body ascending from her dive with the sun reflected in every glistening drop on her skin. And when she had shaken her head and sent a rainbow spray around her, his breath had caught in his throat, and he had known in the deepest reaches of his soul that he had fallen in love with this bewitching sea nymph. *An impossible love that could never be returned.*

The realization had overwhelmed him. How was he going to deal with this? Agostino had told him earlier that Neve's visit to Valdoro would end in a couple of days, and then she and her mother would be returning to Canada. He had felt a series of unbearable twinges in his heart from wanting Neve but knowing his desire could not be reciprocated. Fate wouldn't allow it. Davide had immediately felt deflated, already anticipating the impending loss… Neve would be gone tomorrow, and he would be left with this torturous flame in his chest.

*He had to meet her.*

The thought had made his breath falter and his heart thump erratically. If he couldn't have anything else with Neve, at the very least he had wanted a few moments with her. A moment, even. To tell her how he felt, and to hear her response. His gut had told him that she had felt something, too… He had seen it in her eyes.

It had been too much to hope that Neve had fallen in love with him, as well, but Davide had been prepared to accept that. *Or at least, he thought he had been.* Some primeval instinct had been telling him that he just had to let her know, even if it was the last time he saw her lovely face.

He had stolen a last glance in Neve's direction. She had had her back to him as she and her mother enjoyed their picnic lunch. Unable to bear staying at the beach any longer, he had given Agostino a nudge and they had shaken off their beach towels and headed back to Valdoro. While cooling off with a gelato at a bar near the town square, Davide had devised a plan to meet with Neve. He would write Neve a note, and Agostino would make an excuse to show up at the villa with the pretense of talking to his mother and figure out a way to deliver it personally to Neve.

With any luck, Neve would agree to meet him at the bakery down the street, where they could sit down and he could treat her to a cappuccino and a pastry while divulging his feelings to her. It would be a perfectly respectable meeting place that would look like a casual encounter to anyone who might be frequenting the shop.

Staring across to the twinkling indigo sky, Davide felt a sharp twinge as he recalled how stupidly love-struck he had been, waxing poetic in a note that now seemed ridiculous with his naive and laughable choice of words.

Signorina Neve,

Only our eyes have met, and forgive me for being bold, but you have pierced my heart with your beauty. I feel that it is in our destiny to meet. With all my respect, I wish to see you before you depart for Canada. I only ask for a few moments of your time so I can express what is in my soul. My intentions are honorable…

If you can grant me this gift, I will be forever indebted. I will be at Michelina's Bakery after it reopens later this afternoon.

D.

Davide felt a tingle along his nerve endings as he thought about his imminent reunion with the girl who had so thoroughly put him in his "place" with her harsh reply. How would he react? How would *she*? His jaw clenched. Maybe he shouldn't have hired Neve Wilder so quickly. Maybe she had every right to know who her boss was before agreeing to the job.

*But she wouldn't have agreed to the job if she had known it was you…*

Davide felt a jolt. His inner voice was right. But somewhere deep inside the pain that was still trapped in his heart, was the pulsing desire to see Neve again. And keeping his identity from her—at least until she arrived—was the *only* way he could make that happen.

# CHAPTER THREE

"MY GOODNESS, NEVE, you could have told me about this job opportunity sooner." Lois Wilder's voice was half-scolding, half-offended. "Hearing this a day before your flight hardly gives me a chance to process all this." She waved her hands helplessly, indicating Neve's open suitcase.

*Or interfere in some way*, Neve couldn't help thinking. "There's nothing to process, Mom. And I was busy finishing up my school year. You know I have no time to chat when I'm in the middle of report cards and end-of-school activities."

Lois expelled a sigh of frustration. "But, darling, had I known, I could have booked a flight, as well. Not that I would have expected to be put up at the same place as you," she added quickly. "I still have my friends at Villa Morgana. I'm sure they would be thrilled to have me visit."

"This is not a vacation, Mom. It's a job. Six days a week." Neve tried to keep her voice steady. "And I'm sure that on the seventh day I'll be too exhausted to do anything but rest." Neve was inwardly horrified at the thought of her mother coming to Valdoro. Knowing her, she'd find a way to insinuate herself in Neve's work and leisure time. No, she had to make it clear to her mom—without being mean—that she should stay home.

"Mom, I can't discuss the details, but this assignment

is highly sensitive. I will not be able to spend *any* time with you at all. And besides—" Neve had a brain wave "—you're hosting that big event in a week—the annual technology symposium—at the company, remember?"

Lois frowned. "Yes, of course. I suppose I can't miss that, seeing as how your dad started it all…" Her eyes began to mist. "Although the thought of returning to the special place where your dad and I…" She sniffed and pulled out a tissue from her designer purse. "May he rest in peace."

"Mom, I really have to finish packing. It's going to be a long couple of flights, and I need to get to bed early. It's only been two days since school ended, and I haven't even had a chance to unwind." Neve continued folding light cotton tops, Capri pants and dresses into her medium-size suitcase. She hoped her mother would take the hint.

Lois peered into the suitcase. "Don't forget your sun protection, Neve. You know how quickly you freckle." She took a step forward to scan Neve's face. "And you might start thinking about using some wrinkle cream. I have a new tube in my purse…"

"Thanks, but no thanks, Mom. I like the natural look." Neve realized that her tone was more clipped than she intended, but she had to stop her mother before she offered another dozen suggestions or reminders. "I'm twenty-six, Mom. I can handle this."

Lois raised her professionally shaped eyebrows. "I forgot to ask. Who is your employer? Can you give me his number? And make sure he has mine, in case of an emergency. Oh, and how much is he paying you for this job? Is the flight included?"

"Mother, you need to go, or it'll be midnight before I'm done here." Neve put an arm around her mother's shoulder and gently ushered her to the door of her apartment.

"I'll text you the information. Don't worry, it's all good."
She gave her a hug. "See you at the end of the summer."

"Let me know as soon as your flight lands, Neve. I'll
be waiting anxiously."

"I will, Mom," Neve replied wearily. "Good night."

*"Buon viaggio,"* Lois called out before Neve closed
the door. "And watch out for those Southern Italian men!"

Neve gave a sigh. She always felt somewhat energy-
depleted after spending time with her mother. She often
wondered at her mom's clinginess; she certainly hadn't
been like that while Neve was growing up. Could it be
that Lois had realized that some of her maternal skills had
been lacking back then—especially after her husband's
death—and was feeling guilty and trying to make up for it?

Neve had a hard time with it. At this point in her life,
she didn't need her mother hovering over her. Lois's controlling and opinionated ways were grating, and Neve often
felt her patience dwindling around her.

It wasn't that she didn't love her mother; she just wanted
her to loosen the apron strings. No—she wanted Lois to
untie them completely, and to fold the apron and put it
away. It had gotten to the point where Neve had actually
contemplated moving out of town. And then she had gotten her current job as a kindergarten teacher, which had
prevented any further plans of relocating.

Neve checked the time and quickly finished packing,
pushing away any more thoughts about her mother. All
that was left to do now was to have a soothing bath and
go to bed. And tomorrow, after a leisurely breakfast, she'd
head to the airport. She thought of the plush orca she had
purchased for Bianca—the perfect West Coast gift for a
child—and smiled. Difficult and troubled though Bianca
might be, Neve was confident that she could help her.

Lucia Michele had provided more details about Bianca's

ROSANNA BATTIGELLI                    39

situation, her daily routines and Neve's trip arrangements
in a subsequent email, including the fact that Bianca's
uncle would be covering all her travel and food expenses.
*How very generous, and obviously very wealthy*, Neve
had thought, and had wondered what he did for a living.

Feeling her eyelids start to droop, Neve pulled the
stopper and stepped out of the tub, shivering despite the
warmth of the room. She wrapped her terry-cloth robe
around her and dried herself briskly before changing into a
knee-length nightshirt. Under the covers, she let out a deep
sigh. *She was really doing this.* Her travel clothes were laid
out, and she was ready to fly to Italy and be a nanny! She
hugged her pillow and let the memories of sun-drenched
days, delicious Southern cuisine and the magical Ionian
Sea lull her to sleep.

Davide drummed his fingers on his desk. He checked the
time on his cell phone. Neve's plane should be landing in
minutes at the Lamezia International Airport. Tomaso,
his occasional driver, would be waiting for her, holding a
card up with her name on it. Hopefully, there wouldn't be
a delay in claiming her luggage. If complications arose,
Tomaso would take care of them.

Davide wondered if Neve still spoke some Italian. The
second time he saw her on her balcony, he had smiled and
said, *"Ciao, signorina."* She had hesitated, given a quirk
of a smile, and replied, *"Ciao."* It came out sounding more
like the English "chow," and, embarrassed, she quickly repeated it with less of an aspiration at the start of the word.
He had nodded in approval, and as he continued walking,
he couldn't resist looking back and saying, *"Ciao, bella."*
But she had already gone in.

Davide had tried to push recurring thoughts of her away
after she had left Valdoro and returned to Vancouver. But if

he had managed to accomplish that even temporarily during the day, he had been plagued by dreams of her at night.

His zio, Francesco, had noticed his malaise and had encouraged Davide to confide in him. *Is it about a girl?* He had eyed Davide with furrowed brows. Davide had been too embarrassed to talk about his feelings. *Especially to his uncle the priest. How could he have possibly discussed his unquenchable desire for Neve, and his feelings of bitterness and humiliation?*

"The best thing is to concentrate on your studies—and perhaps frequent Sunday mass a little more often," his uncle had solemnly suggested.

Davide smirked. He had taken his uncle's advice about his studies, but not so much on the second suggestion. Davide had had an issue with God and the whole destiny thing, and at twenty-two, forgiveness was not a strong male virtue. Davide had still gone to mass on special occasions, like the main holidays and an occasional funeral mass for a family friend, but other than that, he had stayed away. Besides, he had had goals he needed to accomplish.

*And he had.* He gave a bitter laugh as his gaze fell on the copy of his award-winning novel on his desk. Maybe he should thank Neve personally for *her* part in his literary success. Maybe he should have included a few words about her in his acceptance speech. After all, it was *her written words* that had ignited the chain of events leading up to the writing of his book.

*Let it go*, an inner voice whispered. Davide took a deep breath. *Indeed.* Why should he continue to be bitter about the words and actions of a teenage girl? He was a man now. His young ego may have been bruised then, but surely he was mature enough to have moved on?

Davide thought he had dealt with all those immature emotions, but he couldn't deny the sharp twinge in the core of his heart when Neve's face had appeared on the screen. She was still beautiful. *Bellissima*. He had watched the interview a few times after Lucia had gone home. Studied Neve's face as she spoke. Paused to go over her every feature. He had drunk in the sight of her like a man coming across a source of water after days of walking in a scorching-hot desert.

Could he handle her living in the castle with him, interacting with him daily, watching her deal with his beloved niece? *Only time would tell...*

His phone indicated a text. He checked the message, written in Italian.

Signorina Wilder has arrived. We are on our way.

Va bene, Davide replied swiftly.

He set down his phone, strode over to the credenza and poured himself a shot of brandy.

# CHAPTER FOUR

As soon as Neve stepped out of the plane, the dry July heat enveloped her like a swaddling blanket. She was glad she had packed light. Her carry-on contained her laptop and a few emergency items in case her luggage was lost. And in her one piece of luggage, which she would shortly claim, there were just enough items to last her three weeks. She would alternate clothes over her two-month stay, and if she really got tired of wearing the same thing, she'd go to any one of the outdoor markets and buy something new. After all, she wasn't there to be in a fashion parade; she was there for work.

Neve took a moment to text her mother that she had arrived, and joined a slow-moving throng to get clearance from the uniformed officials. She then proceeded to the baggage claim area. She looked eagerly for a middle-aged man holding a sign with her name on it, as Lucia Michele had indicated in her email, and when she had spotted him, she waved and walked briskly toward him. He welcomed Neve in Italian and introduced himself as Tomaso Rocco. She smiled back at him and thanked him in Italian for having come to the airport to pick her up and drive her back to her employer's house.

Neve noticed that his eyebrows had lifted at the word *casa*. Maybe he was surprised that she could speak Italian. She had studied it since her trip to Italy as a teenager, and made it a point to use it with her Italian landlady and landlord, so she felt fairly comfortable communicating right away with Tomaso. Strangely enough, he switched to a faltering English after she had spoken.

"Would you care for a refresh before we proceed?" Tomaso pointed to a nearby kiosk. "Or a *panino*?"

Neve smiled. "*Grazie*, Signor Tomaso, but I had a nice meal on the plane. I wouldn't mind finding a ladies' room, though."

He nodded and once she returned, she positioned herself near one of the conveyors to scan the moving luggage. A few minutes later she spotted the suitcase with two extra-large stickers of the Canadian flag and the Italian flag placed side by side. Tomaso deftly grabbed it and a few moments later they were driving south along the coast. Neve was glad that Tomaso was not a man of many words, as the view around her had her total attention. She caught her breath at the shimmering expanse of the Gulf of St. Euphemia in the Tyrrhenian Sea, and the pastel-colored facades of villas and apartments. The familiar sight of oleander trees, with their profusion of white, pink and fuchsia blooms, growing not only around homes but also along endless stretches of railroad tracks, made Neve think of an impressionist painting, with its mesmerizing combination of multicolored strokes.

Despite the stifling heat of the afternoon, Tomaso had opted to roll the windows down instead of putting on the air-conditioning, and Neve actually didn't mind as she breathed in the sweet scent of the oleander blossoms perfuming the air.

Before long Tomaso had changed direction and was heading inland. The view changed from seascape to hills and valleys, with miles and miles of olive groves.

Neve loved the look of the olive trees, with their gnarled branches and silver-green foliage. She started as the vehicle jerked to a sudden stop, and Neve, turning her head, discovered the cause: a herd of goats crossing the road. The goatherd ambled by, waving at Tomaso, and he gave a resigned wave back. "People not like to hurry here," he said to Neve in his broken English. He drummed his fingers on the steering wheel. "You understand? Sometimes is like a thousand years ago."

"I understand." Neve stifled the urge to chuckle. "It's like time standing still."

Tomaso gave her a baffled look and then exclaimed as some of the goats started to backtrack. He gave a quick blast of the horn and the goats finally crossed over. Neve settled back to enjoy the magnificent views as the road snaked its way through what she discovered as she checked her map, was the Aspromonte mountain range. *The Bitter Mountains.*

She couldn't help a slight shiver as she recalled reading about some of the nefarious happenings within the dark recesses of the heavily wooded slopes. Stories of bandits, or *briganti.* Some had been the Italian counterpart to Robin Hood, but others were immortalized in folk songs for their notorious deeds.

Neve marveled at some of the hamlets perched on top of a hill. Some had been abandoned for years, and the houses were crumbling in areas. But even these ghost towns, with their borders of cactus pear plants and hillsides of golden broom, had a mysterious and romantic air about them, conjuring all kinds of stories in her imagination.

Totally absorbed in the mountain landscape, with its dark gullies and sheer cliff sides with often no guardrails, Neve found herself holding her breath. It was like seeing everything with new eyes. Perhaps at eighteen she had had other things—or people—that had grabbed her attention, but now the mountains, trees and the scintillating waters were even more majestic and striking than she remembered.

Tomaso started whistling an old folk tune; she had heard it at a festival during her last trip to Italy. She knew the title, *Calabrisella Mia*, and if her memory served her right, it was about a young man who spotted a young lady washing clothes at the public fountains and was captivated by her. Well, maybe nobody went to do laundry at the fountains or by the river anymore, but Valdoro still celebrated the chivalry of the "old days" at their annual summer festival, the *Festa della Calabrisella*, where couples dressed up in traditional vintage clothing and danced the *tarantella*.

The hamlet came alive for the festivities, with its numbers swelling from visitors near and far. Merchants sold their artisanal goods in an outdoor market in Valdoro's *piazza* during the day, and everything from stuffed eggplants to fried calamari and cuttlefish were sold in the town banquet hall in the evening before the outdoor activities resumed, with musicians performing back in the square until midnight.

Neve's mouth watered at the memory of the food fair, and in particular, the sizzling stuffed zucchini flowers that she loved, their golden orange blossoms filled with a chunk of *fontina* cheese, and then floured and quickly deep-fried. Neve hoped she would be able to attend with Bianca, or during her day off.

"*Ecco!* We are approaching Valdoro," Tomaso suddenly exclaimed, and Neve realized she had been lost in her thoughts and had missed the road signs. She sat up straighter and wondered at how much of what she saw seemed completely new. And then she saw the fork in the road that led right into Valdoro.

"The Pasticceria Michelina!" She recognized the peach-colored facade of the bakery on the same street as the Villa Morgana. "They had the best marzipan cookies and cannoli! Could we stop?" She would love to buy some treats for Bianca.

"I'm sure you will have time to go back soon enough," Tomaso said with a tone of regret. "But your employer is waiting and expects us very shortly."

*Was her employer that inflexible? She wouldn't have taken more than five minutes to get what she wanted...* Neve started as Tomaso suddenly swerved to follow the left fork, which took them away from the main road.

"Wh-where are you going?" Neve said, confused. "I thought we were going to Valdoro."

"We are still in Valdoro, *signorina*. Your boss lives on the—how do you say?—outside skirts."

Neve smiled, but didn't correct him. As Tomaso drove farther along, fewer and fewer homes appeared, and then suddenly, there was nothing but stretches of olive groves, uncultivated land bordered with endless cactus pear bushes and what looked like giant aloe vera plants, and massive clay hills. Tomaso veered into a side road, and Neve realized he was starting to ascend a path that wove its way around a mountainside, giving her flashes of the Ionian Sea through the dizzying blur of trees.

Neve's stomach gave a flip at the change in elevation. *Who would build way up here? Was there a cluster of homes at the summit?* She had seen photos of mountaintop villages or monasteries all over Italy, and they had always made her catch her breath, trying to imagine the toil of the men and mules employed to carry out such a task centuries ago.

Neve closed her eyes at one point. There were no guardrails at all, and the thought of the vehicle skidding down the mountain made the butterflies in her stomach crash wildly into each other.

*"Siamo arrivati,"* Tomaso announced after what seemed like an eternity.

Neve felt the car come to a stop. She opened her eyes and allowed her stomach to settle for a moment. Tomaso came around to open her door, and she stepped out hesitantly, thanking him. He nodded and as he went to retrieve her luggage, Neve's gaze shifted eagerly to her employer's house. She froze and then felt a slow tremble along her nerve endings.

*This was no house.* Neve's gaze traveled from one side of the centuries-old castle to the other. *A castle! Was she dreaming?* She pinched her hand. No, no dream. And no wonder that Tomaso had had that funny expression when she thanked him for picking her up to take her to her employer's "house." Parked outside were three other vehicles, one an electric blue that dazzled in the sun. As they approached, the golden bull brand confirmed her guess: a Lamborghini. The second one was a red Alfa Romeo, and the third, a Fiat Cinquecento.

Neve followed Tomaso numbly toward the massive rounded portico. The low heels of her sandals clicked on the granite slabs of the walkway, and she felt as if she was walking into a fairy tale. The few scattered clouds seemed to be within reach, and the air was fresh at this elevation. Neve breathed in the scent of the nearby pine trees. They seemed to be twinkling with the sun's rays poking through spaces in their thick boughs. The sun gleamed off the casement windows, and Neve wondered if her employer was watching from behind one of them. She swallowed. *What was she in for?* She felt an inner shiver and had a feeling that there were a lot more unexpected things to come.

Tomaso ignored the heavy iron knocker and pressed a

buzzer on a panel below. Okay, so there was one modern touch, but what if her employer was an eccentric?

*She knew next to nothing about him. Who was this enigmatic boss who lived at the top of a mountain and who hadn't wanted his identity revealed? And how could he be raising his niece here, so isolated from other people? From kids?*

A hundred questions swarmed her mind, but they dissipated when the doorknob turned. She bit her lip.

The door opened with a slight creak, and Neve was almost expecting to see a disheveled, wild-haired scientist or inventor type, dressed in a lab coat and smelling of formaldehyde and carrying a beaker with some swirling concoction. *What appeared was anything but.*

She looked up to meet the unsmiling and spectacled gaze of a thirty-something man who was hardly the Frankenstein she had envisioned. The fresh citrus scent of his cologne tingled her nostrils. He hadn't shaved, but that didn't detract from his attractiveness. *No*, his well-groomed scruff was absolutely charming. *If only he would remove his sunglasses.* Somehow, Neve felt at a disadvantage...

His dark brown hair was cut short but revealed curls on the top, and he had a firm, straight nose and strong jaw. And perfect lips. Although she didn't want to stare, Neve couldn't help taking in his physique in a two-second glance that wandered from his face to his body, noting the broad shoulders and snug-fitting sleeves; the crisp black shirt open at the neck, with buttons tapering to a flat stomach; and the tailored cream trousers and polished black shoes. *Italian leather, of course.*

Neve's heart did a flip at the way he was staring at her when her gaze returned to his face. He smiled, revealing a dimple that was the icing on the cake as far as she was concerned, and she began to reciprocate but realized with a gulp that he was directing it to Tomaso, who stood behind her with her suitcase in hand. He opened the door wider and directed Tomaso in Italian to carry her suitcase to her room. When Tomaso disappeared, he looked appraisingly at her, and the half smile that still lingered on her face began to waver.

But then he held out his hand and flashed her a smile. "*Benvenuta*, Signorina Wilder."

Neve would have truly felt his welcome was genuine, had the coolness of his tone not indicated otherwise.

From his study window, Davide had watched Neve come out of his Fiat van. His pulse had quickened with her every step toward the castle. The way the sun had caught in her hair and made it shimmer had taken his breath away. Her calf-length, pale lavender dress, with its filmy skirt layers and uneven hem, made her look like a mystical fairy. All she needed to do was to kick off her shoes and dance around the castle grounds…

*Stop! What are you doing? This fairy wanted to have nothing to do with you, remember? She made it quite clear that you were below her. And she's not here for any reason other than to take care of Bianca.*

Davide realized he was clenching his jaw and relaxed it. The fact was, Neve Wilder had had the best credentials for the job, and he had to forget what she had been like at eighteen. What had devastated him at the time—*and afterward*—had probably not affected her one bit. She had most likely forgotten the whole incident. *And maybe him, as well*… In any case, he had no intention of bringing it up…unless *she* did.

Making his way down the gleaming oak staircase to the main floor, Davide had thought of how opportune it was to have arranged for Bianca to be away for a few days. Thank goodness Bianca enjoyed spending time with Lucia, his trusted research assistant and friend. Davide didn't know how he would have gotten through these past few months without Lucia's help. She had been there to pick up the pieces after he had dismissed the last three nannies, and for that he would be eternally grateful. Lucia was married with no children of her own but had grown up in a large family, and had a wonderful way with children.

Davide was grateful that Lucia had gained Bianca's trust, but Lucia wasn't there to be a nanny. After the disappointments of the past, he intended to discover whether Neve Wilder was truly the right choice. He'd decided not to introduce Bianca to her new nanny right away, and risk upsetting her if he had to fire Neve.

Davide was sure that he would be able to determine if Neve's character was genuine, or if she had just put on a good act during the interview. And if his judgment *had* been faulty, he'd waste no time in sending her back to Vancouver.

David had stipulated that Neve would have a "trial period" in the contract, but he had omitted to mention that Bianca wouldn't be there at that time. He shrugged, his mouth twisting.

*His prerogative. He* was the boss.

When Davide had opened the thick wooden door, he had felt a surge of electricity zip through his veins. His gaze had flown first to Neve, then he had smiled at Tomaso to bring up Neve's luggage to her room. "The one in the turret," he had directed, and then had focused his attention to Neve. Nothing in her gaze had indicated that she had recognized him. *Good. Maybe that was for the best...* But her smile had suddenly faltered...and then he had realized that his expression had hardly been welcoming.

No matter what he thought of her, he had reminded himself that he had to be civil, for Bianca's sake.

Davide had forced himself to smile, and despite the hard, twisted knot in his gut that he had lived with for the past eight years, faking his welcome had made him feel like a cad.

Now he swore inwardly as he saw something shut down in her blue-green eyes. She had perceptively picked up on his less than genuine gesture.

Neve had not even been in his presence for a minute, and he was feeling emotional turmoil. Realizing now that he was staring at her, he cleared his throat and tried softening his tone. "I apologize, Signorina Wilder. I've had little sleep these past few months. It has been a very difficult time, as you can imagine." He offered her his hand.

Her aquamarine eyes widened. "Yes, of course, *signor.*" She gave his hand a gentle squeeze. "I'm very sorry for your loss…and Bianca's."

The touch of her hand in his, albeit brief, ignited his nerve endings.

He nodded and focused on what she was saying. *Were her eyes actually misting?* "Thank you. May I take your carry-on?" He wanted to veer away from any further mention of his sister and brother-in-law. The last thing he wanted was to be emotional in front of her.

Fortunately, Tomaso's reappearance distracted them both. Davide thanked him and offered him a cool refreshment, but Tomaso respectfully declined. "My wife texted me to say her eggplant parmigiana would be ready when I get home," he chuckled. "And believe me, she makes the best *melanzana alla parmigiana.*"

"I don't blame you for hurrying back." Davide nodded. "It's not every man who can go home to a good meal—and a good woman," he added drily. He shook Tomaso's hand,

and as Tomaso headed toward his Fiat Cinquecento, Davide motioned for Neve to enter the castle. He could see that Neve was impressed by what she saw. He gave her a few moments as she took in the rich oak staircase curving sensuously to the second level, the vaulted ceiling and pale mint walls, the luxurious peach marble tiles and the gleaming walnut and oak inlaid furniture pieces, including the round central table, enhanced by a large crystal vase filled with fresh flowers of every color. Davide had them delivered and arranged once a week. He enjoyed the look and scent of them in the foyer—the mix of peony and oleander, jasmine and rose, and any other combination of flowers native to Calabria.

"I imagine you're tired after your trip, Signorina Wilder. I'll show you to your room." He gestured toward the staircase.

Neve hesitated for a moment before nodding, and as she proceeded gracefully up the stairs, Davide couldn't stop his gaze from sweeping over her. Her dress molded to the curves of her body, and its flared and layered skirt swayed with her hip movements. Davide swallowed as his eyes swept farther downward along the length of her calves and to her low-heeled sandals. She suddenly stopped on the landing, and he looked up too late to stop his body from bumping into hers. She faltered, and his arms instinctively dropped her carry-on bag and reached out to steady her.

For a moment his body went into shock. The feel of her trim waist almost completely encircled by his hands made his nerve endings sizzle. His mouth was inches away from her neck, and, oh, how he had often dreamt of—

He felt her stiffen. And he remembered that his fantasies of holding her in his arms, of brushing a path of kisses against her neck before moving upward to taste her coral lips, had died with his hopes long before, splintering like the waves that dashed against the boulders on the shore.

*"Mi scusi,"* he apologized curtly, moving away to pick up her bag. He preceded her down the hall, walking past a half-dozen doors until he stopped at a curved section, one of the four turrets in the castle. Davide wanted her in the spare room next to Bianca, and both were across the hall from his bedroom and his study.

Not that he had any ungentlemanly intentions toward Neve. No, despite his undeniable attraction to Neve *still*, his pride would not allow him to even venture in *that* direction. She was here to do the job he had hired her for. Nothing more, nothing less. He opened the thick, rounded door. "I hope you will be pleased with this room, Signorina Wilder."

She glanced past him and her mouth opened in wonder. Turning, she gave him a dazzling smile. *"Pleased?* This is every girl's dream come true," she breathed. "A castle and a room fit for a princess—I feel like I'm in a fairy tale…" She went straight to the casement window to check out the view. The breeze rippled through her hair, and Davide felt a twist in his gut at the reality that she was actually here in person.

"I'm glad you like it." He gave her a piercing look as he set down her bag. "Just keep in mind, though, that your experience here may not be like the fairy tales you're familiar with. And hopefully, you'll last longer than the previous three princesses…"

# CHAPTER FIVE

NEVE STARED AT the door that had just closed behind him. She felt foolish now for having gushed about the place; he must have thought her materialistic, or at the very least, fanciful. And she had a strong feeling that fanciful was not what he wanted in a nanny.

Neve looked around. She wondered what kind of a job her boss had to allow him to renovate an ancient castle in such a lavish manner. There had been nothing in sight to enlighten her in any way about this. Perhaps he had inherited money and didn't have to work…

She had grown up accustomed to a wealthy lifestyle, but *this*, this place was over-the-top. The floor was a stunning pale rose marble with veins of gold. The bed stood in the center of a rich Renaissance-style rug. The duvet and pillow shams had the dreamy colors of an impressionist painting, with assorted custom pillows in turquoise and gold. The massive armoire matched the gleaming wood of the bed and the night tables, and on the top of each end table stood an antique lamp with carnelian tassels hanging from the rim of each shade. A luxurious burgundy recliner was positioned by the window.

This was obviously decorated for a woman's use, Neve thought, eyeing the ornate dressing table against one wall. *Had her boss designed it for his lady? Or wife?* She hadn't seen a ring on his finger, which didn't necessarily mean he wasn't married. Neve felt her stomach tighten at the thought of how his hands had felt around her waist. With his gorgeous looks, how could she even think he wasn't attached in one way or another? Those hands of his were probably in high demand…

Neve forced herself to stop that train of thought. *What was the matter with her?* She was here not even an hour, and already she was thinking about her boss in a way that an employee should not be.

She strode to the mahogany four-poster bed, with its matching step-up stool. After removing her sandals, she climbed up to sit on the bed. Much as she wanted to lie down and have a nap, Neve's mind was too preoccupied to let herself sleep. On the plane trip, her thoughts had kept returning to the little girl that she would soon meet. *Would Bianca be upset or hostile to yet another nanny showing up?* Not that there had been any mention of her being hostile, but Neve couldn't help wondering at the cause of the dismissal of three previous nannies.

They had obviously displeased Neve's uncle. Could one of them have been negligent in her care of Bianca? Had one been too harsh with her? Or had one of the nannies been more attentive to their boss than to his niece? Neve turned over every possibility that she could think of, and had finally convinced herself to stop. Just because three nannies had disappointed their employer, it didn't mean that *she* would. In any case, all she could do was try her best. Use all the skills and compassion she had to try to reach this little girl.

Neve felt a twinge in her heart, thinking of Bianca's tragic loss. *Not one parent, but two.* A double trauma. And then to be whisked away to a new country where she had nobody but her uncle as family. Neve took a deep breath. *No, this was not going to be a vacation.*

She frowned. And how strange was it that she still didn't know her employer's name? He hadn't introduced himself, and taken by surprise at his appearance, Neve hadn't even thought of asking...

A couple of taps at the door made her start. "*Scusi*, Signorina Neve. I thought you might like some refreshments."

Neve slid off the bed and put on her sandals before hurrying to open the door. He was holding a silver tray with a bottle of water and one of orange juice, a small platter of grapes and golden plums and a variety of cheeses and crackers. He was still wearing his glasses, which Neve found rather unnerving.

"That's very thoughtful. Thank you, Mr...?"

He looked at her intently. "Cortese," he said curtly. "You're welcome." He strode to the dressing table and set the tray down. He walked back to the door and then looked over his shoulder at her. "After you have rested and when you are ready, please come to my study across the hall and we'll go over my expectations..."

Neve's eyebrows arched. *Hadn't Lucia Michele informed her of all his expectations?* She felt her stomach muscles contract. There was something in the way he was looking at her that made her stomach quiver with apprehension. And when exactly was he planning to introduce her to Bianca? He hadn't said anything about her whereabouts. She was most likely having an afternoon siesta, and Neve would meet her afterward...

"I'm not feeling that tired right now, Signor Cortese. But I wouldn't mind having some water and fruit." Neve gave him a tentative smile. "I'll be over in a few minutes, and by then, I'm hoping that Bianca—"

"Bianca's not here," he said swiftly. He swiveled to face her. "She's away for a few days. My assistant—Signora Michele—has a niece visiting, and I arranged for Bianca to spend a few days with them. I thought that we could use the time to review a few things…"

Neve had to stop from gaping as she stared back at him. She felt a shiver run through her. She was alone in a castle miles away from anyone, with a man who had wanted his identity protected. Could she trust him? What if—?

"You have nothing to worry about, Signorina Wilder," he said coolly. "I'm not planning to compromise your virtue." His ebony eyes swept over her body deliberately before locking with hers. "I had you brought here for my niece, not for me." He turned to leave. "And I have no interest in taking up in *that* way with *straniere*."

Neve's stomach tensed at the way his voice had chilled at the word *foreigners*, specifically foreign women. Speechless, she stood watching him, and even after he had shut the door firmly, she stood immobilized for another minute. Finally, she walked over to the dressing table, had a long drink of water and sat down on the stool, her heart racing as if she had just completed a marathon.

She had no choice but to meet Signor Cortese in his study. But first she needed to cool herself off. After finishing the bottle of water, Neve stood up and taking a deep breath, headed for the door.

Davide had left the door of his study open. He heard Neve's door open and shut and her footsteps as she crossed the hall. He remained at his desk, looking out to the view of the countryside and to the strip of azure sea beyond. "Come in," he said curtly when her footsteps ceased at his doorway.

He had been thinking about the startled fawn look on Neve's face when he had told her that Bianca wasn't there.

*I'm not planning to compromise your virtue*, he had stated, and almost blurted afterward, *if your virtue is still intact...*

Davide swiveled to face her, but remained sitting. He gestured to the maroon leather chair in front of her. "Please...have a seat."

He reached beyond his laptop for a file on the left-hand corner of his desk, and slid it toward him. He saw that Neve was gazing at the small pile of books on the other side of his desk.

"So now you know what I do for a living..."

Her eyes widened. *"You're an author?"*

Davide nodded. "I suppose you must have wondered what I did to enable me to buy this place and renovate it." He saw a flush spread over her cheeks.

"Well, it *had* crossed my mind," she admitted, shrugging defensively. "But most writers don't live... I mean... can't live—"

"Like *this*?" Davide smirked. "You're right, Signorina Wilder. I was one of the lucky ones whose first novel—and the only one published so far—was not only awarded the *Strega*, Italy's highest literary award, but was also optioned immediately by a major film company. And a television series is also in the works. If I wanted to, I could retire right now and live happily-ever-after..." The muscles in his jaw flicked. "But I have no intention of retiring. And *happily-ever-after* is not an option right now." He tapped his closed laptop. "Eventually I'll get back to working on my second novel...when Bianca is more settled..."

"I'm sure luck was not the only factor in your success, Signor Cortese."

Neve's soft voice was like a hammer against his heart. No, it hadn't been all about luck. It had been about her rejection, about heartbreak, about losing himself in a fictional world to escape his own reality...

"Perhaps I can read your book while I'm here…"

*No!* Letting her read the story of Serena and Vittorio would be allowing her a glimpse—no, an entire window—into his soul, and he wasn't ready for that… He had revealed a vulnerable part of his soul once to her, only to have it scorched by her harsh words.

"Perhaps," he forced himself to reply nonchalantly. "But I'm sure you'll be too busy tending to Bianca…" He straightened in his chair. "But we're not here to talk about me or my book," he said curtly. "Let's get down to business and not my personal life."

"I'm sorry," Neve replied quickly. "I didn't mean to—"

"Apology accepted."

"I—I hope I haven't offended you."

Davide surveyed her for a moment. The flush on her face had deepened, and her discomfort was palpable. "I'm not offended in the least," he replied crisply. *At least not about the present. The past was a different story…* He leaned forward, out of the direct sunlight. "Now, let's go over Bianca's routines…" He removed his sunglasses, his eyes boring into Neve's.

# CHAPTER SIX

NEVE'S LIPS PARTED with a sudden uptake of breath. His black eyes were so intense…like smoldering volcanic shards. She couldn't pull her gaze away. She felt something stir in her memory… Black eyes that glistened like raven's wings…

Neve felt her heart begin to beat a warning drum against her chest.

*Could it be? The Italian who had made it a point to walk past her balcony every day while she had stayed at the Villa Morgana? Who had shown up at the beach with his friend when she was there with her mother?*

She scanned his face, trying to imagine him eight years younger, without the groomed shadow or styled hair.

*Yes.* Sparks shot through her veins. It was *him*.

Neve stared at him speechlessly. Eight years ago he had had longer hair and no groomed shadow, and he had been more lanky. Now he exuded maturity, worldliness and wealth. With his expensive clothes and styled hair that was short on the sides and back and curling on top, he looked as polished and sophisticated as a model in a magazine. His face had lost its adolescent leanness, and was strong, chiseled—*and heart-stopping*.

What were the chances of *him* being Bianca's uncle and her employer for the summer?

And then her mind stilled. *He had known who she was when he had hired her.* He had watched the interview conducted by his assistant.

Neve didn't think she had changed that much in eight years; she had no doubt that he would have recognized her right away. That is, if he had remembered walking past her balcony at Villa Morgana and gazing at her with such intensity…

She had been young, but not so young that she hadn't been instantly aware of the meaning of his look. It had riveted her, caused the first stirrings of sensuality, made her wonder what it could lead to…and after three days of this, she had felt a molten heat begin to spread throughout her veins even at the anticipation of seeing him return from his work in the countryside.

And then one day he had shown up at the beach. When she had seen him and his friend Agostino, whom she recognized as the son of the housekeeper at Villa Morgana, she had tried to be discreet about watching him. She had directed fleeting glances at his tanned, muscled body, always when her mother was distracted with preparing the picnic lunch or sunning on the beach chair. Neve had brought a book along, and she had held it up in front of her, pretending to read, but all the while, gazing at *him*. She hadn't known his name, and she'd never seemed to have the opportunity to ask Agostino…

And two days before she had to leave Italy, Davide had stopped coming by. The first day Neve had left the balcony with a heavy feeling in her chest. She had pleaded a headache and stayed in her room instead of joining her mother and hosts for dinner. Her appetite had left her. Her mother had checked in on her, but Neve had pretended to be sleeping.

On the evening before their departure, Neve had had

no choice but to join the group, despite the fact that she was feeling even worse.

The next morning she had left Valdoro with a desperate scan of the streets from the backseat of the vehicle that had sped toward the airport. The flight back home had been just as dismal, and for the next few months Neve had felt listless and down. Her mother had claimed it to be a hormone imbalance, and had supplied her with over-the-counter remedies. Neve had pretended to take them, but all the while had flushed them down the toilet.

Her gut had told her that it wasn't pills she needed; it was time. Time to get over the crazy feeling that she had lost someone she had just begun to fall in love with…

Neve's gaze dropped to the name on the book. *Davide Cortese…* How often had she wondered about his name? Carlo, Luciano, Marco, Roberto, Vincenzo… She had gone over every Italian name in the alphabet, trying to guess at his. For a long time he had appeared in her adolescent dreams, and during the day she had found it hard to concentrate on her classes.

When her marks had started to slip, her mother had threatened to send her to a private school and Neve had forced herself to slip out of her malaise and get back to reality. She was in Canada and *he* was in Southern Italy. They were from different worlds, and there was no chance of those worlds colliding…

Yet here she was, eight years later. *In a castle that she'd be living in for two months with him…and his niece.* She shook her head and wanted to pinch herself, but knew it was futile.

*This was not a dream…*

Davide had noticed the changes in Neve's expression. The slight furrowing of her eyebrows suddenly smoothing out, her blue-green eyes widening and her lips parting. And her chest rising with a quick intake of breath. She had recognized him.

So now what?

She would have figured out that he had recognized her from the interview. How would she react? Perhaps she was wondering what his real motive was in hiring her. Or feeling threatened that someone she had spurned eight years earlier had masterminded her return to Valdoro? Maybe she wondered if he was some kind of psychopath who was bent on revenge… He searched her face for any sign of fear, but all he saw was surprise. And confusion. He saw her glance down at his books and back at him. Her cheeks had darkened to a deep shade of pink, the same pink as some of the roses and oleander flowers on his property.

Her eyebrows had lifted in an unspoken question, but Davide wasn't ready to comply with a response. And it didn't look like she wanted to be the first one to bring up the now very obvious elephant in the room…

"*Va bene*, let's discuss your goals concerning Bianca before I reinforce my expectations." His eyes narrowed. "And please respond with specifics about how you intend to achieve those goals."

Davide checked the time on his phone. He had grilled Neve long enough, and to his surprise, she had answered his questions unwaveringly, providing a detailed knowledge of behavioral strategies and demonstrating a genuine empathy toward children. But the color that had suffused her face earlier had dissipated. In fact, she was looking a little pale…

He stood up abruptly. "I think we've discussed enough for now. Once you have rested, please feel free to go down to any of the rooms on the main level or out in the courtyard or gardens." He watched as Neve nodded and turned, the uneven hem of her violet dress swirling to reveal a flash of her thighs. His pulse jumped erratically. Despite the efforts he had made to recover emotionally from Neve, his body was obviously not on board.

Stifling a growl of frustration, he waited until he heard her bedroom door click shut behind her and then busied himself with email, responding to several communications from his publisher, who had been checking on him regularly since Davide had brought Bianca back from Vancouver. Afterward, he went downstairs to make himself an espresso. Sitting with it in the courtyard beyond the kitchen, he couldn't help thinking about Neve.

He forced himself to face a hard fact. *He was not immune to her physical charms.* The eight years of trying to quench his desire for her had been futile. Watching her on his computer screen had activated his pulse, but having her in his presence, within his touch, was a sweet torture that took every ounce of his energy to conceal.

Maybe hiring Neve Wilder, despite her stellar CV and qualifications, had been a mistake. How could he not have imagined the effect that her presence would have on him? Eight years ago he would have given anything to have met her, held her hand, revealed his feelings. But she had denied him even the chance to meet. Then she had left the country, leaving him with a gnawing regret and a crushed spirit.

If he had thought that he could be neutral having Neve as a nanny to Bianca without his emotions being affected, he had been delusional. The feel of her hand in his…just that momentary touch had sent a spiral of heat through him, and his heart had hammered against his rib cage, drowning out some of her words… And then she had told him how sorry she was for his and Bianca's loss, and those azure eyes had started to mist.

*How could he endure two months of having Neve so close? What on earth had he hoped to accomplish, other than to find a nanny who could help Bianca and prepare her for school?*

Davide recalled the flash of recognition on Neve's face. *What was she thinking now? Would she stay, now that she knew who he was?*

He clenched his jaw. *She had to stay.* Whether she liked it or not. Even if she was uncomfortable with him. She had signed a contract. And ultimately, she was here for Bianca, not for *him*. He would stay out of her way as much as possible.

Davide felt the familiar stabs of sadness and concern over Bianca's trauma. Since the accident, she had awoken occasionally during the night with a bad dream. He had made sure to have the room across his set up for her when he brought her back here, and he had always kept his door open to listen for any signs of distress from her.

It had been a trauma for him, too; he had loved Violetta and had been crushed at the news of her and Tristan's deaths. He still shuddered every time he thought about the phone call that night. How his body had gone numb, and then trembled in icy shock. There had been no sleep for the rest of the night. He had paced through the castle like a man possessed, feeling a desolation that was as dark and deep as the Ionian Sea nearby. And a helplessness that he could do nothing for little Bianca while they were oceans apart.

He had known that Violetta's friend Alba would take good care of Bianca until he arrived, and Davide had made her promise that she would let *him* tell Bianca. Like a zombie, he had thrown together a few clothes in a medium suitcase, and had driven straight to Lamezia Airport. He had flown to Rome and then had made two more connections to his final stop in Vancouver.

And he had crashed for a few hours in a hotel before hiring a driver to bring him to Alba's condo.

That had been five months ago. Before that he had still felt young and relatively carefree. Any sense of happiness over his literary success and his progress with his second novel had dissipated like the morning fog at the news of Violetta and Tristan. And the hardest thing that he had ever had to do was to look at Bianca's sweet little face, all lit up over his arrival, and tell her about the accident.

The shadow that had crossed her face, and the cries of *"Mummy! Daddy! I want them to come home!"* while he held her in his arms, had almost done him in, but he had forced himself to stay calm and strong for her sake, and had stayed with her until she had cried herself to sleep. Alba had prepared a spare room for him, but he opted for a spare cot to be brought to Bianca's room, in case she woke up in the night, scared or in shock.

Davide had thanked God countless times that he had been able to fly to Vancouver regularly since Bianca's birth. Violetta had bestowed him with the honor of being Bianca's godfather, and he had been determined to have a special relationship with his niece. He had not wanted Bianca to ever feel that he was a stranger.

Davide had been so grateful that the success of his first novel had provided him with the means to take regular trips and stay connected with Violetta's family.

Since he had brought Bianca home with him, Davide had put his writing on hold. Helping Bianca had been his priority. And still was. But now that Neve was here, he might be able return to his novel in progress. *If she lasted…*

## CHAPTER SEVEN

NEVE OPENED HER EYES, blinking at the unfamiliar light fixture, a chandelier that featured dozens of colorful Murano glass flowers in various states of bloom. And then she remembered where she was. She had returned to her room and emotionally drained, had taken off her sandals and had lain down on the bed. Despite the turbulence of her thoughts, she had felt herself drifting.

Now, checking the time, she realized that she had been napping for almost two hours. Still feeling somewhat groggy, she slid off the bed and ambled to the washroom. After a refreshing shower, she towel-dried her hair, combed it out and slipped on a headband. She opened her suitcase and chose an aqua cotton top and a pair of white Capri pants.

There was no avoiding the situation. She couldn't stay in her room indefinitely. Taking a deep breath, Neve headed downstairs.

She found her way past the elegant dining area to the most spectacular kitchen she had ever seen. From the gleaming granite countertops to the oversize appliances, the room shouted luxury. The new complemented the old, which Neve could see was the original stone hearth and an antique harvest table. In the center of the table was a large terra-cotta jug filled with flowers that Neve did not recognize, but she breathed in their delicate scent and loved the way they made the room homey despite its size.

She started as her boss suddenly spoke behind her.

"Would you like a cool drink or perhaps a cappuccino?"

"Thank you. I'd love a cool drink—*un'aranciata*?"

"Yes, certainly." He opened the restaurant-size refrigerator and grabbed a bottle of orange soda and a beer. "Let's go out into the courtyard…" He strode over to open a large rounded door. "After you."

Neve caught her breath. Was there no end to the wonder of this place? It was a garden of Eden; there was no other way to describe it. Lemon and fig trees. Bay laurel and medlar. Wild rosebushes and a huge grape pergola. And a large trellis, draped with an enchanting canopy of wisteria in full bloom. Glazed pots of every size and color, filled with rosemary, oregano, parsley, sage and thyme. And beyond, a vegetable garden and a profusion of cactus pear bushes.

Davide set down the drinks on an ornate glass table and pulled out a chair for Neve.

She thanked him and sat down. As Neve sipped her orange soda, she gazed at the more rugged terrain across the mountain, and then beyond that, to the cobalt strip of the Ionian Sea. *It was unreal, being here. Never in her wildest imagination had she thought she'd be working in a place like this.* She glanced again at the cultivated areas of the property and imagined all the work that had gone into it.

Neve turned to see Davide sit next to her, a beer in his hand.

"You must have a gardener," Neve said, unable to keep the awe out of her voice.

"You're looking at him," Davide replied curtly.

Neve was taken aback at his tone. *Had she said something that had offended him?* "Oh… I just thought…"

"That someone with my money would have hired help?" He gave a biting laugh. "No, when I bought this place, I decided that I needed to restore it to its previous glory and functionality. Inside and out. And I wanted to do the work outside myself, as I had done on my uncle's farm years ago." His eyes speared hers. "Let's just say that I needed to get over something...and hard, physical labor under our summer Calabrian sun will make you forget just about anything...or *anybody.*"

Neve's heart did a half flip at the intensity of his gaze. Why did she have the gnawing feeling that Davide was inferring something that she would understand? Davide's mouth opened as if he was going to add something, but he promptly shut it, and the look he gave her was almost... *reprimanding.*

Perhaps she was misinterpreting things. *Why would he be reprimanding her?*

Neve glanced away, her cheeks already feeling the effects of the late-afternoon sun. *Or was it more than the sun?*

Davide excused himself as he stood up. "My housekeeper/ cook is away for a week," he said. "So you're going to have to put up with some of my cooking." While Neve sauntered into the garden, Davide went inside to prepare a tomato salad and lemon rosemary chicken scallopini.

He set down the plates on the kitchen island, and he brought out a slightly chilled white Greco wine.

Davide had pulled out a chair for Neve at the kitchen island. *"Buon appetito,"* he said, gesturing for her to start.

"If the rest of your cooking is this good, I won't mind that your housekeeper's away," Neve murmured after her first taste. She glanced across at him shyly. "I can make basic meals, but I must say I was glad that cooking wasn't part of the requirements of this job…"

Davide arched an eyebrow. "I'm surprised…"

Neve's fork paused in midair. "That I'm a mediocre cook?"

"That you'd be so candid about your perceived culinary shortcoming."

Neve shrugged. "I see no need to lie about myself, or pretend I'm something I'm not."

"That's a good virtue for a nanny to have." Davide swirled the wine in his glass without averting his gaze.

They ate in silence for a few moments, and Davide wondered if it was the right time to venture into the past and confront Neve about the letter. *About how less than virtuous she had been in the way she had treated him…*

No; now was not the time. Neve had just arrived today. It wasn't fair to bombard her with something that had happened eight years ago, and that had probably bothered *him* a lot more than her. He would have to be patient and wait for the right opportunity…

Lucia would be bringing Bianca back after two days, leaving him tomorrow and the day after to evaluate Neve's character and suitability to take care of Bianca. Tomorrow he planned to take Neve to the market. He wanted to observe and interact with her in a variety of settings, with a variety of people. If any red flags went up in his mind, he could address them with her and then decisions would be made.

Davide offered Neve coffee, but she declined, thanking him for the lovely meal before excusing herself to return to her room. He watched her leave, and after setting the dishes in the dishwasher and turning it on, he decided to turn in, as well.

Lying in his king-size bed with his sheets pulled back,

Davide listened to the night sounds outside his windows, unable to sleep. He heard an owl, and a few minutes later, a kestrel. He shivered involuntarily, despite the warmth of the night.

Neve had been in his castle only one day, and already she had begun to affect him. From what he could determine today, she would be good for Bianca.

But would she be good for *him*?

# CHAPTER EIGHT

NEVE'S PHONE ALARM woke her up and she rolled over to silence it on her night table, her eyes still closed. Her first thought was what to wear for school, and then her eyes flew open. School was over. She stared up at the ceiling, looked down at the unfamiliar quilt and gazed around her without lifting her head off the pillow. Her mind cleared. She was in Davide Cortese's castle, and she had been hired for the summer as nanny to his niece, Bianca.

But it would be a couple of days more before Bianca returned. *A couple of days more for Davide to ascertain whether she would be right for the job.*

Neve stretched and rolled off the bed, almost losing her balance when she missed the stepping stool. She wondered what Davide had planned for today…and her nerve endings began to tingle… She didn't blame Davide for wanting to ensure that she would work out; what unnerved her was knowing that she'd be alone with him…

*Stop. Now. Focus on what you're here for…*

Neve headed to the bathroom, opting for a shower. She marveled again at the spaciousness and luxury around her. The wooden shutters on the two casement windows were open, and the sun splashed into the room, which was bigger than the kitchen in her apartment back in Vancouver. Everything gleamed, from the marble floor to the granite countertop and silver fixtures. The crystal chandelier, casting its prismatic colors on the opposite wall, was intertwined with a sculpted garland of leaves and roses in various states of bloom. Neve couldn't believe how lifelike they looked.

Eyeing the enormous claw-foot tub, she imagined it would be better suited for two, and she couldn't stop the thought that perhaps Davide had made use of it in the past...

Lathering herself in the shower, question after question filled her mind: *Why had Davide stopped walking past Villa Morgana? Had he been sorry to see her go? Had he married? What had made him choose such a remote location in which to live? And besides wanting a qualified nanny for Bianca, had he hired her for another reason?*

She'd have to be patient for the answers. *If he ever chose to enlighten her.*

After changing into a striped coral T-shirt and mint Capri pants, Neve made her way down to the kitchen. Davide was having an espresso but put his demitasse down and stood up, greeting her with a *"Buon giorno*, Signorina Neve. *Espresso o cappuccino*?"

Neve returned the greeting. *"Cappuccino, grazie."*

Moments later Davide returned with Neve's cappuccino and a tray of biscotti and assorted pastries. A platter of fruit was already on the table, along with little tubs of yogurt.

Neve thanked him again and took a sip of her cappuccino. She eyed the assorted pastries. *Were they from the Pasticceria Michelina?* She chose an almond brioche with custard filling and after taking her first eager bite, she couldn't help sighing with pleasure.

A smile flashed across Davide's face, showing perfectly straight white teeth. A warm feeling spread inside her at how *absolutely gorgeous* he looked when the outside edges of his eyes crinkled… "I'm going to enjoy these while I can," she said, tilting her head in feigned defiance. "*When in Rome*, as they say…" She took another bite.

"You have custard on your nose, *signorina*," he informed her drily.

"Oh!" Neve gave an embarrassed laugh. "It's a good thing you told me before I ended up swimming in custard."

Davide gave a wry laugh. He leaned across the table to wipe the custard off Neve's nose with a napkin. She blinked and then reached for a marzipan pastry and popped it into her mouth, her gaze locking with his as he brought his cup to his lips.

God in heaven, he was having some unholy thoughts. And memories of Neve swimming while he and Agostino watched… Davide set down his demitasse. The image of Neve swimming now—

"I—I wasn't expecting you to be working here as an author…"

"You mean to be doing your job with me around?" His eyes pierced hers. "I suppose that wasn't mentioned in any of the correspondence. Well, now you know." He watched Neve's blue-green eyes blinking a little more rapidly than before. "Don't worry, *signorina*, I won't be following you like a lost puppy." He gave a curt laugh but this time, his raven eyes were devoid of humor. "You do understand that the three of us will be spending certain times of the day together?" He leaned toward her, murmuring, "I am hoping that we will be able to establish a workable routine… for the sake of my niece."

"Of course, Signor Cortese," she replied, this time a little stiffly. "I am here to do my job, and nothing else."

*And nothing else…* Was she referring to their mutual

flirting eight years ago, signaling that she had no intention of venturing in that direction? *And why should she?* She had made it quite clear in her note that she considered him below her. He nodded and abruptly stood up.

"Since Bianca is not here and it's a beautiful day, I thought you might want to consider going for a ride in the countryside to the market in Reggio."

"I…well, yes, okay. That would be…nice."

His gaze swept over her face and bare arms. "Did you bring a sun hat? The temperature was thirty-two degrees Celsius an hour ago. The sun will bake your fair skin."

"Yes, I have one in my room." Neve stood up and started to gather the cups and dishes, but Davide put up his hand. "Please leave those. You are not here as a housekeeper. That is not your *place*."

"But your housekeeper's not here…"

"I'll take care of them." His voice brooked no argument. "I'll be waiting for you in the foyer."

Davide held the door of his Alfa Romeo open for Neve, his eyes sweeping over the curves of her slim body and the soft lines of her profile. He rolled up his sleeves and took his place behind the wheel. He caught a whiff of Neve's perfume, a delicate floral scent that reminded him of an awakening spring garden. A glance her way confirmed she had fastened her seat belt, and he repressed his desire to linger on the curves of her body so tantalizingly close to him. He was glad she was looking out her window, though, reluctant for her to see the desire in his eyes.

*He couldn't deny it.* He still desired her, despite her past rejection of him. Despite the eight years that he had tried to extinguish that desire. But what good would it do to let her know how he felt? Or to show her? *And risk being rejected once again?* He reached for his sunglasses and concentrated on driving. *No, he needed her now for one purpose only.* And that was to do the job she had been hired to do.

As he maneuvered his way carefully down the mountainside, he noted how rapt Neve was with the view. She was leaning forward in her seat, taking in the stretches of woodland, the dizzying drops of ravines and the dazzling blue of the Ionian Sea. Several times she swayed toward him when he rounded a corner, and once her bare arm skimmed his forearm. The unexpectedness of her soft skin against his made him swerve slightly, and he cursed inwardly for his reaction. *Stay in control, man*, he berated himself.

When he reached the turnoff at the bottom of the mountain leading to the main coastal highway, he inserted a CD of classic Italian hits from the yearly Sanremo Music Festival, and for the next forty minutes, drove along the coast. The market he was heading to was in the capital city of Reggio di Calabria, and not sure if he had mentioned this to Neve, he turned down the music and told her.

Neve's eyes lit up. "Oh, wonderful! We had come to Reggio to take the ferry across to Sicily, and we did have time to go to the museum to see the famous Bronzi di Riace, but we missed the market."

"And what did you think of the bronze sculptures?" He was interested about her impression of the eight-foot-high statues discovered in the sea near the boundary of the Marinas of Riace and Camini. They were thought to be representations of Greek warriors created during the era of Greek colonization of Southern Italy.

Neve flashed him a curious look. "They were…amazing, just like the other items in the museum. I loved ancient history when I was a teenager—and I still do—and I remember thinking it would be great to become an archaeologist and go on digs and discover something fabulous."

She laughed, a sweet, gurgling sound that reminded him of the brook on the outskirts of Valdoro.

"So what made you decide on teaching?"

She laughed again. "I realized I liked kids more than digging."

He couldn't help chuckling. He stole a glance at her and felt his pulse jump. *She looked so...fresh and wholesome.* And now that he was physically closer to her than he had ever been in Italy, he could see the sprinkling of freckles over her nose and part of her cheeks. *Charming.*

"I babysat a lot in my final years of high school and through university." Neve paused, smiling, as if she was remembering some of those moments. "We lived in an upscale neighborhood with lots of CEOs, both male and female. Lots of late evenings, social events, staff parties, last-minute business trips. And kids of all ages. Bouncy babies all the way up to testy teens." She gave another tinkling laugh. "I never had to work at another job. I spent many evenings and most weekends looking after all these kids. And plenty of overnights, too."

"It sounds like you enjoyed it, that it wasn't a—what is the word?—chore? Most teenagers would rather be out socializing...and on dates." He kept his eyes on the road, but when she didn't respond right away, he glanced quickly at her. *Had her cheeks become more flushed?*

"I wasn't much of a socializer," Neve murmured. "I was kind of shy..."

Davide didn't know how to respond. This picture of Neve was so different from the one he had drawn up after she sent him that note. A picture that had grown more and more dark, at least when it came to Neve's personality.

She was confusing him. *Making him doubt his previous perceptions.* Maybe he had misinterpreted her note based on his insecurities at the time. He *had* felt somewhat inferior. Not inferior in character, but in wealth and status. His ancestors had been landless laborers and his parents, although they had managed to acquire a piece of land to farm, had enough food to provide for their family, but barely enough for extras.

Davide and Violetta had worked alongside their parents after school and on weekends to carry out all the seasonal rituals: drying tomatoes in the summer sun, picking mushrooms in the fall, harvesting vegetables and fruits, picking olives, getting them pressed into oil, growing and picking the winter greens and seeding in the spring. The only socializing they had done was at communal activities, such as the chestnut roast in early winter, or during the religious processions for their town's patron saint, San Nicola. And it had been even more work-intensive after their parents had died.

No wonder Violetta had jumped at the opportunity for a new life in another country. After she had married Tristan, Davide had been left to carry out most of the work on the farm, since their uncle had obligations not only in Valdoro but also in the next community. It was after Neve's message that Davide had felt the stirrings of dissatisfaction in what he had been doing. He had wanted *more*. And fortunately, when he had expressed his desire to pursue his masters degree, Zio Francesco had sold the farm, actually relieved to not have to worry about its upkeep. He had divided the money three ways, and had provided Davide with the means to continue his studies, Violetta with a cash endowment and a nest egg for himself. Sadly, his uncle had died during Davide's last year at university.

A series of honking and bleating made Davide slow down and then come to a full stop. A herd of goats was haphazardly crossing the road, and traffic had stalled on either side to let the animals pass. The goatherd ambled along as if he had all the time in the world, oblivious to some of the impatient calls from the vehicles. His dog was scrambling about, doing its job, its sharp barks adding to the cacophony.

Neve had leaned forward, clearly delighted with the whole scene. Their windows were rolled down, and Davide couldn't help laughing at some of the more colorful remarks aimed at the goatherd, who grinned good-naturedly and ambled on.

"The market's not far now," Davide said. "A couple of minutes…" He maneuvered his way through several congested streets, looking for a place to park, and then finally pulled into a spot two blocks away. "Wait here a moment," he told Neve, and climbed out of the vehicle to go around to her side. He opened the door and held out his hand. "*Prego*. Please allow me…"

Her turquoise eyes widened and she hesitated briefly before taking his hand. As she stepped out, she used her left hand to put on her sun hat and as she took a step forward, she stumbled over one of his feet. Davide immediately encircled her with his other arm and helped her regain her balance. "I'm beginning to think you're deliberately trying to trip me, Signorina Neve," he said wryly. "Three strokes and you're out." He smiled, attempting a joke.

"It's three *strikes*," she blurted.

Davide watched Neve's face flush before his eyes.

"Yes, of course," Davide replied gruffly when the different meanings had registered. "My English is not always… exact." He let go of her. "My apologies." *Now, how was he supposed to get that suggestive image out of his mind?*

A few people walked past, smiling at them.

"*Che bella coppia.*" He heard a lady say. "*Avranno dei belli bambini in famiglia.*"

*What a beautiful couple. They'll have beautiful babies in their family.*

Neve must have heard it also, and for a second their gazes locked and the sounds around them seemed to meld into a distant hum.

It took every ounce of Davide's energy to keep the stab of pain in his heart from showing on his face.

# CHAPTER NINE

NEVE COULDN'T BE SURE, but she thought she saw something flicker in Davide's expression.

A momentary crease in his forehead, as if a headache had started. Had the lady's comment hit a nerve? Had Davide been struck by a surge of grief at the mention of family? After all, his family had been shattered with the loss of his sister and brother-in-law. And how could he *not* feel the loss that Bianca was experiencing?

Neve felt a rush of empathy toward Davide. *Poor man.* What an enormous responsibility he had on his shoulders. She didn't doubt that he loved his niece, but from her experience with single parents of children in her class, he would need a lot more to sustain him in the difficult months, and maybe years, ahead.

She wondered if Davide had been able to express his grief to anyone. This made her think of the loss of her father, and how she had wished she had been able to share her grief with her mother... Feeling a prickle behind her eyes, she averted her gaze. She was relieved when they finally reached the market grounds.

The sights, smells and sounds made an instant impression on Neve, and for a moment she just stood there, gazing around at the colors and bustling crowds. Her nose crinkled at the strong smell of fish and seafood. A nearby vendor had a swordfish on display, its two halves glistening on a heavy plank, its eyes glassy. *"Pesce spade, pesce spada, signore e signori.* Swordfish, ladies and gentlemen. Fresher than a gentleman from the south of Italy!"

The nearby crowd erupted in laughter, and Neve couldn't help joining in. She saw that Davide had a smirk on his face.

Neve was looking forward to going through the vendor stalls and finding something unique to the area for herself. Suddenly, she felt as if everything was right in her world. This is where she was supposed to be, in a market in Southern Italy, among the bustling crowds, surrounded by bursts of color and the sounds of parents cajoling or scolding, their children laughing or crying, and couples bartering with animated gestures to vendors who were just as animated.

Neve had studied the standard Italian, but she was able to pick up some of the Calabrese dialect she heard and couldn't help smiling at the singsong nature of the voices of two women perusing the products displayed on the table at the next stall.

When they reached the stall, the ladies had moved on, and Neve was able to clearly view the delicate lingerie items displayed on the lacy tablecloth below.

Neve felt her cheeks tingle with heat and she didn't dare look at Davide. There were samples of silky bras and panties, sold separately or in sets, in colors ranging from delicate pastels to dusky purple, red and black. There were also exquisite nighties with Venetian lace accents in elegant boxes. Her gaze lingered on a filmy coral nightgown with intricate rose lace edging. *If she had been here on her own, she might have been tempted to buy it...*

The vendor was an attractive man in his late thirties or early forties, and the way he was sizing up her size and shape made Neve want to squirm, especially with Davide looking on. To add to her mortification, the vendor winked at Davide and suggested he treat "his lady" with a *regalino da ricordare*, a gift to remember. And then a second wink.

Neve felt as if she were melting under a bright spotlight. She gave a self-conscious laugh. *"No, grazie,"* she told the vendor and turned away. "I was thinking of a different kind of souvenir," she murmured to Davide in English. "Like something for the kitchen."

"But you can use any of these items in the kitchen," the vendor replied with a laugh.

Neve's cheeks burned. She hurried past to the next stall, which featured handbags and shoes. A few stalls farther down, they came to one selling pottery. Although the stalls provided some shade with their awnings or large beach-style umbrellas, Neve felt the Calabrian heat affecting her. Her hat helped, but even with her T-shirt and Capri pants, she felt overdressed and overheated.

She closed her eyes for an instant and felt herself swaying slightly. And then she felt Davide's arms bracing her, the citrus scent of his cologne tingling her nostrils. "You need water," he said huskily, his touch and words jolting her. She blinked at him wordlessly. "You stay here. I'll go buy some."

Davide called to the vendor, who quickly ushered Neve toward a chair behind his main display table. She sat gratefully, but was annoyed with herself for her momentary weakness. Davide came back with two bottles of water. He opened one and handed it to Neve.

The water wasn't refrigerated, but it refreshed her all the same. She drank half the bottle without stopping. Davide finished his bottle and then offered to hold Neve's while she looked around. "You're sure to find something you like for your kitchen here," he said, a gleam in his eyes.

Neve handed him the bottle and nodded, her pulse reactivating. She quickly turned to the collection of pottery. Davide chatted with the vendor while Neve looked over the items, but as she tried to decide on the glazed or unglazed ones, she sensed his gaze on her...

Neve's head was bent, her strawberry-blond hair falling in front of her. The sun reflected in the strands, made them look like gilded waterfalls. He caught his breath.

What were the chances of a nanny called Neve taking care of his niece, Bianca? Snow and white. *Snow White.* He felt a corner of his mouth lifting. As the vendor moved away to attend to a customer, Davide couldn't help thinking about fate again. Fate and fairy tales.

Fairy tales had their dark elements, both physical and psychological, and his and Bianca's lives had certainly had their share of those. And they also usually involved a physical and inner journey—with periods of isolation, daunting challenges and malevolent forces—finally leading toward a happy ending.

Well, he had often felt moments of isolation. Some longer than others. Even during all the social and public events celebrating the success of his first novel. Davide had had no shortage of female company, with beautiful women seeking his attention—and he had sometimes taken what was offered—but despite the satisfaction of his physical needs, his emotional needs had remained unfulfilled. He hadn't known what exactly he was looking for—and he still wasn't sure—but none of his dates had tempted him to make a serious commitment.

As for challenges, the one of raising Bianca had to be the most difficult of any he had faced. He had had no other choice, given the loss of her parents. But it was a challenge he had embraced. He had loved Bianca from the moment he had seen her, and taking care of her was now at the top of his list of priorities, challenges and all. Davide felt a twinge in his chest. Hadn't his uncle done the same for him and Violetta after both their parents had died?

Noticing that Neve was paying for some items, Davide strolled toward her. Neve had chosen a set of three unglazed terra-cotta jugs, the small one about the size of a lemon and the largest about the size of a small teapot.

She handed them to the vendor, who proceeded to arrange them in a sturdy bag with bubble wrap. "I love things that are made from the earth," she told him in Italian. "And not mass-produced. These are lovely. I have the perfect spot for them in my kitchen."

The vendor beamed and told Neve that his family had been making them for several generations, and now he was teaching the trade to his grandchildren.

Neve thanked him with a smile and was about to take the bag, but Davide reached for it first. "I'll carry it," he said. "You can keep looking. You have about forty minutes before the market closes."

Neve shrugged, smiling, and continued going in and out of the market stalls, trying on bracelets and bangles, sunglasses and sandals. Davide suddenly realized that he felt a lightness that he couldn't remember feeling for a very long time. *Or was it contentedness?*

On the way back to the castle, Davide put on some quiet music and, glancing in Neve's direction a few times, he noticed that her eyelids were drooping.

When he finally brought the vehicle to a stop, Neve shifted a little but didn't wake up.

Her chest was rising and falling gently with her every breath. Davide's gaze settled on her mouth and he felt desire sizzle through him. Right or wrong, he wanted to reach over and taste those lips, feel their curves, savor them oh…so…slowly.

He closed his eyes for a second. *What was he doing?* He couldn't risk losing Neve as a nanny because of his unwanted advances. *Don't ruin a good thing.* Davide's eyes fluttered and he realized with a start that he had actually started to lean toward Neve. He was about to move back, but a flicker made him look across at Neve. *Too late.*

Neve was wide awake. Her eyes were so close to his that Davide felt like he could dive right in and swim in their blue-green depths.

He gave her a crooked smile. "I was just about to wake you, *Snow White.* We're home…"

# CHAPTER TEN

AFTER WAKING UP in the car last night to Davide's intense gaze only inches away—and feeling his breath gently fanning her face—it had taken every bit of Neve's self-control not to close the gap and kiss him. To finally feel the lips of the one who had ignited her desire eight years earlier. After a few seconds of holding her breath, she exhaled in relief when Davide moved away.

*Kissing her boss before she officially began her job would not have been a good choice. Nor a very professional one.* Walking briskly toward the castle, carrying her bag of pottery souvenirs, Neve reminded herself that although they had been attracted to each other from afar in Valdoro eight years ago, and there was obviously a magnetic force that still existed, encouraging any involvement with Davide Cortese under the current circumstances would be not only unwise, but also foolhardy.

In the foyer, Davide asked if she'd like to join him for a drink or a cup of tea in the kitchen. She thanked him but declined, her cautious inner voice sounding off warning signals.

Besides, she was feeling the jet lag…

Davide gazed at her speculatively. "All right, then, before you turn in, I want to ask you…"

She paused and waited, her curiosity piqued.

"I'm flying to Milan tomorrow for a meeting with my publisher at one. Bianca won't be back until the day after. Why don't you join me? At least you'd get to see another part of Italy." He raised his eyebrows. "While I'm at the meeting, you can visit the Duomo and the Galleria if you like. Are you familiar with these places?"

Neve's eyes widened. "Only from what I've seen in books or videos."

The stunning Gothic cathedral that had taken nearly six centuries to build was a place she had always wanted to visit, and who wouldn't want to peruse the shops of the famous gallery next to it? A spiral of excitement wound its way through her, and she gave him a tentative smile. "I'd love to go. Will we be taking a train? I suppose we'll have an early start, then?"

Davide's mouth curled in amusement. "Not too early. I've chartered a private plane. Once my meeting is over, we can meet in the Galleria, and then later, fly back. We'll have dinner on the plane." He nodded. "All right, then. *Buona notte*, Signorina Neve. *Sogni d'oro*."

Neve watched him head toward the kitchen. *Yes, she would certainly have sweet dreams tonight...*

Davide concealed a smile as he watched Neve's childlike delight as the private plane picked up speed on the runway at the airport in Valdoro and soon nosed its way upward. The sky was a brilliant blue with no clouds, perfect conditions to enjoy the view. Neve kept track of the flight progress, exclaiming when they flew over the wooded and mysterious landscapes of Sicily and farther north toward Naples, where the dark, looming mass that was Vesuvius made her visibly shiver.

Their conversation was limited to discussion about the

places they passed, with Neve asking questions and Davide answering them.

When the male flight attendant brought them lunch, Neve's eyes widened at the sight of the steaming risotto with porcini mushrooms, served on white china with gold edging and accompanied by gold-plated cutlery and white wine that Davide had selected. The second dish consisted of a platter with calamari, cuttlefish and other seafood delights lightly fried to perfection. Strong coffee and a tiramisu mousse ended the meal.

At Milan's Linate Airport, a black limousine was waiting for them. It wound its way through the busy streets and made its first stop near the Duomo and Galleria. Davide walked with Neve to the massive sculpted doors of the cathedral. "I know you'll enjoy the tour," he said, "and afterward, you can begin your shopping adventure. I'll text you when my meeting is over, and you can meet me at the front doors of the Galleria." He gave her a pleasant smile and waited until she had disappeared into the cathedral before striding toward the limo.

The two-hour meeting to discuss his second novel went as well as could be expected, given that he hadn't made any progress with it since his sister and brother-in-law's deaths. His publisher asked him how he and Bianca were doing, and after a shared espresso, had him go over the story line. As Davide recounted what he had written so far and what he still had to accomplish, he felt the desire to write re-igniting within him. Shaking his publisher's hand and bolstered by his encouragement, Davide left with the resolution to return to his novel...

Neve was waiting for him at the entrance of the Galleria. She had a couple of shopping bags, one of them from the Duomo and one from a bookstore. He raised an eyebrow.

"I bought a reproduction of a painting in the cathedral,"

she told him, her eyes sparkling, "and in the Galleria, I found a book about brigandage in Calabria. And a pictorial history of Milan that has a lovely section on the history and architecture of the Duomo, which I absolutely loved!"

During the flight back to Valdoro, Davide opened up his laptop and started to review the chapters he had written so far. Neve divided her attention between her books and the view. At one point he watched her unnoticed, rapt in her book. He shut down his laptop. The click made her look up and glance at him across the aisle.

"So other than babysitting and becoming a teacher, what else is there to know about Neve Wilder?" He gazed at her quizzically. "You read, you enjoy traveling, you appreciate good food. What am I missing?"

Neve closed her book. "Um, I'm not sure what you're asking…"

"Do you ski, have a particular hobby, go out dancing on Friday night—"

Neve burst out laughing. "I'm too exhausted from teaching all week to go out dancing on Friday night. Usually I just curl up with a good book or movie and veg."

*"Veg?"*

"Relax." She smiled. "And yes, I ski. And swim and hike. I like to be outdoors as much as I can…"

He glanced at her ring hand. Neve caught his gaze and blushed.

"And no, I don't have a boyfriend…at the moment," she said a little defensively. And then she cocked an eyebrow at him. "And you?"

"I'm too exhausted from parenting Bianca to go out dancing on Friday nights," he said, his mouth quirking. "And I don't ski—didn't have time to learn while working on the farm and doing my graduate studies—but I do swim and hike. And enjoy gardening, as you already know."

Neve was looking at him intently, waiting for him to go on, and a curious sensation washed over him. *She wanted to know if he had a love interest...*

"I'm happily unattached," he added bluntly, and turned to the approaching flight attendant, who announced that their dinner was ready.

They lowered their trays, their conversation over, and were served a plate of ricotta cheese and spinach cannelloni in a roasted tomato sauce followed by a mixed salad and pork tenderloin medallions. Dessert was a variety of fresh fruit.

Relaxing with his espresso, Davide thought that the day with Neve had worked out pretty well.

*And he had to admit that Signorina Neve had some redeemable qualities after all...*

At the castle Neve thanked Davide for allowing her to join him on his trip to Milan. She would make it an early night, she said, stifling a yawn, and was looking forward to meeting Bianca in the morning.

Davide went upstairs to his study and placed his laptop on his desk before heading to his room. In bed, he stared at the opposite wall for a long time, watching the shaft of moonlight change with the movement of the clouds. He thought about the woman in the room across his, and how today he had not seen any indication of snobbery or arrogance. He closed his eyes, not sure if the contentedness he was feeling stemmed mostly from his time with his publisher or with Neve Wilder.

# CHAPTER ELEVEN

NEVE WOKE UP before her phone alarm went off. She had heard voices a little earlier and footsteps leading to the room next to hers. Bianca was back. As Neve finished dressing, she felt a flutter of anxiety at her imminent meeting with the child. Generally, she had plenty of confidence when dealing with kids. But with Davide Cortese watching her...

As she put on her sandals, she heard a cry and then another.

Was Bianca rebelling at the thought of meeting *her*? Neve inhaled deeply. *Coraggio*, she told herself. *You can do this*. Before she could change her mind, she opened the door and stepped into the hallway.

Davide rushed into Bianca's room after her first cry. Lucia had dropped her off a half hour earlier, and she had been playing quietly with her toys while he had gone to his study to return a phone call to his publisher. Now she was sitting on her bed, her face puckered in a frown. Her braids had come undone and she was holding the ribbons within two tight little fists.

Davide sat next to her and put his arm around her. "*Che c'è*, Bianca? What's the matter, sweetheart?"

"My hair's wrecked and I want to go to the market!"

Her voice ended in a wail, and Davide's jaw tightened as he wondered what strategy he could use to prevent Bianca's distress from escalating into a tantrum.

"Come, Bianca, let me fix your hair in pigtails. And then you can have breakfast and you'll feel better."

"I don't want pigtails!" Bianca's voice rose. She slid off the bed. "And I'm not hungry! I want to go to the market today!" She ran out of the room, crying, "I want Mommy and Daddy!"

Davide strode quickly after her. He stopped short in the hall. Neve and Bianca were sprawled on the floor, and Bianca was staring at Neve, looking dazed. Neve's shapely legs were exposed and realizing that her dress had hiked up, Neve quickly readjusted it, her cheeks flushed as she met his gaze.

Davide rushed to help them both up. Bianca stood there wide-eyed while he helped Neve.

After making sure that neither of them had bumped their head, Davide said wryly, "I see you've both hit it off with a bang. Bianca, this is Signorina Neve, your new nanny. *Signorina*—my niece."

Neve shifted her gaze to the little girl in the white shirt and red jumper who had instinctively reached for her uncle's hand. Bianca had delicate features, with eyes the color of caramel, and the longest lashes Neve had ever seen on a child. Her hair was golden brown and had tumbled down, showing the pleats from her previously tight braids. Her eyes held a gleam of curiosity and at the same time, suspicion.

"*Ciao*, Bianca." Neve smiled warmly. "I'm so glad you and I didn't crack like Humpty Dumpty when we fell." She made her eyes widen deliberately. "Can you imagine? Your poor uncle would have had to pick up all the pieces and put us back together," she laughed. "And what if he got the pieces wrong and I ended up with your hair? And you with mine?"

Bianca's mouth twitched. And then she giggled. "You're silly!"

Neve smiled, relieved. Appealing to a child's sense of nonsense was one of the strategies that often helped defuse a situation in her classroom.

"Please join me and Bianca for breakfast," Davide said, his gaze shifting to her.

"Only if Bianca doesn't mind having a silly nanny around." Neve winked at Bianca.

"I don't mind," Bianca said brightly, tugging her uncle's hand. "Come on, Zio Davide, I'm hungry."

Neve caught a flash of surprise in Davide's eyes. *And was that a flicker of approval in his gaze?* A warm rush swirled throughout Neve's body as she recalled how his gaze had swept over her when she had lain on the tiled floor... Blinking, she returned to the present. "I'd like you to come into my room a minute, Bianca. I have a little something for you..."

"That wasn't necessary," Davide said curtly. At Bianca's crestfallen expression, he added, "but it was kind of you."

He stood in Neve's doorway as Bianca pulled the blue tissue out of the gift bag excitedly and then reached inside. He could only see Bianca's profile from where he stood, and the lips that were starting to quiver as she stared at the plush creature in her hand. *An orca.* Davide groaned inwardly. It was probably the worst gift Neve could have brought for Bianca.

Bianca burst into tears, threw down the orca and ran out the door. Davide didn't stop her.

She headed to her room, and he would go there very

shortly. But first, he had to explain Bianca's reaction to Neve, who looked as if she had just received an unexpected slap on the cheek.

"I—I…" She looked at him with her mouth open. "I don't know why…"

"I'll tell you why." He rubbed his jaw tiredly. "Bianca's father worked as a tour guide at a whale-watching company in Steveston." He picked up the plush toy. "This just reminded her that her daddy is dead."

"I'm so sorry." Neve's voice broke. "I didn't know—"

"No, you didn't," Davide said, and the words sounded even more abrupt and bitter than he had intended as he left Neve's room.

Today was Neve's first official day of work as Bianca's nanny. *How long would she last?*

## CHAPTER TWELVE

Neve sat down on the edge of her bed. Only minutes with Bianca and she had already screwed up. But how was she to have known? She had bought the orca from a vendor at the Granville Island Public Market in Vancouver, thinking it would be the perfect West Coast gift. Neve bit her lip. She could see now that working here would be full of ups and downs. She had imagined that it might be, but the positive start between her and Bianca had given her false hope.

Of course there would be outbursts and episodes such as this one. Bianca was sensitive, and how much more sensitive could a situation be than one where both your parents were suddenly gone from your life? *Forever.* She had lost one parent, and *that* had devastated her…

No; it was not going to be an easy job. And having Davide around much of the time would be even harder. Watching her with those gleaming black eyes…

They were not the eyes that had made her adolescent hormones do a wild dance, though. *Eyes that had hinted of passion and promise…*

Neve hadn't seen that look in the guys she had dated. And not that there had been many… After her trip to Italy, none of the guys at university had appealed to her. Somehow, their appearance and manner always seemed so…so young and immature. And none of them had looked at her with the same intense gaze as Davide had…

She had dated a couple of guys, three years apart, but there had been no sparks. Both had been more interested in trying to get to know her physically than in making an emotional connection. She hadn't welcomed the pressure; she had wanted to *feel* something before making *that* kind of commitment.

Neve started at the sudden knock at her door.

"May I come in?" Davide's voice was calm.

Neve's pulse began to thrum. "Yes." She took a deep breath as he entered. "How's Bianca?"

Davide took a few steps toward her then stopped. "She has calmed down," he said, his gaze steady. "I told her that you wanted to give her a special gift. Then I suggested that every time she felt sad about her daddy, she could give the whale a hug. And her daddy would be happy, because he would feel the hug, too."

Neve felt her heart swelling. "Thank you. That was very insightful… You've given Bianca something concrete to do to deal with her feelings of loss." She stood up and gazed at him, smiling with relief. "Is it okay if I go and see her now?"

Davide's mouth curved briefly. "Yes, of course."

He made a half turn then glanced back at her appraisingly. His gaze flew to the unmade bed, lingered there for several seconds, and returned to her. "I hope you're finding this room comfortable and meeting your standards," he said, his dark eyebrows lifting.

Neve had felt a current sizzle its way through her veins at the way Davide's gaze had swept over the bed, taking in her nightie tossed among the sheets. Feeling the warmth in her cheeks, she nodded quickly. "It's very comfortable, thank you."

Davide nodded abruptly, opened his mouth to reply, but at that moment his phone rang.

"*Buon giorno*, Lucia," he said warmly, and with a quick nod at Neve, strode out the door, his voice carrying down the hall. Neve felt a twinge as he gave a deep laugh.

Neve bit her lip. Would Davide ever laugh like that with *her*? Or speak about the past? Enlighten her as to why he had suddenly stopped going by the Villa Morgana? There were so many things she wished she had the nerve to ask him... But now was not the time. She closed the door behind her and hurried to Bianca's room.

Davide was putting his phone away and telling Bianca that he would take her for a gelato in town and that they would go to the market another day.

Bianca gave a happy squeal and ran to him. "Is Signorina Neve coming, too?"

Neve liked the way Bianca addressed her name the Italian way, just like *he did*. She smiled at Davide expectantly.

Davide felt his jaw tighten. "No. Signorina Neve is not coming." He saw Neve's smile disappear. "She can come next time." Although he had been speaking to Bianca, he had kept his gaze on Neve. Davide saw her open her mouth as if to disagree with him and then shut it, a deflated look in her eyes. She was disappointed. And maybe a little hurt.

*Had he wanted to hurt her? Give her a taste of what rejection felt like?* He pushed aside those thoughts impatiently. No, it was not his intention to strike back at Neve this way; he simply wanted to go over a few things with Bianca before Neve began her duties as nanny.

The puzzled expression in Neve's eyes at his abrupt "no" puzzled *him*. And that fawn-like innocence in her expression wasn't helping to ease his conscience. As he strode away, the satisfaction that he had thought he'd feel turned out to be more like a twinge of remorse. He stopped and turned around. She deserved an explanation, at least.

"Bianca and I may visit friends in town for a while," he said, "or we might not. In any case, I'd like to go over a few things with her before you take over as nanny…" He paused to see if she would respond, but she just nodded. "If you're hungry, feel free to go down to the kitchen and help yourself to anything in the refrigerator," he added gruffly. *"Ciao."*

Davide closed the side door of his Fiat van and then settled Bianca into her car seat in the back. Driving, he occasionally glanced in the rearview mirror at Bianca. She was hugging her whale, and Davide felt his heart constrict. He marveled at a child's capacity for forgiveness and wondered cynically about his own propensity for it.

*Tesoro mio.* Bianca *was* a treasure—and his now, to cherish, love and raise. He swallowed hard. He couldn't bring back her parents, but he would do everything in his power to make her happy. And making sure she had the right nanny was at the top of his list.

As Davide drove down the mountainside, an image of Neve flashed in his mind, and the momentary furrowing of her brows when he said she was not joining him and Bianca. A split-second action, but long enough to indicate that she felt hurt, confused that he would exclude her so soon after meeting Bianca.

Could it be possible that Neve had totally forgotten how she had treated him in the past, how she had insulted him by telling him to "remember his place"? Maybe to someone else, those words might not have been a big deal, but they had delivered a sizeable blow to his ego. *And heart.*

The words on the note might have been civil in and of themselves, but he had had no trouble reading between the lines: *You're not good enough to be with me. You're inferior. Poor. You have no business trying to associate with someone in a class above you...*

Davide enjoyed his second espresso at the Pasticceria Michelina while Bianca worked happily away at her hazelnut gelato. For a long time he had avoided coming to this bakery that had evoked so many painful memories and dashed hopes...

Davide checked the time on his phone. He didn't want to head back to the castle just yet. And he hadn't really intended to visit friends in Valdoro; he had just needed some space. *Time to think.* Time to process the reality of having Neve Wilder living under the same roof with him and Bianca...and most important, to make sure Bianca was ready to be with her new nanny...

When they arrived at the castle, there was no sign of Neve. Davide's pulse relaxed. He helped Bianca prepare for an early bedtime, and after reading her a story in Italian from the collection he had bought her, he gave her a gentle kiss on the forehead. *"Buona notte, tesoro,"* he murmured. He set the book down on the night table and went to sit in the rocking chair in the corner as he always did until he was sure Bianca had fallen asleep.

Davide had never imagined how a parent must feel until he had assumed the care of Bianca. Yes, he had visited her in Vancouver, but he had never had to provide for her in a material or emotional way. It had been the latter that had changed him. And it had made him aware of how Bianca had felt, bewildered and shaken...the same way *he* had felt, losing his father and his mother soon after.

Sometimes, the ache of growing up without either of his parents had made him withdraw from situations where he'd have to witness his friends interacting with their families in their homes or at community events. It wasn't that he had begrudged them their happiness; it was just that it made his own sense of loss that much more acute. He had felt more comfortable being by himself, either working on the farm or in his room, losing himself in books and later, writing...

Before the accident, he had had only himself to take care of. Now he had a child. Not his biologically, but as close as it could possibly get. He no longer had the freedom he had enjoyed as a bachelor and celebrated author, but he didn't care. Although the deaths of Violetta and Tristan had catapulted him into a whirlpool of grief and loss, they had also given him a new awareness of the fragility of life and his responsibility of raising Bianca.

He had embraced that responsibility without any hesitation. Bianca belonged with him. He would protect her, care for her and provide every opportunity for her. He had loved her from the moment he had seen her, a week after she was born.

Davide felt a twinge at the memory of Violetta holding Bianca up to him, her dark eyes shining with pride and love. She had swaddled Bianca in a soft pink blanket, and her tiny face, perfectly round and with open eyes, had melted his heart.

Noting Bianca's rhythmic breathing, Davide turned off the lamp and switched on her night-light. The two espressos he had had would keep *him* up for a while. Maybe now was a good time to go to his study and review the research notes that he had abandoned months ago...

As he left Bianca's room, he glanced across to the rounded door of Neve's bedroom. *Would she be in bed? Or by her window, looking out to the sea?* There was no light emerging from the crack at the bottom of the door, and no sounds of movement. He imagined Neve in her filmy nightie, her hair reflecting the shaft of silvery light from the moon…

Davide strode down the hall to his study and turned on his desk lamp. For a moment he tapped his fingers on the polished walnut desk. *Who was he kidding?* He was too restless to concentrate on his research notes. Sighing, he turned off the lamp and went to his room, hoping sleep would come quickly.

# CHAPTER THIRTEEN

AFTER DAVIDE AND BIANCA had left, Neve had gone downstairs and out into the courtyard with a book, but she hadn't been able to concentrate. Why would Davide rush Bianca off so quickly after they had just met? She wondered at the real reason why Davide had been so adamant about her staying behind. Had she simply imagined that his gaze had hardened for a moment, as if she had done something to displease him?

Whatever it was, she was determined to find out what the problem was.

*And then maybe he'd look at her again like he had eight years ago...*

The tread of shoes in the hall outside her room had briefly registered in her light slumber, but Neve hadn't fully awakened until she heard a series of shrieks sometime later. She jolted upright, disoriented, and then consciousness hit her like a wave.

*Bianca. Was she having one of her nightmares?*

She grabbed the matching robe and hurriedly put it on, tying the straps before bolting out the door.

Bianca's door was partially open, and Neve didn't hesitate. In seconds she was at Bianca's side. Bianca was sitting up, her face puckered and streaked with tears.

"You're safe, Bianca," Neve murmured, putting an arm around her. "You must have been dreaming. I'm here."

"And *I'm* here."

Davide's voice made them both direct their gazes to the doorway. In several strides he had reached the bed, and had crouched down to kneel on the mat. Taking Bianca's hands, he gave them a kiss and then met Neve's gaze. "You can go back to bed," he said curtly. "I'll take care of this."

Neve felt a stab of hurt. She had been hoping to comfort Bianca with a little rhyme she had shared with her kindergarten students after reading them a story about having bad dreams. "I just—"

"I want her to stay," Bianca cried, tugging at her uncle's hands.

Neve saw Davide's jaw tighten, the muscles flicking as he gazed from Bianca to Neve.

"If you wish, and if Signorina Neve doesn't mind," he said gruffly.

"I don't mind at all," Neve said. She glanced at the bookshelf nearby. "Maybe I can read Bianca a story…"

Bianca's face brightened. She clambered out of the bed and ran to grab a book. Neve felt her heart melting at the sight of Bianca in her nightshirt, her golden-brown hair streaming down her back, her slender legs bronzed from the summer sun.

Although she kept her eyes on Bianca, Neve was very conscious of Davide's proximity. *And gaze.* He was still on his knees and inches away from her own. An image of his head cradled in her lap flashed in her mind, and her hand caressing his hair, and she felt a series of sparks shoot through her. She was sure her cheeks were flaming and she was glad when Bianca jumped back on the bed between them.

"This is my favorite," she said, turning the book to reveal the cover: *Bianca Neve.* "I'm in it!" She looked up at Neve, her eyes fluttering as if she just realized something. "And so are *you*! Can you read it to me?"

"I don't think Signorina Neve can read Italian," Davide said brusquely. "I'll read it."

"I can read it," Neve said quickly. "I studied Italian in high school and at university."

*"Va bene."* Davide nodded, crossing his arms.

Neve's heart flipped. *She had expected him to leave the room.* Bianca thrust the book toward her. Neve felt as if she was on a stage with the spotlight gleaming down on her. Lifting the cover that displayed Snow White in the arms of the prince, she turned to the first page, took a deep breath and started reading…

*"C'era una volta…"*

Davide felt something tighten in his chest at the sight of Neve reading in Italian to Bianca. As if someone was squeezing his heart. He tried not to wince. Was he resentful of Neve? Jealous? No… The pain came from the thought that his sister, Violetta, should be the one tucking Bianca in at night, comforting her after a bad dream, reading her a story. Not a stranger. He swallowed and felt himself clenching his teeth.

*He was angry.*

Angry that God had taken away his only sister. Angry that at least one of Bianca's parents couldn't have survived. *Furious* with God that Bianca had to suffer this loss at so young an age. And frustrated that he didn't have all the answers to making things better for Bianca. *And himself.*

He stroked Bianca's hair absentmindedly. *Poor child.* He felt a protective surge run through him. He squeezed his eyes tightly to stop the tingling at the backs of his lids.

When they reopened, they settled on Neve. He watched

the flitting of expressions on her face as she became each character on the page. Heard the lilting cadence of her voice in an Italian that was charming, with only a few syllabic mistakes. Saw how totally absorbed she was, looking up regularly to meet Bianca's enthralled gaze. *She must be a wonderful kindergarten teacher.*

This thought collided with the impression he had held about her for the past eight years. *She was spoiled, entitled, arrogant, a tease.* She had teased him with her gaze every day on that balcony, hadn't she? She had appeared around the time he was returning from the farm. Had sat there with a book, or a cool drink, or had stood watering the flowers. Except for the first time their gazes locked, she hadn't averted her gaze, which, even from several paces away, reflected a mutual attraction. And a hundred thoughts had flitted through his mind, a hundred ways that he could try to meet her and get beyond the stage of just devouring her with his eyes…

And then she had shattered any hopes he might have had by expressing her true feelings in that note… She had probably gotten a real kick out of imagining his reaction upon reading it…

*"E vissero felici e contenti…"*
*And they lived happily-ever-after…*

He started at Bianca's sudden clapping. All signs of distress from her dream had gone. Neve's face was flushed, her mouth curved in a smile as she gazed at Bianca.

He felt the initial tightness in his chest suddenly dissolve. No matter what Neve had done in the past, she had done something just now that he couldn't fault. For the second time today she had made Bianca smile and laugh.

He had worried that Bianca would never display the lightheartedness that was part of her character before the accident, the lightheartedness inherent in most children.

He had done everything possible to lift her spirits these past few months, even when his own spirit had felt dead. After what seemed like an unbearably long stretch, she had finally rewarded him with a smile, then two, and he had cheered inwardly, knowing that she had started to move along the lengthy road toward healing.

But she was still a long ways off. *And so was he.*

He stood up. "Well, Bianca, now you can have a good sleep. Say good-night and thank-you to Signorina Neve." He riveted his gaze to Neve, who stood up promptly.

Bianca complied and gave Neve a shy smile before putting her arms around her uncle's neck and kissing him on the cheek. She settled under the covers and Davide tucked her in.

"*Buona notte*, Bianca," Neve said softly.

Davide flicked off the light switch, leaving only a night-light on. When he and Neve were in the hall, he gazed down at her. Despite the shadows under her eyes, she was still a beautiful woman. And in minutes, she would be taking that robe off and going to bed herself…

His pulse quickened. *Don't go there*, his inner voice reminded him. *You've tormented yourself enough over the years, imagining her…*

"*Buona notte*, Signorina Neve," he said huskily, "*e grazie.*"

"*Buona notte,*" she said with a quick nod. "And you're welcome." She turned toward her room in the turret.

He watched until the last thing he saw was the swirl of her robe and the door clicking shut.

# CHAPTER FOURTEEN

NEVE WOKE UP with a dream that she was lost in a dark cleft of the Aspromonte mountains, and that she was calling for help, but the only response she got was from the howl of an Apennine wolf. She sat up in a sweat, her breathing accelerated, and despite the earliness of the hour, knew she couldn't get back to sleep.

After a quick shower Neve wrapped a turquoise towel around her head and put on the white robe that was hanging on the back of the door. She'd take a minute to check on Bianca.

Neve glanced across the hall. Davide's door was partially open. She felt a quiver run through her, wondering if he was still sleeping…

She hurried into Bianca's room and smiled at the sleeping figure. *Poor baby*, she needed the rest. Back in her room, Neve retrieved a paperback from her handbag and plopped down into the burgundy recliner by the window.

When she heard movements in Bianca's room, Neve put down her book and checked the time. She was shocked that two hours had gone by. She hurried over and saw that Bianca had changed into a T-shirt and shorts. Neve greeted her warmly and told her to wait while she changed, and then they could go down to the kitchen together.

Neve decided on a red skort and a white peasant-style top with short, gathered sleeves. As she slipped on white sandals, her phone signaled an incoming text. She glanced at the series of long messages and felt herself tensing. *Had her mother forgotten that she would be busy with her job?* Before she left the room she quickly replied.

Working; will text later.

Bianca was not at her window seat. Neve hurried to check the washroom, and wondered if Bianca had decided to go to the kitchen on her own. She'd have to make it clear to Bianca to follow her instructions and not take off anywhere without her.

Neve flew down the stairs and by the time she reached the kitchen she was breathless. Davide was at the stove, but he was alone. She looked past the doors leading to the courtyard. No sign of Bianca. She met Davide's narrowed gaze. "Bianca promised to stay in her room while I got dressed," she blurted. "I couldn't have been more than five minutes."

Davide shut off the gas element and the look he gave Neve made her stomach twist. "Bianca cannot be left unsupervised. Not even for five minutes. There are too many dangerous spots around the castle for a child. She could go wandering off and topple over a ledge or bluff." He strode quickly out of the kitchen, adding harshly, "I've lost my sister. I can't risk losing Bianca, too."

She followed him out and watched as he took the steps three at a time. "I'm going to see if she's in one of the unused rooms of the castle." He paused to glance at her. "You check the main rooms."

Neve nodded, shuddering at the thought of Bianca in

one of the scenarios Davide had mentioned. She wouldn't be able to live with herself if Bianca got hurt, or worse…

*No, that's not going to happen,* she tried to convince herself. *Bianca will show up.*

"Bianca!" Davide's booming voice echoed in the halls. Neve's heart pounded as she checked Bianca's room again, her own room, and then hesitated a moment when she came to Davide's bedroom. She couldn't *not* check it…

The room was breathtaking. *Masculine.* And elegant, with a double-sided marble fireplace dividing his room and en-suite bathroom. The floor was a huge expanse of gleaming hardwood, the walls a sage green, the bed coverings a pewter gray. The sight of them pulled back and rumpled from Davide's sleep made her pulse kick up. Could Bianca be under the bed? Neve called out for her and was about to look under it when she heard Davide's loud voice in the hall. And then Bianca's faint, "I'm here, Zio Davide."

Neve rushed out and saw Davide disappear into his study. She strode over and paused at the door. Bianca was crawling out from under Davide's desk, a sheepish look on her face, and Davide was standing by, his eyebrows furrowed and his jaw muscles tensed.

"Why did you not stay in your room and wait for Signorina Neve as she asked?" Davide's voice was calm but firm. "You can't just run off, Bianca."

Bianca's lip started to tremble. "But I wanted to play hide-and-seek."

"You were told to stay put. You *have* to follow instructions, Bianca. From me or from your nanny."

Bianca burst into tears and ran out of the room, barely glancing at Neve. Davide started to follow but stopped at the doorway and gave Neve a piercing look. "I think you need to address this with Bianca, as well. *Now.*" He strode out of the room.

Neve took a deep breath. As she followed Davide into Bianca's room, she knew she had a double challenge: to get her message across to Bianca and to show Davide that she was as competent as she had made out to be in her application and interview.

Bianca had thrown herself facedown on her bed, her crying reduced to quiet sniffling. Neve spotted the plush orca on Bianca's night table and picked it up. She sat down gently at the side of the bed. "You know, Bianca, I love to play hide-and-seek." She saw Davide raise an eyebrow, probably wondering where she was going with this. "And we can play after lunch. But first, we need to go over the rules, so nobody is in danger."

Bianca turned over to one side and wiped her eyes. "What danger?"

Neve made her eyes widen. "Well, I've never been in a real castle before, and I'm afraid I might get lost on my own. And end up in the dragon's den," she added, making her voice tremble.

"We don't have a dragon," Bianca sniffed. "That's just in fairy tales."

"Are you sure?" Neve looked around fearfully. "I thought every castle had a dragon."

Bianca scrambled to sit cross-legged next to Neve. "Silly Miss Neve!" She took Neve's hand. "I'll stay beside you, I promise. And don't be scared. If there was a real dragon, Zio Davide would protect you!"

*I would?* Davide's eyes narrowed and glinted like shards of obsidian. And then he smiled and Neve caught the twinkle in them. "Of course I would." He sat next to Bianca and put an arm around her, giving Neve a thumbs-up sign at the same time.

Neve felt a warm glow spread throughout her body. She

hadn't been sure that her strategy would work with Bianca, but it had and Davide had approved.

Davide was the first to rise. "I'll get back to making lunch." He ruffled Bianca's hair. "Maybe Signorina Neve can tame your hair first." He gazed at Neve. *"A presto."*

Neve nodded, her words sticking in her throat. *Yes, I'll see you soon. Gladly.*

She watched him leave, then stood up and smiling, held out a hand to Bianca.

Davide found himself humming as he stirred the sliced cherry tomatoes in the pan where he had first sautéed onions and garlic in extra-virgin olive oil. He had already put the spaghetti into the boiling salted water. All the ingredients were from his garden, the oil from his olive groves and the pasta was locally made and sold. He rinsed a generous sprig of basil that he had snipped off one of the plants in the courtyard and added it to the pan.

As Davide set three place mats on the harvest table, with his at one end, and Neve's and Bianca's on either side of him, he replayed the scene between Neve and Bianca in his mind. Neve had known exactly what strategy to use to get Bianca to come around. She hadn't been stern or raised her voice. She had relied on her own understanding and experience with children to get her message across. And she had done it by tapping into Bianca's imagination and by communicating with her at her level. *Brilliant.*

*Who was this Neve Wilder?*

Yes, she was the beauty who had made his heart flip almost a decade ago. His Juliet on the balcony of Villa Morgana. The girl whose eyes had branded his every time he had walked past… And not one day had gone by since they had exchanged the first gaze that Davide hadn't thought about her, dreamt about being with her. But she had turned him down, hadn't even wanted to meet him. Every silent message that he had intercepted from her eyes had turned out to be wrong.

And now she was *here*. Sometimes he thought he must be dreaming and that he'd surely wake up and Neve wouldn't be in his castle. Nor would Bianca. But then reality would pinch him. *Hard. Really hard.* Bianca was an orphan and Neve was here as a result…

How could sadness and happiness be so intertwined?

Davide stopped at the sudden jolt of awareness. Yes, he was sad, terribly sad about the loss of his sister and brother-in-law. And even sadder for Bianca's loss. But he could not deny that happiness had somehow found a way to take root in the hardened core of his heart. He had felt twinges of happiness, contentedness and hope…all in the short time since Neve had arrived.

And it…felt…good. It made him almost want to forget the past. *Almost.* Maybe he and Neve would have the opportunity to delve into it while she was here. And then maybe not. But at the moment Davide didn't care. He had lunch to serve.

The aroma of freshly made tomato sauce with basil filled the air. Davide set the cutlery down and returned to the stove to check the pasta. *Perfect.* Davide drained the spaghetti, transferred it into a large colorful bowl that had been his mother's and mixed in some sauce. At the sound of approaching footsteps, Davide felt a surge of anticipation. He set the bowl on the table, and glancing up, he saw Neve and Bianca walking hand in hand toward him, the look on both their faces melting his heart.

# CHAPTER FIFTEEN

NEVE HADN'T REALIZED how hungry she was until the scent of tomato sauce reached her before she even entered the kitchen. When she and Bianca walked into the room, Davide flashed them a grin.

"After *you*, ladies," he said, pulling out Neve's chair on his right and Bianca's on his left.

"*I'm* not a lady, Zio Davide!" Bianca giggled.

"Okay, little girl, but try to eat like one, *va bene*?"

"Okay." Bianca took her fork and twirled the spaghetti expertly and plopped it into her mouth.

Neve felt a little self-conscious. She hadn't really thought about all the time that she would be spending with Bianca and her uncle. She twirled her spaghetti mindfully, careful not to end up with a massive amount on her fork, and had her first taste. *Wow.* She had eaten Italian food numerous times in restaurant chains, but she couldn't remember any of them imparting this kind of instant impression on her.

She had a second forkful. "This is delicious," she murmured, glancing at Davide. *"Grazie."*

"Where are my manners?" Davide suddenly rose and went to a side cabinet that revealed itself to be a wine cooler. He pulled out a bottle, opened it and poured it into two wineglasses before returning to set them on the table.

"Here's to dragons and damsels who can handle them," he said, leaning forward to offer Neve a glass. Then he clinked glasses, his black eyes piercing into hers.

Neve felt her nerve endings pulsate. She averted her gaze to breathe in the wine's aroma, then brought the glass to her lips. *Exquisite. And strong.* Perfect choice with the tomato sauce.

Neve sat back, her body relaxed from the combination of delicious food and drink.

"Can we go play hide-and-seek now, Zio Davide?"

Davide nodded. "A quick game."

Neve was relieved at Bianca's query. She offered to help with the dishes, but Davide waved them on. "I'll join you in a minute," he said. "Bianca can start showing you around the garden."

The sultry heat of the midafternoon sun was palpable as soon as Neve stepped outside into the courtyard with Bianca. Neve was awed by the organized rows of flowering plants and pots bursting with herbs. One planter contained the largest rosemary bush she had ever seen. She couldn't resist snipping a sprig and pressing it together and inhaling its sharp aromatic scent.

Neve followed Bianca, who was skipping along the rows of plants, bushes and trees. Lemon trees with lemons almost the size of grapefruit. A trellis with cascading wisteria and rows of oleanders, with blooms of white, pink and fuchsia. *This place was magical.*

Neve recognized the large, flapping leaves of a fig tree and paused gratefully in its shade. Even with her sun hat on, the heat was stronger than she remembered.

"Perhaps we should wait for later in the evening to indulge Bianca with a game of hide-and-seek. It won't be so hot then."

Davide had come up right behind her. Neve turned,

startled, and her shoulder brushed against him. She sprang back as if she had touched a live wire and was instantly embarrassed at her reaction. Davide didn't move. His eyes narrowed slightly, though, and he gazed at her intently. "Thank you for the way you handled the issue with Bianca earlier," he said quietly. "I didn't expect that kind of approach."

Neve felt a coil of pleasure at his words. "Sometimes you have to turn into a child to get your message across to another child," she replied a little breathlessly. "What I mean is, you have to put yourself in their shoes, try to reach them at their own level."

"And you did," he said, nodding. "You have a way with children," he added huskily. "You must be a wonderful teacher."

Neve didn't know what to say. The unexpected series of compliments from Davide had made her tingle all over. And he had taken a step closer to her. Was he intending to—?

"Zio Davide! Signorina Neve! Are you coming?" Bianca had stopped skipping and had turned around, her hands on her hips, looking stern even from where they stood.

Davide chuckled. "We've been told. Shall we? I haven't played this game since I was a kid."

Davide gestured for Neve to walk ahead of him. He had to get a handle on his emotions. He had almost embraced her. Thank goodness that Bianca had called out.

Once they reached Bianca, Davide went over the rules. No climbing trees, no going past the border of cactus pear bushes. Neve could be "it." Home base would be under the fig tree, and Neve would count slowly to twenty while Davide and Bianca went to find a hiding spot.

"Remember, no peeking!" Bianca cried.

"No peeking," Neve promised, crossing her heart.

"Is everybody ready?" Davide looked from Bianca to Neve. Bianca clapped excitedly. Neve nodded, her cheeks flushed. "Okay, Signorina Neve, take your spot." He waited till she reached the fig tree. He winked at Bianca. They watched as Neve turned toward the trunk of the tree, covered her eyes and started counting. Davide waited to see where Bianca was heading and then took the opposite direction.

He couldn't believe he was doing this. *Playing a children's game with the girl he had fallen for eight years ago.* How could he have ever predicted this would happen? That he'd be raising his orphaned niece and hiring that very girl—*woman*—as her nanny? Davide shook his head and chose a grassy spot between a row of bushy magnolia trees and a cactus pear grove. He heard Neve call out, "Ready or not, here I come!"

*Why was his heart thumping?* He heard Neve's footsteps padding away, and then Bianca's little gasp and more running, and then suddenly footsteps moving in his direction. Davide waited silently, and when he caught a glimpse of her through a space in the oleanders, he considered making a dash for "home." He'd wait another few seconds... and maybe she'd turn right around. Turn she did, before suddenly pivoting and charging right around the corner. *And into him.*

Davide had just managed to stop them both from landing in the cactus pear grove, which would have been much more painful than the body slam Neve had just given him. His arms had automatically shot out and wrapped themselves around her like a vise while his legs stood firm as he took the blow. Fortunately for them both, her head had hit his chest and not his nose or mouth. They could have easily ended up with either a broken nose or teeth knocked out.

For a moment Neve's head lay flat against his chest and

if his heart had been thumping before, now it was clanging. *She was in his arms.* He could feel her chest heaving against his, and the knowledge that only two thin layers of material lay between them made his abdomen muscles tighten with a longing that almost hurt.

And then, as if she had just come to, Neve lifted her head to gaze up at him. Her eyes were wide and startling this close. An ocean of turquoise with teal depths. And dark pupils that seemed to drill right into him. Her lips parted as if she wanted to say something, and that was when something inside Davide broke loose. He lowered his head and covered her lips with his, savored their fullness, top and bottom. He expected her to push him away, tell him he was out of line, but when she didn't, he pressed her even closer to him, cupping the back of her head, and deepened his kiss. Wave after wave of desire washed over him, and if he didn't have Bianca around, he'd—

*Bianca!* He broke away from Neve so suddenly that he almost felt light-headed.

"You tagged me good," he rasped. "Now you better see if you can find Bianca."

Neve blinked and bolted away from him.

NEVE DIDN'T KNOW how she had managed to continue playing after Davide had kissed her. She had found Bianca hiding behind a giant ceramic planter and had proceeded to chase after the squealing child who managed to get "home" without being tagged. Davide had had his turn being "it" and Neve's heart had done an anxious dance, wondering if he would attempt to kiss her again.

What had felt like ages in his arms with that first kiss had actually been only about half a minute. Just enough time to send her spinning into another universe.

She had seen stars when she had slammed into him. Or rather, *felt* them. They weren't like the stars in cartoons when two people collided, but a shower of dazzling little orbs that made all her nerve endings tingle. And when his lips had touched hers…she had felt something bursting inside her, and she had realized that the awakening she had felt at eighteen had suddenly been reactivated in a rush of adult desire and passion.

They had to talk. Clear the air. And she had to find out, once and for all, the reason for Davide's disappearing act eight years ago.

The game had tuckered Bianca out. Neve had accompanied her to her room, and after washing up, Bianca had willingly gone for a nap, holding her orca tight against her. Neve had closed her shutters and then gone to her own room to shower.

Now, as she lathered herself with the mandarin-scented body wash, Neve couldn't help shivering at the memory of Davide's arms around her. And his lips taking possession of hers...

She rinsed and dried herself and instead of getting dressed right away, slipped on a teddy. She might even try to have a nap herself. Since they had had a later lunch, Davide had said that they would have dinner at about eight or eight-thirty. She wouldn't mind a little rest and some time to collect her thoughts before going down to talk with him.

Just as Neve lay down on her bed, her damp hair wrapped up in a towel, her phone rang. She reached for it and moaned. *Her mother.* What now?

"Hi, Mom," she said, trying not to sound testy. "I guess you didn't read my last text."

"Now, Neve, I'm just trying to make sure you're all right. And I called deliberately in the afternoon Italy time, when most people are having a siesta."

"Mom, I know you mean well, but you don't have to worry about me. I'm not a teenager anymore."

"Well, you *are* in a foreign place. And much as I love Italy, you still have to be careful. You'll be there for two months, and you don't have experience—"

"I certainly do. That's why I applied for this job, remember?"

"I didn't mean in teaching, darling. I meant in the world of men—"

"I'm not here to be with men, Mother," Neve retorted.

*"Really?"*

"Well, just make sure you don't take up with any of the locals." Her tone sounded as if she was wrinkling her nose. "People in those small towns talk, and your name will be sullied."

"Mom, it's the twenty-first century, for God's sake. Things *have* changed in the last hundred years." Neve felt her jaw muscles tighten.

"And by the way, you barely gave me any details about this nanny job you've taken on. Who are the parents?"

"There are no parents. The little girl's an orphan."

"Oh. Poor girl. Well, who hired you, then?"

"The girl's uncle. He's her godfather and guardian."

"Is he married?"

Neve heard the sharp edge in her mother's voice. *Where was she going with this?*

"No, Mom. And I don't have time for this interrogation. I have to get back to work."

"But—"

"Sorry, gotta go. Bye, Mom."

Neve was too agitated to try to have a rest. If only her mother would respect her wishes and give her some space. Maybe next time she would just not answer the phone...

She changed into a tangerine halter dress and sandals, then unwrapped the towel and went to sit by a window to comb and dry her hair. She returned to the washroom to check her appearance and decided to add a touch of eyeliner and a hint of green eyeshadow, finishing with a dab of orange-red lipstick. Now she was ready to face Davide. And talk.

She took a deep breath and left her room. Davide's bedroom door was shut but the door of his study was half-open. She strode quickly to it before she could change her mind. Her pulse spiked at the sight of him, his broad back to her, his laptop open.

Davide had taken a shower, too; his hair was still damp, the tendrils curling at the top of his head. He was wearing a white T-shirt that outlined his shoulder muscles and black jeans that fitted his body perfectly. He was looking at the screen intently, scrolling through it with one hand while cupping his chin with the other.

Was he doing research for his novel? Neve felt a surge of pride, thinking of how hard he had worked to accomplish his goals over the years…

An image flashed in her mind of the first time she had seen him, returning midday from a farm or somebody's property, his hands and face earth-stained, his clothes dampened with sweat. Standing on her balcony at Villa Morgana, what had captivated her instantly had been his eyes. Black and intense, looking up at her as if he had been struck by a vision. They had set off a series of sparks inside her that she had never felt with anyone else, before or since.

Neve swallowed and knocked gently. Davide immediately shut his laptop and swiveled in his chair to face her, his brows furrowed. She saw his eyes narrow and quickly scan over her before returning to meet her gaze. He lifted his eyebrows but remained silent.

"I—I think we need to clear up a few matters, Signor Cortese."

"And I think you can call me Davide now that we've gotten to know each other a little more," he returned smoothly "Come in, Neve." He gestured to one of the recliners.

Neve walked over and sat down, a strange drumming in her chest. He always pronounced her name the Italian way—and she liked it—but this time, something in the deep resonance of his voice made her nerve endings tingle.

He rolled his chair over the hardwood floor and stopped a few feet away from her.

They sat looking at each other for a few moments, and unable to hold it in any longer, she blurted, "You had stopped passing by the Villa Morgana a couple of days before I left for Canada. You had made me think that—"

"That I wanted you?" he said huskily, leaning forward. "Or should I put it more delicately…that I wanted to meet you?"

Neve bit her lip. She was no longer a somewhat naive eighteen-year-old. Still a little shy, maybe, but there was no reason why she couldn't be frank. "Yes."

He cocked his head as if she was a puzzle to him. *"And…?"*

She frowned. "And I wanted to know why…"

Davide looked at her as if she had two heads. "You know perfectly well why, Neve. Have you lost your memory?"

Neve felt the heat in her chest rising to her neck and face. "I don't understand what you're saying. I was there for two days after, waiting for you, but you just stopped showing up."

Davide let out a laugh, but there was no humor in it. "You made it quite clear in your note that you wanted nothing to do with me."

Neve's jaw dropped. *Was she in another dimension?* "Wh-what? What note?"

Davide stared at her intensely for a moment, then rose to return to his desk. Neve watched him open the drawer and then reach into it farther. He returned to sit across her and held out a folded note in his hand.

Davide wasn't sure if her memory was defective, or if she was pretending not to remember—for whatever reason—but she couldn't deny the contents and meaning of the note she was now reading intently.

He had it memorized, imprinted in his mind like a hot branding iron:

I will *not* meet you. Your bold request is inappropriate and not appreciated. You would do well to remember your place.

Davide watched her read the note again, before turning it over and discovering *his* message. She looked up at him, blinking as if in shock.

"I did not write that note." Her voice cracked. "But I know who did." She handed it back to him, her hand trembling.

Davide's heart had jolted at her words. And at the emotions flashing in her eyes in mere seconds. Shock. Awareness. Defeat. *And pain.* In an instant he knew she was telling the truth.

The realization pierced him to the core. "Who?" he ground out.

She bit her lip again and he saw that her eyes were misting. "My mother."

She dropped her head in her hands, pressing them against her eyes. "I can't believe it."

Davide felt his stomach begin to churn. "Are you sure, Neve?"

Neve nodded, still holding her head. "That's her handwriting."

"Why?" He couldn't control the edge of anger in his voice.

Neve let her hands drop limply in her lap. She looked across at him and said nothing. Her eyes had darkened like an angry winter sea. But there was a sadness in them that made Davide want to take her in his arms and hold her.

He took a long, deep breath and reached for her hands, caressing them softly with his own.

And that was when she burst into tears. He rose and gently but firmly pulled her up to cradle her in his arms.

He let her sob against his chest, soaking his T-shirt, while he stroked her head and back. The warmth of her tears against his neck ignited his primeval instinct to protect his woman, and he embraced Neve even tighter.

He lowered his head to brush her forehead with light kisses, and when her sobs began to subside, he tilted her chin up to his and kissed her as thoroughly as he had done in the garden. *In the way that he had dreamed about thousands of times in the past eight years.* He tasted salt from her tears and after gently wiping them away, he kissed her over and over, wanting every kiss to make up for the pain her mother had caused her. *And him.*

He still wanted to know why Neve's mother had done this. But he wasn't going to push Neve into answering. He could wait, now that the main mystery had been solved. "Bianca will be waking up soon," he murmured in Neve's ear. "We can talk later." He brushed a kiss on her temple. "Why don't you go and check on her, and then we can all go for a ride into town." He looked deeply into her eyes. "How do you feel about a gelato or some cannoli at the Pasticceria Michelina?"

The look in Neve's eyes made his heart and stomach flip.

Her lips slowly stretched into a smile. And then she stood on tiptoe to answer him with a kiss.

*A kiss that made him forget that eight lonely and bitter years had ever gone by...*

NEVE SPLASHED COOL water over her face in her bathroom. Her stomach was still churning, thinking about her mother. How could she? She had had no right to manipulate Neve's life in the way that she had. Neve's first impulse had been to call her mother immediately, ream her out, but then had changed her mind. She had to think this one through.

Her mother had gone too far, interfering with Neve's business, her *private* business. She had been eighteen that summer. Old enough to accept a young man's invitation to meet, for God's sake. But no, Lois Wilder had to stick her controlling finger into Neve's life, poking it where it didn't belong. *Again*. Intercepting and responding to a note that had been meant for *her*.

Davide had asked why but Neve had been reluctant to explain just then. She had needed time to process what this all meant, how she would handle things with her mother and how she and Davide would deal with this new knowledge.

Neve knew exactly why Lois had done it.

*Because she was a snob.*

Neve had never liked this character trait of her mother's. Lois had always liked to flaunt her money, display her status through the clothes and jewelry she wore, or by the different cars she drove. And she had wanted Neve to do the same. "The way you look is *everything*, darling," she had said to Neve on numerous occasions. In fact, she had drummed it into Neve's head since kindergarten.

And she hadn't appreciated Neve's reluctance to comply.

Over the years Lois had cajoled, flattered or even scolded Neve in order to get her to be more like *her*. Subtly and not so subtly criticized Neve's choice of clothes as being too *common* and had tried to discourage Neve from associating with some of her friends whose families she had deemed to be in a lower financial or social status than theirs. Lois's eagle eyes had often judged people based on the way they looked.

*So no wonder that Davide hadn't passed inspection.* Her mother would have instantly been horrified, having noted Davide's dusty and dressed-down appearance. Neve remembered all too clearly how her mother had yanked her back into her room when she had caught her smiling at him across the street. And she obviously hadn't liked the way Davide had been staring and smiling back.

But how had she managed to intercept Davide's note and send it back? Neve felt another surge of anger toward her mother, but she took a few deep breaths, counted to ten and then headed to Bianca's room. They were going to be driving to the special place where Davide had wanted to meet, and the last person Neve wanted there was her mother, even if it was only in her thoughts.

The bakery's facade hadn't changed, but the interior had been modernized to appear retro, Davide told her with a smile. The owners had purchased the adjacent building so they could add a pizzeria and a bigger seating area.

Neve liked the look of the place. The round tables had pastel-colored surfaces with chrome edging and legs. Their colors of coral, robin's egg blue and buttercup yellow made the place cheery.

Neve noticed that people had turned to look at them

with unconcealed curiosity. Some greeted Davide and he smiled or waved back, but he did not introduce her to any of them. "If I do, I'll never have a moment with you alone," he murmured as he led her and Bianca to a table near the front window. "I hope you don't mind."

"Not at all." She smiled, relieved. "I'm not really in the mood for socializing." *I'd rather keep you to myself.*

Davide pulled out a chair for Neve and Bianca, placing Bianca between them.

"Zio Davide, can we order pizza? I'm starving." Bianca rubbed her tummy for emphasis.

Davide chuckled as he checked the time on his phone. "No wonder. You haven't eaten in at least five hours." He glanced at Neve. "Is pizza okay with you? We can have something sweet afterward." His gaze lingered on her lips before returning to lock with hers.

*I already had something sweet...your kisses.* "You pick. I'm sure I'll enjoy whatever you choose."

Davide ordered a *pizza alla melanzana.* "Something I'm almost sure you've never had—pizza with roasted eggplant," he said, flashing her a smile. "You might as well try new things while you're here…"

The way that Davide was looking at her was making her heart do jumping jacks in her chest. She lost herself in their depths for a few moments, imagining what would have happened if she had met Davide here eight years ago… Would she have let him charm her and take her to a more private place? Would he have kissed her? Made her melt like she had after his searing kiss in the garden?

The waiter came over with three glasses of water and Davide immediately stood up and greeted him with a hug before introducing him as Agostino.

*"Piacere."* Neve smiled. "Pleased to meet you." She

wondered why he seemed a little flustered all of a sudden, looking from Davide to her, and then back to Davide.

Agostino greeted Bianca and placed a paper place mat in front of her with a box of crayons before returning to the kitchen with their order.

"My childhood friend," Davide explained. "His mother worked at the Villa Morgana eight years ago. You might have seen him around... And he's the one I asked to deliver the note to your room."

Neve frowned. "Now that you mention it, he *does* look a little familiar."

"Well, from the looks of it, some of the locals here are probably thinking the same about *you*."

Neve glanced casually over her shoulder and met several smiles. She smiled back shyly and turning back to Davide, murmured, "They're *staring* at me."

"Why wouldn't they be staring? *Sei bellissima...*"

Neve flushed at his compliment.

"Besides, this isn't a big town. Word gets around. People know I've hired a nanny for Bianca, and they're curious." His mouth twitched. "It's in their nature."

Agostino returned with their pizza, its aroma making Neve's mouth water. The cheese on top was golden brown, with thin rounds of roasted eggplant spread all over. Neve had her first bite and nodded her approval at Davide. "My new favorite pizza," she said. "It's heavenly."

"I was drawing heaven," Bianca piped up, holding up her drawing. "See? There's Mommy and Daddy."

Neve swallowed. Bianca's drawing had a spiky sun in one corner and some clouds over mountains, with two stick figures standing on one cloud. They looked like they were holding hands. All around them, Bianca had drawn hearts. Neve glanced at Davide, and the look in his eyes made her heart hurt.

* * *

Davide had lost his appetite. Seeing Bianca's creation had given his heart such a jolt that for a moment, he wished that he were alone with the pain. And yet, seeing the empathy and compassion in Neve's eyes made him want to be alone with her, so she could comfort him as he poured out his grief and mourned his losses.

Months ago he had tried to be stoic at Violetta and Tristan's funeral, but there had been moments that had simply been too much. Seeing his little niece standing next to the coffin had been one of those moments, and he had not been able to hold back the tears. He had picked her up and they had both cried, Bianca clinging to him with big, sorrowful eyes that had haunted him ever since.

Her drawing was simple but so profound. Davide was shaken by the symbols that immediately flashed in his mind as he scanned the page, symbols that had come naturally to Bianca. The sun shining brightly and the mountains to represent her parents' ski trip. The stick figures on the clouds to show her parents up high, where heaven was. And finally, the detail that pierced his heart: the stick figures with hands joined.

Whereas *he* had questioned his faith and beliefs after the accident, here was a five-year-old who had suffered a trauma no child should ever have to suffer, yet her beliefs were clearly evident in her drawing. Beliefs that had obviously originated from her upbringing by two loving parents. And the hearts all over the page showed the reciprocation of that love.

There was no car in the drawing, or anything resembling a sign of the accident. Davide let out a long breath. "That's a beautiful and very special drawing, Bianca," he murmured, putting his arm around her shoulders. "We will have to frame it." He bent down to give her a kiss on the head. "Your *mamma* and *papà* would be very proud of you, as I am."

Bianca nodded as she bit into her second piece of pizza, seemingly unperturbed at the moment.

But Davide could tell that Neve was not going to eat much more. He called Agostino over and requested a box so they could take the unfinished pizza home.

Davide ordered an espresso for himself and Neve, and a spumoni gelato for Bianca. He held his hand up when Neve offered to contribute to the cost. "You are not paying for meals, remember?" He looked at her sternly. "That's part of your working conditions."

"Thank you, Signor Davide," Neve said, blushing as she added a touch of sugar to her espresso.

"And I told you to drop the *signor*, remember?" Davide gazed at her with raised eyebrows. "Since we're now on more...*familiar* terms?" He watched her light flush deepen and her eyelashes flutter briefly, causing a wave of desire to pulsate through his body.

Seeing that Bianca had finished her gelato, Davide paid the bill and said goodbye to Agostino, adding quietly that he'd be in touch soon. He held the door open for Neve and Bianca and ushered them into his van. He made sure Bianca's seat belt was fastened properly and climbed into the driver's seat. He glanced over at Neve. She was holding Bianca's drawing, a wistful look on her face. And then she looked over and caught his gaze. He had almost expected her to look away, but she held his gaze for five seconds...then ten...

"Zio Davide, I'm tired. Are we going home?"

Davide gave a start and looked back at Bianca. "Right now, *tesoro*. Close your eyes and rest. We'll be home in no time."

In minutes Bianca was asleep. As Davide maneuvered

his way out of town, he could feel the tension that had settled on his neck and shoulders. He would relax in his whirlpool bath when he got home. It had been an emotionally draining day, and he needed to digest what had happened—*and what was happening*—between him and Neve.

There were still plenty of questions that he wanted to ask her about her mother. And he was sure that Neve had questions of her own. It had sounded like Neve and her mother had issues that had originated in Neve's adolescent years. Or maybe earlier. At the very least, Lois Wilder was controlling and manipulative. *Had she been jealous of Neve?* Most mothers *wanted* their daughters to find a nice guy. But she had found a way to stop her daughter from meeting with him. Had she done the same with other guys?

Davide felt a chill as he remembered the words on the note. *You would do well to remember your place.* Maybe the issue hadn't been with Neve, but with *him*. Of course! He hadn't fit Lois's image of *a nice guy*. He had been grimy and dusty from his work on the farm… She must have cringed at the thought of her upper-class daughter stooping to meet *a farmer*.

Anger and disgust swirled in his gut. He couldn't abide snobbery. And he felt a stab of remorse for all the years that he had thought that it was Neve who had been the snob. *Eight wasted years.* Years of bitterness, regret and humiliation.

But maybe they hadn't been wasted. Those words that Lois had written—dripping with disdain—had actually pushed Davide to elevate his goals. This had eventually led to the writing of his novel, which had catapulted him to a level of success that he had only ever dreamed of. So in that sense, those eight years hadn't been wasted, but on the other hand, almost a decade of his and Neve's lives had been controlled by a force neither of them had been aware of. The force that was Lois Wilder.

Davide didn't know how things would be proceeding with Neve from this point on, but he knew one thing for sure: the feeling that had settled in his heart when he had first seen Neve had never disappeared. It may have flickered, like a match's flame on a windy day, but now, with the truth finally out in the open, the flicker was becoming stronger and stronger. All the judgments he had made about Neve after reading that note had dissipated when he had seen that stricken look in her eyes. The raw pain that she had been deceived by her own mother, by some one she had thought she could trust. And that look had pained him also, knowing that Neve had been hurt.

As Davide wound his way up the mountain, he suddenly thought of the novel that he had put on hold since the accident. Taking care of his sister's and brother-in-law's affairs after their accident had taken all his time and emotional energy. And once Bianca had returned to Southern Italy with him, he had spent time with her during the day and evening, trying to adapt to a new life that included a child.

He had hired a nanny right from the beginning, and then another, and a third, but each one had fallen short of his expectations. The first had exaggerated her qualifications, the second had crossed the line by snooping and the third had wanted to get to him through Bianca. All had violated his trust.

During all of this Davide hadn't felt the desire to return to his writing. So he had done the next best thing—continued his research. He had set this novel in the late nineteen-fifties, during the last great wave of Italian immigration to other parts of the world. Reading and compiling facts and significant details of that era had kept him moving forward, even if the creative part of it was on hold.

Fortunately, the resounding success of his first novel afforded him whatever time he needed to move through his grief and mourning without the worry about a paycheck not arriving. And even though his publisher and editor had been anxiously awaiting his next literary offering, Davide had refused to put pressure on himself. He knew that the desire to write would return, sooner or later.

And it *had*, especially after seeing that *look* in Neve's eyes. The utter defeat, mixed with shards of pain. A look that he could envision on his heroine's face after her discovery of her husband's infidelity in their newly adopted country—a scene that he had been about to write the night that he had gotten the call from Bianca's babysitter in Vancouver…

As Davide drove the final stretch onto his property, the lights he had had installed casting an amber glow on different sections of the castle, Davide felt a ripple of excitement run through him. *He would return to his writing tonight.*

# CHAPTER EIGHTEEN

BIANCA WAS TOO tired for a bath and a story before bed. And earlier, too tired to walk into the castle. Davide had carried her from the van into the castle and up the winding staircase. Neve had followed, a warmth spreading throughout her body at Davide's tenderness toward his niece. And at the sight of his strong back and arm muscles…

The sudden image of him carrying *her* up the stairs made her pulse quicken and she was glad he wasn't able to see her face at that moment, probably close to the same color as her hair.

Davide kissed Bianca good-night and excused himself. Neve helped Bianca change and get into bed, and when Neve tiptoed out of her room, Davide reappeared from his study. He offered Neve a chamomile tea or a cool drink, and she hesitated for a moment, trying to read his expression in the dimmed hall lighting.

*Would this lead to further discussion about the past and her mother's part in it? Or encourage something more intimate?* A wave of exhaustion washed over her then, and although she was very tempted, she made herself decline his offer. "Thanks, but I… I think the best thing is for me to get to bed. Today has been somewhat overwhelming…"

He closed the distance between them and took her hands in his. The way his thumbs were circling gently over her palms was triggering a series of red-hot currents through her. And when she thought that she was close to letting out a soft moan, he brought her hands to his lips, planted a firm kiss on both of them and brought them gently down. "*Anche per me*, Neve. Also for me."

Davide looked deep into her eyes—activating another delicious swirl in the pit of her stomach—and murmured, "I have some work to do, but we will see each other in the morning. *Va bene?*"

"*Va bene,*" she managed to reply a little breathlessly. Of course it was okay with her. Neve watched him retreat into his study, leaving the door half-open, and she entered her room, almost regretting that she hadn't accepted his offer.

As soon as she stepped into the large, claw-foot tub in her en-suite bathroom, enveloped by the sweet, soothing fragrance of the floral bubble bath, she knew she had made the right choice. *At least for tonight.*

The muscles in her body were more tense than she had realized. Neve closed her eyes, glad she had dimmed the lights, and focused on doing some deep breathing exercises. After twenty or so minutes, she stepped out of the perfumed water, feeling much more mellow and relaxed. Wrapping herself in an oversize towel, she padded to her bed. She had put on a shower cap to expedite her bath routine, so she didn't have to worry about drying her hair. She switched on the night-light near the door to the en suite and turned off the Murano chandelier in her room.

Neve lay on top of the bed for a few minutes, enjoying the warm breeze from the open shutters. She felt like a pampered princess in her luxurious turret room. Before her eyelids became too droopy, she shifted to turn back the covers, and then flung her towel on the edge of the bed. The thought *did* occur to her to walk over to the armoire where she had hung up her nightie, but her limbs refused to cooperate.

The cool satin sheet against Neve's bare skin made her snap out of her lethargy. She felt a slow, sensual tingle along her nerve endings with every brush of her body against the satin, and the thought of Davide so close by in his study ramped up the sensations even more. With a sudden shiver, she pulled the top satin sheet over her and squeezed her eyes shut. She had to stop imagining Davide walking through that door and coming to her...

*He was her boss!* No matter that there had been sparks between them eight years ago, sparks that hadn't needed much to flare up since she had arrived. She could not encourage any kind of involvement with Davide while she was employed by him. Yes, it would be sweet torture, living under his roof and erecting an emotional barrier to prevent him from getting closer. But there was no other option, unless she quit her job and went home.

And she didn't have the heart to do that to Bianca. The child had had enough traumatic changes in her life, and Neve wasn't about to become the fourth nanny who hadn't worked out. The poor child needed some stability, and Neve had every intention of fulfilling her part of the contract and ensuring that Bianca was ready for kindergarten. She could see—and she knew Davide could, too—that Bianca was already warming up to her.

Neve inhaled deeply. She could only take it one day at a time. And even *that* might prove to be more difficult than she could imagine...

Exhausted, Neve closed her eyes and curled to one side, tucking the sheet under her chin, and willed herself to sleep.

Davide stared at the paragraph he had just finished typing up on the laptop. He frowned, his fingers drumming the keys softly without actually typing. Then he changed a few words, read it over again and smiled. He was back on track!

He rubbed his eyes and then checked the time on his cell phone. After 3:00 a.m. Well, he had accomplished what he had meant to do. The scene was done, and he felt emotionally spent but exhilarated at the same time.

Davide sat back in his leather office chair and let his shoulders relax. He dipped his head, moved it to one side and then the other, stretching his neck and then his shoulders. The sound of footsteps in the hall made him swivel. His first thought was that it was Bianca, but a couple of seconds later Neve appeared at the half-open door, her cotton robe tied loosely at her waist.

Her hair was tousled, framing her face in feathery strands, and her eyes were blinking, as if surprised to see him there.

"I—I woke up and thought I heard something," she said, her voice husky. "I opened my door and saw your light. I thought maybe you had forgotten to turn it off… so I was going to."

Davide couldn't help smiling. "Thank you for being concerned about my light bill, Neve."

Her mouth quirked on one side and her gaze flew to his computer. "Well, I guess I'll let you get back to whatever you were doing…"

Davide waited till her gaze returned to his. "No, don't go just yet… Come in."

He saw her hesitate and then pull the strap of her robe tighter around her. She walked tentatively toward him, stopping several feet from his desk. His laptop was still open, with the last page of his chapter on the screen. Davide saw her gaze fly to it quickly and then back to him.

He closed the laptop and stood up to face her.

"I have something I'd like to give you. A little gift to

express my gratitude for doing such a great job with Bianca." He held out a copy of *La Figlia Dei Borboni*. "The English translation is in the works."

Davide felt a swirl of pleasure as Neve's eyes widened, along with her smile. She took the book gingerly as if it was a priceless treasure. She scanned the cover and then turned it over to read the blurb. And then she flipped the first couple of pages to where he had inscribed it.

*Per Neve,*
*Con ammirazione e gratitudine.*

*For Neve, with admiration and gratitude.*
She looked up at him, her eyes a misty azure.

"*Grazie,* Davide," she said, blinking but unable to stop the teardrops from slipping out onto her cheeks.

He groaned softly and took the book out of her hands and dropped it on the desk. He pulled her close against him, wrapping one arm around her back and raising his other hand to press her head gently against his chest. He breathed in the fresh scent of her hair and held her for timeless moments, letting all his senses experience the intimacy he had dreamed of for years.

And then his need for her made him tilt her face toward him and hungrily seek her lips. When they opened almost immediately for him, an exquisite current ran through him as he tasted the fruit that had been denied him for almost a decade. *Madonna mia*, he thought, his breath ragged. He pulled away to trace a path of kisses down her silky neck, and with impatient hands, he tugged at the ties of her robe until it fell away.

Her sudden gasp at the touch of his hands over the thin nightie beneath her robe sent his heart catapulting against his rib cage. His lips sought hers again while one hand slid under her nightie. And then another gasp. With a muffled groan, Davide swept her up in his arms and carried her to his bedroom.

"I've been waiting a lifetime to make you mine, Neve," he breathed against her ear before setting her down on his king-size bed. He had so much he wanted to say to her…

*But he let his passion say the rest…*

# CHAPTER NINETEEN

WHEN NEVE WOKE UP, she was alone in her own bed. A series of images flashed through her mind and made her pulse do hurdles. Had she been dreaming? There was no way that she and Davide had...

They *had*.

And her body was still thrumming from his touch.

*The way he had begun his tender exploration, so slowly and gently, as if she were a delicate flower.*

And the feel of his lips and touch becoming more passionate...and thorough...

He had sent her to the stars and back. There had been few words...his eyes had relayed everything she had needed to know. And afterward she had nestled against him, cocooned by his strong arms, his breath warm against her neck. *This is how she had always imagined lovemaking would be...*

Neve had wished she could have stayed there until morning, but they both knew that Bianca could wake up at any time.

Davide had helped her with her nightie and dressing gown, and had carried her back to her room. After a final passionate kiss, he had left, and Neve had eventually succumbed to a deep, contented sleep.

The unexpected ring of her cell phone gave Neve an

unpleasant jolt, and she reached for it on her night table, irritated at the interruption of her thoughts. Blinking, she read the text message.

Neve, I can't believe you didn't tell me you were living in a castle! And that your boss is the celebrated author Davide Cortese! Not that I knew about him before, lol, but my sources in Valdoro texted me to tell me that the two of you had been seen in Michelina's Bakery, of all places! So, 'fess up, darling. Is something going on that I should know about? Did you meet him online through a dating service? Is that why he hired you as nanny to his niece?

Neve paused, her stomach in knots. She could not believe that even this far away from home, her mother was still sticking her nose in her private business. And of course her mother's "sources" were her friends at the Villa Morgana. An employee at the villa had either been at the bakery when she and Davide had been there with Bianca, or else someone at the bakery had told a friend who had then told another friend…

And how was she supposed to respond to her mother's query? What had happened between her and Davide was too fresh, too private. And the last person she wanted to know about it was the person who had contrived—and succeeded—in preventing them from ever meeting. Neve still had to confront her mother about *that*.

But maybe her mother didn't know that Davide was the fellow she had responded to so disdainfully years ago… In any case, Neve needed to downplay the situation and convince her mother that there hadn't been any involvement between her and Davide.

No, Mom, we didn't meet through an internet dating site. I was hired because of my credentials and experience with children. And I had no idea he was an author when I accepted the position.

Her mom was quick to reply.

Well, I hope he's paying you well. If he's living in a castle he must be loaded. And I hear his book has been optioned for a film!

Neve's jaw clenched as she wrote back.

You don't have to worry about what he's paying me, Mom. And I have to go now. Bye!

She was about to turn off her phone, but her mother quickly texted again.

Well, I'll see you soon, darling, because I've booked a flight for Italy! I'll be in Valdoro before you know it! My flight leaves tonight. But don't worry. I don't expect to be put up in the castle of your prince—oops—boss, lol! I'll be with my friends at the Villa Morgana, of course! Arrivederci, bella! Can't wait to see you and meet him!

A moment later Lois texted Neve her flight number.

Neve stared openmouthed at her cell phone. And then she turned it off, not bothering to reply.

*How could she stop her mother from coming? Stop her from interfering with her life?*

Neve bit her lip, her nerves jangled. Her mother could not be stopped when she put something in her head. And her impulsive decision to return to Valdoro must have something to do with her discovery of Davide's status.

For as long as Neve could remember, her mother had

taken every opportunity to associate with people of distinction. So why would things be different now? Neve frowned at the thought of her mother's imminent arrival. Lois would be sure to find a way to show up at the castle and try to ingratiate herself with Davide.

And how would Davide feel when he found out about her mother's plans? Lois had humiliated him, and Neve wouldn't blame him if Davide wanted nothing to do with her. Surely he would see right through Lois...

Neve's attraction to Davide had nothing to do with his money or status. Yes, she was thrilled for his success, but the spark that connected them had been created in the past. It hadn't mattered to her then that he had come from humble beginnings, and it didn't matter to her now. If Davide had remained a farmer, she would still be attracted to him. What mattered to her was his devotion to his niece, and how he had put aside his work to make Bianca his priority and help her adjust to life without her parents.

Neve had to give Davide a lot of credit for accepting and carrying out his role as godfather. And her heart bled for the grieving he must have felt at the tragic news—and still must be feeling...

A rush of tenderness swept through her as she thought of ways to comfort Davide. Not just by taking care of Bianca, but by taking care of *him*. Neve felt a sudden longing that she had never felt with any other man, and it made her catch her breath.

*She wanted Davide.*

Not just in the physical sense, but in every way imaginable. She wanted to nurture that spark from eight years ago into red-hot flames that would burn for a lifetime. She had disappeared from his life once, but fate had brought them back together. She couldn't ignore or throw away the second chance offered to them, even if Davide *was* her boss.

*But what if Davide doesn't feel the same? What if he's just needing something—somebody—to help him get through his grief? What makes you think he would want you permanently in his life?*

Neve faltered at her inner voice. Maybe Davide *had* needed a physical release after the grief and pain of the past few months. She felt her cheeks burn at the memory of his passion, and how he had managed to make her reciprocate, even though it had been her first time…

Neve bit her lip as her thoughts took a dark turn. Perhaps one of the three "princesses," as Davide had called Bianca's nannies, had had a physical relationship with him before he tired of her and dismissed her. Neve frowned. Did she *really* know what Davide's true character was like? Maybe what she had seen on the outside was just a mask…

A gorgeous mask that she had fallen for. *Hard.*

*No*, she couldn't believe—*didn't want to believe*—that Davide had made love to her for the sole purpose of physical gratification. She couldn't possibly have misread the tenderness in his eyes, and that look of wonder…

Neve checked the time on her phone. Davide had told her to sleep in; he would see to Bianca's breakfast and *hers*, when she came down to the kitchen. Neve smiled. She'd have a quick shower first, and maybe she'd be in time to watch Davide make the frittata he had promised her…

In the stillness of dawn, Davide watched the sun rise up like a gleaming orange persimmon on the horizon, and the pale blue sky brightening with streaks of pink and gold. He had already been up for an hour, gone to make himself an espresso and returned to his room to enjoy it.

For the first time since Bianca had come to live with him, Davide had woken up without feeling like the proverbial weight of the world was on his shoulders. Without the responsibility of parenting seeming so *serious*.

Not that it wasn't serious, but since Neve had taken over as nanny, Davide had experienced some of the lighter moments of raising a child, and he had enjoyed them. Like the game of hide-and-seek. Bianca had laughed and he had, too, watching her squeal when Neve had gotten close enough to tag her.

Davide felt his nerve endings tingle at the thought of Neve. Not in a game of tag, but in his arms last night, *in his bed*. He hadn't planned it and he would have stopped the second she had shown any sign that she wanted him to stop… *But she hadn't*.

Discovering that *he had been the first* had taken Davide straight to heaven with the wonder of it. He had felt humbled, exhilarated and emotional all at once, and he had been careful to rein in his passion…until she was ready.

Bianca's call and knock on the door forced him to suppress any further thoughts of Neve.

He called out for Bianca to enter and she joined him on his leather chair, her orca with her, which, she told him matter-of-factly, she had named "Berry." Sitting on his lap, she watched the sun's ascent with him and told him about the whales she had seen with her father, called "Granny" and "Onyx." Davide listened quietly, inwardly rejoicing that Bianca was starting to talk about her parents without bursting into tears.

And then she proclaimed that she was hungry. Chuckling, he headed downstairs with her, and after preparing her cereal and milk, went out to the garden to get snippets of parsley and green onions for the frittata. He whistled a tune that had been a hit a decade earlier, performed at the Sanremo Music Festival. Whenever it had played on the radio, his heart had felt a twinge. It had haunted him then with its romantic melody, but no more.

Davide took out a bowl and as he beat the eggs with a mixture of milk, chopped parsley and pecorino romano, the cheese he preferred with its sharp bite, Neve walked into the kitchen. Davide stopped whistling, and his hand stopped beating. He took in Neve's sleeveless coral dress with its big retro buckle that emphasized her slender waist, and its skirt that flared and reached just above her knees. A matching headband made her look like a fifties glamour girl.

"*Buon giorno*, Neve." If Bianca wasn't with them, he'd have called Neve *cara* or *bella* or *tesoro mio*. But he couldn't very well call her *dear* or *beautiful* or *my treasure* in front of his niece. At least…not yet. He motioned for her to join Bianca at the table. "I'm keeping my promise to cook for you," he murmured as she walked by him. "Are you hungry?"

She paused and fixed him with a wide-eyed glance. Lashes fluttering open and closed like exotic fans. Eyes with an intensity that sent coils of electricity spiraling throughout his body.

"Very," she said, and then noticing that Bianca was watching her, made a fierce expression, adding, "I'm as hungry as the wolf in *The Three Little Pigs*."

Bianca let out a little squeal. "You can't have my cereal!" she laughed.

Davide resumed beating the eggs. Neve had such a remarkable way with kids. She made Bianca smile and laugh, and after the sadness and tears since the accident, hearing that little tinkling sound come out of Bianca's mouth, and seeing her brown eyes literally sparkle at Neve's silliness, Davide couldn't help but smile and laugh himself.

It felt strange to feel lighthearted. The past few months had been anything but. He had wondered sometimes if he and Bianca would ever laugh again. Her previous nannies had not elicited anywhere near the kind of reaction Bianca had demonstrated with Neve. All three had left him disillusioned with their less-than-honorable motives. He had been determined to find the right nanny for Bianca, one who was genuinely interested in helping her, and not using her as a means to get to *him*.

Aware of Neve's eyes occasionally shifting from Bianca to him, Davide heated the pan with extra-virgin olive oil and sautéed the chopped onions before adding the egg mixture. When the edges started curling in, he flipped the frittata over by sliding it first on the bottom of the pan lid and then quickly flipping it over into the hot pan. When both sides were golden brown, he transferred it to a large plate, cut it into wedges and brought it to the table, along with a plate of tomato slices and a crusty roll.

"I'll let you serve while I get the coffee," he said, and returned moments later with an espresso for himself and a cappuccino for Neve.

Bianca finished her wedge of frittata quickly and went out into the courtyard.

When she had gone, Davide looked closely at Neve. "Don't you like it?" He looked pointedly at her half-finished plate.

"No… I mean, yes, it's very tasty. It's just that…" She met Davide's gaze directly and then looked down, her shoulders slumping. When she looked back at him, her brows were furrowed and her lips were pursed.

"I don't know how to tell you this," she finally ventured.

Davide's stomach twisted. *Was she going to tell him that she regretted last night? That she now wanted to leave?* He leaned forward, elbows on the table, and hands clasped together in front of his mouth. The euphoria he had felt in his chest from just being with Neve started to seep out of him. Bracing himself, he said brusquely, "Just tell me."

Neve took a deep breath. "My mother is coming to Valdoro. She wants to meet you."

# CHAPTER TWENTY

THERE—IT WAS OUT. Neve watched Davide closely, wanting to see what his first gut reaction would be.

*It wasn't what she had expected.*

The frown on Davide's face had relaxed, and unclasping his hands, his mouth had become visible, showing a crooked smile. "Why?"

"*Why?* Because she's curious, impulsive. Her friends at the Villa Morgana told her that we had been seen at the bakery." At Davide's puzzled look, she felt herself flush in embarrassment. "They told her about *you*. Your success, your castle, your…"

"Wealth," he finished, nodding. "And she wants to come and see for herself what high society circles her daughter has gotten herself into…" His black eyes gleamed. "Does she know who I am?"

Neve gazed at him for a moment, her heart contracting. *No, her mother had no idea who Davide was as a person. She was interested in Davide Cortese as a celebrated author who lived in a castle and was "loaded."* But Neve knew that Davide was referring to the past…

"No…she wouldn't know that you were the one she wrote the note to…" Neve sighed.

"The last thing I wanted was my mother around," she said, her voice breaking. "I'm sorry."

Davide leaned forward and grasped her hands. "You don't need to be," he said huskily, his thumbs caressing her palms. "Is she expecting to stay here?"

"No, thank God." Neve felt her shoulders relax. "She'll be staying with her friends at the Villa Morgana."

Davide released one hand to cup her chin. "That's just a peach," he chuckled.

Neve couldn't help breaking into a smile. *"Peachy,"* she corrected.

"Yes, just peachy." He gave a deep laugh. "Or we could have prepared a room for her in the castle dungeon."

Neve laughed. "Is there really a dungeon?"

Davide's eyes twinkled. "It's a cellar, and it actually has a secret tunnel that leads to a cave in the mountainside… Apparently, it was a hiding place for brigands in the eighteen-sixties."

*"Brigands?"* Neve stared at him incredulously. *"Really?"* She couldn't help shivering. "And the owner of the castle knew about it?"

"Probably. He may have been sympathetic to the brigands' cause. They were rebelling against the ousting of the Bourbon regime during Italy's Unification, mostly because of the hardships suffered by the peasants after the formation of the new government. The owner—a baron whose family had enjoyed the privileges of the old order for generations—probably used the brigands to covertly rebel against the government himself."

"Oh, my," Neve murmured. "Sounds like a very dangerous time."

Davide nodded. "It's a period known as *il decennio di fuoco*—the decade of fire. The government went after the brigands and employed the National Guard to find and capture them. *And* their women, the *brigantesse*."

Neve stared. "Their women went into hiding with them?"

"Some, but if they were captured, the law was generally more lenient with them, sentencing them to life imprisonment in a workhouse."

"That was more *lenient*?"

"More lenient than having them hanged or shot. Sadly, some ended up in the latter category."

Neve gave another shudder. She looked across at him with a sudden curiosity. "Do you know if…if any of your ancestors might have been *briganti*?"

Davide's eyes narrowed, glinting amusement. "Possibly. When I was researching the municipal archives, I came across the names of some distant relatives who had disappeared around that time…"

Neve's mouth dropped. She imagined the castle engulfed in fog over a century and a half earlier, and a brigand with Davide's features furtively making his way through the castle tunnel with his *brigantessa*, and hiding out in the dark mountain cave. The brigand would have wrapped his cloak over his woman and she would have snuggled against him, trying not to think about the bats clustered in masses on the walls and ceiling…

Davide's laughter shattered her thoughts. "Wh-what?" She blinked at him.

"You looked horrified for a moment. Did the thought of my possible brigand heritage shock you?"

Neve looked at him sheepishly. "No… I was just thinking about the bats in the cave."

Davide's burst of laughter made Bianca run over to them.

"Zio, can we go to the beach this morning?" She turned excitedly toward Neve. "Did you bring a swimsuit?"

Neve glanced at Davide. "Don't feel you need to… I'm sure you have some work you might like to do…some writing?"

"I can do that later. I have a better imagination at

night…" Davide's gaze locked with hers for so long that Neve began to feel a flush spread to the most vulnerable zones of her body.

He glanced at the time on his cell phone. "We can leave in twenty minutes or so. I have a quick call to make to my publisher." Davide grinned at them. "You ladies get what you need—sunscreen, hats, a good book… Have you read the latest Strega Prize–winning novel?" he said teasingly. He gave Neve a wink. "*Ciao.* I'll meet you in the foyer."

Davide watched Neve and Bianca walk toward the staircase, with Bianca reaching for Neve's hand. He felt a rush of warmth at his niece's gesture. She trusted Neve.

*And so did he.*

With a lightness he thought he'd never feel again, Davide called his publisher in Milan to tell him that he had returned to the writing of his novel. They discussed a few details and timelines, and then Davide scheduled another meeting with him for the middle of the week. *And he could take Neve with him again…*

Whistling, Davide returned to the kitchen. His publisher had been thrilled, and he was just as thrilled. But right now he had other things to think about, like packing up a few items for the beach. They would be there till around noon, and Bianca would be sure to get hungry.

He found a large insulated bag in the pantry and set it down on the table. He decided to keep it simple: panini and some cheese, olives and tomatoes. He gathered up a few more items from the fridge and a bottle opener. And finally, he added a bottle of red wine and two crystal glasses, wrapped up in several tea towels.

Davide thought about Neve's initial words, *I don't know how to tell you this*, and how he had braced himself for Neve's declaration that she regretted what had happened between them and that she would be resigning, no longer able to work for him under the circumstances… The tension had put his stomach in knots.

But those knots had instantly relaxed with Neve's announcement that her mother would be coming to Valdoro. Not that he was exactly delighted with the news, but it was something that wouldn't cause his heart to break, like Neve's leaving would do.

Davide froze with a sudden realization. *He didn't want Neve to leave.*

Not now…*or ever.*

# CHAPTER TWENTY-ONE

NEVE ACCOMPANIED BIANCA to her room first and helped her with her swimsuit and clothes to wear over it. Bianca insisted on bringing Berry the orca with her. While Bianca waited in Neve's room, Neve changed into a red one-piece swimsuit in her en-suite bathroom, and then slipped on a pair of white shorts and a green eyelet peasant blouse.

As she brushed her hair in front of the dressing table in her room, Bianca came over and watched. "Can I brush your hair?" she said suddenly. "My mommy used to let me brush hers...and then she would brush mine. She would call me *principessa* when she did my hair."

Neve's heart ached at the sad note in Bianca's voice. She handed Bianca the brush. "Yes, of course you can, Bianca." She leaned forward so she was eye to eye with the child. "I know you miss your dear mommy, Bianca. And your daddy. Just remember that they love you, and they want you to be happy."

"But why did they have to die and leave me all alone?" Bianca's lips started to quiver.

"Sweetheart, you're not alone," Neve said softly. "You have your Zio Davide. He loves you, and your mommy and daddy chose him to take good care of you. That's why they made him your godfather when you were born."

Bianca's face puckered into a frown. "Did they *know* they were going to die?"

"No, love. Just try to remember that when you're missing them, think of something beautiful, like an angel, or a twinkling star, or a rainbow, and think of them being right beside it. *Imagine it.*" She smiled brightly. "Your mommy and daddy will always be in your heart and mind and memories, Bianca. And in your imagination."

"But that's *make-believe*," Bianca said, her chocolate-brown eyes widening. "I want it to be *real*."

"When you *believe*, it feels real," Neve said, trying to keep her voice steady. "Now how about I pick a special name for you? Your mommy called you 'princess,' and since you're taking such good care of your little whale, I'd like to call you—" she pretended to think "—Queen of the Orcas! How does that sound to you, *Your Majesty*?"

"I like it, Miss Neve!" She grinned and proceeded to brush Neve's hair.

"And how about you just call me Neve?"

"Okay, but can I sometimes call you Snow White?"

A gentle cough made them both look toward the doorway. Davide was leaning casually against the door frame. *How long had he been there? Had he heard Bianca's words about her parents?*

Neve caught a glimpse of sadness on Davide's face. Or was it just her imagination?

"My telephone conversation didn't take as long as I thought it would," he said. "I came up to tell you we could leave as soon as you were ready." His jaw muscles flickered. "So let's go, Snow White and Queen of the Orcas! Your carriage awaits!"

"I should call you Miss Italy with the colors you're wearing, Neve," Davide murmured, his gaze sweeping over her again. That green peasant top that she had positioned just slightly off her shoulders, those white shorts that hugged her curves and the red peeking through the eyelets of her cotton blouse… *Bellissima.*

She didn't reply, and as she walked past him with Bianca, she just gave him a twitch of a smile, her blue-green eyes startling in their clarity.

During the drive down the mountain to the beach, Davide put on a CD of Bianca's favorite tunes, and she hummed along while alternately throwing her orca up in the air and catching it, or making it dance to the rhythm of the song.

Davide had deliberately planned the musical distraction. He had caught much of the conversation earlier between Neve and Bianca. When he had arrived at Neve's bedroom door, she was telling Bianca that she knew that she missed her mommy…

Neither of them had seen him, and there hadn't been the opportunity to announce his presence, so he had waited in the doorway. And the words Neve had communicated to Bianca had made something shift inside him, creating room for his heart to expand. The feeling had been so exquisite that he had almost cried out. It took everything he had to act casual, to hide the revelation that his body—and soul—had just revealed to him.

*He loved Neve.* He loved her gentle spirit with Bianca, her compassion, her understanding of how to help a grieving child. She had come up with a way to empower Bianca to hold on to her parents through her memories and her imagination. He had felt a prickling behind his eyes at her words. They had sparked something in him, as well—the realization that he could handle his grief in the same way.

Moreover, he had felt a wave of regret about the opinion he had harbored about Neve for nearly a decade. He had been so wrong. So…very…wrong. Well, he would do whatever it took to make it right. He no longer wanted her just as a nanny for Bianca. He wanted her for himself, too, if she would have him.

*Yes, he wanted her to spend a lifetime with him. As his wife. As his fairy-tale princess. As his lover. As the guardian of his little Queen of the Orcas.*

Davide wanted the three of them to be a *family*, to share everything a family shared.

He stole a glance at Neve. She was swaying gently to the music and singing the words to the nursery rhymes. Davide felt like his heart would burst. He needed to tell her how he felt, but he would be patient and wait for a time when they could be alone.

His assistant Lucia had texted him earlier to say that she was babysitting her niece Rosalia again, and could she pick up Bianca later in the afternoon and bring her back the following day? Davide had agreed. Bianca needed to be with kids her own age and he was grateful to Lucia for arranging regular visits.

He couldn't help smiling. Tomorrow would be the day, then. After Bianca left, he would take Neve for a special drive through the countryside to one of his favorite seaside spots. They would share a wonderful dinner, and afterward he would reveal what was in his heart.

*And with any luck, she would accept his proposal.*

The road from the castle veered off to a private road at the base of the mountain that was available to him exclusively, and after a few final twists in the road, they arrived at the beach.

Davide parked the van at the end of the path, and they had walked several hundred feet to the beach.

The pale, silky length of it seemed endless, stretching as far as the eye could see in either direction. Davide watched Neve taking it all in, and he felt a spiral of pleasure that he could share this place—*his place*—with her.

She darted an awe-filled glance at him, and her blue-green eyes were as dazzling to him as the sun-speckled waters of the Ionian Sea.

Bianca immediately plunked herself down on the sand and while she played with her sandcastle toys, Davide set up the beach umbrella and the lounging chairs that he and Neve had carried from the van. He proceeded to take off his T-shirt and jeans, leaving only his swim shorts.

He'd wait a while before plunging into the sea.

Out of the corner of his eye, he could see Neve doing the same. At the sudden flash of red, he turned, and the combination of the curves emphasized by the silky red swimsuit and her shapely legs made his heart flip wildly against his rib cage. She must have known he was watching her, because a soft flush had crept into her cheeks. She immediately sat down and pulled a book out of her bag. *La Figlia Dei Borboni.*

He was so tempted to tell her that he didn't want her to go back to Vancouver, that he wanted her to stay… There was no doubt in his mind that she was physically attracted to him, as he was to her. The passion they had shared had rocked his world. But was that enough for Neve to uproot her entire life and move to Italy?

He had to find a way of convincing her to stay…and never disappear out of his life again.

He lay back on the reclining beach chair. "I'm going to let myself heat up a little more before I dive in," he told her huskily. "I'll leave you to your reading. Oh, by the way, my assistant Lucia will be coming by later this afternoon to pick up Bianca. She's babysitting her niece again, and she asked if Bianca could go over and stay the night. Lucia will bring Bianca back tomorrow."

Neve nodded and lay back herself, but only a couple of minutes had passed before Bianca called out for her to help build a sandcastle. Neve put away Davide's book and sauntered over to Bianca, who handed her a yellow pail. "Can you get some water, Neve?"

"Yes, at once, oh Queen of the Orcas." Neve curtsied and with a smile, went to do Bianca's bidding.

Davide watched them together between half-closed lids. He felt drowsy and...*content*. The world—or at least *his world*—suddenly felt right. *Maybe this is what starting to heal feels like*, he thought in wonder. Shards of pain replaced by rays of hope.

It was just too bad that Lois Wilder would be arriving soon, like a meteor about to crash into his world.

# CHAPTER TWENTY-TWO

IT TOOK NEVE'S every effort not to constantly glance at Davide's body. He was lying back on his chaise longue, his sunglasses on. His leanness a decade ago had become solid muscle, and as her gaze swept over his chest and sculpted muscles of his abdomen and legs, she quivered inside, remembering how that body had felt against her...

And although she had nodded nonchalantly at the news that Bianca would be having a sleepover, her nerve endings were tingling at the thought of spending a night alone with him in the castle...

When he suddenly sat up, she started, and spilled the bucket of water she had been carrying, splashing herself and Bianca.

"I think it's time for a real splash," he chuckled. "Come on, Bianca."

Bianca dropped her beach toys and ran to clasp Davide's hand. "Come on, Neve," she called.

Neve followed and moments later they were all immersed in the gentle ebb and flow of the surf. Davide's hands firmly held Bianca's as she bobbed and kicked her legs. Not long after the first exhilarating dip, Neve's body acclimatized to the temperature of the water, and with the sun beaming down, it actually started to feel balmy. The taste of the salt water, the turquoise waves glittering with millions of specks of light and the glistening body of Davide…it was all making her feel quite heady…

Afterward, Davide spread out the picnic lunch he had prepared: panini and a variety of luncheon meats, cheeses and condiments. He met Neve's gaze and tilted his head to direct her attention to Bianca. Bianca's little cheeks were full, and while she happily munched away, she broke off little bits of cheese from her plate and pretended to feed it to her orca.

Neve smiled and when her glance returned to Davide, he was grinning back at her. Seeing his eyes crinkle at the edges, his delight and love for Bianca reflected in their depths, Neve felt both joy and sadness. Joy for having witnessed the depth of Davide's feelings for his niece, and sadness, knowing that she herself was only a temporary addition in their lives.

Yes, Davide and Bianca were a family…and maybe one day Davide would meet someone he wanted as his wife and godmother to his niece…and then their little family would grow… Feeling a sudden prickle behind her eyelids, Neve turned away, pretending to watch the surf.

"When did you say your mother was arriving?" Davide asked moments later.

Neve groaned. "I hadn't. But if she made all her connections, she should be getting in around three at the Villa Morgana. And she'll probably want to make her way here sometime after that. I'm sure she'll text right away."

"Shall we return to the castle and get ready for her arrival, then?" He smiled at her. "Pull out the red carpet?"

"Please, Davide, you don't have to do anything special, especially after the way she treated you."

His smile widened. "I…was…teasing, Neve. I don't have a red carpet." He looked over at Bianca. "I see our queen is feeling drowsy. She'll have a good nap when we get back." He gazed back at Neve, lifting an eyebrow. "Shall we pack up?"

Neve checked her phone anxiously. Her mother had settled into Villa Morgana and had texted Neve to say that she was ready to be picked up. Could her boss send a driver out to the villa?

Neve had relayed her request to Davide, apologizing for her mother's assumption that "her boss" would take care of her travel arrangements. "I'm sure she could have hired someone through her friends at the villa," she said, her cheeks heating up in frustration.

Davide's lips quirked. "She's obviously expecting the royal treatment. Shall I pick up Her Highness in my Lamborghini or Alfa?"

Neve stared at him. *"Really?"* She shook her head. "Is there not a taxi she can take?"

Davide's eyebrows lifted. "Well…there *is* a taxi driver I know who hasn't been getting much work. His name is Santo. Why don't I call him?"

"Perfect." Neve sighed, relieved.

"And I'll call the Pasticceria Michelina and order a box of pastries. Santo can pick them up on his way here. The least I can do is to offer her a *caffè* and biscotti," he said, winking at Neve.

Bianca was still napping when Neve heard the taxi arrive. She was waiting in the foyer, sitting in one of the two wingback chairs with a magazine. Davide had gone to work in his study and must have seen the taxicab from his window. He joined her, wearing black trousers and a crisp white shirt, unbuttoned at his neck. He flashed Neve a smile that sent her pulse skittering. "Are we ready for this?"

Neve sighed. "Do we have a choice? I should apologize in advance for anything she might say or—"

"You don't have to apologize for anything," Davide said firmly. "And don't worry on my account. I can take care of myself." He reached for her hand and gave it a squeeze. "And you can, too. Take care of yourself, I mean." He opened the thick door and motioned for Neve to precede him. *"Coraggio,"* he murmured close to her ear as they walked out.

"Neve!"

Neve watched her mother scramble out of the taxicab and begin striding toward her. She was wearing a light blue pantsuit and nude pumps. Even from this distance, Neve could see that she was frowning. The cab driver followed more leisurely, holding the box from the bakery. Lois slowed down as she caught sight of Davide's cars, and her frown seemed to deepen. As if she suddenly realized where she was, she stopped and gazed up at the castle and the view around it.

Neve and Davide closed the gap between them. Neve gave her mother a dutiful hug and then stepped back to introduce Davide.

Neve saw Lois's gaze sweep over him. *Recording every bit of data her senses took in.*

The fresh, citrus scent of his cologne, his styled hair, his gold chain, his expensive shirt and pants, his gleaming leather shoes…

Davide courteously held out his hand and Lois took it with a smile, also scanning his fingers for gold.

When Davide excused himself to go and retrieve the package from the cab driver, Lois turned so that only Neve could see her face.

"Neve, I can't believe that your boss is living like a king here—" she gestured toward the luxury vehicles "—and the best he could do was to send a cab! The driver reeked of cigarettes and garlic, and his air-conditioning was not working." She brushed off her pants as if germs were still clinging to them. "Could you not have asked your boss to pick me up himself?"

"I'm sorry, Mom, but he was not available at the time." *She hated to lie, but she could hardly tell the truth...*

Lois sniffed. "Well, I heard some things down at the villa, including the fact that your boss comes from a *farming* background."

"Mom, *please*. He's my boss and his background does not concern me. Nor should it concern you." Neve felt her hackles rising. Five minutes hadn't gone by and her mother was already saying things that grated on her. "And at the moment, you are his guest."

"May I offer you some refreshment, Signora Wilder?"

Neve and her mother both started at the voice behind them.

"I would like that, thank you." Lois nodded imperiously. "That dreadful cab had no air-conditioning and I thought I was going to pass out."

*"Prego,"* Davide said, gesturing toward the castle. As her mother marched off ahead of them, Davide caught Neve's eye and winked. She exhaled slowly, shaking her head, and went inside.

Neve could tell that her mother was impressed, despite the nonchalant set of her shoulders. Lois's gaze was taking in every luxurious piece of furniture, the shiny marble floor and the curving sweep of the staircase. Davide directed her into the dining area and kitchen and asked if she would like tea, coffee or a cold drink.

"For now, a cold beverage, thank you, Signor Cortese." Lois glanced around as if she expected a butler or maid to suddenly show up. "I imagine you employ a large staff to maintain the place," she said casually.

Davide glanced at her, smiling thinly. "Not large, no." He handed her a glass of iced tea and poured another one for Neve. "Shall we proceed into the courtyard?" Davide took the tray with the two drinks and set it down on the bistro table. He pulled out a chair for her and Neve before going back to get the box of pastries.

Neve saw her mother's sculpted eyebrows lift when he returned. "I'm presuming that my daughter's reputation will remain intact while she's here?"

*"Mother!"*

"Now, Neve, I'm sure Signor Cortese can understand a mother's protectiveness…"

Neve shot her mother an icy look. "I'm going to check on Bianca," she said stiffly. Her stomach churning, she left, resisting the urge to slam the door behind her.

"Well, it seems my daughter doesn't appreciate my directness," Lois said before taking a sip of her iced tea. "A mother has to look out for her daughter's best interests," she sniffed, checking her manicured nails.

Davide leaned back in his chair and crossed his arms, his eyes pinning hers. "Have you ever thought, Signora Wilder, that your daughter can look out for her own best interests? She's not a child anymore…"

Lois blinked. "Have you ever raised a daughter? Because if you haven't, you couldn't possibly understand."

Davide felt a twinge in his chest. "I'm raising my niece, Bianca," he said curtly.

"Well, then, Signor Cortese, you can understand my point." Lois looked at him with a triumphant smile.

"And I can understand Neve's point," he said without smiling. "She can make decisions on her own."

"Apparently." Lois nodded. "Applying for this position and getting hired was quite a surprise to me."

"She was the most qualified of the applicants," Davide said crisply. "And she has not disappointed. In fact, *signora*, your daughter's personality and skills with my niece have exceeded my expectations."

"I'm glad to hear it. She's quite valued as a teacher back home. She had passed up the opportunity to work in the family computer business and chose teaching instead."

"She chose well. Neve is a natural around children and I'm glad she accepted the position of nanny for Bianca." He leaned forward and looked at her squarely. "So tell me, why have *you* come back to Valdoro?"

She looked taken aback that he would ask such a question. "I thought it would be nice to catch up with my friends at the Villa Morgana. And check in on Neve. Spend time with her on her days off."

Davide's eyebrows lifted. Neve had been right. Her mother couldn't untie the apron strings. Well, maybe it was time someone gave her a hand...and a firm one at that.

"Well, I'm afraid you're going to be disappointed, *signora*. I've already made arrangements to take your daughter sightseeing on her days off. It's the least I can do for her exceptional care of Bianca."

Lois blinked at him. "Really? Why would you—?"

"Because I've wanted to be with your daughter since I saw her eight years ago."

"You've what? Wh-what are you saying?" Lois sputtered. "What do you mean?"

Davide reached into his pocket and handed her the note. She read it, flipped it over, then looked up at him sharply, before reading the note again. "*Y-you* were the one who wanted to meet Neve?"

He nodded and took back the note. "And you were the one who kept it from happening." His words were stone cold.

Despite being in the shade, Lois reached for her napkin to wipe her forehead. "I—I won't apologize for that. Neve was young and—"

"She was eighteen," Davide replied curtly. "And I was—"

"You were out of line," Lois snapped. "And not suited—"

"Because I was working on a farm and therefore too lowly for your daughter?" Davide kept his voice steady, despite the agitation that he felt in his gut. "Tell me, *signora*, how did you manage to intercept the note? My friend, Agostino, slid it under Neve's door after going to the villa to give his mother a message…"

"I saw him do it and take off, and fortunately Neve hadn't come out of the shower." Lois fell silent for a moment, lost in her thoughts. "I replied and put it back in the envelope and then placed it under the flowerpot by the front door, as per the instructions on the envelope." She gazed at Davide defensively. "I did what I thought was right."

"I can't argue that," Davide replied coolly. "And we can't change the past. Or your feelings that I should remember my *place*. What's done is done." He leaned forward. "But things are different now. Neve is an adult and it would be nice if you treated her like one and stopped trying to control her life. She doesn't need your approval or your interference. *And neither do I.*"

Lois opened her mouth as if to protest, then promptly shut it. She stared at Davide for a few moments. "Well, *I've* been told."

Davide looked hard at the woman who had manipulated Neve's life since she was a child—and still seemed reluctant to relinquish total control. Eight years ago he might have had a difficult time confronting someone like her, but now he had no qualms about expressing his feelings, and no fears that he had to remember his *place*. "I think if you really gave it some thought you'd see that you deserved it, Signora Wilder. *You* were the one who was out of line."

Davide's piercing gaze didn't falter. He watched the play of emotions on her face: the furrowing of eyebrows, the arrogant tilt of her head at his effrontery and the wide-eyed blinking, probably from the shock of being brought down a few pegs.

Davide stood up. "Now, if you'll excuse me, I'll go and see if Neve is ready to come back down." He nodded and began to walk away. When he got to the door, he turned around. "Oh, by the way, Signora Wilder, your daughter is old enough to make adult decisions about her reputation. You would do well to let go of those apron strings…"

He met Neve as she was coming down the stairs. "I have some work to do," he said. "I'll listen for Bianca." He shook his head and gave an exaggerated sigh, aware that she was wondering how things had gone between him and her mother. "I think you and your mother might need some time alone…"

Davide took the remaining stairs two at a time, and after peeking into Bianca's room and seeing that she was napping soundly, he went to his study. He would give Neve and her mother ten minutes or so, and then go back down. After checking his email and replying to some of the messages regarding his planned renovations on another section of the castle, Davide checked his phone.

He'd give them a few more minutes…

Realizing it was rather dim in the room, he strode over to open the heavy shutters. The voices of Neve and her mother were suddenly audible, and although it hadn't even occurred to him that they'd be within hearing distance, and he had no intention of eavesdropping, the words Neve was saying immobilized him.

He had caught the last part of her sentence, the words

"peasant" and "unrefined" in a tone that clearly reflected her disgust. "Did you actually think I would give up my virginity to him? I had no intentions of sinking that low…"

Davide felt his heart crack as if someone had taken a hammer to the stone that it had instantly become. He missed Lois's reply. Neve went on, "He's not the same man he was back then, Mother. He's not in the same *place*. He's got money—lots of money—and more status than you could dream of—" Her voice sounded triumphant, as if she had just landed the biggest prize in the lottery.

Davide closed the shutters with a bang, not caring that they would hear him. He paced the room, disillusionment taking root in his gut and spreading tentacles of anger throughout him, constricting his heart to the point where he felt like collapsing.

*Neve was a great actress*, he thought bitterly, his hand gripping the back of his chair. And now he knew her true feelings. She may not have been the one who wrote that note, but clearly she was just like her mother, phony and obsessed about money and status. *And just as deceitful as the three nannies he had fired.*

Davide wanted to smash the chair against the wall. Neve wasn't interested in him as a person; no, she was obviously thrilled that she had hooked a guy who had an income and status even higher than hers. *Which is why she had allowed him to take her to his bed…* She had obviously thought it was a good trade…

He clenched his jaw so hard that the pain shot through to his temples. If Neve's note had devastated him eight years ago, her words moments ago had shattered every last ounce of trust and hope that had regenerated in his soul since she had arrived in Valdoro…

And now he'd have to go and face them both; mother and daughter, cut from the same rich cloth. His mouth twisted. He would keep his composure while Neve's mother was at the castle. *Put on the best act of his life.* And he would save his moment of reckoning with Neve till later...

He heard Bianca call out. His heart twisted, not only for himself, but for the way Bianca would feel when he eventually told her that Neve would no longer be staying as her nanny...

# CHAPTER TWENTY-THREE

NEVE FELT A tightening in her jaw as she walked into the courtyard. What exactly had her mother bargained for, coming to the castle? And how was she supposed to do her job with her mother around? As her mother gazed at her expectantly, Neve felt her stomach twist with anxiety.

What *she* really wanted was to confront her mother about her manipulative and controlling actions to prevent her from meeting with Davide. Her need to manage Neve's life a decade ago, and even now. Would Lois ever change?

Well, it was time *she* did. Perhaps she had subconsciously allowed her mother to keep controlling her life. Perhaps *she* hadn't been ready to let go of the apron strings.

*Not anymore.*

There was no time for small talk. Lois had arrived against her wishes, made plans to come to the castle, had expected Davide to drop everything to accommodate her and pick her up, and had even had the effrontery to insinuate that he was making Neve do housekeeping along with her nanny duties.

It *was* time for her to stand up to her mother.

"I'm surprised you were civil to my boss, Mom," she said curtly. "But then again, he's not a *peasant* and *unrefined* as you thought him a decade ago. Did you actually think I would give up my virginity to him? I had no intentions of sinking that low…"

Her mother opened her mouth to reply, but Neve wasn't ready to let her have her say. "I wouldn't be sinking so low as to sleep with anyone unless I was in love with him. I can't believe you wrote that note, Mom. *Really?* What were you afraid was going to happen? That he would whisk me up into the hills and have his way with me? *Come on*, I hardly had the personality to allow *that* to happen!" She shook her head angrily. "It's so sad that you couldn't even trust me."

"It wasn't *you* I didn't trust, darling. It was *him*. I imagined it was the young fellow who had been making eyes with you. *I saw what was in them.*"

"Good God," Neve sputtered. "Admit it, Mom. You thought he was *below* me. *Us.* You didn't want me associating with *a farmer*." Her cheeks burned. *"You would do well to remember your place,"* she mimicked.

"A mother has to look out for her daughter's best interests," her mother said, dabbing her forehead with her napkin.

"No, you have always looked out for *your* best interests," Neve shot back. "He's not the same man he was back then, Mother. He's not in the same *place*. He's got money—lots of money—and more status than you could dream of. And when you found out about my boss, you had to come here to see how Davide's position and status could benefit *you* in some way."

"I came here because I care about you, Neve. It's hard to relinquish motherhood. You'll find that out for yourself one day."

Her mother sounded hurt, but Neve wasn't finished. "You don't have to relinquish motherhood. You just have to relinquish control." She took a deep breath. "And you don't care about me as much as you care about *you* and how you appear to your high society circles," Neve retorted. "I'm done with all of it." She glared at her mother. "If you really care about me, you'll leave and let me do my job here."

"Well… I've been told. *Again*," Lois huffed. "I can't undo what I did eight years ago, Neve. And I'm sorry you feel the way you do about me." She turned to grab her handbag. "I hope you will eventually find it in your heart to forgive me. And don't worry. I won't bother you anymore while I'm in Valdoro."

She started to walk toward the entrance to the kitchen, then stopped to pull a smaller bag out of her handbag. "This is a little something for Bianca. I'll leave it on the kitchen counter."

Neve stared at the retreating figure of her mother. Deflated, she took the box of pastries and followed her inside. Davide and Bianca were approaching. Bianca let go of Davide's hand and ran up to Neve. Davide introduced Bianca to Lois.

"Are you coming to live with us, too?" Bianca asked.

Lois gave an embarrassed laugh. "No, dear. I was just here for a visit."

"I'll drive your mother back to the Villa Morgana," Davide said coolly. "Bianca can stay and have a treat. I won't be long."

After they left, Lois walking stiffly past her, Neve tried to ignore the churning in her stomach. She gave Bianca a snack of almond cookies and milk, and after putting the pastry box in the fridge, Neve took the bag that was on the counter. "Come and open your gift, Bianca," she said brightly, not wanting to show Bianca how shaken the confrontation with her mother had left her.

Bianca ran over and pulled the tissue from the bag, letting it fall to the floor in her excitement. Neve picked it up and when her gaze shifted to the gift in Bianca's hand, she gulped.

It was a photo frame with a three-dimensional angel on one side. The top of the frame showed a sky with glittering stars, and the angel's arms were uplifted to hold one of them. The text at the bottom of the frame read: *Love never dies; it's true. Like the stars in the heavens, our love shines for you.*

And she had included a card.

To Bianca,
    For you to keep a special photo of your mommy and daddy.
God bless you.
Lois Wilder.

Neve didn't know how she had kept it together after seeing her mother's gift and note. She had set the picture frame on the counter, holding her tears back, and had ushered Bianca upstairs to get her overnight bag ready. Signora Lucia would be arriving to pick up Bianca later in the afternoon, Davide had said, which could be anytime now.

She arrived before Davide got back. Neve answered the door to greet her and Rosalia, and after Bianca had rushed to give them both a hug, Neve chatted with Lucia briefly and wished them all a good time. Neve almost lost her balance when Bianca unexpectedly turned around and hugged her around the waist. "*Arrivederci*, Bianca Neve," she giggled, before following Lucia out to her car.

Neve closed the door and promptly burst into tears.

# CHAPTER TWENTY-FOUR

NEVE WAS STILL standing there moments later, staring out toward the dark strip of the Ionian Sea, when Davide returned. She felt the corners of her eyes prickling, and as he walked toward her, her tears prevented her from seeing him clearly. She wiped them hastily with her hands, and when her vision cleared, Davide was next to her, but instead of the look of concern that she was expecting, his face was expressionless, except for the hard line of his mouth.

She frowned. "What's the matter, Davide? Did my mother say something to upset you?"

He gave a harsh laugh. "No, it's not what your mother said that upset me." His eyes glinted. "It's what I heard *you* say..." He gestured toward the door. "Let's take this inside. I need a drink."

Neve followed him numbly. *What had she said to have caused Davide to speak to her so icily?* When they were in the kitchen, he poured himself a shot of brandy. She waited by the island, her stomach twisting apprehensively.

After he had downed it, he poured himself another one. Neve's heart thudded in her chest. *Why was he acting this way?*

"Davide, what is going on? Why—?"

"Why do I want to drink myself into oblivion tonight?" he rasped. "I'll tell you why, Signorina Neve." He spat out her name as if it was poison. "Because I hate myself for having trusted you. For believing that you…that you had *feelings* for me." His eyes narrowed. "What a fool I was, to think that you were any better than your mother." He swallowed his second drink. "You and your mother are a great team," he sneered. "You were both disgusted eight years ago when I was a *peasant* and *unrefined*, but how quickly you both changed your tune when you found out I had plenty of money and status…" He reached again for the bottle.

"No! Davide, don't! Please!" Neve grabbed his arm. "I don't know where you got these ideas…"

Davide's gaze swiveled to her hand and frowning, he pried her fingers off him. "You can cut the act now, Neve. I got those ideas from *you*, from what you said to your mother in the courtyard." He raked his hand through his hair. "Here, let me refresh your memory: *Did you actually think I would give up my virginity to him? I had no intentions of sinking that low…* But you had no problem sinking into my bed when you discovered I had more money and status than you could ever imagine. You and your mother can shake hands," he said icily. "And you can start packing. I'll have Lucia book the first possible flight back to Vancouver."

Neve froze as Davide brushed past her to stalk out of the room and into the courtyard.

*"Oh. My. God."*

She felt her eyes welling up. The glare he had fixed her with had pierced her to the core. *Such disgust in the depths of his eyes…* Neve blinked, but she could not stem the flow of tears. *How could Davide believe she had been so conniving?* With a sob, she ran up to her room and collapsed on the bed, letting herself cry until she was depleted.

When she got up and went to splash cold water on her face, she looked at the bathroom mirror and cringed at her red-rimmed eyes and mottled cheeks. With a heavy heart, she took her suitcase and started packing her clothes into it. Halfway through, she stopped.

*What was she doing?* She was not going to abandon Bianca, and she certainly wasn't going to accept Davide's damning judgment of her.

She *had* to find him and convince him that he had been wrong…

Davide's garden had always been a place of relaxation for him, but this time, his nerves were too jangled to allow him any hope of destressing. He had strode past the spot where he had kissed Neve and the pain that was already throbbing in his chest had intensified. He had to get out of there and away from the castle. Drive anywhere to distance himself from Neve.

He had just entered the kitchen when Neve appeared and planted herself in front of him, her eyes puffy and red.

"You said you were a fool, Davide. And you *were*, to believe those words you obviously heard without listening to the whole conversation. And I'm not leaving this castle, let alone this country, dammit, until I make you understand." Her eyes bored into his. "I'm not losing you again."

Davide's jaw tensed and he gripped the edge of the island chair. But as Neve kept talking, the muscles in his face and hand began to relax.

"I love *you*, not your money, Davide, and I would be happy living in a cave with you." Neve's eyes glittered. "And I've loved you from the day you stared at me across the road with your beautiful black eyes…"

When she was done, Davide groaned as he pulled her to him tightly. "I'm so sorry, *tesoro*. When I heard you say those words to your mother, my heart crumbled…" He brushed soft kisses on her cheeks. "Don't cry, *amore mio*."

As he reached for the box of tissues on the counter, his gaze fell on the photo frame. He picked it up and raised an eyebrow at Neve.

"My mother brought that for Bianca," Neve said, choking on her words.

Davide read the text on the frame. He set the frame down and closed his eyes. It felt like someone was squeezing his heart. *Hard.* He opened his eyes when he felt Neve wrap her arms around him. He swallowed.

"I miss her," he said, his voice cracking. "Why did this have to happen? To them, to Bianca… *She didn't deserve this.*"

"No child does."

Neve's soft voice and the compassion in her eyes pierced Davide's heart. He felt the pain and grief that he had been holding back for Bianca's sake begin to seep out. Letting out a moan, he broke away from Neve and went to sit down on the leather couch in the living room. He covered his face in his hands and tried to control the dam that was about to break within him. But when Neve came over to sit next to him and put her arm around him, the dam collapsed. He let the grief for the loss of his sister and brother-in-law burst out of him in deep sobs.

The feel of Neve's fingertips caressing his temples and face was calming. He inhaled and exhaled deeply. And then he turned to face her, looking deep into her eyes. He brought her fingers to his lips and brushed them with soft kisses. "Let's get out of here, *tesoro*," he murmured. "I want to take you somewhere special tonight."

## CHAPTER TWENTY-FIVE

NEVE FELT RENEWED after her shower. She quickly dried off and chose a midnight-blue halter dress that fell just above her knees and a shimmering rose shawl. In case Davide was planning a walk along the coast, Neve decided on a pair of dressy navy sandals with laces that tied up at her calves. The anticipation of the evening and night ahead with Davide all to herself had her pulse spiking. Trying to keep her hand steady, she applied some dark brown eyeliner and a gentle brush of blue eyeshadow. And a rose lipstick to match her shawl.

She left her hair down but used her curling iron to give it extra body, and satisfied with the way she looked, she grabbed a navy clutch and made her way downstairs.

Davide was waiting in the foyer. He stood up when he saw her at the top of the stairs and strode over to the end of the stairway to wait for her. As she approached the final curve of the stairway, Neve could see the approving spark in his eyes as his gaze swept over her.

She reciprocated the gaze, her heart drumming at how incredibly handsome he was, with his well-fitting dark gray trousers and maroon shirt emphasizing his strong, muscled body. He was holding a single rose in his hands, and as she reached the bottom step, he held it out to her with a smile that sent her heart leaping.

Davide held out his other hand and led her outside toward his Lamborghini. Moments later, as he began the curving descent down the mountainside, Neve held her breath. She gasped at a few hairpin turns, and on one them, her hand impulsively shot out to grasp hold of Davide. He just smiled and when he reached the base of the mountain, he veered off in the direction of the interior, and not the coast, as he had originally mentioned.

"I'm heading to the *other* coast," he said, flashing Neve a grin. "And before too long, we'll be passing through the Aspromonte mountain range." He raised an eyebrow. "Brigand territory in the eighteen-sixties…"

The countryside took on a muted aspect as twilight set in. They passed through vast stretches of olive groves and craggy limestone hills, their shapes and shadows lending a haunting quality to the landscape. With the sensual thrum of the engine and the luxurious comfort of the vehicle, Neve couldn't help but relax, and she settled back in her seat and allowed her eyelids to close…

A soft pressure on her lips woke her up and her eyes blinked open. Davide's face was inches away from hers. She felt her pulse accelerate.

"We're here, Neve. And you must not have been under a deep spell, since it took only one kiss to wake you up…"

Neve quickly straightened in her seat. "Where are we?"

"In the Marina di Scilla, about twenty-two kilometers north of Reggio di Calabria on the Strait of Messina. *Andiamo*, the place where I want to take you is in walking distance."

Davide had parked on the side of the street flanking the beach. He climbed out of the car and opened the door for Neve. She stepped out and stood mesmerized by the yellow lights illuminating the clustered three-story houses across the beach and up the promontory to the castle that rose out of the hill, with its stark sides and square windows overlooking the hamlet and the strait. It looked like something out of a fairy tale.

"That's the Castello Ruffo," Davide said. "It was built by the priests in a time when they needed to protect themselves against Saracen invasions. Nowadays it's used for exhibitions and conferences."

Lampposts illuminated the stretch of beach where people were strolling, children were playing and others were dining. The aromas from the beachside restaurants were making Neve's mouth water.

As they walked along the road, with Davide's arm around her, Neve felt a contentedness she had never felt before. And despite the earlier confrontation with her mother, Neve resolved to make things right between them. Lois's thoughtfulness toward Bianca had touched her, and she hoped that they could work out their problems and come to a new understanding. And maybe in time, Davide could forgive her mother, as well.

Davide turned into a narrow alley that meandered past terraced steps and balconies festooned with geraniums and bougainvillea. These houses were steps from the strait, and the faint scent of salt and fish hung in the air.

A few moments later he was ushering Neve into an exclusive waterfront *trattoria* with a terrace that jutted out over the water. The waiter, who greeted Davide by name, led them to a table in a far corner of the terrace. The lights illuminating the terrace were reflected in the water around them, and with the movement of the waves, it gave Neve the impression that they were suspended above twinkling stars.

Davide pointed to the breakers in the distance. "That's the site of the sea witch, Scylla, the whirlpool personified in Greek mythology as a female monster devouring sailors and impeding the way of the hero Odysseus…" He turned to her, his gaze piercing. "You know, Neve, when I first saw you on my computer screen, I thought you might very well be a sea witch, with those mesmerizing eyes…"

Neve pretended to pout. "That wasn't the first time you thought me a witch."

At Davide's puzzled look, she added, "After you got that note and thought that I had written it…you must have thought me cruel and heartless."

Davide couldn't lie. "I was confused," he murmured. "What I had seen—or thought I had seen—in your eyes was so different from what I had seen written on that note."

"Did you hate me?" she whispered.

"I was crushed," he rasped, "but I never hated you. I admit, it was hard on my ego. But I think I despised myself, for not being your equal, for not being good enough for you."

"That was my mother's opinion, not mine. I wish I had seen the note…" Neve said wistfully.

"It wasn't meant to be…at least not then. If you had come, we might have stolen a kiss. But our destiny was not to meet that night, but eight years later. Our time is *now*."

The waiter approached and Davide ordered an aperitif for both of them and fried calamari as an appetizer followed by eggplant parmigiana and grilled swordfish.

After the waiter left, Davide rose and took Neve's hand. The way she looked in her blue dress and filmy shawl sent his pulse racing. He led her to the railing and for a few moments they looked up at the stars and the lights twinkling in the water. And then, with a muffled groan, he pulled her closer and inhaled the sweet floral scent at her temples.

"I suffered, Neve, losing you before I could even tell you how I felt… But maybe I would have suffered even more if I had spent treasured moments with you and then had had to let you go. Who would have ever believed that destiny would lead us to one another again?"

"I never really believed in destiny before…until now," Neve sighed, resting her head against his chest.

Out of the corner of his eye, Davide saw the waiter set down the drinks and appetizer on their table, but he didn't want to let Neve out of his arms. *Or out of his life.*

"I'm hungry," he whispered huskily against her ear. "For you." He drew back so she could see the love and passion in his eyes. "*Ti amo, tesoro mio.* You are my treasure, Neve, and I will love and honor you for the rest of my life, if you will have me. And Bianca."

Neve's eyes glistened. "*Yes.* I wouldn't have it any other way!" She gave him a lingering kiss. "*Ti amo*, Davide," she told him breathlessly. "And I'm just as hungry." She let out a tinkling laugh. "Let's eat, and we can have *dessert* back at the castle."

By the time they arrived at the castle, Neve was feeling drowsy from the effects of their fabulous dinner and wine. Before she knew it, Davide had scooped her up in his arms and was carrying her into the castle and up the stairs…

He deposited her gently on his bed and removed her shoes. "Don't move," he ordered gruffly and disappeared into his walk-in closet. When he returned, he was carrying a decorative box. He held it out to her somewhat sheepishly.

Neve glanced through the transparent cover and recognized the filmy coral nightgown she had liked at the market. She blinked in disbelief, and then gave Davide a teasing smile. "Either you were psychic or just confident."

"Impulsive and hopeful would be more accurate." He gave her a scorching kiss. "Would you like to wear it tonight, Bianca Neve, or on our honeymoon?"

# EPILOGUE

*Two weeks later*

DAVIDE GOT DOWN on one knee in the same spot where Neve had collided into him when they had first played hide-and-seek. He reached into his vest pocket and pulled out a silver box. When he opened it, Neve gasped. The platinum ring was stunning, with an exquisite two-carat diamond and four small diamonds on either side of the band.

"The eight diamonds represent the years I waited," he said huskily, taking her left hand and slipping the ring on her third finger. "And the round diamond represents my infinite love for you—"

"Can I come in now, Zio Davide?" Bianca called out impatiently, a few steps away.

Davide let his head drop in feigned despair and Neve laughed.

Bianca rushed into the space, her orca in hand. "Can I be your flower girl?" she cried excitedly, clasping Neve's arm.

Neve bent down and gathered Bianca in a hug. "I wouldn't dream of having anyone else, *tesoro*."

"Oh, Bianca!" Lois Wilder joined them, throwing her hands up. "I told you I'd give you the signal when to go in, sweetheart," she said. "Oh, well!" She looked at Neve and Davide, who was still down on one knee, and smiled. "It's time for all of us to celebrate. Come on. I'm treating at the Pasticceria Michelina!" She gave Neve a hug. "I think I owe you two *that*, at the very least. Congratulations, darling!"

After Lois and Bianca had left, Davide held out his hand. Neve slipped her hand into his, and perched herself on his knee, her eyes glittering along with her ring. "*Sposami*, Neve," he said huskily.

Neve looked deep into Davide's eyes. "*Sì*, of course I will marry you, *amore*."

She leaned forward, but suddenly his knee shifted and she lost her balance, sending them both tumbling onto the grass, and the scent of the pink magnolia flowers was as sweet as their kiss.

\* \* \* \* \*

# FIANCÉ IN NAME ONLY

## MAUREEN CHILD

To my mom, Sallye Carberry, and my aunt, Margie Fontenot, for too many reasons to list. They are the original Matriarchs. Love you.

# One

"Sorry about this," Micah Hunter said. "I really liked you a lot, but you had to die."

Leaning back in his desk chair, Micah's gaze scanned the last few lines of the scene he'd just finished writing. He gave a small sigh of satisfaction at the death of one of his more memorable characters, then closed the lid of the laptop.

He'd already been working for four hours and it was past time for a break. "Problem is," he muttered, standing up and walking to the window overlooking the front of the house, "there's nowhere to go."

Idly he pulled out his cell phone, hit speed dial, then listened to the phone ring for a second or two. Finally a man came on the other line.

"How did I let you talk me into coming here for six months?"

Sam Hellman laughed. "Good to talk to you, too, man."

"Yeah." Of course his best friend was amused. Hell, if Micah wasn't the one stranded here in small-town America, he might be amused, too. As it was, though, he didn't see a damn thing funny about it. Micah pushed one hand through his hair and stared out at the so-called view. The house he was currently renting was an actual Victorian mansion set back from a wide street that was lined by gigantic, probably ancient, trees, now gold and red as their leaves changed and died. The sky was a brilliant blue, the autumn sun peeking out from behind thick white clouds. It was quiet, he thought. So quiet it was damn near creepy.

And since the suspense/horror novels Micah was known for routinely hit number one on the *New York Times* bestseller list, he knew a thing or two about *creepy*.

"Seriously, Sam, I'm stuck here for another four months because you talked me into signing the lease."

Sam laughed. "You're stuck there because you never could turn down a challenge."

Harsh but true. Nobody knew that about Micah better than Sam. They'd met when they were both kids, serving on the same US Navy ship. Sam had run away from his wealthy family's expectations, and Micah had been running from a past filled with foster homes, lies and broken promises. The two of them had connected and then stayed in touch when their enlistments were up.

Sam had returned to New York and the literary agency his grandfather had founded—discovering, after being away for a while, that he actually *wanted* to be a part of the family business. Micah had taken any construction job he could find while he spent every other waking moment working on a novel.

Even as a kid, Micah had known he wanted to write books. And when he finally started writing, it seemed the words couldn't pour out of his mind fast enough. He typed long into the night, losing himself in the story developing on the screen. Finishing that first book, he'd felt like a champion runner—exhausted, satisfied and triumphant.

He'd sent that first novel to Sam, who'd had a few million suggestions to make it even better. Nobody liked being told to change something they thought was already great, but Micah had been so determined to reach his goal, he'd made most of the changes. And the book sold almost immediately for a modest advance that Micah was more proud of than anything he'd ever earned before.

That book was the precursor of things to come. With his second book, word-of-mouth advertising made it a viral sensation and had it rocketing up the bestseller lists. Before he knew it, Micah's dreams were a reality. Sam and Micah had worked together ever since and they'd made a hell of a team. But because they were such good friends, Sam had known exactly how to set Micah up.

"This is payback because I beat you at downhill snowboarding last winter, isn't it?"

"Would I do something that petty?" Sam asked, laughter in his voice.

"Yeah, you would." Micah shook his head.

"Okay...yeah, probably," Sam agreed. "*But*, you're the one who took the bet. Live in a small town for six months."

"True." *How bad could it be?* He remembered asking himself that before signing the lease with his landlady,

Kelly Flynn. Now, two months into his stay, Micah had the answer to that question.

"And, hey, research," Sam pointed out. "The book you're working on now is *set* in a small town. Good to know these things firsthand."

"Ever heard of Google?" Micah laughed. "And the book I set in Atlantis, how'd I research that one?"

"Not the point," Sam said. "The point is, Jenny and I loved that house you're in when we were there a couple years ago. And, okay, Banner's a small town, but they've got good pizza."

Micah would admit to that. He had Pizza Bowl on speed dial.

"Like I said, in another month or so, you'll feel differently," Sam said. "You'll be out enjoying all that fresh powder on the mountains and you won't mind it so much."

Micah wasn't so sure about that. But he had to admit it was a great house. He glanced around the second-floor room he'd claimed as a temporary office. The ceilings were high, the rooms were big and the view of the mountains was beautiful. The whole house had a lot of character, which he appreciated, but damned if he didn't feel like a phantom or something, wandering through the big place. He'd never had so much space all to himself and Micah could admit, at least to himself, that sometimes it creeped him out.

Hell, in the city—any city—there were lights. People. Noise. Here, the nights were darker than anything he'd ever known. Even in the navy, on board a ship, there were enough lights that the stars were muted in the night sky. But Banner, Utah, was listed on the International Dark-Sky roster because it lay just beyond a ridge that wiped out the haze of light reflection from Salt Lake City.

Here, at night, you could look up and see the Milky Way and an explosion of stars that was as beautiful as it was humbling. He'd never seen skies like these before, and he was willing to acknowledge that the beauty of it took some of the sting out of being marooned at the back end of beyond.

"How's the book coming?" Sam asked suddenly.

The change in subject threw him for a second, but Micah was grateful for the shift. "Good. Actually just killed the bakery guy."

"That's a shame. Love a good bakery guy." Sam laughed. "How'd he buy it?"

"Pretty grisly," Micah said, and began pacing the confines of his office. "The killer drowned him in the doughnut fryer vat of hot oil."

"Damn, man…that is gross." Sam took a breath and sighed it out. "You may have put me off doughnuts."

Good to know the murder he'd just written was going to hit home for people.

"Not for long, I'll bet," Micah mused.

"The copy editor will probably get sick, but your fans will love it," Sam assured him. "And speaking of fans, any of them show up in town yet?"

"Not yet, but it's only a matter of time." Frowning, he looked out the window and checked up and down the street, half expecting to see someone with a camera casing the house, hoping for a shot of him.

One of the reasons Micah never remained in one place too long was because his more devoted fans had a way of tracking him down. They would just show up at whatever hotel he was staying in, assuming he'd be happy to see them. Most were harmless, sure, but Micah knew "fan" could turn into "fanatic" in a flash.

He'd had a few talk their way into his hotel rooms, join him uninvited at dinner, acting as though they were either old friends or long-lost lovers. Thanks to social media, there was always someone reporting on where he had been seen last or where he was currently holed up. So he changed hotels after every book, always staying in big cities where he could get lost in the crowds and living in five-star hotels that promised security.

Until now, that is.

"No one's going to look for you in a tiny mountain town," Sam said.

"Yeah, that's what I thought when I was at the hotel in Switzerland," Micah reminded his friend. "Until that guy showed up determined to pummel me because his girlfriend was in love with me."

Sam laughed again and Micah just shook his head. Okay, it was funny now, but having some guy you didn't know ambush you in a hotel lobby wasn't something he wanted to repeat.

"This is probably the best thing you could have done," Sam said. "Staying in Banner and living in a house, not a hotel, will throw off the fans hunting for you."

"Yeah, well, it should. It's throwing me off, that's for sure." His scowl tightened. "It's too damn quiet here."

"Want me to send you a recording of Manhattan traffic? You could play it while you write."

"Funny," Micah said, and didn't even admit to himself that the idea wasn't half bad. "Why haven't I fired you?"

"Because I make us both a boatload of money, my friend."

Well, Sam had him there. "Right. Knew there was a reason."

"And because I'm charming, funny and about the only

person in the world who's willing to put up with the crappy attitude."

Micah laughed now. He had a point. Right from the beginning, when they'd met on the aircraft carrier they'd served on, Sam had offered friendship—something Micah had rarely known. Growing up in the foster care system, moving from home to home, Micah had never stayed anywhere long enough to make friends. Which was probably a good thing since he wouldn't have been able to *keep* a friend, what with relocating all the damn time.

So he appreciated having Sam in his life—even when the man bugged the hell out of him. "That's great, thanks."

"No problem. So what do you think of your landlady?"

Frowning, Micah silently acknowledged that he was trying to *not* think about Kelly Flynn. It wasn't working, but he kept trying.

For the last two months, he'd done everything he could to keep his distance because damned if he didn't want to get closer. But he didn't need an affair. He had to live here for another four months. If he started something with Kelly, it would make things…complicated.

If it was a one-night stand, she'd get pissy and he'd have to put up with it for four more months. If it was a long-running affair, then she'd be intruding on his writing time and spinning fantasies about a future that was never going to happen. He didn't need the drama. All he wanted was the time and space to write his book so he could get out of this tiny town and back to civilization.

"Hmm," Sam mused. "Silence. That tells me plenty."

"Tells you nothing," Micah argued, attempting to convince both himself *and* Sam. "Just like there's nothing going on."

"Are you sick?"

"What?"

"I mean, come on," Sam said, and Micah could imagine him leaning back in his desk chair, propping his feet up on the corner of his desk. He probably had his chair turned toward the windows so he could look out over Manhattan.

"Hell," Sam continued, "I'm married and I noticed her. She's gorgeous, and if you tell Jenny I said that I'll deny it."

Shaking his head, Micah looked down and watched Kelly work in the yard. The woman never relaxed. She was always moving, doing something. She had ten different jobs and today, apparently, still had the time to rake up fallen leaves and bag them. As he watched, she loaded up a wheelbarrow with several bags of leaves and headed for the curb.

Her long, reddish-gold hair was pulled into a ponytail at the back of her neck. She wore a dark green sweatshirt and worn blue jeans that cupped her behind and clung to her long legs. Black gloves covered her hands, and her black boots were scarred and scuffed from years of wear.

And though she had her back to the house, he knew her face. Soft, creamy skin, sprinkled with freckles across her nose and cheeks. Grass-green eyes that crinkled at the edges when she laughed and a wide, generous mouth that made Micah wonder what she would taste like.

Micah watched her unload the bags at the curb, then wave to a neighbor across the street. He knew she'd be smiling and his brain filled with her image. Deliberately, he turned his back on the window, shut the image of Kelly out of his mind and walked back to his chair. "Yeah, she's pretty."

Sam laughed. "Feel the enthusiasm."

Oh, there was plenty of enthusiasm, Micah thought. Too much. Which was the problem. "I'm not here looking for a woman, Sam. I'm here to work."

"That's just sad."

He had to agree. "Thanks. So why'd you call me again?"

"Damn, you need to take a break. You're the one who called me, remember?"

"Right." He pushed one hand through his hair. Maybe he did need a damn break. He'd been working pretty much nonstop for the last two months. No wonder this place was starting to feel claustrophobic in spite of its size. "That's a good idea. I'll take a drive. Clear my head."

"Invite the landlady along," Sam urged. "She could show you around since I'm guessing you've hardly left that big old house since you got there."

"Good guess. But not looking for a guide, either."

"What are you looking for?"

"I'll let you know when I find it," Micah said, and hung up.

"So how's our famous writer doing?"

Kelly grinned at her neighbor. Sally Hartsfield was the nosiest human being on the face of the planet. She and her sister, Margie, were both spinsters in their nineties, and spent most of their days looking out the windows to keep an eye on what was happening in the neighborhood.

"Busy, I guess," Kelly said, with a quick glance over her shoulder at the second-story window where she'd caught a glimpse of Micah earlier. He wasn't there anymore and she felt a small twist of disappointment as she turned back to Sally. "He told me when he moved in that he would be buried in work and didn't want to be disturbed."

"Hmm." Sally's gaze flicked briefly to that window, too. "You know, that last book of his gave me nightmares. Makes you wonder how he can stand being all alone like that when he's writing such dark, scary things…"

Kelly agreed. She'd only read one of Micah's seven books because it had scared her so badly she'd slept with a light on for two weeks. When she read a book, she wanted cheerful escape, not terror-inducing suspense. "I guess he likes it that way," she said.

"Well, everybody's different," Sally pointed out. "And I say thank goodness. Can you imagine how boring life would be if we were all the same?" She shook her head and her densely-sprayed curls never moved. "Why, there'd be nothing to talk about."

And that would be the real shame as far as Sally was concerned, Kelly knew. The woman could pry a nugget of information out of a rock.

"He is a good-looking man though, isn't he?" Sally asked, a speculative gleam in her eyes.

*Good-looking?* Oh, Micah Hunter was well beyond that. The picture on the back of his books showed him as dark and brooding, and that was probably done purposefully, considering what he wrote. But the man in person was so much more. His thick brown hair was perpetually rumpled, as if he'd just rolled out of bed. His eyes were the color of rich, dark coffee, and when he forgot to shave for a day or two, the stubble on his face gave him the air of a pirate.

His shoulders were broad, his hips were narrow and

he was tall enough that even Kelly's own five feet, eight inches felt diminutive alongside him. He was the kind of man who walked into a room and simply took it over whether he was trying to or not. Kelly imagined every woman who ever met him had done a little daydreaming about Micah. Even, it seemed, Sally Hartsfield, who had a grandson as old as Micah.

"He is nice looking," Kelly finally said when she noticed Sally staring at her.

The older woman sighed and fisted both hands on her hips. "Kelly Flynn, what is wrong with you? Your Sean's been gone four years. Why, if I was your age…"

Kelly stiffened at the mention of her late husband, automatically raising her defenses. Sally must have noticed her reaction because the woman stopped short, offered a smile and, thank heaven, a change of subject.

"Anyway, I hear you're showing the Polk place this afternoon to a couple coming in from California of all places."

Impressed as well as a little irked, Kelly stared at the older woman. Honestly, Kelly had only gotten this appointment to show a house the day before. "How did you know that?"

Sally waved a hand. "Oh, I have my ways."

Kelly had long suspected that her elderly neighbors had an army of spies stationed all over Banner, Utah, and this just cemented that idea. "Well, you're right, Sally, so I'd better get going. I still have to shower and change."

"Of course, dear, you go right ahead." She checked the window again and Kelly saw frustration on the woman's face when Micah didn't show up to be watched. "I've got things to do myself."

Kelly watched the woman hustle back across the street,

her bright pink sneakers practically glowing against all of the fallen leaves littering the ground. The ancient oaks that lined the street stretched out gnarly branches to almost make an arbor of gold-and-red leaves hanging over the wide road.

The houses were all different, everything from small stone cottages to the dignified Victorian where Kelly had grown up. They were all at least a hundred years old, but they were well cared for and the lawns were tidy. People in Banner stayed. They were born here, grew up here and eventually married, lived and died here.

That kind of continuity always comforted Kelly. She'd lived here since she was eight and her parents were killed in a car accident. She'd moved in with her grandparents and had become the center of their world. Now, her grandfather was dead and Gran had moved to Florida, leaving the big Victorian mansion and the caretaker's cottage at the back of the property to Kelly. Since living alone in that giant house would just be silly, Kelly rented it out and lived in the smaller cottage.

In the last three years, the Victorian had rarely been empty and when it wasn't rented out by vacationers, the house and grounds had become a favorite place for weddings, big parties and even, last year, a Girl Scout cookout in the huge backyard.

And, she thought, every Halloween, she turned the front of the Victorian into a haunted house.

"Have to get busy on that," she told herself. It was already the first of October and if she didn't get started, the whole month would slip past before she knew it.

Halfway up to the house, the front door opened and Micah stepped out. Kelly's heart gave a hard thump, and down low inside her she felt heat coil and tighten. Oh, boy. It had been four long years since her husband, Sean, had died, and since then she hadn't exactly done a lot of dating. That probably explained why she continued to have this over-the-top reaction to Micah.

Probably.

He wore a black leather jacket over a black T-shirt tucked into the black jeans he seemed to favor. Black boots finished off the look of Dangerous Male and as she admired the whole package, her heartbeat thundered loud enough to echo in her ears.

"Need some help?" he asked, jerking his head toward the wheelbarrow she was still holding on to.

"What? Oh. No." *Great, Kelly. Three. Separate. Words. Care to try for a sentence?* "I mean, it's empty, so not heavy. I'm just taking it around to the back."

"Okay." He came down the wide front steps to the brick walkway lined with chrysanthemums in bright, cheerful fall colors. "I'm taking a break. Thought I'd drive around. Get my bearings."

"After two months of being in Banner?" she asked, smiling. "Yeah, maybe it's time."

His mouth worked into a partial smile. "Any suggestions on the route I should take?"

She set the wheelbarrow down, flipped her ponytail over her shoulder and thought about it. "Just about any route you take is a pretty one. But if you're looking for a destination, you could drive through the canyon down to 89. There are a lot of produce stands there. You could pick me up a few pumpkins."

He tipped his head to one side and studied her, a flicker of what might have been amusement on his face. "Did I say I was going shopping?"

"No," she said, smiling. "But you could."

He blew out a breath, looked up and down the street, then shifted his gaze back to hers. "Or, you could ride with me and pick out your own pumpkins."

"Okay."

He nodded.

"No," she said. "Wait. Maybe not."

He frowned at her.

Having an audience while she argued with herself was a little embarrassing. She could tell from his expression that Micah didn't really want her along so, naturally, she really wanted to go. Even though she shouldn't. She already had plenty to do and maybe spending time with Micah Hunter wasn't the wisest choice, since he had the unerring ability to stir her up inside. But could she really resist the chance to make him as uncomfortable as he made her?

"I mean, sure," she said abruptly. "I'll go, but I'd have to be back in a couple of hours. I have a house to show this afternoon."

His eyebrows arched high on his forehead. "I can guarantee you I won't be spending two hours at a pumpkin stand." He tucked his hands into the pockets of his jacket. "So? Are you coming or not?"

Her eyes met his and in those dark brown depths, Kelly read the hope she would say *no*. So, of course, she said the only thing she could.

"I guess I am."

# Two

"Why are you buying pumpkins when you're growing your own?"

They were already halfway down the twisting canyon road. The mountains rose up on either side of the narrow pass. Wide stands of pine trees stood as tall and straight as soldiers, while oaks, maples and birch trees that grew within those stands splashed the dark green with wild bursts of fall color.

"And," Micah continued, "isn't there somewhere closer you could buy the damn things?"

She turned her head to look at his profile. "Sure there is, but the produce stands have the big ones."

Kelly could have sworn she actually *heard* his eyes roll. But she didn't care. It was a gorgeous fall day, she was taking a ride in a really gorgeous car—even though it was going too fast for the pass—and she was sitting beside a gorgeous man who made her nervous.

And wasn't that a surprise? Four years since her husband Sean had died and Micah was the first man to make her stomach flutter with the kind of nerves that she had suspected were dead or atrophied. The problem was, she didn't know if she was glad of the appearance of those nerves or not.

Kelly rolled down the window and let the cold fall air slap at her in lieu of a cold shower. When she got a grip, she shifted in her seat to look at Micah. "Because I grow those to give away to the kids in the neighborhood."

"And you can't keep some for yourself?"

"I could, but where's the fun in that?"

"Fun?" he repeated. "I've seen you out there weeding, clipping and whatever else it is you do to those plants. That's fun?"

"For me it is." The wind whipped her ponytail across her face and she pushed it aside to look at him. "Besides, if I was going to take lessons on fun from somebody, it wouldn't be you."

He snorted. "If you did, I'd show you more than pumpkins."

Her stomach swirled a little at the implied promise in those words, but she swallowed hard and stilled it. He was probably used to making coded statements designed to turn women into slavering puddles. So she wouldn't accommodate him. Yet.

"I'm not convinced," she said with a shrug. "You've been in town two months and you've hardly left the house."

"That's work. No time for fun."

"Just a chatterbox," she mumbled. Every word pried out of him felt like a victory.

"What?"

"Nothing," she said. "So, what's your idea of fun then?"

He took a moment to think it through, and said, "I'd start with chartering a private jet—"

"Your own personal jet," she said, stunned.

He glanced at her and shrugged. "I don't like sharing."

She laughed shortly as she thought about the last time she'd taken a flight out of Salt Lake City airport. Crowded onto a full flight, she'd sat between a talkative woman complaining about her grandchildren and a businessman whose briefcase poked her in the thigh every time he shifted in his seat. Okay, she could see where a private jet would be nice. "Well sure. Okay, your jet. Then what?"

He steered the Range Rover down the mountain road, taking the tight curves like a race-car driver. If Kelly let herself worry about it, she'd be clinging to the edges of her seat. So she didn't think about it.

"Well, it's October, so I'd go to Germany for Oktoberfest."

"Oh." That was so far out of her normal orbit she hardly knew what to say. Apparently, though, once you got Micah talking about something that interested him, he would keep going.

"It's a good place to study people."

"I bet," she murmured.

He ignored that, and said, "Writers tend to observe. Tourists. Locals. How people are interacting. Gives me ideas for the work."

"Like who to murder?"

"Among other things. I once killed a hotel manager in one of my books." He shrugged. "The guy was a jackass so, on paper at least, I got rid of him."

She stared at him. "Any plans to kill off your current landlady?"

"Not yet."

"Comforting."

"Anyway," he continued, "after a long weekend there, I'd go to England," he mused, seriously considering her question. "There's a hotel in Oxford I like."

"Not London?"

"Fewer people to recognize me in Oxford."

"That's a problem for you?" she asked.

"It can be." He took another curve that had Kelly swerving into him. He didn't seem to notice. "Thanks to social media, my fans tend to track me down. It gets annoying."

She could understand that. The photo of Micah on the back of his books was mesmerizing. She'd spent a bit of time herself studying his eyes, the way his hair tumbled over his forehead, the strong set of his jaw.

"Maybe you should take your photo off your books."

"Believe me, I've suggested it," Micah said. "The publisher won't do it."

Kelly really didn't have anything to add to the conversation. She'd never been followed by strangers desperate to be close to her and the farthest she'd ever traveled was on her last flight—to Florida to visit her grandmother. England? Germany? Not really in her lifestyle. She'd love to go to Europe. Someday. But it wouldn't be on a private jet.

She glanced out the window at the familiar landscape as it whizzed past and felt herself settle. Micah's life was so far removed from her own it made Kelly's head spin just thinking about it.

"One of these days," she said suddenly, shifting her gaze back to his profile, "I'd like to go to Scotland. See Edinburgh Castle."

"It's worth seeing," he assured her.

Of course he'd been there. Heck, he'd probably been *everywhere.* No wonder he stuck close to the house. Why would he be interested in looking around Banner, Utah? After the places he'd been, her small hometown probably appeared too boring to bother with. Well, maybe it wasn't up to the standards of Edinburgh, or Oktoberfest in Germany, but she loved it.

"Good to know," she said. "But until then, I'll plant pumpkins for the kids." She smiled to herself and let go of a twinge of envy still squeezing her insides. "I like everything about gardening. Watching the seeds sprout, then the vines spread and the pumpkins get bigger and brighter orange." Smiling, she continued. "I like how the kids on the street come by all the time, picking out the pumpkins they want, helping water, pulling weeds. They get really possessive about *their* pumpkins."

"Yeah," he said wryly. "I hear them."

He never took his eyes off the road, she noted. Was it because he was a careful driver, or was he just trying to avoid looking at her? Probably the latter. In the two months he'd been living in her Victorian, Micah Hunter had made eluding her an art form.

Sure, he was a writer, and he'd told her when he first arrived in town that he needed time alone to work. He wasn't interested in making friends, having visitors or a guided tour of her tiny town. Friendly? Not so much. Intriguing? Oh, yeah.

Could she help it if tall, dark and crabby appealed to her? Odd though, since her late husband, Sean, had been blond and blue-eyed, with an easy smile. And *nothing* about Micah was easy.

"You don't like kids?"

Briefly he slanted a look at her. "Didn't say that. Said I heard them. They're loud."

"Uh-huh," she said with a half smile. "And didn't you say last week that it was too quiet in Banner?"

His mouth tightened but, grudgingly, he nodded. "Point to you."

"Good. I like winning."

"One point doesn't mean you've won anything."

"How many points do I need then?"

A reluctant smile curved his mouth, then flashed away again. "At least eleven."

Wow. That half smile had come and gone so quickly it was like it had never been. Yet, her stomach was swirling and her mouth had gone dry. Kelly took a breath and slowly let it out again. She had to focus on what they were talking about, *not* what he was doing to her.

"Like ping-pong," she said, forcing a smile she didn't feel.

"Okay." He sounded amused.

"All right, good," Kelly said, leaning over to pat his arm mostly because she needed to convince herself she could touch him without going up in flames. But her fingers tingled, so she pulled them back fast. "Then it's one to nothing, my favor."

He shook his head. "You're actually going to keep score?"

"You started it. You gave me a point."

"Right. I'll make a note."

"No need, I'll keep track." She looked ahead because it was safer than looking at him. Then she smiled to herself. She'd gotten him to talk and had completely held her own in the conversation—until her imagination and hormones had thrown her off.

As long as she could keep those tingles and nerves in check, she could handle Mr. Magnetic.

For the next few days, Kelly was too busy to spend much time thinking about Micah. And that was just as well, she told herself. Mainly because the minute they returned from their pumpkin-shopping expedition, Micah had disappeared and she'd gotten the message.

Clearly he wanted her to know that their brief outing had been an aberration. He'd slipped back into his cave and she hadn't caught a glimpse of him since. Probably for the best, she assured herself. Easier to keep her mind on her own life, her own responsibilities if the only time she saw Micah was in her dreams.

Of course, that didn't make for restful sleeping, but she'd been tired before. One thing she hadn't experienced before were the completely over-the-top, sexy-enough-to-melt-your-brain dreams. She hated waking up hot and needy. Hated having to admit that all she really wanted to do was go back to sleep and dream again.

"And don't start thinking about those dreams or you won't get any work done at all," Kelly told herself firmly.

It wasn't hard to push Micah into the back of her mind, since she juggled so many jobs that sometimes she just ran from one to the next. Thankfully, that gave her little opportunity to sit and wonder if sex with Micah in real life would be as good as it was in her dreams.

Although if it was, she might not survive the experience.

"Still," she mused, "not a bad way to go."

She shook her head, dipped a brush into the orange tempera paint, wiped off the excess, then painted the first of an orchard of pumpkins onto the Coffee Cave's front window. Of all her different jobs, this was her favorite. Kelly loved painting holiday decorations on storefronts.

But she was also a virtual assistant, she ran websites for several local businesses, and was a Realtor who had just sold a house to that family from California. She was a gardener and landscape designer, and now she was thinking seriously about running for mayor in Banner's next election, since she was just horrified by some of the current mayor's plans for downtown. As she laid the paint out on the glass, her mind wandered.

Kelly had a business degree from Utah State, but once she'd graduated, she hadn't wanted to tie herself down to one particular job. She liked variety, liked being her own boss. When she'd decided to go into several different businesses, a couple of her friends had called her crazy. But she remembered Sean encouraging her, telling her to do whatever made her happy.

That had her pausing as thoughts of Sean drifted through her mind like a warm breeze on a cool day. A small ache settled around her heart. She still missed him even though his features were blurred in her mind now— like a watercolor painting left out in the rain.

She hated that. It felt like a betrayal of sorts, letting Sean fade. But it would have been impossible to keep living while holding on to the pain, too. Time passed whether you wanted it to or not. And you either kept up or got run over.

On that happy notion, Kelly paused long enough to look up and down Main Street. Instantly, she felt better. Banner was a beautiful little town and had been a great place to grow up. Coming here as a heartbroken eight-year-old, she'd fallen in love with the town, the woods, the rivers, the waterfalls and the people here.

Okay, Banner wasn't Edinburgh or Oxford or wherever, but it was…cozy. The buildings were mostly more than a hundred years old with creaky floors and brick walls. The sidewalks were narrow but neatly swept, and every one of the old lampposts boasted a basket of fall flowers at its base. In another month or so, there would be Christmas signs up and lights strung across the streets, and when the snow came, it would all look like a holiday painting. So, yes, she'd like to travel, see the world, but she would always come home to Banner.

Nodding to herself, she turned back to the window and quickly laid out the rest of the pumpkin patch along the bottom edge of the window.

"Well, that looks terrific already."

Kelly turned to grin at her friend. Terry Baker owned the coffee shop and made the best cinnamon rolls in the state. With short black hair, bright blue eyes and standing at about five foot two, Terry looked like an elf. Which she didn't find the least bit amusing.

The two of them had been friends since the third grade and nothing had changed over the years. Terry had been there for Kelly when Sean died. Now that Terry's military husband had deployed for the third time in four years, it was Kelly's turn to support her friend.

"Thanks, but I've got a long way to go yet," Kelly said, taking a quick look at the window and seeing a spot she'd have to fill in with a few baby pumpkins.

"Hence the latte I have brewed just for you." She held out the go-cup she carried.

"Hence?" Kelly took the coffee, savored a sip, then sighed in appreciation. "Have you been reading British mysteries again?"

"Nope." Terry stuffed her hands into her jeans pockets. "With my sad love life, I'm home every night watching the British mysteries on TV."

"Love lives can be overrated," Kelly said.

"Right." Terry nodded. "Who're you trying to convince? Me? Or you?"

"Me, obviously, since you're the only one of us with a man at the moment."

Terry leaned one shoulder against the pale rose-colored brick of her building. "I don't have one, either, trust me. It's impossible to have phone sex on an iPad when half of Jimmy's squad could walk in at any moment."

Kelly laughed, grabbed another brush and laid down a twining green vine connecting all of the pumpkins. "Okay, that would be awkward."

"Tell me about it. Remember when he called me as a surprise on my birthday and I jumped out of the shower to answer the call?" Terry shuddered dramatically. "I can still hear all the whistles from his friends who were there in the room."

Still laughing, Kelly said, "Well, that'll teach Jimmy to surprise you."

"No kidding. Now we make phone appointments." Terry grinned. "But enough about me. I hear you and the writer went for a long ride the other day."

"How did you—" Kelly stopped, blew out a breath and nodded. "Right. Sally."

"She and her sister came in for coffee yesterday and told me all about it," Terry admitted, tipping her head to one side to study her friend. "The question is, if there was something to know, why didn't I already know it?"

"Because it's nothing," Kelly said, focusing on her painting again. She added shadows and depth to the curling vines. "He took me to buy some pumpkins."

"Uh-huh. Sally says you were gone almost two hours. Either you're really picky about your pumpkins or something else was going on."

Kelly sighed. "We went for a ride."

"Uh-huh."

"I showed him around a little."

"Uh-huh."

"Nothing happened."

"Why not?"

Kelly just blinked. A couple of kids on skateboards shot down the sidewalk with a roar that startled her. "What?"

"Honey," Terry said, stepping close enough to drop one arm around Kelly's shoulders. "Sean's been gone four years. You haven't been on a single date in all that time. Now you've got this amazing-looking guy living in the Victorian for six months and you're not going to do anything about it?"

Laughing a little, Kelly shook her head again. "What should I do? Tie him up and have my way with him?"

Terry's eyes went a little dreamy. "Hmm…"

"Oh, stop it." But even as she said it, a rush of heat filled Kelly. She only enjoyed it for a second or two before tamping it right down and mentally putting out the fire.

Honestly, she didn't want or need the attraction she felt for Micah. He clearly wasn't interested and Kelly had already loved and lost. She really had zero interest in a romance. Of any kind.

"Okay, fine," Terry said, laughing. "If you're determined to shut yourself up in a closet, wrapped in wool or something, there's nothing I can do about it. But I swear, if the CIA ever needs more spies, I'm going to recommend Sally and Margie. Those two have their fingers on the pulse of everything that happens in town."

And lucky Kelly lived right across the street from them. Sean used to laugh when he saw the older ladies, noses pressed to the windows. He would sweep Kelly into an elaborate dip and kiss her senseless, saying, *"The reason they're so nosy is no one's ever kissed them senseless. So let's give them something to talk about."*

That memory brought a sad smile that she just as quickly let slide away. Remembering Sean meant not only the good times, but the pain of losing him. She'd lost enough in her life, Kelly told herself firmly.

First her parents when she was just a kid, then her grandfather, then Sean. Enough already. And the only way to ensure she never went through that kind of pain again was to never let herself get that close with anyone again.

She had Terry. Her grandmother. A couple of good friends.

Who needed a man?

Micah's image rose up in her mind and she heard a tiny voice inside her whisper, *You do. He's only here temporarily, why not take advantage? There's no future there, so no risk.*

True, Micah would only be in Banner for four more months, so it wasn't as if—no.

*Don't think about it.*

Sure. That would work.

"You know," Terry said, interrupting Kelly's stream of consciousness, "there's a guy in Jimmy's squad I think you'd really like..."

"Oh, no." Kelly shook her head firmly. "Don't go there, Terry. No setups. You know those never go well."

"He's a nice guy," her friend argued.

"I'm sure he's a prince," Kelly said. "But he's not *my* prince. I'm not looking for another man."

"Well, you should be." Terry folded her arms over her chest.

"Didn't you just say there was nothing you could do about it if I wanted to lock myself in a closet?"

"I hate seeing you alone all the time."

"*You're* alone," Kelly reminded her.

"For now, but Jimmy will be home in another couple of months."

"And I'm happy for you." Deliberately, Kelly turned back to her paints. She picked up the yellow and a small brush, then laid in the eyes on the first pumpkin. With the bright yellow, it would look like the pumpkin was lit by a candle. "I had a husband, Terry. Don't want another one."

From the corner of her eye, Kelly saw her friend's shoulders slump in defeat. "I didn't say I wanted you married."

"But you do."

"Not the point," Terry said stubbornly. "Sweetie, I know losing Sean was terrible. But you're too young to live the rest of your life like a vestal virgin."

Kelly laughed. "The virgin ship sailed a long time ago."

"You know what I mean."

Of course she did. Terry had been saying pretty much the same thing for the last two years. She just didn't understand that Kelly was too determined to avoid pain to ever take the kind of risk she was talking about. Loving was great. Losing was devastating, and she'd already lost enough, thanks.

"Yeah, I do, and I appreciate the thought—"

"No, you don't," Terry said.

"You're right, I don't." Kelly glanced at her friend and smiled to take the sting out of her words. "Honestly, you're as bad as Gran."

"Oh, low blow," Terry muttered. "She's still worried?"

"Ever since Sean died and it's gotten worse in the last year or so." She focused on the paints even while she kept talking. "Gran's even started making noises about moving back here so I won't be lonely."

"Oh, man." Terry sighed. "I thought she loved living in Florida with her sister."

"She *does*." Kelly crouched down to paint in the faces of three other pumpkins. "The two of them go to bingo and take trips with their seniors club. She's having a great time, but then she starts worrying about me and—"

Her cell phone rang and Kelly stood up to drag it from her jeans pocket. Glancing at the caller ID, she sighed and looked at Terry. "Speak of the devil…"

"Gran? Really?" Terry's eyes went dramatically wide. "Boy, her hearing's better than ever if she could catch us talking about her all the way from Florida!"

Kelly laughed. With a wince of guilt, she sent the call to voice mail.

"Seriously?" Terry sounded surprised. "You're not going to talk to her?"

"Having *one* conversation about my lack of a love life is enough for today."

"Fine." Terry held up both hands in surrender. "I'll back off. For now."

"Thanks." She tucked her phone away and tried not to feel badly about ditching her grandmother's call.

"*But*," Terry added before she went back into the cof-

fee shop, "just because you're not interested in a perma-
nent man…"

Kelly looked at her.

"…doesn't mean you can't enjoy a temporary one. I'm
just saying."

After she left, Kelly's brain was racing. *A temporary
man.* When she went back to her painting, she was still
thinking, and as an ephemeral plan began to build in her
mind, a speculative smile curved her mouth.

# Three

Micah hated cooking, but he'd learned a long time ago that man cannot live on takeout alone. Especially when you're in the back end of beyond and can't get anything but pizza delivered.

He took a swig of his beer and flipped cooked pasta into a skillet with some olive oil and garlic. Adding chopped tomatoes and sliced steak to the mix, he used a spatula to mix it all together. The scent was making him hungry. Most people would think it was way too early for dinner, but Micah didn't eat on a schedule.

He'd been wrapped up in his book for the last several hours, hardly noticing the time passing. As always happened, once the flow of words finally stopped, he came out of his cave like a grizzly after six months of hibernation.

"Hi."

Micah turned to look at the open back door. It was late afternoon and the cool air felt good. Of course, if he'd known he'd be invaded, Micah would have kept the door shut. Too late now, though, since there was a little boy standing there, staring at him. The kid couldn't have been more than three or four. He had light brown hair that stuck up in wild tufts all over his head. His brown eyes were wide and curious and there was mud on the knees of his jeans and the toes of his sneakers. "Who are you?"

"I'm Jacob. I live there." He waved one hand in the general direction of the house next door. "Can I go see my pumpkin?"

The sizzling skillet was the only sound in the room. Micah looked at the kid and realized that he was one of the crew who made so much noise in Kelly's garden. That still didn't explain why the kid was here, talking to Micah. "Why are you asking me?"

"Cuz Kelly's not here so I have to ask another grown-up and you're one."

Can't argue with that kind of logic. "Yeah. Sure. Go ahead."

"Okay. What're you doin'?" Jacob came closer.

"I'm cooking." Micah glanced at the boy, then, dismissing him, went back to his skillet. "Go look at your pumpkin."

"Are you hungry, too?" The boy gave him a hopeful look.

"Yeah, so you should go home," Micah told him. "Have lunch." What time was it? He looked out the window. The sky was darkening toward twilight. "Or dinner."

"I hafta see my pumpkin first and say good-night."

That was a new one for Micah. Telling a vegetable

good-night. But the boy looked so…earnest. And a little pitiful in his dirty jeans with his wide brown eyes. Micah didn't do kids. Never had. Not even when he *was* a kid.

He'd kept to himself back then, too. He'd never made friends because he wouldn't have been able to keep them. Moving from home to home to home kept a foster kid wary of relationships. So he'd buried his nose in whatever books he could find and waited to turn eighteen so he could get out of the system.

But now, staring into a pair of big brown eyes, Micah felt guilt tugging at him for trying to ignore the kid. The feeling was so unusual for him he almost didn't recognize it. He also couldn't ignore it. "Fine then. Go ahead. Say good-night to your pumpkin."

"You hafta open the gate for me cuz I'm too little."

Rolling his eyes, Micah remembered the gated white-picket fence Kelly kept around her garden patch. She'd told him once it was to discourage rabbits and deer. Even though the deer could jump the fence with no problem, she wanted to make vegetable stealing as hard as possible on them.

With a sigh, Micah turned the fire off under his skillet, and said goodbye to the meal he'd just made. "All right." Micah looked at the boy. "Let's go then."

A bright smile lit the kid's face. "Thanks!"

He hustled out of the kitchen, down the back steps and around to the side of the house.

Micah followed more slowly, and as he walked, he took a second to appreciate the view. All around him fall colors exploded in shades of gold and red. The dark green of the pines in the woods beyond the house made them look as if they were made of shadows, and he idly plotted another murder, deep in the forest.

"I could have some kid find the body," he mumbled, seeing the possible scene in his mind. "Freak him out, but would he be too scared to tell anyone? Would he run for help or run home and hide?"

"Who?"

Coming back to the moment at hand, Micah looked at the child staring up at him. "What?"

"Who's gonna run home? Are they scared? Is it a boy? Cuz my brothers say boys don't get scared, only girls do."

Micah snorted. "Your brothers are wrong."

"I think so, too." Jacob nodded so hard his hair flopped across his forehead. He pushed it back with a dirty hand. "Jonah gets scared sometimes and Joshua needs a light on when he sleeps."

"Uh-huh." Way too much information, Micah thought and wondered idly if the kid had an off switch.

"I like the dark and only get scared sometimes." Jacob shifted impatiently from foot to foot.

"That's good."

"Do you get scared?"

Frowning now, Micah watched the boy. For a second he was tempted to say no and let it drop. Then he thought better of it. "Everybody gets scared sometimes."

"Even dads?"

Micah had zero experience with fathers, but he suspected that the one thing that would terrify a man was worrying about his children. "Yeah," he said. "Even dads."

"Wow." Jacob nodded thoughtfully. "I have a rabbit I hold when I get scared. I don't think my dad has one."

"A rabbit?" Micah shook his head.

"Not a real one," Jacob assured him. "Real ones would be hard to hold."

"Sure, sure." Micah nodded sagely.

"And they poop a lot."

Micah hid the smile he felt building inside. The boy was so serious he probably wouldn't appreciate being laughed at. Did all kids talk like this? And whatever happened to not talking to strangers? Didn't people tell their kids that anymore?

"There it is," Jacob said suddenly, and pointed to the garden as he hurried to the gate and waited for Micah to open it. Once he had, Jacob raced across the uneven ground to one of the dozen or more pumpkins.

Micah followed, hands in his jeans pockets, watching the kid because he couldn't very well leave him out here alone, could he? "Which one?"

"This one." Jacob bent down to pat the saddest pumpkin Micah had ever seen.

It was smaller than the others, but that wasn't its only issue. It was also shaped like a lumpy football. It was more a pale yellow than orange, and it had what looked like a tumor growing out of one side at the top. If it had been at a store, it would have been overlooked, but here a little boy was patting it tenderly.

"Why that one?" Micah asked, actually curious about what would have made the kid pick the damn thing.

Jacob pulled a weed, then looked up at Micah. "Cuz it's the littlest one, like me." He looked at the vines and all of the other round, perfect orange blobs. "And it's all by itself over here, so it's probably lonely."

"A lonely pumpkin." He wasn't sure why that statement touched him, but he couldn't deny the kid was getting to him.

"Uh-huh." Smiling again, Jacob said, "None of the other kids liked him, but I do. I'm gonna help my mom draw a happy face on him for Halloween and then he'll feel good."

The kid was worried about a pumpkin's self-esteem. Micah didn't even know what to say to that. When *he* was a kid, he'd never done Halloween. There'd been no costumes, no trick-or-treating, no carving pumpkins with his mom.

Micah had one fuzzy memory of his mother and it drifted through his mind like fog on a winter night. She was pretty—at least, he told himself that because the mental picture of her was too blurred to really tell. She had brown hair and brown eyes like his and she was kneeling on the sidewalk in front of him, smiling, though tears glittered in her eyes. Micah was about six, he guessed, a little older than Jacob. They were in New York and the street was busy with cars and people. He was hungry and cold and his mother smoothed his hair back from his forehead and whispered to him.

*"You have to stay here without me, Micah."*

*Fear spurted inside him as he looked up at the dirty gray building behind him. The dark windows looked like blank eyes staring down at him. Worried and chewing his bottom lip, he looked back at his mother. "But I don't want to. I want to go with you."*

*"It's just for a little while, baby. You'll stay here where you'll be safe and I'll be back for you as soon as I can."*

*"I don't want to be safe, Mommy," he whispered, his voice catching, breaking as panic nearly choked him and he felt tears streaking down his face. "I want to go with you."*

*"You can't come with me, Micah." She kissed his fore-head, then stood up, looking down at him. She took a step*

back from him. "This is how it has to be and I expect you to be a good boy."

"I will be good if I can go with you," he promised. He reached for her hand, his small fingers curling around hers and holding tight, as if he could keep her there. With him.

But she only walked him up the steps, knocked on the door and gave Micah's fingers one last squeeze before pulling free. Fear nibbled at him, his tears coming faster, and he wiped them away with his jacket sleeve. "Don't leave..."

"You wait right here until they open the door, understand?"

He nodded, but he didn't understand. Not any of it. Why were they here? Why was she leaving? Why didn't she want him to be with her?

"I'll be back, Micah," she said. "Soon. I promise." Then she turned and left him.

He watched her go, hurrying down the steps, then along the sidewalk, until she was lost in the crowd. Behind him, the door opened and a lady he didn't know took Micah's hand and led him inside.

His mother never came back.

Micah shook off the memory of his first encounter with child services. It had been a long, confusing, terrifying day for him. He was sure he wouldn't be there long. His mother had said so. For the first year, he'd actually looked for her every day. After that, hope was more fragile and, finally, the hope faded completely. His mother's lies stuck with him, of course.

Hell, they still lived in a tiny, dark corner of his mind and constantly served as a reminder not to trust anyone.

But here, in Banner, those warnings were more silent

than they'd ever been for him. Watching as Jacob carefully brushed dirt off his pumpkin, Micah realized that this place was like stepping into a Norman Rockwell painting. A place where kids worried about pumpkins and talked to strangers like they were best friends. It had nothing at all to do with the world that Micah knew.

And maybe that's why he felt so out of step here.

That's how Kelly found them. The boy, kneeling in the dirt, and the man standing beside him, a trapped look on his face—as if he were trying to figure out how he'd gotten there. Smiling to herself, Kelly climbed out of her truck and walked toward the garden at the side of the house. Micah spotted her first and his brown eyes locked with hers.

She felt a jolt of something hot that made her knees feel like rubber, but she kept moving. She had to admit it surprised her, seeing Micah here with Jacob. She hadn't pictured him as the kind of guy to take the time for a child. He was so closed off, so private, that seeing him now, walking through a fenced garden while a little boy talked his ears off gave her a warm feeling she couldn't quite describe.

"What're you guys up to?" she asked as she walked closer.

"I showed Micah my pumpkin," Jacob announced. "He likes mine best, he said so."

"Well, of course he did," she agreed. "Yours is terrific."

The little boy flashed Micah a wide grin. Micah, on the other hand, looked embarrassed to have been caught being nice. Interesting reaction.

"It's okay I came over, right?" Jacob asked, looking

44       FIANCÉ IN NAME ONLY

a little worried. "Micah was cooking, but he opened the gate for me and stuff."

"Sure it's okay," Kelly told him.

"Okay, I gotta go now," Jacob said suddenly, giving his pumpkin one last pat. "Bye!"

He bolted through the gate and tore across the back-yard toward the house next door.

Micah watched him go. "That was fast."

Kelly laughed a little, then looked over at Micah. "You were cooking?"

He shrugged. "I was hungry."

She glanced at the lavender sky. "Early for dinner."

"Or late for lunch," he said with a shrug. "It's all about perspective."

What did it say about her that she enjoyed the sharp, nearly bitten off words he called a conversation? Kelly wondered if he'd been any easier with Jacob, but somehow she doubted it. The man might be a whiz when typing words and dialogue, but actually speaking in real life appeared to be one of his least favorite things.

"So, why keep the fence when you told me it doesn't stop the deer?

She looked around at the tall, white pickets, then walked toward the still-open gate. Micah followed her. Once through, she latched the gate after them and said, "Makes me feel better to try. Sometimes, I could swear I hear the deer laughing at my pitiful attempts to foil them."

He looked toward the woods that ran along the back of the neighborhood and stretched out for at least five miles to the base of the mountains. "I haven't seen a single deer since I've been here."

"You have to actually be outside," she pointed out.

"Right." He nodded and tucked his hands into his jeans pockets.

"There's a lot of them and they're sneaky," Kelly said, shooting a dark look at the forest. "Of course, some of them aren't. They just walk right into the garden and sneer at you."

He laughed and she looked at him, surprised. "Deer can sneer?"

"They can and do." She tipped her head to one side to stare at him. "You should laugh more often."

He frowned at that and the moment was gone, so Kelly let it go and went back to his first question. "The fence doesn't even slow them down, really. They just jump right over it." Shaking her head, she added, "They look like ballet dancers, really. Graceful, you know?"

"So why bother with the fence?"

"Because otherwise it's like I'm saying, *It's okay with me guys. Come on in and eat the vegetables.*"

"So, you're at war with deer."

"Basically, yeah." She frowned and looked to the woods. "And, so far, they're winning."

"You've got orange paint on your cheek."

"What? Oh." She reached up and scrubbed at her face.

"And white paint on your fingers."

Kelly held her hands out to see for herself, then laughed. "Yeah, I just came from a painting job and—"

"You paint, too?"

"Oh, just a little. Window decorations and stuff. I'm not an artist or anything, but—"

"Realtor, painter, website manager…" He just looked at her. "What else?"

"Oh, a few other things," she said. "I design gardens, and in the winter I plow driveways. I like variety."

His eyes flared at her admission and her stomach jumped in response. Not the kind of variety she'd meant, but now that the thought was in her brain, thank you very much, there were lots of other very interesting thoughts, too. Her skin felt heated and she was grateful for the cold breeze that swept past them.

Kelly took a deep breath, swallowed hard and said, "I should probably get home and clean up."

"How about a glass of wine first?"

Curious, she looked up at him. "Is that an invitation?"

"If it is?"

"Then I accept."

"Good." He nodded. "Come on then. We can eat, too."

"A man who cooks *and* serves wine?" She started for the back door, walking alongside Micah. "You're a rare man, Micah Hunter."

"Yeah," he murmured. "Rare."

Naturally, she was perfectly at home in the Victorian. She'd grown up there, after all. She'd done her homework at the round pedestal table while eating Gran's cookies fresh out of the oven. She'd learned to cook on the old stove and had helped Gran pick out the shiny, stainless steel French door refrigerator when the last one had finally coughed and died.

She'd painted the walls a soft gold so that even in winter it would feel warm and cozy in here, and she'd chosen the amber-streaked granite counters to complement the walls. This house was comfort. Love.

At the farmhouse sink, Kelly looked out the window at the yard, the woods and the deepening sky as she washed her hands, scrubbing every bit of the paint from her skin. Then she splashed water on her face and wiped that away, too. "Did I get it all?"

He glanced at her and nodded. "Yeah."

"Good. I like painting, but I prefer the paint on the windows rather than on me."

Kelly got the wine out of the fridge while Micah heated the pasta in the skillet. She took two glasses from a cabinet and poured wine for each of them before sitting at the round oak table watching him.

What was it, she wondered, about a man cooking that was just so sexy? Sean hadn't known how to turn the stove on, but Micah seemed confident and comfortable with a spatula in his hand. Which only made her think about what other talents he might have. Oh, boy, it had been a long time since she'd felt this heat swamping her. If Terry knew what Kelly was thinking right this minute, she would send up balloons and throw a small but tasteful party. That thought made her smile. "Smells good."

He glanced over his shoulder at her. "Pasta's easy. A few herbs, some garlic, olive oil and cheese and you're done. Plus, some sliced steak because you've gotta have meat."

"Agreed," Kelly said, taking a sip of her wine.

"Glad to hear you're not one of those *I'll just have a salad, dressing on the side* types."

"Hey, nothing wrong with a nice salad."

"As long as there's meat in it," he said, concentrating on the task at hand.

"So what made you take up cooking?"

"Self-preservation. Live alone, you learn how to cook."

Whether he knew it or not, that was an opening for questions. She didn't waste it. "Live alone, huh?"

One eyebrow lifted as he turned to look at her. "Did you notice anyone else here with me the last couple of months?"

"No," she admitted with a smile, "but you do write mysteries. You could have killed your girlfriend."

"Could have," he agreed easily. "Didn't. The only place I commit crimes is on a computer screen."

"Glad to hear it," she said, smiling. Also glad to hear he could take some teasing and give it back. But on to the real question. "So, no girlfriend or wife?"

He used the spatula to stir the pasta, then gave her a quick look. "That's a purely female question."

"Well, then, since I am definitely female, that makes sense." She propped her chin in her hand. "And it was very male of you to answer the question by not answering. Want to give it another try?"

"No."

"No you won't answer or no *is* the answer?"

Reluctantly, it seemed, his mouth curved briefly into a half smile. "I should know better than to get into a battle of words with a woman. Even being a writer, I don't stand a chance."

"Isn't that the nicest thing to say?" But she stared at him, clearly waiting for his answer. Finally he gave her the one she was looking for.

He snorted. "No is the answer. No wife. No girlfriend. No interest."

"So you're gay," she said sagely. Oh, she knew he wasn't because the two of them had that whole hot-buzz thing going between them. But it was fun to watch his expression.

"I'm not gay."

"Are you sure?"

"Reasonably," he said wryly.

"Good to know," she said, and took a sip of wine, hiding her smile behind the rim of her glass. "I'm not, either, just so we're clear."

His gaze bored into hers and flames licked at her insides. "Also good to know."

Her throat dried up so she had another sip of wine to ease it. "How long have you been a writer?"

"A writer or a published writer?" he asked.

"There's a difference?"

He shrugged as he plated the pasta and carried them to the table. Sitting down opposite her, he took a long drink of his wine before speaking again. "I wrote stories for years that no one will ever see."

"Intriguing," she said, and wondered what those old stories would say about Micah Hunter. Would she learn more about the closed-off, secretive man by discovering who he had been years ago?

"Not very." He took a bite of pasta, "Anyway, I've been published about ten years."

"I don't read your books."

One eyebrow lifted and he smirked. "Thanks."

She grinned. "That came out wrong. Sorry. I mean, I read one of your books a few years ago and it scared me to death. So I haven't read another one."

"Then, thank you." He lifted his glass in a kind of salute to her. "Best compliment you could give me. Which book was it?"

"I don't remember the title," she said, tasting the pasta. "But it was about a woman looking for her missing sister and she finds the sister's killer, instead."

He nodded. "*Relative Danger*. That was my third book."

"First and last for me," she assured him. "I slept with the light on for two weeks."

"Thanks." He studied her. "Did you read the whole book? Or did you stop because it scared you?"

"Who stops in the middle of a book?" she demanded,

outraged at the idea. "No, I read the whole thing and, terror aside, it ended well."

"Thanks again."

"You're welcome. You know, this is really good," she said, taking another bite. "Your mom teach you how to cook?"

His face went hard and tight. He lowered his gaze to his plate and muttered, "No. Learned by trial and error."

Sore spot, she told herself and changed the subject. She had secret, painful corners in her own soul, so she wouldn't poke at his. "How's your book coming? The one you're working on now, I mean."

He frowned before answering. "Slower than I'd like."

"Why?"

"You ask a lot of questions."

"The only way to get answers."

"True." He took a sip of wine. "Because the book's set in a small town and I don't know small towns."

"Hello?" Laughing, she said, "You're *in* one."

"Yeah. That's why I came here in the first place. My agent suggested it. He stayed here a couple of years ago for the skiing and thought the town would work for my research."

"*Here*, here?" she asked. "I mean, did he stay at the Victorian?"

"Yeah."

"What's his name?"

"Sam Hellman. He and his wife, Jenny, were here for a week."

"I remember them. She's very pretty and sweet and he's funny."

"That's them," Micah agreed.

Kelly took a drink of her wine. "Well, first, I'm glad

your agent had a good time here. Word of mouth? Best advertising."

"For books, too," he agreed.

"But if you want to use the town for its setting and ambience, it might help if you left the house and explored a little. Get to know the place."

He ate for a couple of minutes, then finally said, "Getting out doesn't get the typing done."

Kelly shrugged and set down her glass. "But you can't get to know the town by looking through a window, either. And, if you don't know what it's like here, you've got nothing to type anyway, right?"

"I don't much like that you've got a point."

Kelly grinned. "Well, that makes two points for me, doesn't it? I'm still winning."

Unexpectedly, he laughed and the rich, warm sound seemed to ripple along her spine.

"Competitive, aren't you?"

"You have no idea," Kelly admitted. "I used to drive my grandparents crazy. I was always trying to be first in my class, or the fastest runner or—"

"Your grandparents still live here?"

"No." She picked up her wineglass and watched the light play on the golden wine. "My grandfather died six years ago and my grandmother moved to Florida to live with her sister a year later." Kelly took a sip, let the cold liquid ease her suddenly tight throat. "When my husband died four years ago, Gran came home for a few weeks to stay with me."

"You were married?" He spoke quietly, as if unsure exactly what to say.

No surprise there, Kelly thought. Most people just immediately said, *I'm sorry.* She didn't know why. Social convention? Or was it just the panic of not being able to think of anything else?

She lifted her gaze to his. "Sean died in a skiing accident."

"Must've been hard."

"Yeah," she said, nodding. "It was. And thanks for not saying you're sorry. People do, even though they have nothing to be sorry about, you know? Then I feel like I have to make them feel better, and it's just a weird situation all the way around."

"Yeah. I get that."

The expression on his face was sympathetic and that was okay. Telling someone your husband was dead was a conversation killer. "It's okay. I mean, no one ever really knows what to say, so don't worry about it." Another sip of wine to wash down the knot in her throat. "Anyway, it wasn't easy to get Gran to go back to her new life— she thought she was abandoning me. And I love that she loves me, you know? But I don't want to be a worry or a burden or a duty—not really a duty, but that little nudge of worry. I don't want to be that, either." She took a breath and smiled. "Whoa. Rambling. Anyway, Gran's still worried, and unless I can convince her I'm just fine, she's going to move back here to keep me company."

"And that's a bad thing?"

She looked at him. "Yes. It's bad. She's having a blast in Florida. She deserves to enjoy herself, not to feel like she has to move back to take care of an adult granddaughter."

Nodding, Micah leaned back in the chair, never taking his gaze from hers. "All right. I can see that. So you know what you want. How're you going to manage it?"

Good question. There was a ridiculous idea worming its way through her mind, but it was so far out there she felt weird even entertaining the idea while Micah was here.

"I don't know yet." She smiled, had another sip of wine and said, "But, hey, as fascinating as my whirlwind life can be, enough already. I've given you my story. What's yours?"

He stiffened. "What do you mean?"

"Well, for starters," Kelly said, "have you ever been married?"

Micah shook his head. "No."

Kelly just stared at him, waiting. There had to be more than just a no.

Finally, he scowled and added, "Fine. I was engaged once."

"Engaged but not married. So what happened?"

"It didn't take." His features were tight, like the doors of a house locked against intruders.

Okay, that was obviously a dead-end subject. "You know, for a writer—someone supposedly good with words—you're not particularly chatty."

He snorted and the tension left him. "Writers *write*. Besides, men aren't 'chatty.'"

"But they do talk."

"I'm talking."

"Not saying much," she pointed out.

"Maybe there's not much to say."

"Oh, I don't believe that," Kelly told him. "There's more, you're just stingy about sharing."

He started to speak—no doubt protest, Kelly told herself, but she stopped him with another question.

"Let's try this. You're a writer and you travel all over the world, I know. But where's home?"

"Here." He studiously avoided her gaze and concentrated on the pasta.

"Yeah," she said. "For now. But before this. Where are you from?"

"Originally," he answered, "New York."

Honestly, it would probably be easier if she asked him to *write* the information and let her read it. "Okay, that's originally. How about now—and not this house."

"Everywhere," he said. "I move around."

She hadn't expected that. Everyone was from *somewhere*. "What about your family?"

"Don't have any." He stood up, took his plate to the sink, then came back for his wineglass. Lifting it for a drink, he looked at her. "And I don't talk about it, either."

Message was clear, Kelly thought. He'd put up his mental No Trespassing signs. His eyes were shuttered and his jaw was tight.

Whatever bit of closeness had opened up between them was over now. Funny that while they were talking about *her*, he was all chatty, but the minute the conversation shifted to him, he clammed up so tightly it would take a crowbar to pry words from his mouth.

It surprised her how disappointed she was about that. Since Sean died, she hadn't been as interested in a man as she was in Micah. And for a while, as they sat together sharing a meal, she'd felt that buzz humming between them like an arc of electricity. And now it was fizzling out. The expression on his face told her he was waiting for her to pry. To ask more questions. And since she hated being predictable, Kelly said simply, "Okay."

Suspicion gleamed in his eyes. "Just like that."

"Everybody's got secrets, Micah," she told him with

a shrug. "You're entitled to yours." Tipping her head to one side, she asked, "Why so surprised?"

"Because most women would be hammering me with questions right now."

"Well, then, it's your lucky day, because I'm not like most women." Besides, hammering him wouldn't work.

"Got that right," he muttered.

She heard that and smiled to herself as she carried her dishes to the sink, then turned for the back door. Kelly didn't want to leave, but she knew she should. Otherwise, she might be tempted to be like every other woman in the world and try to get him to open up some more—which would be pointless and exactly what he expected.

"So, thanks for lunch or dinner or whatever. And the wine."

Micah was right behind her. "You're welcome."

His voice came from right behind her. At the open doorway, she turned and almost bumped into his chest.

"Oh, sorry." Wow, was his chest really that broad, or was she just so close it *looked* like he was taking up the whole world? Heat poured from his body, reaching for her, tingling her nerve endings. And he smelled so good, too.

Kelly shook her head, and ignored the flutter of expectation awakening in the pit of her stomach. Deliberately, she fought for lighthearted, then tipped her head back and smiled up at him. "You know, I think I should get another point."

"For what?"

"For surprising you by not asking questions." She held up three fingers and gave him a teasing smile. "So that makes it three to nothing my favor and don't you forget it."

"Not a chance in hell you would *let* me forget, is there?"

"Nope." Kelly grinned. "And how nice that you know me so well already."

"That's what I thought." He studied her as if he were trying to figure out a puzzle. But after a second or two, he nodded. "You want to keep score? Then add this into the mix."

He pulled her in close and kissed her.

# Four

Everything inside Kelly lit up like a sparkler, showering her head to toe in red-hot flickers of heat and light. Instinctively, her eyes closed and her body swayed closer to him. His mouth covered hers and his arms came around her, molding her to him, and she lifted both arms to hook them around his neck.

It had been so long since she'd been kissed she was dizzy with the sensations pouring through her. God, she'd forgotten how sensations poured through her system in a kiss, the tangle of feelings that erupted. She couldn't think. Couldn't have spoken even if she had wanted to pry her mouth from his. His tongue stroked hers and the groans lifting from her throat twisted with Micah's, the soft sounds whispering into the twilight.

Breathing was becoming an issue, but she didn't care. She wanted to revel in the feeling of her body awakening as if from a coma. Fires quickened down low inside her and a tingling ache settled at her core. Need clawed at her and she moved in even closer to him. She might have stood there all night, taking what he offered, feeling her own desires tearing at her. But, as suddenly as he'd kissed her, he ended it.

Tearing his mouth from hers, he lifted his head to look down at her. From Kelly's perspective, his features were blurry. She swayed unsteadily until she slapped one hand to the door frame just for balance. As her mind defogged, her vision cleared and her heart rate dropped from racing to just really fast.

He still held her waist in a tight grip, and when he looked down into her eyes, Kelly saw that *his* eyes were a molten brown now, shot through with the fires that were burning her from the inside out.

"I think that makes it three to one now, doesn't it?" His voice was low, a deep rumble that was almost like thunder.

Points? Oh, yeah. Kelly's brain was just not working well enough at the moment to count points. But since her body was still smoldering, she had to say, "Oh, yeah. Point to you."

He gave her a slow, satisfied smile.

Reluctantly, her mouth curved, too. "You're enjoying this, aren't you?"

"I'd be a fool not to," he admitted.

"Yeah. Well." She lifted one hand to touch her fingers to her lips. "Let's not forget, I've still got three points to your one."

His smile faded and his eyes flashed as he let her go. "But the game's not over yet, is it?"

"Not even close to finished," she said, then turned

and started the short walk home. She felt him watching her as she walked away and that gave her a warm rush, too. Kelly had the feeling that this game was just getting started.

She couldn't wait for round two.

Micah watched her go for ten agonizing seconds, then he shut the door firmly to keep himself from chasing after her. God, he felt like some girl-crazed teenager and that just wasn't acceptable. He was a man who demanded control. He didn't do spontaneous. Didn't veer from the plan he had for his life. And that plan did *not* include a small-town widow who tasted like a glimpse of heaven.

He wanted another taste. Wanted to feel her body pressed to his, the race of her heart, the warmth of her arms around his neck.

"Damn it." He took a deep breath to steady himself, but her scent was still clinging to him and it invaded his lungs, making itself a part of him.

His own heartbeat was a little crazed and his jeans felt like an iron cage around his hard body. Micah didn't know what had made him grab her like that. But the urge to taste her, hold her, had been too big to ignore. If he'd been thinking clearly, he never would have done it. The problem was, every time he was around Kelly, thinking was an impossible task.

"Maybe Sam's right," he told himself. "Maybe an affair is the answer." Something had to give, he thought. Because if he spent the next four months as tied up in knots as he was at the moment, he'd never get any writing done.

Something to think about.

* * *

Kelly walked home across the wide front lawn, mind racing, nerves sizzling from that unexpected but amazing kiss. She stopped halfway to the carriage house, turned around and looked at the big Victorian.

In the deepening twilight, the house looked as it had to her when she was a child—like a fairy tale. The house was painted a deep brick red with snow-white trim that seemed to define every little detail. Three chimneys jutted up from the shake roof, indicating the tiled fireplaces—in the living room, the master bedroom and the kitchen. The wide, wraparound porch was dotted with swings, chairs and tables, inviting anyone to sit, enjoy the view and visit for a while. Double front doors were hand-carved mahogany with inset panes of etched glass. The last of the sunset glanced off the second-story windows, making them glow gold, and downstairs a lamp in the living room flashed on, telling Kelly exactly where Micah was in the house.

She lifted one hand to her mouth as she looked at that light, imagining him striding through that front door, marching across the yard to her and kissing her again. God, one kiss and all she could think was she wanted more.

"Oh, man, this could be bad..." Deliberately then, as if to prove to herself she *could*, she turned away and continued to the cottage.

It was a smaller version of the big house. Same colors, same intricate trim, made by a long-dead craftsman more than a hundred years ago. Just one bedroom, bathroom, living room and kitchen, the cottage was perfect for one person and normally, when Kelly stepped inside, it felt like a refuge.

She'd moved out of the Victorian not long after Sean's death because she simply couldn't bear the empty rooms and the echo of her own footsteps. Here, in this cottage, it was cozy and safe and, right now, almost suffocating. But that was probably because she still felt like there was a tight band around her chest.

Kelly dropped into the nearest chair and snuggled into the deep cushions. The comfort and familiarity of the cottage didn't relax her as it usually did. Shaking her head, she sighed a little and told herself to get a grip. But it wasn't easy since Micah Hunter had a real gift when it came to kissing. So, naturally, she had to wonder how gifted he was in…related areas. Oh, boy. She was in deep trouble.

The worst part was that she wanted to be in even deeper.

When her cell phone rang, she dug it out of her pocket, grateful for the distraction. Until she saw the caller ID. Guilt rose up and took another healthy bite out of Kelly's heart. She'd forgotten all about returning her grandmother's call. Seeing Micah, sharing a meal with him, had thrown her off, and then that kiss had completely sealed the deal on her mind, shutting down any thought beyond *oh, boy*!

Taking a breath, she forced a smile into her voice and answered. "Hi, Gran! I'm sorry, I just didn't have a chance to call you back before."

"That's okay, honey," her grandmother said. "I hope you were out having fun…"

Kelly sighed a little and leaned her head back against the cushioned chair. She could hear the worry in her grandmother's voice and wished she couldn't. Ever since Sean died, Gran had been worried and it didn't seem to be easing. If anything, it was getting worse. As if the older Gran got, the more she was concerned about eventually leaving Kelly on her own.

Kelly had been trying for months to convince Gran that she was fine. Happy. But nothing worked because the only thing Gran would accept was Kelly in love and married again. She wanted her settled with a family and no matter how many times Kelly told her that she didn't need a husband, Gran remained ever hopeful.

Even knowing that Kelly had just been kissed until her brain melted wouldn't be enough to satisfy Gran. Not unless she and Micah were married or—

Suddenly, the idea she'd played with earlier came back to her. Maybe it was the kiss. Maybe it was sitting across that table from Micah, talking, laughing, sharing dinner. Whatever the reason, Kelly made a decision that she really hoped she didn't come to regret. "Actually, Gran," she said, before the still-rational corner of her brain could stop her, "I was with my fiancé."

"*What?* Oh, my goodness, that's wonderful!"

The joy in her grandmother's voice made Kelly smile and wince at the same time. Okay, yes, technically she was lying to her grandmother. But, really, she was just trying to give the older woman some peace. The chance to enjoy her life without constant worries about Kelly. That wasn't a bad thing, was it? It's not like she was pretending to be engaged for her own sake. This was completely altruistic.

"Tell me everything," Gran insisted. "Who is he? What does he do? Is he handsome?"

"It's Micah Hunter, Gran," she said, hoping a lightning bolt didn't streak out of the sky and turn her into a cinder. "The writer who's renting the Victorian for six months."

"Oh, my, a writer!"

Kelly's eyes closed tightly on another wince, but that didn't help because Micah's image rose up in her mind and gave her a hard look. She ignored it.

"He's very handsome and very sweet." Oh, it was a wonder her tongue didn't simply rot and fall out of her mouth. *Sweet?* Micah Hunter? Sexy, yes. Prickly, oh, yeah. But she'd seen no evidence of sweet. Still, it was something her grandmother would want to hear. And as long as Kelly was lying through her teeth to the woman who had raised her, she was determined to make it a *good* lie.

"When did this happen?" Gran asked. "When did he propose? What does your ring look like?"

Before Kelly could answer, Gran covered the receiver and shouted, "Linda, you won't believe it! Our girl is engaged to a writer!"

Gran's sister squealed in the background and Kelly sighed.

"I'm putting you on speaker, sweetie. Linda wants to hear the story, too."

Great. A command performance. Boy, it was a good thing they didn't do video chatting.

"It just happened tonight," Kelly blurted. Her grandmother's friends in Banner no doubt gave her updates on Kelly, so she would know that nothing had happened between her and Micah any sooner.

"How exciting!" Linda exclaimed, and Gran shushed her.

"Tell us everything, honey," Gran urged. "I want details."

"He cooked dinner tonight," Kelly continued, and consoled herself that at least that part of the story wasn't a lie. "He proposed while we were sitting out on the porch."

"Oh, that's lovely." Gran gave a heavy sigh and Kelly felt terrible.

She was already regretting this, but she was in so deep now there was no way to back out without admitting she had lied. Nope. Couldn't do it.

"Yeah, it was lovely." Kelly nodded and kept going, making it as romantic as she could for her grandmother's sake. The woman loved watching Hallmark movies and had been known to cry at particularly touching commercials, so Kelly knew Gran would expect romance in this story.

Thinking fast, she said, "He had flowers on the porch and those little white twinkle lights hung from the ceiling. Music was playing, too," she added, telling herself to remember all of these details. "He brought out a bottle of champagne and went down on one knee and when I said yes, he kissed me."

Kissed her brainless, apparently, because otherwise why would she be inventing all of this? Oh, God, just remembering that kiss had her blood humming and heat spiraling through her body. One kiss and she was making up an engagement.

*What was she doing?*

"Well, good, I'm so glad to hear he gave you romance, sweetheart. I'm so happy for you." Her grandmother sniffled a little and her sister said, "Oh, Bella, stop now. The girl's happy. You should be too."

"These are happy tears, Linda, can't you tell?"

"They're still tears, so stop it."

Kelly grimaced. Could you actually be *devoured* by guilt?

"Pay no attention to my sister," Gran said softly. "You know, honey, since you lost Sean, I've been so worried."

"I know." Kelly told herself she was doing the right thing. She was easing an old woman's heart. Making her happy. It wasn't hurting anyone. Not even Micah, really. He was only here temporarily. Heck, he didn't even have to meet her grandmother. And, when he left in four months, Kelly would simply tell Gran that they'd broken up. Maybe the very fact that Kelly had been engaged, however briefly, would be enough to assure Gran that she didn't have to worry so much.

"Will you take a picture of your ring and send it to me?"

*Oops.* She looked at her naked ring finger and sighed.

"Um, I don't have a ring yet," Kelly said.

"The man thought of twinkle lights but didn't bother with a ring?" Linda asked.

The two women together were really hard to stand against. "Micah wants to wait until we go to New York so we can pick one out together."

"New York?" Linda's tone changed. "How exciting!"

"Hush, Linda," Gran told her sister. "When are you going to New York, sweetie? Can you send me pictures? I'd love to show the girls at bingo."

"Sure I can, Gran." *Oh, my God, stop talking, Kelly.*

But the lies kept piling on top of each other until any second now, she'd be buried beneath a mountain of them. There was no way to stop now. She'd started all of this and she had to follow through because admitting a lie to her grandmother was simply impossible.

"I don't know when we're going to New York though…" That was true, at least. "He's busy with work and I've got Halloween coming up and—"

Gran clucked her tongue and Kelly muffled a groan.

"Well, you both just have to take the time for each other," Gran told her firmly. "Work will always be there, but this is a special time for you two."

*Oh, it was special, all right.* And wait until she told Micah about all of this. That scene promised to be extra special.

"Why a New York ring?" Linda demanded. "They don't sell rings in Utah?"

"Well," Kelly said, making it up as she went along, "when I told Micah I'd never been to New York, he insisted on flying me out there in a private jet so he could show me around. So, we really want to wait on the ring until then."

"Oh, my goodness," Gran whispered. "Linda, can you imagine? Private jets."

"He must be rich," Linda said thoughtfully.

"Course he is," Gran told her. "Haven't we seen his books just everywhere? Don't tell him we don't read his books because they're too scary, though, all right dear?"

"Sure, I won't tell him," Kelly promised.

"You know," Aunt Linda said, "I saw a documentary on those private jets not long ago. They've got *bedrooms* on those jets. You could live on them, I swear."

Kelly couldn't sit still anymore. She lunged out of the chair, walked to her tiny, serviceable kitchen and threw open the fridge. Grabbing the bottle of chardonnay, she pulled out the cork and took a swig straight from the bottle. Oh, if Gran could see her at that moment. Sighing a little, Kelly got a wineglass from a cabinet and poured herself what looked like eight ounces. It might not be enough.

"Well," Gran continued to argue with her sister.

"They're not looking to live on the plane, for heaven's sake, and you just keep your mind out of bedrooms."

"Nothing wrong with a good romp," Linda told her sister. "It would do you good to try one."

Kelly took a big gulp of wine. She didn't want to know about her grandmother's sex life. Or her aunt's, for that matter. Actually, she didn't want to know they *had* sex lives.

"What's that supposed to mean?" Gran sounded outraged. "Just because you don't have standards…"

"I have standards," Linda countered, "but they don't get in the way of a good time."

This argument could go on all night, Kelly knew. The two women loved nothing better than arguing with each other. Drinking her wine, Kelly told herself that while they were arguing about their men friends, they weren't interrogating Kelly about *her* love life. That was something, anyway.

Halfheartedly listening to the two of them, Kelly had enough of a break from her lie fest that she had the time to start worrying about breaking all of this to Micah. How was she supposed to explain it to him when she could hardly figure out herself why she'd started all of this?

She stared out the kitchen window at the yard and the stately Victorian where the man she was using shamelessly was currently living, unaware that he'd just gotten engaged. Oh, boy.

"When's the wedding?" Linda asked suddenly.

"She's *my* granddaughter," Gran said tightly. "I'll ask the questions here. When Debbie gets engaged, then it'll be your turn. Kelly, when's the wedding, honey?"

Kelly's cousin Debbie had already insisted that she and her girlfriend were *never* getting married because the two grans would drive her insane. Kelly could understand that. After all, she'd already lived through one wedding where Gran had made and changed plans every day. If she ever really did get married again one day, she'd elope. Vegas sounded good.

But, for now, Gran was waiting for an answer and since Kelly couldn't tell the truth, she told another lie. It seemed she was on a roll.

"Oh, the wedding won't be for a while yet," she hedged, and had another drink of wine. At this rate, she was going to pass out in another few minutes. "I mean, Micah's got this book he's working on and then he has to do other writing stuff—" Oh, God, that sounded weak, even to her. What did writers have to *do*? "Um, book tours and research trips for the next book, so we probably won't be able to get married for at least another six months, maybe even a year. It all depends on Micah's work." There. That was reasonable, right?

"Wonderful," Gran said, and Kelly released a breath she hadn't realized she'd been holding. "That gives us plenty of time to *plan*. You'll have the wedding at the Victorian, of course…"

"Oh, of course," Kelly agreed, rolling her eyes so hard she heard them rattle.

"Or," Linda argued. "You could get married on the beach right here in Florida. Next summer, maybe?"

"I don't know, Aunt Linda…"

"Why would you want to get married on a beach?" Gran snorted. "All that sand in your shoes and the wind ruining your hair and seagulls pooping all over the place."

"It's romantic," Linda insisted.

"It's dirty," Gran countered.

"Oh, God," Kelly murmured, so quietly that the other two women on the line didn't hear her.

Completely wrapped up in their argument, the ladies didn't notice when Kelly went quiet and that was good. Carrying her wine back to the living room, Kelly dropped into a chair again and listened with only half an ear to her grandmother and aunt.

She didn't have to pay attention now. Kelly knew that she'd be hearing nothing but plans for the next four months—until Micah left and she could break this imaginary engagement. Supposing, of course, that she could talk Micah into going along with this in the first place. If she couldn't, then what? She'd have to claim insanity. That would be the only excuse accepted by her family.

Guilt was becoming such a familiar companion she hardly noticed when it dropped into the pit of her stomach and sat there like a ball of ice. Wine wouldn't melt it, either, though she gave it her best shot.

Her grandmother was talking about white dresses while Linda insisted that white was outdated and Kelly wasn't a virgin, anyway.

A snort of laughter escaped her throat and Kelly was half-afraid it would turn into hysteria. Shaking her head, she tried to figure out the best way to approach Micah about the story she'd created. Once she hung up the phone, Gran would be calling all of her friends in Banner to share the happy news, so Micah had to be prepared for questions. And for behaving like a man in love so she could keep her grandmother blissfully unaware for four short months.

Oh, boy. Lying got out of hand so quickly Kelly could only sit and stare blankly at the wall opposite her. Really, even when a lie seemed like the best idea, it wasn't. No one ever looked far ahead as to what that lie was going to look like once other people picked it up and ran with it. But it wasn't as if she'd had a whole lot of options. She wasn't dating anyone, so she'd had to name Micah. She couldn't let her grandmother give up her new life and sacrifice herself on the altar of Sad Lonely Granddaughter.

But, even though she knew she was doing the right thing, the hole she'd dug for herself was beginning to feel like a bottomless chasm.

At least, she *hoped* it was bottomless. Otherwise, the crash landing she was going to make would be spectacular.

Micah woke up irritated. Not surprising since what little sleep he had gotten had been haunted by images of Kelly Flynn.

"Your own damn fault," he muttered. "If you hadn't kissed her…"

The taste of her was still with him. The feel of her body, warm and pliant against his. Her eager response had fired his blood to the point that it had taken everything he had just to let her go and back off.

Hell, the woman had been making him nuts for the last two months. Sexy, smart and a wiseass, Kelly was enough to bring any man to his knees.

"But damned if I will," he muttered darkly, and got out of bed. Disgusted with himself *and* her, he stalked to the bathroom, turned the water on to heat up, then stood under the shower. He let the hot water slam into his head, hoping it might wash away the last of the dreams that had tormented him and had had him waking up hard as iron.

Naturally it didn't work. It was like her features were imprinted on his brain. Her wide green eyes, the way she had lifted one hand to her lips when their kiss ended. Her smile, her ridiculous insistence on keeping track of "points" scored.

Shaking his head, he saw her in the stupid pumpkin patch talking about her war with deer, of all things. Micah had never *seen* a deer. He closed his eyes and reminded himself that he didn't want or need a woman. But maybe that was wrong, too. If he was fantasizing this much about the landlady, it had clearly been too long since he'd been with a woman.

"Gotta be it," he murmured, shutting off the water and stepping out of the tiled, glassed-in shower. "That's the reason I can't stop thinking about a woman who doesn't even know when she has orange paint on her face."

He dried off, then walked into the bedroom, not bothering to shave. Hell, he'd gotten so little sleep he'd probably slit his own throat if he attempted it.

"What I need to do is put this out of my head and get to work." Losing himself in a grisly murder was just the thing to take his mind off finding Kelly and dragging her here to his bed.

He pulled on a pair of black jeans, then tugged a forest green T-shirt over his head. Micah didn't bother with shoes. It might be gray and cold outside, but inside the old house was toasty. All he wanted was some coffee and then some quiet so he could create another murder.

As soon as he opened the bedroom door, the unmistakable scent of fresh coffee hit him hard. But it wasn't just coffee. It was bacon, too. And toast. "What kind of burglar breaks into a house to make breakfast?"

He started down the long staircase, his bare feet silent on the sapphire-blue carpet runner. Two months here and he still felt like a stranger in this big old house with its creaky doors and polished, old-world style.

He couldn't complain about anything. The house had been updated over the years and boasted comfortable furniture, every amenity and a view from every window that really was beautiful. But it was a lot more space than he was used to. A lot more quiet than he was happy with. Being solitary was part of being a writer. After all, the bottom line was sitting by yourself at a computer. If you needed people with you every damn minute, then writing was not the job for you.

But even solitary creatures needed sensory input from time to time. And being on your own in a house built for a family of a couple dozen could be a little unsettling. Hell, as a mystery/horror writer, Micah could use this house, the solitude and the woods behind the property as the perfect setting for a book.

As that thought took root in his mind, he stopped at the bottom of the stairs, considered it and muttered, "Of course I should be using this house. Why the hell aren't I?"

He continued on through to the kitchen, his senses focused on the tantalizing scents dragging him closer even while his mind figured out how big a rewrite he was looking at. To move his heroine from a small apartment in town to this big house, he'd have to change a million little things. But, he told himself, the atmosphere alone would be worth it.

A cold winter night, the heroine closed up in her bedroom, a fire burning as the wind shrieked and sleet pelted the windows. Then over that noise, she hears something else. Someone moving downstairs—when she's alone in the house.

"Oh, yeah," he told himself, nodding, "that's good. I like it."

He hit the swinging door into the kitchen, stepped inside and stopped dead. Kelly stood at the stove, stirring scrambled eggs in a skillet. Morning sunlight danced in her hair, making the red and gold shine like a new penny. Her black yoga pants clung to her behind and hugged her legs before disappearing into the tops of the black boots on her feet. She half turned toward him when he came in. Her pale green long-sleeved shirt had the top two buttons undone, giving Micah just a peek at what looked like a lacy pink bra.

Instantly his body went hard as stone again. He swallowed the groan that rose in his throat. Wasn't it enough that she'd tormented him all damn night? Why was she here first thing in the morning? Cooking? God, he needed coffee.

And the only way to get it was to deal with the woman smiling at him.

# Five

"What're you doing?"

"Cooking." She smiled at him and Micah felt every drop of blood drain from his brain and head south.

After turning the fire down under the pan, she walked to the coffeemaker, poured him a cup and carried it to him.

"I made breakfast." She sounded bright, cheerful, but her eyes told a different story. There was worry there and a hesitation that put Micah on edge.

Whatever was going on, though, would be handled best *after* coffee. He took his first sip of the morning and felt every cell in his body wake up and dance. How did people survive without coffee?

After another sip or two, he felt strong enough to ask, "Why?"

"Why what?"

One eyebrow lifted. "Why are you here? Why are you cooking?"

"Just being neighborly," she said, and he didn't believe a word of it.

"Yeah." He walked to the table, sat down and had another sip. "I've been here two months. This is the first time you've been 'neighborly.'"

"Well, then, shame on me." She stirred the eggs in the pan and neatly avoided meeting his gaze. Not, Micah told himself, a good sign.

"You're not really good at prevarication."

Her eyes widened. "Oh. Good word."

"And," Micah added wryly, "not very good at stalling, either."

She sighed heavily. "Okay, yes, there is something I need to talk to you about, but after breakfast, okay?"

He grabbed a slice of bacon, took a bite and chewed. When he'd swallowed, he sent her a hard look. "There. I ate. What's going on?"

Taking a deep breath, she turned the fire off under the eggs before facing him. "I need a husband."

Not enough coffee, he told himself. Not nearly enough. But he said only, "Good luck with that."

"No," she corrected quickly. "Not a husband, really. I just need a fiancé."

"Again. Happy hunting." He got up to refill his coffee and thought seriously about just chugging it straight from the pot.

"Micah, I need you to pretend to be my fiancé." After she blurted out that sentence, she grabbed her own cup and took a drink of coffee.

He leaned back against the granite counter, feeling the cold of the stone seep through his T-shirt and into his bones. He crossed his bare feet at the ankles, kept a tight grip on his coffee mug and looked at her. "That seems like an overreaction to one kiss."

"What?" She flushed, flipped her hair behind her shoulders and said, "For heaven's sake, this isn't about the kiss. Though, I admit, it gave me the idea..."

More confused than ever, he could only say, "What?"

"Oh, man, this is harder than I thought it would be." She dropped into a chair at the table, grabbed a slice of bacon and took a bite. "I don't even know how to say all of this without sounding crazy."

"I'll give you a clue," he said softly. "Just say it. Don't lie to me, either, trying to soften whatever it is that's going on. Just say it."

"I wasn't going to lie to you."

"Good. Let's keep it that way."

"Okay." She nodded, took another breath that lifted her breasts until he got another peek at that lacy bra, then started talking. "When I went home last night, my gran called and she started in on moving back again because I'm so alone, and before I knew what I was saying, I told her that she didn't have to worry about me being lonely anymore because I'm engaged. To *you*."

Well, he'd wanted the truth. Micah shook his head, walked to the table, sat down opposite her and waited. Objectively, as a writer, he couldn't wait to hear the rest of this story, because it promised to be a good one. As a man with zero interest in marrying *anyone*, he felt itchy enough that he snatched another piece of bacon and bit into it.

Her green eyes were flashing and her chin was up defiantly, but she chewed at her bottom lip, and that told him she was nervous. That didn't bode well.

"You have to understand, Micah. Gran's my only family and she was so sad after my grandfather passed away." She folded both hands around her coffee mug. "Then she moved to Florida with her sister, my aunt Linda, and she was happy again. Then Sean died and she came home to be with me and she started worrying and the sorrow crept back into her eyes, her voice, everything. It was like she was being *swallowed*, you know?"

No, he didn't know. He didn't have family. Didn't have the kind of deep connections she had, so he couldn't be sure if he'd have reacted the same way she did or not. But just looking at Kelly told him that she was emotionally torn in a couple of different directions.

"I finally convinced her to go back to her life by telling her I needed time alone—which wasn't a lie," she added. "And being away from here, the memories of Grandpa and Sean, helped her and she was happy again. Micah, she's determined to come back here and protect me. To sacrifice her own happiness on the altar of what she thinks of as my misery."

"*Are* you miserable?" he asked, interrupting the stream of words pouring from her.

"Of course not." She took a sip of coffee. "I mean, sure, I get lonely sometimes, but everybody does, right?"

He didn't say anything because what *could* he say? She was right. Even Micah experienced those occasional bouts when he wished there was someone there to talk to. To hold. But those moments passed, and he realized that his life was just as he wanted it.

"But when I told her I was engaged to you…" Kelly sighed helplessly. "She was so happy, Micah, that from there, I just grabbed the proverbial ball and ran with it."

"Meaning?"

"Oh." She put her head in her hands briefly, then looked up at him again. "I told her how romantic your proposal was—"

"What did I do?" Now he was just curious. He couldn't help it. This was all so far out there that it didn't even seem real. It was like watching a movie or reading a book about someone else.

Still worrying her bottom lip, she said, "You set up a candlelit dinner on the porch around back and you had roses everywhere and music playing and little twinkle lights strung over the ceiling…"

He could *see* it and thought she'd done a nice job of scene setting. "Well, I'm pretty good."

She gave a heavy sigh. "You're laughing at me."

"Trust me," he said. "Not laughing."

"Right." She nodded, swallowed hard and said, "Anyway, then you went down on one knee and asked me. But you didn't have a ring because you want to take me to New York to pick one out."

"That's thoughtful of me."

"Oh, stop." She tossed her slice of bacon onto her plate. "I feel terrible about all of this, but I was so worried that Gran was going to hop on the first plane out of Florida…" She plopped both elbows on the table and cupped her face in her palms again, making her voice sound weirdly muffled when she added, "Everything's just a mess now and if I call her back and tell her it never happened, she'll think I lied—"

"You *did* lie."

She looked up at him. "It was just a little lie."

"So now size *does* matter?" He shook his head.

"Oh, God. How can you even make jokes about this?"

"What should I do? Rant and rave? Won't change what

you told your grandmother. But I never understood," Micah said, watching her as misery crossed her face, "how people could convince themselves that *little* lies don't matter. Lies are never the answer."

"Oh." She smirked at him and Micah was pleased to see the snap and sizzle of her attitude come back. "Mr. Perfect never lies?"

"Not perfect," he told her tightly. "But, no, I don't."

"You've never had to tell a lie to protect someone you care about?"

Since he had only a handful of people he gave a flying damn about, the answer was an emphatic no. Micah didn't do lies. Hell, his mother's lie—*I'll come back for you. Soon...*—still rang in his ears. He would never do to someone what she had done to him with that one lie designed, no doubt, to make him feel better about being abandoned.

He scrubbed one hand across his face. It was too damn early to be hit with all of this and maybe that's why Micah wasn't really angry. Confused, sure. Irritated? Always. But not furious. A part of him realized he should be mad. He was used to people trying to use him to get what they wanted. It was practically expected when you were rich and famous. And those people he had no trouble getting rid of.

But Kelly was different. He looked across the table at her and noted the worry in her eyes. Why was he so reluctant to disappoint her? Why was he willing to give her the benefit of the doubt when he never did that for anyone else? She was *lying* to her grandmother. That wasn't exactly a recommendation for trustworthiness. And yet...

"Why me?" he asked abruptly. He got up, walked to the coffeepot and carried it back to the table. He filled both of their cups, then set the pot down on a folded towel. Staring at her from across the table, he said, "There have to be some local guys you could choose from. Pick someone you know. Someone who knows your grand-mother and might want to help you out with this."

She took a gulp of coffee like it was medicinal brandy and she was swilling it for courage. "Why you? Who else could I tap for this? Gran knows everyone in town. She'd never believe a sudden engagement to Sam at the hard-ware store. Or Kevin at the diner. If anything romantic had been going on between me and someone in town, her friends would have told her about it already."

Irritating to realize she had a point.

"But you're a mystery," she continued, leaning toward him. "She knows I have a famous writer living here, but no one in town could have told her anything about you. You hardly ever leave the house, so, for all anyone knows, we could have been carrying on some torrid affair right here in the house for the last two months."

*Torrid affair?* Who even talked like that anymore? But as archaic as the words sounded, they were enough to make breathing a little more difficult and Micah's jeans a little tighter. Still, he shifted his mind away from what his body was feeling and forced it to focus on what she'd said.

Kelly wasn't doing this because he was rich. Or for the thrill of claiming a famous fiancé. He was her choice because no one in town knew him. Because her grand-mother would believe her lie. So it wasn't *him* so much that she wanted. Probably any single renter would have done. That made him feel both better and worse.

"That's why I picked you. You're perfect."

*Perfect*, he thought wryly. *And handy.*

"Why should I go along with this?" Not that he was

considering it, he assured himself. But he was curious what she'd come up with.

"As a favor?" she asked, throwing both hands high. "I don't know—because you're a fabulous human being and I'm flawed and you feel sorry for me?"

He snorted.

She sighed and scowled at him. "Micah, I know it's a lot. But this is really important to me. Gran's happy in Florida. She has friends, a nice life with her sister. She's enjoying herself and I don't want her to give it all up for *me*."

He heard the sincerity in her voice, read it in her eyes and knew she meant every word. And he wondered what it would be like to love someone so much you were willing to do whatever it took to make them happy? But since he avoided all closeness with everyone, he'd never know.

Hell, he'd broken off his own real engagement because, bottom line, he couldn't bring himself to trust the woman he'd proposed to. He didn't believe she loved him—because she hadn't known the *real* him. He hadn't allowed her to peek behind that curtain, so he couldn't trust that she would still care for him if she ever found out that he was a man whose past haunted every minute of his present. So he'd ended it. Walked away and vowed he'd never do that again.

Yet here he was, actually considering another engagement? This one based on a lie?

"Micah, I don't want anything from you."

He laughed shortly. "Except an engagement to fool an old woman, the lies to keep the pretense going, and a trip to New York to pick out a ring…"

"Oh, God." She flushed and shook her head. "Okay, yes, I do want you to pretend to love me. But you won't have to lie to Gran—"

"Just everyone else you know."

"Okay, yes—" She winced a little as she admitted that. "But there won't be a trip to New York and there won't be a ring, either. I can keep postponing our *trip* when I talk to Gran and—"

"More lies."

"Not more lies, just a bit more emphasis on the original lie," she argued. Frowning, she met his gaze squarely and said, "If you think I *want* to be dishonest with my grandmother, you're wrong. I love her. I'm only doing this because it's the best thing for *her*."

He drank his coffee and felt her steady gaze focus on him. As if she could will him to do this just by staring at him. And, hell, maybe it was working. He was still here and listening, right?

She must have sensed that he was weakening because she leaned toward him, elbows on the table. Did she know that the vee of her blouse gaped open wider, giving him a clear and beautiful view of the tops of her breasts?

"I'll sign anything you want, Micah," she said. "I know you probably have lots of people trying to get things from you—"

Surprised that she seemed to have picked that thought right out of his mind, he watched her carefully.

"But I'm not. Really. If you're worried I'll sue you or something, you don't have to. I don't want anything from you. Really. Just this fake engagement."

In his experience, everyone wanted something. But Micah was intrigued now. "And when I leave town? What then?"

"Then," she said, heaving a sigh as if she already dreaded it, "I'll tell Gran we broke up. She'll be upset, but this *engagement* will buy me some time. Gran will be able to stay in Florida without worrying and…" She took a breath, then lifted her coffee cup for another sip. "Maybe I'll think of a way to convince her to stay there even if I'm not engaged."

He didn't like it, but Micah couldn't see where this ploy was going to cost him anything, either. He'd only be in town four more months, and then he'd be gone and this would all be a memory. Including the fake engagement. And, he had to admit, the longer he looked at Kelly, seeing the worry in her eyes, hearing it in her voice, the more he wanted to ease it. He didn't explore the reasons he was wanting to help her out because he wasn't sure he'd like the answers.

"All right," he said, before he could think better of it.

"Whoop!" Kelly jumped out of her chair, delighted. She came around the table, bent to him and gave him a hard, quick hug. Then she stood up and smiled in relief. "That's so great. Thanks, Micah. Seriously."

That hug had sent heat shooting straight through him, so he needed a little space between him and Kelly. Fast.

"Yeah," he said, rising to put the coffeepot back on its burner. He turned around to face her. "So what do I have to do?"

"Nothing much," she assured him, and joined him at the counter, closing the distance he'd just managed to find. "Just, when we're around people in town you have to act like you're nuts about me."

"Oh." Well, he thought, that would be easy enough. Not that he was in love with her or anything. Sure, he liked her. But what he felt for her was more about extreme *lust*. So, he could sure as hell act like he *wanted* her, because he did. Now more than ever.

What he didn't want was a wife. Or a fiancée. But he'd

never wanted *anything* in his life more than he wanted Kelly in bed.

She looked insulted as she stared up at him. "Oh, come on," she said. "You don't have to look so horrified about pretending to love me. It won't be that hard to do."

*Hard?* Not a word Micah should be thinking about at the moment. Staring into her green eyes was almost hypnotic, so Micah shifted his gaze slightly. "Yeah," he said with just a hint of sarcasm, "I think I can handle it."

She laid one hand on his arm, and once again a flash of heat shot through him. "I really appreciate this, Micah. I know it's weird, but—"

"It's okay, I get it." He didn't. Not really. How the hell could he understand real family? He'd lost whatever family he had when he was six years old. But, as a writer, he did what he always did. He put himself in someone else's point of view. Tried to look at a situation through their eyes. Over the years, he'd been in the minds of killers and victims. Children and parents.

Yet, he was coming up blank when he tried to figure out what Kelly was thinking, feeling. In fact, she was the one woman he'd ever known who was as damn mysterious as the stories he created. Ironic, he told himself, since he made his living inventing mysteries—and now he was faced with an enigma he couldn't unravel.

It wasn't just Kelly confusing him. It was what being near her did to him that had him baffled.

And he didn't like the feeling.

A couple of hours later, Kelly was at Terry's house, wishing she was anywhere else.

"I tell you to have a steamy affair and you say no," Terry mused thoughtfully as she tapped one finger against her chin. "But you *do* get engaged. Sure that makes sense."

Kelly hung her head briefly, then lifted it to look at her best friend. Terry's place was just a block or two off Main Street. It was a small old brick house with a great backyard and what Terry called *tons of potential.* She and Jimmy were completely rehabbing the old place that Kelly had found for them, a little at a time. The living room was cozy, the kitchen was fabulous, the bathroom was gorgeous—and the rest of the house still needed work.

Sitting on her friend's couch sipping tea and eating cookies was pure comfort. Which Kelly really needed at the moment. In fact, it almost took the sting out of what Terry was saying.

"It's crazy," Kelly agreed. "I know that."

"Good for you," Terry said, injecting false cheer into her voice. "Always best to recognize when you've completely lost your mind."

"You're not helping."

"Of course I'm not helping." Terry shook her head, sending the silver hoops at her ears swinging. "For Pete's sake, Kelly, what were you thinking? You're setting yourself up for God knows what, and now there's no way out."

Kelly knew all of that, but hearing it made her feel worse somehow. Honestly, she still wasn't sure what had made her come up with this idea in the first place. And she sure didn't know why Micah had agreed.

Actually, when she'd first started talking to him that morning, she was positive he'd give her an emphatic no and tell her to get out. But the longer she talked, the more she saw him change, his features changing from irritated to sympathetic to amusement and finally acceptance.

Kelly still could hardly believe he'd agreed to this, but she was super grateful he had. Yes, it was a mess, but at least for the short term, her grandmother was happy and wasn't trying to give up her own happiness for Kelly.

"You should have heard Gran though, Terry," Kelly said softly, remembering. "She was so happy when I told her Micah and I were engaged."

Terry's concerned frown only deepened. "Sure, until you 'break up.'"

Okay, yes, that conversation with her grandmother wasn't one Kelly was looking forward to. But she'd find a way to soften the disappointment. "Yeah, but until then, I've got time to think of a way to keep her from worrying."

"Well, I hope your next plan is as entertaining as this one."

Scowling, Kelly picked up a lemon cookie drizzled with thin caramel stripes and took a bite. Seriously, nobody made better cookies than Terry. People clogged up her tiny coffee shop just to buy the baked goods. And they weren't wrong to do so.

"You're my best friend," Kelly said. "You're supposed to be on my side."

"And if you wanted to rob a bank or drive off a cliff, I should just pick up my pom-poms and cheer you on?"

"That's hardly the same thing as—"

Terry held up one hand. "I'm sorry. You refused a blind date, then got engaged, instead."

"Fake engaged."

"I stand corrected." Terry finished off her tea and set the cup on the coffee table in front of them. "Really, though, I'm on your side, Kelly. I'm just not sure what your side *is*."

"If it makes you feel any better, neither am I." It had all seemed so reasonable when she'd thought of it the night before. But facing Micah with it a couple of hours ago had shaken her a little. Still, Kelly knew this was the best thing to do. The *only* thing, as far as she could tell. Gran was happy, and Kelly didn't have to worry about the older woman giving up her new life.

Micah was fine with it—okay, maybe *fine* wasn't exactly right. *Resigned* might be better. Either way, though, Kelly was getting what she wanted: a reprieve for her worried grandmother.

As far as pretending feelings for the town's benefit, she could pretend to be in love with Micah. She would just have to keep reminding herself that it wasn't real.

Because, honestly, one kiss from that man had melted away every reservation she'd had. Every vow she'd ever made to *not* get involved with another man had simply melted under the incredible rush of heat enveloping her during that kiss. God, even remembering it could set her on fire.

So, okay, this pretense would be a little risky for Kelly. Micah Hunter was the kind of man who could slip past a woman's defenses if she wasn't careful. Even defenses as strong as hers. So Kelly would be *very* careful.

She popped the last of the cookie into her mouth, then said, "Okay, enough 'torture Kelly' time."

"Oh, I'm not nearly finished," Terry told her.

"Fine. We'll pick it up again later, but, for now, are you going to help me with the load of plywood I need to pick up or not?"

"Sure." Terry shrugged and pushed off the couch. "Get engaged, then build a haunted house. What could be more normal?"

Kelly reached for another cookie as Terry picked up the plate and cups to take back to the kitchen. Sighing, Terry said, "And I bet you want to take some cookies home with you."

"That'd be great," Kelly said. "Thank you, very-best-friend-in-the-world-who-is-always-on-my-side-and-only-wants-what's-best-for-me."

Laughing, Terry shook her head and said, "I'll put some in a bag for you."

Kelly grinned as she tugged on her sweatshirt. "Thanks. And to respond to your earlier statement… *normal* is way overrated."

But, while she waited for Terry, Kelly's smile faded and her brain raced. Images of Micah rose up in her mind, and instantly a curl of something dangerous spun in the pit of her stomach.

Yeah. Maybe this fake engagement wasn't such a great idea, after all.

# Six

Micah came out of the house as soon as he saw the two women struggling to pull sheets of plywood out of the back of Kelly's truck.

"So much for getting any work done," he muttered, and made a mental note to tell Sam that if this book went in late, it would be *his* fault. How the hell was Micah supposed to get work done when Kelly was always interrupting? Even when she wasn't there, thoughts of her plagued him, interfering with his concentration and leaving him staring into space as he willed his body into submission.

Hell, how did *any* writer work when they had people coming in and out of their lives? There was just no way to concentrate on your fictional world when the *real* world kept intruding.

As he approached, he noticed for the first time that Kelly's truck had definitely seen better days. It had once been red, but now was an oxidized sickly pink. There were rust spots along the bottom of the body, no doubt caused by all the salt used on winter roads to prevent skidding. There was an old dent in the back right fender, and he had a feeling the inside of the damn thing was no prettier than the outside.

Frowning, he remembered that Kelly had said she plowed driveways and roads during the winter. Did she use this truck? Of course she did, and it probably hadn't even occurred to her that it looked as if it was on its last legs. He didn't like the idea of her out in some snowstorm in a broken-down truck, freezing to death in the cab while she waited for someone to dig her out of a snowdrift—and, yeah, sometimes being a writer was a bad thing. His mind was all too willing to make up the worst-possible scenario of any given situation just to torture him. He shook off the vague ideas and focused on the now.

He was down the front steps and headed across the lawn before either woman noticed him. Kelly had her back to him, but the tiny woman with dark hair and wide silver hoops at her ears spotted him.

Tipping her head back, she stared at the gray sky and shouted to whoever might be listening, "Thank you!"

Looking back at Micah, she grinned. "Well, hi, gorgeous. You must be the new fiancé. I'm the best friend, Terry."

"Good to meet you." It was impossible to *not* smile back at a woman who looked like a seductive elf. "I'm Micah."

Kelly jolted upright from where she was bent over trying to lift one end of the boards. Seductive elf or not, the only woman Micah could see was Kelly. Her hair was back in a ponytail, her gray sweatshirt was paint stained, and her worn denim jeans were ripped high on her right thigh. She must have changed into work clothes after she'd left him that morning. And even in what she was wearing right now, she looked amazing.

She dropped the plywood sheets she was trying to maneuver, and they clattered when they hit the truck bed. Straightening up, she smiled a little nervously. "Um, hi, Micah. This is Terry."

"Yeah, we met." He walked closer, looked into the truck bed, then up at Kelly. "What's all this for?"

She pushed one stray windblown lock of hair out of her face. "Every year I build a haunted house for the kids."

That didn't even surprise him. "Of course you do."

Kelly kept talking. "Last year Terry's husband, Jimmy, helped me out, but he's deployed this year."

Terry sat on the edge of the truck. "I think Kelly misses him almost as much as I do."

"Today I do," Kelly agreed. Her heart flipped over as Micah's gaze was fixed on her with the wariness of a man waiting to see if a suspicious package will explode. And of course she *had* to look absolutely hideous. "So, Micah, can you help carry these boards to the front of the house?"

"I can." He dropped both hands onto the side of the truck. "Does it get me a point?"

"A what?" Terry asked.

"No," Kelly said, smiling because he was acting as he always had around her. Things weren't awkward and she'd worried about that. Oh, she knew he was as good as his word and that he'd act like her lover in public. But she'd been afraid that asking him to do this for her might make things weird between them in private. "This is a favor. Not a point earner."

"What points are we talking about?" Terry looked from one to the other of them.

"Hmm," he mused, "seems to me I already did you a favor earlier. If I do this one, as well, that's two in one day. Is there any kind of payoff for a favor?"

"What'd you have in mind?" Kelly's stomach did a fast spin and roll. Honestly, the man's eyes were so dark that when they were fastened on her, as they were now, she could feel the earth beneath her feet slide and shift.

"Another kiss," he said.

All of her breath left her in a rush.

"Okay," Terry murmured. "This is getting interesting. Wait a minute. Did he say *another* kiss?"

Kelly paid no attention to Terry because she couldn't see anything but Micah. It took everything in Kelly not to vault over the side of the truck and lock her mouth onto his. Just the thought of being held close to him again made her want it more than anything. But she had a question first. "Why?"

He shrugged and his broad chest sort of rippled beneath his black T-shirt. "You said we needed to put on a show in front of people, right?"

"Yeah…" she said, "but Terry doesn't count."

"Thanks very much," Terry said, "however, since Jimmy's gone, I wouldn't mind seeing a red-hot kiss. A little vicarious living would do me worlds of good."

"Pay no attention to her," Kelly advised.

"I wasn't talking about Terry," Micah said, his gaze flicking briefly to a point over Kelly's shoulder. "I was talking about the two old women watching from their window."

"Oh, God…" Kelly murmured. She'd forgotten all about her neighbors, but the two sisters probably had their noses pressed to the glass.

"Hi!" Terry shouted as she turned to wave at Sally and Margie.

The curtains dropped instantly, blocking the women from view. But Kelly knew they were still there. Watching. Hoping to see something worth gossiping about.

"So? Is it a deal?" Micah asked.

Kelly sighed. This had been all her idea, after all. "Deal."

She moved to the side of the truck and Micah reached up to grab her at the waist. His hands were big and strong and hot enough to sear her skin right through the fabric of her shirt. He lifted her out of the truck bed as if she weighed nothing and then let her slide slowly along his body until she was standing on her own two feet again.

By the time her feet hit the ground, Kelly's insides were sizzling and her brain was fogging over. Her hands at his shoulders, she stared up into his brown eyes and read a wild mix of desire and amusement there. She couldn't have said why that particular combination appealed to her, but it did. "Well," she asked after a long minute of simply staring into each other's eyes, "are you going to kiss me?"

"Nope."

Surprised, she tried to pull away, but his hands only tightened on her waist. "Fine. But I thought you wanted a kiss for a favor."

"Yeah," he said, his gaze sliding over her face before meeting hers again, "but this time, *you* kiss *me.*"

Another swirl of hot nerves inside, but she had to admit it was only fair. He'd surprised her with their first kiss, and now she wanted to surprise him with just how hot a kiss could be if she knew it was coming. Giving him a faint smile, Kelly went up on her toes and slanted her mouth over his.

He held on to her but didn't take the lead. This show was all Kelly's. She parted his lips with her tongue, slid into his mouth and felt his breath catch in his throat. She explored his mouth, tasting, plundering. Spearing her fingers through his hair, she turned her head slightly to one side and groaned as he finally surrendered to the fire building between them. He clutched her tightly to him and tangled his tongue with hers until Kelly's mind splintered and floated out of her head to blow away in the cold breeze.

"Niiiiccceee…" Terry's voice was no more than a buzz that Kelly barely registered.

Kelly's heart banged against her ribs. She held on to Micah because if she didn't, she'd have keeled over from the rush of sensations pouring through her. His hands fisted at her back and held her so tightly to him she felt the hard length of him pressing into her belly. She rubbed against him, torturing them both. Knowing he felt what she felt, wanted what she wanted, only made her own feelings that much deeper. More intense.

God, she wanted to feel his skin beneath hers. She wanted to feel his heavy weight on top of her. Feel his hard body sliding into hers…

"Um, guys?" Terry's voice came again, hesitant but insistent. Then she got louder, demanding they hear her. "*Guys!* You realize you're about to get way out of control right in the front yard?"

In a daze, feeling a little drunk, Kelly pulled her head back and turned to look blearily at her friend. "What?"

"Damn." Terry fanned herself with both hands. "I think that's enough of a show for now or you'll kill Sally and Margie."

"What?" Kelly asked again, and then realization slammed into her, and she turned to Micah and dropped her forehead on his chest. She could hardly believe what had just happened. If Terry hadn't spoken up, who knows what might have happened? "Oh, God."

"Yeah," Micah said tightly as he struggled to even out his ragged breathing. "I think Terry's right. I'll just get those boards for you now. Where do you want them?"

"Okay, that's good. Um, right in front of the porch," she whispered, and he let her go. Amazing how *alone* she felt without the strength of his arms wrapped around her middle.

Still a little shaky, she leaned against the truck and watched while Micah lifted a few of the huge plywood sheets and, balancing them on his shoulder, carried them to the front of the Victorian. His muscles stretched and shifted beneath his shirt. His black jeans hugged his behind and his long legs, and her mouth went dry just watching him.

"Honest to God," Terry murmured in her ear, "if you don't jump that man immediately, you're not the brave, intrepid Kelly I know."

"It's not that easy," Kelly said, gaze locked on him.

"Why the hell not?" Terry gave Kelly's shoulder a nudge. "You want him. He clearly wants you. I almost went up in flames just watching, and I can tell you that after seeing that kiss, when I get home, I'm video chatting Jimmy and hoping he's alone."

"That's different," Kelly grumbled. "You're married."

"And you're *engaged*," Terry reminded her. "For God's sake, take advantage of it."

But that hadn't been part of their deal, Kelly told herself. Was it fair to try to alter their agreement now? Then she remembered the grinding pressure of his mouth on hers and knew that he'd be okay with changing the rules. The question was, could she keep her emotions separate from the physical desire engulfing her? And could she live with herself if she *didn't* act on what she was feeling?

Micah walked back across the yard for the next load and Kelly's gaze fixed on him. Black jeans. Black boots. Black T-shirt. Dark brown hair ruffling in the cold breeze. Brown eyes that met hers for one long, blistering moment.

And she knew that, complicated or not, deal or not, she had to have him.

Micah ignored the noise from the front of the house for the next two hours. He heard the constant hammering, the arguing between Kelly and Terry and told himself it had nothing to do with him. What did he care about haunted houses? Besides, he had work to do. If thoughts of Kelly and that kiss ever left him the hell alone.

Scowling, he glared at the computer screen, rereading what he'd just written. His heroine was in deep trouble and getting in deeper every second. She was wandering the woods, looking for a lost child, and had no idea there was a killer right behind her.

Grimly he kept typing, in spite of the fact that his jeans were so tight he felt he was going to be permanently injured. He kept tasting Kelly on his lips and told himself that it didn't matter. It had been for show. To impress the neighbors and show them that Kelly's fiancé was crazy about her. The fact that it had impacted *him* so much wasn't the point.

Points. Kelly and her points. What was it now, three to one with her in the lead? Hell, if she'd brought it up at the time, he'd have awarded her five more points for that kiss today. He felt like her mouth was permanently imprinted on his. If he lived to be a hundred, he'd still be able to bring back the taste of her and the feel of her in his arms while the cold wind danced around them.

"This isn't getting any work done," he muttered, and stood up from the desk. It wasn't until that moment that Micah realized how quiet it was. The hammering had stopped, and there was no more good-natured shouting from Kelly and Terry.

He walked to the window and looked out. At that angle, all he could see were the tops of plywood panels the two women were fixing together and standing in front of the porch. But it seemed that work on the haunted house was over for the day. Good. No noise meant not being reminded of Kelly. With no thoughts of Kelly, maybe he'd get some pages written.

"Where did she go?" he muttered an instant later, drumming his fingers on the window frame. "And why do you care?"

He didn't, of course. Curiosity didn't translate into *caring*.

Shaking his head, Micah walked to the desk and it felt like the computer screen was glaring at him, mocking him for stopping in the middle of a damn sentence. Well, he didn't have to be insulted by his own tools. He slammed the laptop shut and stalked out of the office. Work wasn't happening. Relaxing wasn't happening. So he'd try a beer, the game on TV and a chance to shut off his mind. Micah took the stairs, then turned and headed for the kitchen.

He never made it.

Kelly stepped through the swinging door from the kitchen into the dining room and stopped dead when she saw him. Everything in Micah tensed and eased at the same time.

Her hair tumbled wild and wavy around her face and down over her shoulders. Her eyes were bright and locked on him like laser beams. Micah's breath caught in his chest as a tight fist of need closed around his throat.

"Surprised to see me?" she whispered.

"Yeah." He nodded. "A little. But then you seem to be full of surprises."

"I'll take that as a compliment," she said, and moved a couple steps closer to him.

"You should." Micah walked toward her, too, one slow step at a time. "I never know from one minute to the next what you're going to do." He didn't admit how much he liked that about her. Didn't mention that he saw her *everywhere*. That images of her were dancing through his brain 24/7. Hell, he didn't even like admitting that to himself, let alone her.

Kelly's eyes flashed and his insides burned.

"Like being here now for instance," Micah said quietly. "What're you doing, Kelly?"

"I came to ask you a question."

He blew out a breath. "What is it?"

"Pretty simple, really," Kelly said, moving still closer.

He could have reached out and touched her, but Micah curled his hands into fists to keep from doing exactly that. After that kiss this afternoon, he was sure that if he held on to her now, he might not let her go again.

"There's a lot of…tension between us, Micah."

He snorted. "Yeah, you could say that."

She kept talking as if he hadn't spoken at all. "I mean, that kiss today? I thought the top of my head was going to blow off."

Micah reached up and rubbed the back of his neck. "I felt the same."

"Good," she said, nodding. "That's good."

"Kelly…" He was at the ragged edge of his near-legendary control. Her scent was reaching for him, and the look in her spring-green eyes was tempting him to just let go. "What're you getting at?"

"Well, we're both grown-ups, Micah," she said, tipping her head back to look at him.

"Yeah," he said tightly. "That might be part of the problem."

She laughed shortly. "True."

Her hair fell in a red-gold curtain behind her, and a light floral scent that clung to her skin seemed to surround him. "But, since we *are* adults, there's a simple way to take care of that tension." She took a breath and held it. When she spoke again, the words tumbled from her in a rush. "I think we should just go to bed together. Once we do that, we'll both be able to relax and—"

Control snapped at the suggestion he'd been hoping for. Micah grabbed her, speared his fingers through her hair and held her head still for his kiss. He poured everything he felt into it. The unbearable frustration that had tortured him for two months. The wild, frantic need that disrupted his sleep every night. The desire that pulsed inside him like an extra heartbeat.

She groaned, fueling the fire enveloping him, and kissed him back with the same fierce hunger that was clawing at him. Her hands moved up and down his back, up into his hair, then clutched at his shoulders.

Micah's brain simply shattered. He didn't need it anyway. The only thing either of them needed now was their own willing bodies. When Micah tore his mouth free of hers and gasped for air, Kelly grinned at him. "I guess that's a yes?"

Surprise after surprise.

"No, it's a *hell yes*," he corrected, then picked her up and slung her over one shoulder in a fireman's carry.

"Hey!" Hands against his back, she pushed up and swung her hair back in an attempt to see him. "What're you doing?"

He glanced back at her and rubbed one hand over her behind until she shifted in his grasp.

"This is faster. No time to waste," he told her, and headed for the stairs again.

"Right." She rubbed her own palms over his back, then down to his butt. "Hurry."

He took the stairs two at a time, his long legs making short work of the distance separating them from the nearest bed. He covered the hallway in a few long steps, walked into his bedroom and tossed her onto the mattress.

"Whoop!" She laughed as she bounced, then her gaze met his and all amusement fled. "Oh, I'm so glad you didn't say *thanks, but no thanks*."

"Not a chance of that," Micah assured her, and yanked his T-shirt off over his head.

Kelly smiled, licked her lips and toed off her shoes before immediately tugging at the button and zipper of her jeans. She squirmed out of them, making Micah's mouth water at his first peek at the tiny triangle of pink lace panties she had on under those jeans.

She kept her gaze locked on his as she worked on the buttons of her long-sleeved shirt and slowly let it slide down off her arms. The pink lace bra matched the panties and displayed more of her breasts than it hid.

He couldn't look away from her. Every breath came loud and harsh in the room. Micah felt like he was straining against a leash that had held him in place for two long months. Now that it was ready to snap, he didn't know what to do first. Where to touch. Where to kiss. Where to lick. He wanted it all. When she took off the bra and panties then tossed them over her head to the floor, the leash finally snapped.

She lay there, her pale skin luminous against the forest-green duvet. Her hair spilled out around her head like a red-gold halo of silk. Her breasts were fuller than he'd imagined, but delicate, too, her dark rose nipples rigid with the desire pumping through her.

His mind simply went blank. Like a starving man suddenly faced with a gourmet feast, Micah froze, helpless to look away from the woman laid out in front of him like a dream.

"Micah...you're wearing too many clothes," she murmured, licking her lips.

"Right. I am." He peeled out of his clothes, and in seconds he was naked and covering her body with his. Her hands slid up and down his back, across his shoulders to his chest and then up to cup his face. When Micah kissed her again, their bodies moved against each other as if they both were looking for that skin-to-skin contact. To revel in the heat. To drown in it. As if to assure each other that they were finally going to ease the raging desperation that had chased them both through torturous days and long, sleepless nights.

He swept one hand down the length of her as he shifted, dragging his mouth from hers to trail kisses along the line of her jaw, the slim column of her throat. She sighed, gasped and arched up into him. Her legs tangled with his, smooth to rough, adding new sensations to those already crashing down on them.

He slid his hand across her abdomen, down her belly to the center of her. To the heat he needed to claim, to bury himself in. She jerked helplessly. To drive her higher, faster, Micah took one hard nipple into his mouth.

Instantly, Kelly writhed in his arms as if trying to escape even while she held his head to her breast to keep him from stopping. "Micah… Micah, this is too much."

"No," he whispered, "not nearly enough." He covered her damp, hot core with his hand and slid first one, then two fingers inside her. She arched into him and his mind splintered at the feel of her generous, oh-so-eager body shaking and twisting in his arms.

His lips, teeth and tongue worked her nipple as his fingers continued to push her toward a release they both needed so badly.

"Stop, Micah," she whispered brokenly.

He lifted his head, questions in his eyes. "You want me to stop?"

Shaking her head, she choked out a short laugh. "Not on your life. I just want more than your hand on me." She was breathless, eyes a little wild, and she'd never looked more beautiful. "If you keep touching me like that, I'm going to climax and I don't want to. Not without you inside me."

Relief flooded him. He'd have had to back away if she'd changed her mind, and Micah knew without a doubt that stopping would have killed him. Knowing that she was simply trying to hold back an orgasm gave him the freedom to push her beyond the ability to fight it.

"One now," he said, stroking that one sensitive nub at her core with his thumb. "More later."

"Oh…my…goodness…" Her fingers dug into his shoulders. Her hips rocked frantically into his hand. She planted her feet and lifted herself higher, higher. He watched as Kelly's eyes glazed. "Micah—I… What are you doing to me? I've never…"

Micah had never been with anyone like her before. What she felt echoed inside him. The taste of her filled him, the scent of her swamped him, and the shattered, hungry look in her eyes fed the fires inside him like nothing he'd ever experienced before.

He hadn't been prepared for this, he thought, frantic himself as he watched her body bow and twist. He'd thought it would be a simple matter of bodies meeting, doing what came naturally. Feeling that sweet flash of release and moving the hell on. But no woman had ever affected him like this. No woman had slipped beneath his defenses, made him crave *her* release as much as his own. He didn't know what any of it meant, and now wasn't the time for trying to figure it out.

Micah felt the first shudder take her, body rippling with too much sensation all at once. She fought for breath, grasping at his shoulders, digging her head back into the mattress, struggling for air as she screamed his name like a prayer to an indifferent god.

His own breath caught in his chest. Mouth dry, heart hammering, body as tight as a bowstring, Micah set her down on the bed and shifted, reaching for the drawer of the nightstand. He pulled it open, grabbed a condom and ripped the foil packet. He had to have her. Now.

"Micah, that was—" She shook her head, at a loss for words. The smile that curved her lips shone in her eyes, as well. "I've never…" She stretched like a happy cat and damn near purred. Then she opened her eyes at the sound of foil tearing.

"Wow. You went out and bought condoms just in case?"

He shook his head. "Nope, had them with me."

"You *travel* with condoms?" she asked, surprise in her voice.

He glanced at her. "Doesn't everyone?"

"Hoping to get lucky, were you?"

"Babe," he admitted as he sheathed himself, "I'm a *guy*. I'm always hoping to get lucky."

Her grin spread as she held out her arms to him. "Well, since I think we're both pretty lucky at the moment, I can't really complain, can I?"

He returned her grin, and as he shifted to part her thighs and kneel before her, he quipped, "So, having a condom handy means a point for me, huh?"

"Oh," she teased, "I don't know about that. I mean *points* are serious business and—"

He slid into her heat, and she went instantly quiet as she shifted a little to accommodate him. Then she groaned and tipped her head back into the mattress.

"Yes," she said. "If you can keep making me feel like—*oh!*—this, definitely a point for you."

"I love a challenge," he whispered. Still smiling, he covered her mouth with his and tangled their tongues in a dance that mimicked the movements of their bodies. She gave as much as she took, Micah thought, and realized that for the first time he was with a woman who was completely herself. There was no pretense with Kelly.

Whatever she felt, she let him know. Her soft cries

and whimpered moans told him exactly what she liked. She was a little wild and he liked it. His mouth moved on hers as his hips rocked, slipping into a rhythm that had her kissing him hungrily, sliding her hands up and down his back, dragging her nails across his skin.

When he was strangling for air, he lifted his head to watch her expressive face as he claimed her completely. Her body held his in a tight, hot embrace, and he gritted his teeth to keep from giving in to the urge to let go. He wanted this to last. Wanted to make her crazy before he finally gave them both what they needed most.

Outside, twilight stained the sky a deep violet. Inside, the only light was in her eyes as she stared up at him, a look of wonder in her gaze. Their hands met, fingers linked, and he felt it when her climax slammed into her. Her body arched, her heels dug into his lower back. She screamed his name, and Micah watched the inner explosions ripple across her face and felt more satisfaction himself than he could ever remember. His heart raced, and his body continued to move in hers, and only when the last of the tremors coursed through her did he let himself go, finally giving up control and diving into the maelstrom, willingly letting it take him.

# Seven

Kelly didn't know how much time had passed. And truthfully, she couldn't have cared less. Her whole body was humming as if her finger was somehow stuck in a light socket and electricity was pouring through her.

Finally, though, when she thought she could speak again, she said simply, "Wow."

"Agreed." Micah's voice was muffled because his face was buried in the curve of her shoulder.

She smiled to herself and stared blankly up at the ceiling. Good to know that he was as shattered as she felt. Micah's body pressed her into the bed and she knew she should ask him to move, but it was so lovely to feel the heavy press of a man's body on hers after so long on her own.

At that thought, Kelly felt a pang of sorrow that peaked and ebbed inside her in seconds. *Sean.* She closed her eyes briefly, as if thinking about him now was a breach of trust, somehow. Which was just stupid and she knew it. But, until today, Sean was the only man she'd ever been with. Hardly surprising that thoughts of her late husband would rise up.

Sean and Micah were so very different in so many ways. Micah's body was stronger, bigger—in every way, she thought with a tiny stab of guilt for the comparison. But it wasn't just their physical differences that set them apart.

With Micah there was laughter along with the sex. Kelly smiled, remembering the teasing about points and traveling condoms. With Sean, lovemaking had been a serious business. Instead of romance and fun, she'd always felt as if Sean had had a mental checklist. *Turn lights off, check. Kiss Kelly, check. Tongue, check. Touch breasts, check.* Their times in bed together had been almost clinical, more of a task to be accomplished.

*God*, she couldn't believe she was even having these disloyal thoughts. Kelly had never told anyone how unsatisfied she'd been in her marriage. Not even Terry. Though she had loved Sean, until now Kelly had believed that she simply wasn't capable of the kind of orgasms that Terry described—*blinding, mind-shattering, earthshaking*. Because in her husband's arms, Kelly had never felt more than a tiny blip of pleasure. Before today, sex had been just a sense of closeness.

She'd had absolutely no idea that there was a tsunami of sensations she'd never experienced.

Kelly opened her eyes and looked at the man she still held cradled to her. In the first few moments with Micah, Kelly had discovered more, *felt* more than she ever had with her husband. And maybe, Kelly thought for the first time, that was the reason she hadn't been interested in going on dates, finding another man. Because being with Sean hadn't been all that great.

She'd long blamed herself for the lack of spark between her and Sean, assuming that she just wasn't experienced enough to really make things heated between them. Now she had to admit that maybe the truth was that she and Sean had been friends too long to make the adjustment to lovers.

"I can hear you thinking," Micah murmured. "Keep it down."

Kelly grinned, grateful he'd interrupted her thoughts. Silently she let go of the past and returned to this amazing moment and the man she'd shared it all with. "Are you sleeping?"

"Yes," he muttered.

She laughed and the motion had his body, still locked inside her, creating brand-new ripples of expectation. Stunned, she couldn't believe she was ready to go again after what had been the most staggering orgasm of her life. Kelly slid her hands up and down his broad back and lifted her hips slightly to recreate that feeling. Instantly she was rewarded with another tiny current of electricity.

He hissed in a breath, lifted his head and looked down at her, one eyebrow arched high. "You keep moving like that and we're going to need a new condom."

Naturally she wriggled again, deliberately awakening a wave of fresh need. Reaching up, Kelly cupped his face in her palms and asked, "How many condoms do you have?"

He rocked his hips against her and she gasped.

One corner of his mouth lifted. "I'm thinking not nearly enough."

Was it bad that her heart did a slow roll and flip at

the sight of his smile? Was it dangerous that she wanted nothing more than to stay here, like this, with Micah smiling down at her, forever? Her heart pounded painfully in her chest and her whole body trembled as he sat back onto his heels, drawing her with him, keeping their bodies locked together.

"Oh, boy." She said it on a sigh as she settled onto Micah's lap. Face-to-face, their mouths only a kiss apart, Kelly was lost in the rich brown of his eyes. His body went deep. She *felt* him growing, thickening inside her, and she swiveled her hips, grinding her core against him to feel even more.

He bent his head to take her nipples, one after the other, into his mouth. Kelly looked blindly around the familiar room, trying to distract herself so she wouldn't climax as quickly this time. She wanted to draw this moment out as long as she could. So she looked at the forest-green walls, the white crown molding, the now-cold white-tiled fireplace and the chairs drawn up before it.

She'd lived here most of her life and knew every corner of the old Victorian; yet, she'd never been more alive than she was at that moment. Never been so in tune with her surroundings, with her own body and with the man currently setting her on fire with a desire sharper, richer than she'd known ever before.

He suckled at her as if trying to draw everything she was within him. Kelly surrendered to the moment, concentrating not on where she was but what was happening. His big hands scooped up her spine and into her hair, fingers dragging along her scalp. Kelly watched him at her breasts while that delicious tugging sensation shot through her body.

Another first. She'd never made love like this—sitting

atop a man so that every stroke of his body into hers was like a match struck. Kelly went up on her knees and slid down slowly, taking him as deep as she possibly could.

When Micah groaned and lifted his head, staring into her eyes, she felt stronger than she ever had. She moved on him again, picking up a rhythm that tormented both of them, and every time she rocked on him, she swore she could feel him touch her heart.

Her breath came in sharp, short puffs as she rode that crest of building pleasure again. How could she have not known all there was to *feel*? To *experience*?

Micah's jaw was tight as he fought for control. He looked into her eyes and dropped his hands to her hips to guide her into a faster rhythm. Bracing her hands on his broad shoulders, Kelly bit her bottom lip, tossed her hair back and stared deeply into Micah's steady gaze. She couldn't look away. Couldn't stop the growing wave of sensation inside her. Sliding her hands from his shoulders, she ran the flat of her palms across the sharply defined muscles of his chest. She ran her thumbnails across his nipples and watched him shudder and grind his teeth in response and she felt…powerful. Knowing what she was doing to this strong man made her feel sexy. Desired.

On his knees, he pushed into her and she twisted on his lap, grinding her pelvis against his, torturing them both, hurrying them along the path to a climax that would, she knew, completely shatter her. She wanted it. More than anything. She raced blindly toward it.

"Micah," she whispered, still scraping her nails across his nipples, still looking into his eyes. "Go faster. Go harder."

"You're killing me," he ground out, then flipped her

over onto her back. Still locked inside her, he drove himself into her, again and again, harder, higher, faster until neither of them could breathe easily. He lifted her legs, draped them across his shoulders and continued his relentless claiming of her.

Kelly shouted and fisted her hands in the duvet beneath her. The world was rocking wildly. He was so deep inside her she thought he might always be there. And she wanted that, too.

Again and again, they moved in a frantic dance designed to end in a splintering of souls, until the world shrank down to the bed alone and nothing outside the two of them mattered. He took her hard and fast and deep and she went with him eagerly.

Kelly called his name over and over again until it became a chant. Lifting her hands, she held on to his upper arms as he braced himself over her and dug her nails into his skin.

"It's coming. Come with me," she said brokenly, voice tearing like wisps of fog in a heavy wind. The tension inside her heightened unbearably. She moved into it, trying to throw herself at the pleasure waiting for her. "Now, Micah. Please, *now.*"

"Come then," he ground out, staring into her eyes. "Let me see your eyes when I take you."

Her release slammed into her like a freight train. She forced her eyes to stay open. She wanted him to see what he was doing to her. What only he had ever done. She quaked and shivered and finally screamed his name in desperation.

And, before the last of the tremors shuddered through her, he called out her name and stiffened as his body joined hers. Kelly held him as he took from her as much as he had given. Then he collapsed, bonelessly atop her, and, shattered, Kelly cradled him in her arms.

It was dark when Kelly woke up. She was a little stiff. A little sore. And a lot desperate for air. Micah was sound asleep on top of her. Couldn't really blame him for being wiped out, but as good as he felt on top of her, Kelly really needed to breathe easier. Shaking her head, she said, "Micah! Micah, roll over."

"What?" Groggy, he lifted his head and opened his eyes. Understanding instantly, he rolled to one side, keeping an arm locked around her middle. "I fell asleep."

"We both did." Taking a deep breath, she curled into his side and just managed to swallow a sigh of satisfaction. "What time is it, anyway?"

"Who cares?" He threw one arm across his eyes.

"Good point."

"Hey," he said. "Another point for me."

"That wasn't a point. That was just a figure of speech. So it's still three to two, my favor."

He smiled. "So I *did* get a point for all of this."

Kelly sighed. By rights she should have given him ten, twenty, even thirty points for everything he'd made her feel. "Oh, boy, howdy."

"I can live with that."

She laughed. "Okay, so, are you hungry? I'm hungry."

He opened one eye. "You're kidding."

"I never kid about food." She went up on one elbow and looked down at him. Oh, my, he was great looking when he was dressed, but *naked*? The man was drool-worthy. Kelly shook her head. If she kept going down that path, she would start something that wouldn't get her fed.

And if she didn't eat soon, she wouldn't have the strength for everything else she wanted to do with Micah. Now that was motivation. "Come on, you've got to be hungry, too."

"Not enough to move anytime soon."

"Really?" Kelly sat up and stretched, feeling looser and more limber than she had in years. "I'm not tired at all. In fact, I feel energized. We should have done this a long time ago."

He stared up at her and frowned.

"What?"

"Seriously?" He studied her as if she were on a slide under a microscope. "You feel great and you're hungry. That's all you have to say?"

Confused, Kelly laughed. "What were you expecting?"

Propping himself up on both elbows, Micah tipped his head to one side. "So you're not going to say that you've been doing some thinking and that we should talk?"

"About what?"

"About your feelings," he said. "And how sex changes things between us and we should figure out where our *relationship* goes from here."

She would have laughed again, but he looked so serious she just couldn't do it. Shaking her head, Kelly held up one hand. "Wait. Is that what most women do? Have sex with you and then ruin it with…*talk*?"

He frowned. "Well, generally, yeah."

She didn't know whether to be insulted that he'd expected her to be like every other woman he'd met in his life—or to feel bad that he had to protect himself against wily women looking to hook him into a relationship he didn't want. So she did neither.

Kelly smiled, bent down and planted a quick, hard kiss on his mouth. "Well, then, I'm happy to surprise you again. I came to you, remember? All of this was *my* idea—"

"Well," he said, "in my defense, I'd had the same idea—I just hadn't approached you with it yet."

"Even if you had, it wouldn't matter." She shrugged. "We're two adults, Micah. We can have sex—really *good* sex—without it meaning hearts and flowers, right?"

Confusion shone in his eyes. "Well, yeah, it's just—"

"What's wrong now?" Hadn't she eased his mind yet?

"Nothing," he said, a scowl tugging at his lips. "It's just, I'm the one who usually gives that little speech. It's weird being on the receiving end."

"Another first." Kelly took a deep breath then blew it out. "Well, I'm done talking. But I could really go for a sandwich."

She scooted off the bed, picked up his discarded T-shirt and pulled it over her head. God, she felt good. "You want one?"

"Sure," he said slowly, thoughtfully. "I could eat."

"Great. I'll see you in the kitchen." Kelly left the room and didn't stop walking until she was downstairs. Then she paused and looked back up toward the room where she'd left him.

She'd told him she didn't want to talk and that was true. What she didn't tell him was that she was starting to feel a lot more for him than she'd planned on. Maybe it was the way he was so hesitant about letting people in. Maybe it was the half smile that curved his mouth so unexpectedly. She didn't know exactly what it was that was growing inside her, but Kelly was pretty sure that she was headed for trouble.

* * *

For the next few days, Micah and Kelly developed a routine that worked for both of them.

Micah spent the mornings working, building his novel page by page while Kelly raced from one job to the next. In the afternoons, they worked together on her Halloween project.

And every night they were together at the Victorian in Micah's bed.

Micah glanced over at Kelly now as she showed three kids how to roll black paint onto the plywood sheets. A reddish-gold ponytail hung down between her shoulder blades and swung like a metronome with her every movement. She wore her favorite worn jeans with the rip on the right thigh, black work boots and a faded red sweatshirt with the slogan Women Do It Better scrawled across the front. There was black paint on her cheek and a smile on her face as she listened to some long, involved story one of the kids told her.

A sharp stab of desire hit Micah so hard, so fast he nearly lost his breath. Hell, the skies were gray and there was an icy wind sliding through the nearby canyon, and Micah felt like his insides were blazing.

He and Kelly had thought to ease the sexual tension between them by sleeping together. Instead, they'd poured gasoline on a smoldering fire and started an inferno. Micah wanted Kelly all the time now. She was constantly on his mind. Her image, her scent, the harsh cries she made when he was inside her, pushing her over the edge.

This had never happened to him before. He should have known, he told himself, that Kelly would be unlike any woman he'd ever met. That had to be why he found her so intriguing. It was the newness factor. Her unpredictable nature. Her ability to keep him guessing, always on his toes. Hell, she *still* hadn't started that whole *we should talk* conversation he kept expecting. And a part of him was waiting for that shoe to drop.

There was no one else in his life who could have gotten him to stand out in the cold putting up plywood walls for a neighborhood Halloween maze. Shaking his head, he didn't know whether to be impressed by her or ashamed of himself.

He emptied his mind and took a good look at what they were building. It wasn't really a haunted house, but more of a passageway kids would have to go through to collect candy on Halloween night. Black walls, fake spiderwebs, a recording of scary sounds and voices, there were also going to be black lights to cast weird shadows and a few ghoulish mannequins to finish it all off.

If anyone had told him a year ago that he'd be in a small town in Utah building scary Halloween stuff, he would have called them crazy. Yet, here he stood.

"How the hell did this happen?" he muttered.

"You said a bad word," Jacob said, frowning up at him.

He looked down at the little boy and sighed. For some reason, this one particular kid had adopted Micah. Apparently, since Micah had taken the kid to visit his pumpkin, that had forged a bond. At least in Jacob's mind.

"What?"

"A bad word," the boy said. "You said *hell*."

"Oh." He rolled his eyes. Really had to watch that, he supposed. But then he wasn't exactly accustomed to dealing with children, was he? Even when he was at Sam and Jenny's place, Micah didn't spend much time with their two kids. In his defense, Isaac was a baby, so the kid didn't have much to say. And Annie, he realized suddenly, was Jacob's age.

Funny. He'd always told himself that he didn't pay attention to Sam's kids because he had no idea how to act with them. But he and Jacob got along so well that the boy had unofficially adopted him. That made him wonder if maybe he should have tried harder to get to know Sam's daughter, Annie.

But at the same time, Micah remembered that he didn't *like* kids. He didn't ask Jacob to hang around all the time, did he? Micah didn't want to get close to anyone. Had, in fact, spent most of his life avoiding any kind of connection.

*And how has that worked out for you?*

He glanced at the little boy kneeling beside him and gave an inner sigh. Now he had to remember to watch his language because a child had decided the two of them were best friends.

"Yeah, well," Micah said finally. "I shouldn't have said the bad word. And don't you say it."

Jacob's eyes went wide. "Oh, I won't cuz once Jonah said *damn* and Mommy made him go sit in his room and he *cried*."

And the ten-year-old probably wouldn't appreciate his little brother sharing that bit of news. Still, nodding sagely, Micah said, "Learn from your brother's mistakes then. Now," he added, "hold the hammer in both hands and hit the nail."

Micah yanked his fingers out of the way just in time, as Jacob's aim was pretty bad. But the grin on the kid's face was infectious. He was clearly proud of himself and loved being thought of as big enough to help like the other kids. Micah smiled at the kid and wondered again just how this had happened to him.

"Can I do another one?" Jacob asked, turning his face up to Micah's.

"Sure," he said, glancing at the bent, smashed nail. Micah would fix them later. For now, let the kid feel important. Memories of his own childhood swept through Micah's mind in an instant. Ignored by adults, he'd taken advantage of their disinterest and learned how to become invisible. He didn't cause trouble. Didn't stand out for good or bad reasons. And because he'd spent every minute trying to not be seen, not once had he *ever* felt important. To anyone.

Micah held out another nail and watched Jacob situate it just right. "Be careful. If you smash your fingers Kelly will get mad."

Jacob laughed delightedly. "No, she won't. But I can be careful."

When his cell phone rang, Micah grabbed it from his back pocket and looked at the screen. "Can you be careful on your own?"

"I can do it. I'm not a baby."

"Right. I forgot." The phone rang again and Micah stood up. "I'll be right back," he told Jacob, then answered the phone as he stepped away from all the hammering and kids' high-pitched voices. "Hey, Sam."

"Hey, yourself," his agent countered. "You haven't called to whine in a few days so I figured you were dead."

Reluctantly Micah laughed. "That's not bad. Giving up the agent life to hit the stand-up circuit?"

"I could," Sam said. "Annie thinks I'm funny."

"Your daughter is three." Micah kept walking until he was ten feet from the small crowd gathered in front of the Victorian. The breeze was stronger out here, without the big house giving any shelter. "She thinks your evil cat is funny."

"Sheba's a perfectly nice cat," Sam pointed out. "With excellent judgment. She likes everyone but you."

"She knows I'm a dog person," Micah said, then frowned. Hell, he didn't know if he was a dog person. He'd never had a pet. Not that he cared. It was just odd to suddenly realize that. But he was always traveling. How was he supposed to take care of an animal if he didn't have a home?

"Great, I'll get you a puppy."

"Do it and die," Micah told him, though it surprised him to realize that a puppy didn't sound like such a bad idea. He scrubbed one hand over his face as if he could wipe away thoughts that had no business in his mind. "If you're calling about the book, it's still coming slowly."

Mostly because instead of just imagining what it might be like to have sex with Kelly, he was spending most of his free time remembering what they'd done together the night before. Hell, it was a wonder he got *any* work done.

"Yeah, this isn't about the book," Sam said. "I'm flying out to California in a couple days. I've got a Friday meeting with an indie publishing house."

Thanks to the internet, independent publishers were springing up all over the place. Most started and disappeared within a span of a few months—just long enough to fulfill and then crush would-be writers' dreams. But a few started small and built a strong list of writers and grew into houses with good reputations and steady sales.

Micah's gaze shifted to Kelly. She was bent over, helping Jacob's older brothers and a girl from down the street apply layers of black paint to plywood. The curve of her behind drew his gaze unerringly, and Micah had to look away for his own sanity.

He started paying attention again just in time.

"So," Sam was saying, "I thought you might want to fly out for the weekend. Take a break from small-town life and visit with an old friend."

It sounded like a great idea to Micah. He'd been here in Banner for more than two months and he could do with a good dose of city life. Plush hotel, room service, noise, people…

"Sold," he said abruptly, then looked at Kelly again. She tossed her ponytail and laughed as Jacob's big brothers started painting each other. Looking at her wide smile, he could only think about getting her away from her home ground. Into some plush, luxurious life where he could seduce her nonstop. "But I won't be coming alone."

"Yeah?" He actually heard the intrigued smile in Sam's voice.

"Thought I'd bring my fiancée with me." He grinned, anticipating Sam's reaction. He wasn't disappointed.

A couple of long seconds filled with stunned silence ticked past before Sam sputtered, "Your *what*?"

"Can't get into it right now. I'll explain when I see you," Micah said, and had to admit he was enjoying leaving Sam hanging on the information front. "Where do you want to meet?"

"I'm staying at the Monarch Beach Resort in Dana Point, and who is this fiancée and when did this happen?"

"Got it," Micah said, ignoring the questions. "When's your meeting?"

"I'm flying in early Friday for a meeting that afternoon. But I'll be staying until Sunday."

"Okay." Micah did some fast figuring. It was Tuesday now—he had plenty of time to arrange for a suite at the hotel and a private jet to get him and Kelly to Orange County. All he had to do was convince her to leave town for a few days. He had confidence in his ability there. "I'll see you then."

"You are *not* going to leave me hanging with no information," Sam complained. "Do you know what'll happen if I go home with this news and no details? Jenny will hound me."

Micah laughed. "Sounds perfect."

"You're gonna pay for this—"

Micah hung up and enjoyed it. Sure, Sam would find a way to get revenge, he told himself. But that's what good friends were for, right?

His gaze locked on Kelly. She must have felt him staring, and something inside him turned when she met his gaze and smiled at him. Her eyes were shining, the curve of her delicious mouth was tempting and when she turned back to the kids and bent down, his gaze locked on her behind again. The woman really had a world-class butt.

His body went tight and hard in an instant. Yeah. A few days away from here. No work interfering for either of them. Just relaxing and enjoying each other. What could be better?

Going online, Micah went to the hotel's website and reserved the Presidential Ocean Suite. He stayed there whenever he was in Southern California and he knew that Kelly would love it. The hotel was top-of-the-line, and this room in particular was damn impressive, with a private balcony that offered sweeping views of the Pacific. Micah smiled to himself as he imagined her on that terrace, the wind in her hair, moonlight making her bare breasts seem to glow. Naked with only the sky, the stars and the sea as witnesses. That's how he wanted her.

All he had to do now was find a way to convince her to take a break from her many responsibilities.


Kelly was flabbergasted.

One of her grandmother's favorite words, it was the *only* one that fit this situation, Kelly told herself. In fact, she was so stunned she couldn't think of a thing to say. And that was so unusual for her, she couldn't remember the last time it had happened.

Micah's invitation had come out of the blue and she'd instantly agreed. True, she had to rearrange the jobs she had lined up, but the chance to get away with Micah was one she didn't want to miss. Being with him was so important to her she was already worrying about what it would be like when he eventually left. But, until then, she wanted to be with him every minute she could be.

She and Terry had made an emergency shopping run to Salt Lake City. It had taken them hours, since Terry had insisted on hitting every single boutique and dress shop in the city, but it had been worth the trip. In her suitcase now, Kelly had clothes suited to a five-star resort.

As soon as Micah told her about the Monarch Bay Resort, Kelly had looked it up online so she'd have some idea of where she'd be staying. The hotel was lovely, elegant. And completely intimidating.

First there had been the limo ride to the airport, then they had been ushered to a private concourse and escorted onto the jet Micah had chartered. Kelly had felt like a queen, lounging in the supple blue leather chairs set into conversation areas. *So* much better than flying like a sardine in an overcrowded can.

She and Micah had sipped champagne and nibbled on strawberries during the short flight. The limo ride to the hotel hadn't flustered her and she'd idly wondered if she was already getting accustomed to being spoiled. But walking into this hotel, where the staff called Micah by name and rushed to do his bidding, and then this spectacular suite... Kelly was simply overwhelmed.

The Presidential Ocean Suite was breathtaking. There was a fireplace, several overstuffed couches and chairs in soft pastels. The carpet was thick and the color of sand. There were vases filled with fresh yellow roses, and there were French doors leading to the private terrace.

The bedroom was huge, with its own fireplace and another set of French doors leading to the balcony they shared with no one. There were crystal chandeliers over the dining table and the bathroom was bigger than her whole cottage back home, with a tub wide and deep enough to swim in and a shower built for a cozy party of five or six, with built-in benches that made Kelly think of any number of things she and Micah could do on them.

And *when* had she become so interested in sex?

Answer, of course—the first time Micah kissed her. He'd created a monster. Smiling to herself, Kelly said simply, "Micah, this is just...amazing. The whole day has been—" She broke off, at a loss for words for the first time in forever. "I wouldn't have missed this for anything."

She walked toward the open terrace doors and caught the shimmer of sunlight on the deep blue of the ocean as it stretched out into eternity. A soft sea breeze danced into the room, ruffling the sheer white curtains.

"I'm glad you came," he said.

"So am I."

Kelly turned to him. He wore black slacks, a dark red dress shirt with the collar open and a black sports coat. He looked comfortable in his surroundings and she realized that *this* was how he lived all the time. He'd told her that he moved from hotel to hotel when he was working, but somehow, even knowing he was rich and famous, she hadn't considered that the hotels he was talking about were really more like palaces.

Kelly tried to imagine living in a place like this and just couldn't do it. The thought of trying to fit into this kind of lifestyle on a daily basis was exhausting. For Kelly, this was an aberration. A step outside her own reality. Okay, more than a step. A *leap*. But the reality was this: as gorgeous as this place was, as glad as she was that she'd come away with Micah, Kelly felt like an interloper here. But, for the next few days, she was going to pretend that she *did* belong, because there was nowhere else she'd rather be.

His gaze locked on her. "Did I tell you before we left that you look beautiful today?"

Kelly flushed, relishing the heat that always raced through her when Micah was near. And now she was doubly glad she and Terry had done so much shopping. Her new black slacks, white silk blouse and deep green brocade vest looked good on her, she knew. And she didn't want to *look* as out of place here as she felt. "You did tell me. Thank you."

He walked across the room to her, took her hand and then led her to the French doors. Stepping onto the terrace, she took a quick look around at the earth-toned tile floor, the table and chairs in one corner and the pair of lounge chairs complete with deep blue cushions and red pillows.

"It just keeps getting better and better," she murmured, and, letting go of his hand, walked to the iron railing and looked out at the sea. The ocean was a deep blue with gold glints of sunlight shining on its surface. Boats with jewel-toned sails skimmed along the waves while surfers closer to shore rode their boards with a grace she envied.

A soft breeze tossed her hair across her eyes. She plucked it free and sighed. "It's like a fairy tale."

"I've pictured you here," he said, and when she turned to look at him, she found his gaze locked on her. "Standing just there, the wind in your hair, a smile on that incredible mouth."

Her heartbeat skittered. "And is the reality as good?"

"Almost," he said, moving in close.

"Only almost?" Her eyebrows lifted and she laughed softly.

"Well, when I pictured you standing there, I was seeing you naked in the moonlight," he admitted, pulling her up against him.

A curl of damp heat settled at her core, and Kelly lifted her head to meet his gaze. Hunger shone in his eyes as he slid his hands down to cup her bottom and hold her tight to his erection. What was it about this man that turned her into a puddle of desires she'd never known before? Why was it he could touch her and send her up in flames? How could one smile from him turn her heart upside down?

She was very much afraid she knew the answers to all of those questions. But now wasn't the time to explore it. The next few days were just for them. To be together. To revel in each other. She didn't want to waste a minute of it.

"Well," she said, when she could breathe past the knot

in her throat, "it's important to make dreams come true. So tonight…"

He hissed in a breath through gritted teeth and held her even tighter to him. "That's a date," he promised, then deliberately took a step back, groaning. "But if I want to show you anything of California, we'd better get going. How about we go down, pick up the car I've got waiting and drive up the coast?"

At that moment, she would have gone with him anywhere.

# Eight

Micah took her up the coast to Laguna where they parked the car and walked along Pacific Coast Highway. They popped into art galleries, bought ice cream from a vendor and swayed in time to a street performer's smooth, slow saxophone performance.

Early October in California meant it was still warm, and with the sun shining down on them, the day couldn't have been more perfect. Then he spotted something in a shop window.

"Come with me," he said, taking Kelly's hand and pulling her into the cool quiet of the jewelry shop. The interior of the shop was cool and dimly lit so that the jewels in the glass display cases could shine like stars in the night beneath lights fixed to the underside of the cabinets. There was a dark red rug on the wood-plank floor, and a grandfather clock ticked loudly into the hushed quiet.

"Micah, what're you doing?"

"I saw something I want to get." He signaled an older man behind the gleaming glass cases filled with diamonds and gemstones.

"May I help you?" He wore round, wire-rimmed glasses. His gray hair was expertly trimmed, and his pin-striped suit complete with vest made him look as though he'd stepped out of the nineteen forties.

"Yeah." Micah glanced at Kelly as she wandered down the glass cases, admiring everything within. Turning back to the man in front of him, he said, "The emerald necklace in the window."

The man brightened. His eyes sparkled and a tiny smile curved his mouth. "One of our finest pieces, sir. One moment."

Kelly wandered back to Micah and leaned into him. "What're you buying?"

"A gift for someone," he said, leaving it at that as the man came back, laid the emerald necklace out on a black velvet tray and waited for their admiration.

"Oh, my, that's gorgeous," Kelly whispered, as if she were in church.

"It is, isn't it?" Micah liked the look of it himself, but he was more glad that Kelly approved of it, too. Square cut, the emerald was as big as his first thumb joint. The setting was simple, with platinum wire at the gemstone's corners and twin diamonds on either side of it, the stone hung on a delicate platinum chain. And the emerald itself, he thought, was exactly the color of Kelly's eyes. That's what had caught his attention in the first place. "Okay, I'll take it."

The older man's eyebrows lifted but, otherwise, he

remained cool and polite. "Of course. Would you like it gift wrapped?

"Not necessary," Micah said, reaching for his wallet and then his credit card. He didn't bother to ask the price. It didn't matter, anyway.

"I'll take care of it straight away," the man said, then looked at Kelly. "I hope you enjoy it." Then he scurried away to ring up the sale, clearly wanting the business done before Kelly talked Micah out of the purchase.

"Oh," she said to the man's back as he left, "it's not for me…"

Her voice trailed off as Micah lifted the necklace from the black velvet and turned to her.

Eyes wide, Kelly looked horrified as she took a step back. "Micah, no."

Again, she surprised him. She hadn't even considered the possibility that the necklace was for her. "You said you liked it."

"Well," she said, "I'd have to be blind *and* stupid to not like it. That's not the point."

"You're right," he said, pushing past her reservations. "The point is, I want you to have it." He stepped behind her, laid the jewel at the base of her neck and ordered, "Lift your hair."

She did, but all the while she was shaking her head. "You can't just buy me something like this out of the blue—"

"Well," he said, voice low and teasing, "you did tell your grandmother that we were going to New York for a ring, so…"

*"Micah."* She turned her head to look at him, and he smiled at her to ease the worried look in her eyes.

When the necklace was secured around her neck, he

moved to stand in front of her. The emerald shone like green fire on her skin and he felt a swift tug of satisfaction seeing her wearing it. "It looks perfect."

"It would look perfect on a three-legged troll," Kelly argued, but her fingers reached up to touch the stone and her gaze slipped to a mirror on the counter to admire it. "It's beautiful, Micah. Seriously. But you don't have to do this. Buy me things, I mean."

No, she wouldn't expect that from him and he found that…refreshing. Most of the women he'd ever been with had anticipated trinkets like this. They'd oohed and aahed over jewelry-store windows or even, on occasion, dragged him inside to let him know in no uncertain terms which piece they'd most like to have. But Kelly didn't want anything from him. Didn't demand anything. She was happy just being with him, and that had never happened before.

And maybe that was why Micah had felt compelled to buy her that damn necklace. He wanted her to have something to remember him by. In a few months, he'd be gone from her life, but every time she looked at that necklace, she'd remember today and she'd…what? *Miss him?* Had anyone, anywhere ever missed him? Had he ever wanted them to? Questions for another time, another place, he told himself.

"I wanted you to have it," he said simply. "It's the same color as your eyes."

"Oh, Micah…" Those big beautiful green eyes filled with tears and, just for a second, he panicked. But Kelly blinked the moisture back and lifted her chin. "You don't want to make me cry. I look hideous when I cry. I'm a sobber. I don't do delicate weeping."

Of course she wouldn't cry. He chuckled—how could

he not? Kelly was one in a million at everything. "Good to know. I'll make a note. No making Kelly cry."

A wry smile curved her mouth briefly, then her shoulders slumped and a defeated sigh escaped her. "I can't stop you from doing this, can I?" she asked, still touching the cold, green stone.

"Already done, so no."

Nodding, she took a breath, let it out again and said, "Fine. Am I allowed to thank you?"

"Only briefly," he told her warily.

"Thank you, Micah," she said, going up on her toes to lay a soft, slow kiss on his mouth. "I've never owned anything more lovely. Whenever I wear it, I'll think of you."

His heart jolted. It was just what he'd wanted, yet hearing her say it he could almost hear the "goodbye" in her voice. He hadn't thought it would bother him, but it did. For the first time in his adult life, he wasn't looking forward to moving on. Frowning, he told himself he would. He had to. Eventually. But Micah didn't want to think about endings today.

Looking at her, the pleasure in her eyes, an emerald at her throat and a smile on that fabulous mouth of hers, all he could say was, "I'll think of you, too."

And he knew he'd never meant anything more.

Later that night, Kelly did a quick spin in place on her three-inch heels, sending the skirt of her new black dress flying. Then she stopped and looked up at Micah. "Today was so lovely. Thank you, Micah."

He shrugged. "It was fun."

It was a revelation, she thought but didn't say. She'd seen Micah in a whole new light. He was famous. Rich. Important. Everywhere they went, people scrambled to please him. Fans—mostly women—had stopped him on the street to coo over him, completely ignoring Kelly's presence. And she'd seen his reaction to all of the notoriety. It all made him uncomfortable. Sure, he was polite to everyone, but there was a cool detachment in everything he did that told Kelly he'd much prefer going unnoticed.

Micah lived a life that was so far removed from Kelly's they might as well have been on different planets. But, for now anyway, they were together. And maybe that was all she should think about.

She strolled across the terrace to the railing and lifted her face into the sea breeze that was soft and cool. Turning her head to him, she said, "I thought the maître d' at dinner was going to cry when you signed his book for him."

Micah poured them each a glass of champagne and carried them to her. Handing her one, he had a sip of his own. "I couldn't believe he had it with him at work."

She laughed and took a drink of the really fabulous wine. Shaking her hair back from her face, she sighed. "I can't believe I'm here. Not just California," she amended. "But here... Here. In this beautiful hotel. With you."

"I'm glad you are," he admitted, then frowned slightly as if he'd like to call the words back.

But it was too late, because Kelly heard them and held them close in her heart. He might not want to care about her, but he did. For now, that was enough for her. Neither of them had gone into this expecting anything but a release of sexual tension. And if she was feeling... more, then she'd just keep that piece of info to herself. He wouldn't want to hear it and she wasn't ready to admit it, anyway.

Pushing those thoughts out of her mind, Kelly turned from the railing, walked to the table and set her champagne flute down. When she turned back to Micah, she smiled and reached behind her back for the zipper. "I think we made a date for this terrace tonight, didn't we?"

She saw his grip on the fragile stem of the flute tighten. "Yeah. We did, didn't we?"

The zipper slid down with a whisper and she lifted both hands to hold the deeply scooped bodice of the dress against her. "And you're sure no one can see us?"

He took a drink and speared her with a look that was so hot, so barely contained, his brown eyes burned with it. "Private terrace. No neighbors. Empty ocean."

"Okay then." Kelly took a breath and let the dress drop to pool at her feet. She'd never done anything like this, and she felt both excited and exposed. But Micah's gaze on her heated her through, and she forgot about feeling self-conscious and instead enjoyed what she was doing to him.

On that shopping trip with Terry, Kelly had indulged in some new lingerie, as well. His expression was all she'd hoped for.

Micah's gaze moved up and down her body before settling on her eyes again. "You're killing me."

"You like?" He more than liked and she knew it.

"Yeah," he ground out. "You could say so. One point for the black lace."

Kelly grinned. "Nice! That makes it four to two, my favor."

"You keep dressing like that, I'll give you all the points you want."

She shook her head slowly and said, "But didn't you say that in your dream I was naked?"

"So you *are* trying to kill me."

"No," she assured him. "Just torture you a little." Slowly she peeled out of the black lace bra, dropping it onto the nearest chair. And, leaving her high heels on, she slipped out of the matching scrap of her panties and stood there with the ocean breeze drifting across her skin like a lover's hands.

"Well," she asked softly, "as good as the dream?"

"Better," he told her, and bent to take a kiss while his hands cupped her breasts, rolling her nipples between his thumbs and forefingers.

Kelly groaned and leaned into him, loving the feel of his hands on her skin. The taste of his mouth on hers. She felt completely wicked and absolutely wonderful.

He dropped one hand to her core and she parted her thighs for his touch. Micah had shown her more about herself, what her body was capable of, than she'd ever have believed possible. And now she wanted him all the time. Craved what happened between them when they were together. He stroked her, explored her, and she whimpered with need as an oh-so-familiar tension crept through her.

His thumb moved over that one sensitive spot and she gasped, moving her hips, trying to feel more, faster. He pushed one finger, then two, inside her and Kelly groaned again, clutching his shoulders, holding on while her body went on another wild ride courtesy of Micah Hunter.

The cold air brushed against her while his warm hands stoked fires inside her. Over and over, he touched, caressed, until she was just on the brink of a shattering climax. Then he stopped and she nearly shrieked.

"Micah—don't—"

"Wait." He lifted her, plopped her onto the table then, as she watched, he parted her thighs and knelt in front of her.

"What're you— Oh, Micah…"

Beneath her, the heavy metal table was cold against her behind, but she didn't feel cold. She felt as if she were on fire. Then Micah covered her center with his mouth and Kelly cried out in surprised pleasure. His lips, tongue and teeth drove her crazy. She threaded her fingers through his hair and held him to her as he continued his delicious torment.

He licked and suckled at the very heart of her, and the sensations rising inside her were powerful. Overwhelming. She had to hold on to him or she was sure she would have simply fallen off the face of the earth. She rocked helplessly in place as he pushed her so high there was no higher to go. Then the crash came and Kelly cried his name in a broken voice and let the sound drift away into the night wind.

Still trembling, she locked her eyes on his as he stood up and looked down at her. "Point to you," she whispered. "That was—"

"Four to three then," he said, scooping her off the table to cradle her close. "I'm catching up."

She smiled because she felt so darn good, but Kelly looked up at him through glazed eyes as she admitted in a whisper, "I've never— I mean no one…"

"I know what you meant," he said softly, his gaze locked with hers. "And if you're interested, there are a lot more firsts headed your way."

"I love to learn," she said, reaching up to briefly cup his face in the palm of her hand. Kelly laid her head on his chest as he carried her through the spacious living area into their bedroom.

Whatever he had in mind, Kelly was ready for it.

The following night, Micah and Kelly had dinner with Sam and Jenny Hellman, then the four of them took a walk around the hotel property. Both women were strolling slowly ahead of the men, and Micah could only guess they were still bonding over their favorite romance author.

Since Sam and Jenny had arrived, the four of them had spent a lot of time together, and Micah was pleased at how well Jenny and Kelly were getting along. Though why it mattered, he told himself, he couldn't have said. It wasn't as if they were all going on vacation together. And unless Sam and Jenny rented the Victorian for ski season again, they wouldn't be seeing each other after this weekend. Once Micah had moved on, none of the others would have any reason to meet. So why did it matter to him that the people he was closest to were becoming friends?

Hell, he didn't know. But that was typical. Since meeting Kelly, Micah had felt off his game. Off balance. And she was doing it to him. Micah's gaze locked on Kelly. She wore a bright yellow dress that made her look like a lost sunbeam in the night. Her hair was long and loose and the wind kept lifting it, as if teasing her. Something inside him stirred and warmth spread through his chest.

"You're sleeping with her, aren't you?"

"None of your business," Micah said tightly, and he knew that was as good as saying *yes*.

"Ah, touchy." Sam nodded thoughtfully. "That's interesting."

"What're you talking about?" Micah kept his gaze straight ahead because looking at Kelly was more fun than looking at Sam.

"Just that you've never minded talking about your women before…"

Micah ground his teeth together. "She's not one of my women," he said. "She's Kelly."

"Also interesting." Sam smiled to himself. "Getting attached, huh?"

"No." He was definitely not getting attached. Of course he cared about her. But there was nothing more than that because he wouldn't allow it. "Leave it alone, Sam."

"Not gonna happen." His old friend punched him in the shoulder and said, "For the first time, you've brought a girl home."

Micah snorted. "Are you crazy?"

"Come on. We both know Jenny and I are as close to family as you've got, and here we are, the four of us, bonding nicely. So I think that says something."

"And I think you should stick to being an agent," Micah told him. "Because the fiction you dream up sucks."

Sam laughed and waved one hand at his wife when Jenny turned around to look at them. "Why not just admit that you and Kelly have something good together?"

Micah sighed and fixed his gaze on Kelly again. The way her hair fell around her shoulders. Her long legs, the way that yellow dress clung to her curvy body. Everything about her appealed to him. And that was enough to make him wary. She was the only woman he'd ever met who had tempted him to look deeper. That made her dangerous.

"Because what we have is temporary." Saying it aloud reinforced what he knew was pure truth. There was no future here.

"Well, I like her."

"Yeah," Micah said grimly. "So do I."

"Well, you don't sound too happy about it."

Micah scowled and wasn't sure if he was directing the expression at his friend or himself. "Why should I be? You know as well as I do I'll be leaving in a few more months."

Although, as he said it, Micah realized that moving on didn't sound as good as it usually did. Strange. Normally, after three months in one place, Micah was already getting restless. Making plans for where he would go next. Polishing up one book and already plotting the next. That was his life. Had been for years. And it worked for him, so why would he even consider changing it?

"And your point is…?"

"Don't say *point*."

"What?"

"Never mind." Micah shook his head. He'd never be able to hear that word again without thinking of Kelly. What were they now? Four to three. He remembered how he'd been awarded that last point and his body went hard as stone.

"This is *temporary*," he said again, emphasizing that last word, more for his own sake than for Sam's.

Sam stared at him as if he had three heads. "It doesn't have to be, that's what I'm saying. Hell, Micah, you're already engaged to her."

And this engagement would end just like the last one, he told himself. Sighing, Micah stuffed his hands into his slacks pockets. "We explained the whole thing to you. It's just a lie for Kelly's grandmother's sake."

"Lies can become truths."

Micah snorted. "No, they can't."

Sam shrugged. "Hey, look at it from my perspective. You guys get married, and Jenny, me and the kids have a place to stay every ski season."

"That's very thoughtful," Micah said wryly.

Sam smiled as he watched his wife stumble, catch herself and keep walking. "Jenny could trip over air, I swear." Sighing in exasperation, he said, "You and Kelly are good together, Micah. Why be in such a damn hurry to throw it away?"

*Because he didn't know what to do with it.*

"You don't buy gigantic emeralds for a woman you don't give a damn about—and thanks for that, by the way. Jenny's already reminded me that her favorite stone is a sapphire."

Micah laughed a little and it felt good to ease the tightness in his chest. "That's your problem. As for the emerald, I just wanted Kelly to have it. That's all."

They were walking through the hotel gardens and past the pool where a couple dozen people splashed in the aquamarine water. The sky was clear, the air was warm and the ocean breeze was cool and damp.

"Why?" Sam asked. "Why'd you want her to have it?"

"Because," Micah said in exasperation. "Just…because."

Sam laughed and Jenny turned around to look at him. He waved her off again and said, "Damn, Micah. No wonder I can get you so much money for your books. You've got a real way with words."

"Drop it, Sam."

Sam stopped. He was a couple inches shorter than Micah, a little heavier and a lot more patient. "Just admit it, man, she's got you. You care about her."

"Of course I care. What am I—a monster?" Micah stared out at the black ocean. "She's a nice woman." *Lame*, he thought. "We have a good time together." *They had a hell of a lot together.* "I like her." *Like. Care.* Hell, even he didn't believe him.

"Must be love."

Micah's head snapped around and his gaze burned into Sam's. "Nobody said anything about love."

Shaking his head, Sam mused, "Damn, you react to that word like a vampire does to a cross."

"I've got my reasons," Micah reminded him.

"Yeah, you do," Sam agreed. He leaned back against the railing behind him, folded his arms over his chest and said, "I'm the first to agree you had a crap time of it as a kid. So I get why you've closed yourself off up until now."

"I hear a 'but' coming," Micah mused.

Sam slapped his shoulder. "That's because you're a very smart man. So here it is. *But,* how long are you going to use that excuse?"

Micah shot him a look that would have had most people backing up with their hands in the air. Not Sam, though.

He gave Micah a bored smile. "Please. Don't bother giving me the Death Stare. It's never worked on me."

Micah rolled his eyes. True. "Fine. But my past is not an excuse, Sam. It's a damn *reason*."

"Because you had a miserable childhood you can't love anyone? That's just stupid." Shaking his head, Sam said, "It's like saying you never had a burger when you were a kid so now you can't have a Big Mac."

Micah scowled.

"Basically, buddy," Sam continued, "you're letting a crappy past mess with your present and future."

Micah ground his teeth together so hard it was a wonder they didn't turn into a mouthful of powder. Having his past reduced to a stupid analogy didn't help the situation any, and Micah felt compelled to defend his decisions on how he chose to run his life. If he wanted to be a footloose wanderer with no connections to anyone, that was his call, wasn't it? If it sounded lonely all of a sudden, that shouldn't be anyone's business but Micah's. And it had *never* mattered to him before, so he'd get over it. He liked being alone. Liked the freedom. Liked being able to pick up and move and have no one miss him. Right?

He frowned to himself over that last thought. Would Kelly miss him when he left? Would she think about him? Because he damn sure knew he would be thinking about her. *Just another reason to leave.*

"Wow," he said finally, "thanks for the analysis. How much do I owe you?"

"This one's on the house," Sam said, ignoring the sarcasm. "At some point," he paused. "Sorry. Used the word 'point' again, and someday you'll have to explain why we're not using it anymore."

Micah choked out a harsh laugh, but Sam wasn't finished.

"You have to decide if you want a life—or if you'd just rather be somebody else's victim for-freaking-ever."

"I'm not a damn victim," Micah muttered, insulted at the idea.

"Glad to hear it," Sam countered. "Now, what do you say we catch up with our women and go get a drink?"

"God, yes."

Sam hustled on ahead to catch up with Jenny and Kelly. Micah smiled in spite of everything as his friend offered each of them an arm and then led them off toward the hotel bar. Kelly turned her head to smile at him, and even at a distance Micah's heart gave a hard jolt.

He hadn't planned on any of this. All he'd wanted was a quiet place to work for six months. He hadn't asked to have Kelly come into his life. And now that she was there, he didn't know what to do about it. Sam meant well, but he couldn't understand what drove Micah. How the hell could he?

When you lived a life in the moment, tomorrows just never came into play. So, like always, Micah wouldn't look to the future—he'd just make the best of today.

Luxury hotels, limos and five-star restaurants made for a wonderful holiday, but after two weeks back at home, it all seemed like a pretty dream to Kelly.

As soon as they'd got home, she had stepped right back into her routine as if she'd never left, and that's how Kelly liked it. Her time away with Micah had been wonderful, but being here in her small town with him was perfect. She never took off the emerald necklace he'd given her so that, even when she was busy with her different jobs and Micah was shut away in the Victorian working on his book, it was like she had him with her everywhere she went.

*Micah.*

"You're doing it again."

Kelly jumped guiltily and grinned at Terry. "Sorry, sorry."

"Where were you?" Terry held up a hand. "Nope. Never mind. I know that look. I have it on my face constantly when Jimmy's home."

Kelly sighed a little, took a sip of her latte and scooted closer to where Terry was rolling out dough for the next batch of cookies for her shop. The kitchen smelled like heaven and, like Terry, was organized down to the last cookie sheet stacked carefully on its rack.

Kelly kept her voice down so the girls running the counter out front couldn't hear her. "Terry, I've never— I mean, I had no idea that— Why didn't you tell me how amazing sex is?"

Terry laughed and shook her head. She picked out a cookie cutter and quickly, efficiently, stamped out a dozen shapes in the dough. Then she carefully lifted each of them to put on a cookie sheet for baking. "Honey, you were married, I thought you knew."

Feeling disloyal again, Kelly said, "It was never like this with Sean. I didn't know feelings could be so *big*. I mean," she said, sighed heavily and closed her eyes briefly to bring back the magic of Micah's hands on her skin. "What he does to me, it's…" She couldn't even find the words to explain and maybe that was best. "I just never want him to stop touching me."

Terry took a moment to fan herself with her hands. "Good thing Jimmy's calling me tonight because I'm dying of jealousy here." Then she took another long look at Kelly and said, "You're feeling guilty, too, aren't you? About Sean, I mean."

"A little." A lot. She didn't mean to compare the two men, but it was inevitable when what she felt with Micah was so much more than anything she'd ever known.

"You don't have to." Terry patted her hand. "Sean was

a sweetie, but it's not like you two were legendary lovers or anything."

"I loved him," Kelly said softly.

"Of course you did," Terry agreed. "In a nice, comfortable, safe kind of way."

Was that what her marriage had been, Kelly wondered? Had she simply married Sean because he'd made her feel safe and settled? If Sean had lived, would they have stayed together? Would they have been happy? Kelly sighed again. There were no answers, and even if there were, they wouldn't change anything.

"He loved you, too," Terry said. "Enough, I think, to want you to be happy, Kelly. So, if Micah makes you happy, then yay him!"

Kelly picked up a finished cookie and took a bite, thinking about what Terry said. "He really does, you know? Every day, it just gets better between us. He's funny and crabby and kind and, God, the man has magic hands. In California, we were together all the time and... look." Leaning in, Kelly reached beneath the collar of her T-shirt and pulled out the emerald.

"Holy Mother of Cinnamon!" Terry all but leaped over the marble counter to lift the emerald with the tips of her fingers. She looked from the stone to Kelly and back again. "Is it real? Of course it's real. Rich guys don't buy junk. I didn't know emeralds *got* that big, for heaven's sake. And those are diamonds...

"Oh my God, I can't believe it took you two weeks to show me!"

Kelly laughed at her friend's reaction. "I just—it's kind of embarrassing. I mean, I told him not to buy it—"

"Of course you did." Terry sighed. "Why are you embarrassed to show me?"

"Because it sort of felt like bragging, I guess."

"Why wouldn't you want to brag about it?" Terry lifted the emerald and turned it back and forth so that the light caught and flashed off it. "That is amazing. If it was mine, I'd wear it stapled to my forehead so everyone would see it."

Laughing, Kelly realized she should have shown it to Terry as soon as she got home. But hiding the necklace wasn't just about not wanting to show off.

It was about the unshakable feeling she had that the emerald had been Micah's way of saying goodbye. Of letting her know that he would be leaving but he wanted her to have something to remember him by. Being Micah, it just had to be an emerald-and-diamond necklace, but the point was, she worried that he was already pulling away.

She'd noticed it more after Sam and Jenny had shown up. It was as if having his friends there had somehow made Micah shut down, go into self-defense mode. Jenny had told her that she'd never seen Micah happier than he was with Kelly. But since their weekend away, he'd drawn more into himself. It was nothing overt, but she *felt* the distance he was slamming down between them, and she had no idea how to get past it.

Yes, this had all started as a lie to make her grandmother feel better, but it had become so much more for Kelly. And maybe, she told herself, this was Karma's way of punishing her for the lie. Make her feel. Make her want. Then deny her. But even if it was, she told herself, she still had three months with Micah and she wouldn't let him leave her emotionally before he actually left.

Ruefully, Kelly admitted, "I can't bring myself to take the necklace off. It's like as long as I wear it, Micah's mine."

"Oh, sweetie, you've got it bad, don't you?"

"I love him." Her eyes went wide and she gasped a little before saying, "Oh, God. I love Micah." Kelly slapped both hands to her stomach as if she were going to be sick. "How could I do this?"

"Are you kidding?" Terry demanded. "Have you *looked* at him lately? It's a wonder it took you this long to fall for him. And that's not even counting the jewelry and the great sex."

Kelly laughed, but it sounded a little hysterical, even to her. She hadn't meant to fall in love, and she knew all too well that Micah would be horrified if she confessed what she felt for him. Heck, he'd probably be nothing more than a blur on his way out the door if he thought she was in love with him.

This had just slipped up on her. She hadn't meant to love him. And it wasn't the luxury vacations. Or the necklace. Or the sex—okay, maybe the sex was part of it. But she'd fallen in love with the *man*.

The man who could look so surprised when she didn't react the way he expected. The man who helped her with her haunted maze. The man who stood with a little boy so he could say good-night to his pumpkin.

"Oh, God," she whispered again. "This isn't good."

"Honey," Terry reached for her hand and squeezed it. "Maybe he loves you, too."

"Even if he did, he probably wouldn't tell me." Kelly shook her head. He'd been pretty clear, hadn't he? One engagement in his past and no desire for another. She could still hear him… *No wife. No girlfriend. No interest.* She closed her eyes and took a breath to try to steady herself. It didn't work.

"This wasn't supposed to be about love, Terry," she

said, and was talking to herself as much as her friend. "This was just…"

"An affair?" Terry shook her head. "You're just not the affair kind of person, sweetie. This was *always* going to end up with you in love."

"You might have warned me," Kelly said miserably.

"You wouldn't have listened," Terry assured her and carried the cookie sheet to the oven. She slid it inside, set the timer and came back again. "You might be upset over nothing. I've seen you guys together and he does feel something for you, Kelly. If it's not love, it's close. So, maybe he won't leave when his time here is done."

"I want to think that, but I can't." Kelly shook her head firmly. She'd already set herself up to have her heart broken. She wouldn't make it harder by holding on to the hope that things would change. "If I believe he'll stay, when he does eventually leave it'll only be worse on me."

"You could *try* to keep him here."

"No." Kelly had some pride, after all. She took another breath, squared her shoulders and lifted her chin. "If I had to *make* him stay then it wouldn't be worth it, would it?"

Terry sighed. "I hate when you're rational."

Kelly laughed sadly. "Thanks. Me, too." She finished off her latte. "He's going to leave, and I'll have to deal with that when it happens. For right now though, he's here. And I've got to go. Micah went to the university library today to do some research—"

"He's never heard of the internet?" Terry asked.

"He's a writer," Kelly said, with a sad smile. "He likes books. Anyway, I want to beat him home because I'm making dinner."

"I thought you said you loved him," Terry quipped.

"I'm not that bad," Kelly argued, though she could

admit that she wasn't the best cook in the world, no one had died from eating what she made.

"Right." Terry turned and headed to the cooling racks. "Why don't I send some cookies home with you and then at least you'll have dessert."

"You're the best."

"So I keep telling Jimmy," Terry said with a wink.

The drive home only took a few minutes, but even at that, her faithful truck wheezed and coughed like an old man forced to run when all he wanted was a nap. Kelly sighed a little, knowing she'd be buying a new one soon.

Micah's car wasn't in the driveway, so Kelly took that as a good sign. She wasn't completely ready to face him yet. The whole *I'm in love* revelation had hit her hard and she needed a bit more time to deal with it.

Grabbing the grocery bags from the passenger seat, she headed into the kitchen through the back door. She had steaks, potatoes for baking, a salad and now the world's best cookies. After she put everything away, she opened a bottle of wine so it could breathe. Because, boy, she needed a glass of wine. Or two. Maybe it would help her settle.

She'd been married, been in love and, yet, this feeling she had for Micah was so huge it felt as if she might drown in it. And she couldn't tell him. Kelly had absolutely no desire to hand him her heart only to have him hand it right back.

She looked around the familiar kitchen as if she were lost and looking for a signpost to guide her home. Micah had stormed into her life with the promise to leave again in six months. Now she was halfway through that timeline and Kelly knew that nothing in her life would be the same without him in it.

"Oh, stop it," she told herself, slapping both hands onto the cold granite counter. "You're feeling sorry for yourself. You're missing him even though he's not even gone yet. So cut it out already." Nodding, she reacted to the personal pep talk by tucking her feelings away. There'd be plenty of time to explore them all later. But for now... "Grab a shower, and put on something easy to take off."

Wow. She was thinking about sex. Again. And had been since... "Micah came into your life, that's when."

Her stomach swirled again as she headed for the stairs. Nerves? Anticipation? Worry? She frowned a little. "Please don't be getting sick, that's all. There's enough going on without that. Besides, it's almost Halloween and there's way too much to do."

Kelly climbed the stairs, walked down the hall, turned into the big bedroom and stopped dead. "Who are you?"

The completely naked stranger propped up against Kelly's pillows stared at her. "I'm Misty. Who're you? Where's Micah?"

# Nine

"Micah?" Kelly stared blankly at the woman. Why was she naked? Why was she here? In *their* bed? And mostly Kelly's brain screamed, *Why are you just standing there talking to her? Why aren't you calling the police?* All very good questions. And still, Kelly started with, "How did you get in?"

"The doors weren't locked." Misty sat up higher in the big bed, clutching the duvet to her bare breasts. Thick black hair fell in tousled waves around her shoulders. She had too much makeup on her wide blue eyes and her lips had been slicked a bright red. As for the rest of her, Kelly didn't want to know.

"You need to get dressed and get out of my house." Kelly folded her arms across her chest and tapped the toe of her boot against the rug. She was hoping to look intimidating. If that didn't work, the sheriff was next.

"*Your* house?" The woman sniffed and settled back more comfortably against the bank of pillows. "Micah Hunter lives here and I don't know what you're trying to pull, but he won't be happy when he comes home to find you."

God, Micah would be home any minute, too. Good thing? Bad? Who could tell?

"How do you know Micah?" Kelly had to wonder at the woman's complete confidence. Was she a girlfriend Micah hadn't told Kelly about? An ex, maybe?

"He's my soul mate," Misty declared dramatically. "I knew it the first time I read his books. His words speak to my *heart*. He's been waiting for me to find him and he won't appreciate *you* being here and spoiling our reunion."

Kelly shook her head. "Reunion?"

"We've lived lifetimes together," Naked Misty intoned with another touch of drama. "In each incarnation, we struggle to find each other again. At last now, we can be together as we were meant."

Baffled, Kelly could only stare at the woman. She was clearly delusional and that might make her dangerous. And she was *naked*. What was going—and that's when the truth hit her.

Naked Misty had to be one of the crazed fans Micah had told her about. He'd said they tracked him down and sneaked into hotel rooms. Sneaking into an unlocked Victorian had to have been a snap. Kelly was now alone with a crazy person who might at any moment decide that Kelly was her competition. She had to get Misty out of the house and she wanted backup for that plan. Finally, she pulled her cell phone from her back pocket.

"I'm calling the police if you're not out of this house in the next minute."

"You can't make me leave." Misty pouted prettily. She probably practiced the look in a mirror. "I'm not going anywhere until I see Micah. He'll *want* to see me," she said, letting the duvet slip a little to display the tops of a pair of very large breasts.

Irritated, Kelly realized she was going to have to burn the sheets, the duvet…maybe the bed. First, however, she had to get rid of Naked Misty.

"Kelly?" Micah's voice came in a shout from downstairs. "Are you here?"

"Well, backup's arrived. It seems you're about to get your wish," Kelly told the woman who was still pouting and using one hand to further tousle her hair to make the best possible impression. Without taking her eyes off the woman, Kelly shouted, "I'm upstairs, Micah. Could you come up?"

The tone of her voice must have clued him in that something was wrong. Kelly heard him come upstairs at a dead run, and when he swung around the corner into the room, he stopped right behind her.

"What the hell?"

"Micah," Naked Misty cried, then sat up straight, threw her arms wide in welcome and let the duvet drop, displaying what had to be man-made breasts of monumental proportions.

Kelly slapped one hand across her eyes. "Oh, I didn't need to see those."

"Me, neither," Micah muttered.

"Who's *she*?" Naked Misty demanded with a finger point of accusation at Kelly.

Micah gritted his teeth, then gave Kelly an apologetic

look before saying, "Kelly's my fiancée. Who the hell are you? No," he corrected. "Never mind. Doesn't matter."

"You're *engaged*?" Misty sputtered and still managed to sound outraged. Betrayed.

"Yeah," Kelly said, then pointedly used Misty's own words in retaliation. "His words speak to my heart."

"How can you be engaged to *her*?"

Insulted, Kelly countered, "Hey, at least *my* breasts are real."

Honestly, she might have laughed at this mess, but the situation was just too weird.

"That's it," Micah ordered, stepping past Kelly to stride to the bed. "Get up whoever you are—"

"Misty."

"Of course you are." He huffed out a breath. "Well, Misty, get out of my bed, get dressed and get out."

"But I *love* you."

"Oh, boy," Kelly murmured. She didn't know whether to feel sorry for Misty or Micah or all three of them.

"No, you don't love me." Micah glared down at the woman until Misty seemed to shrink into the covers.

Kelly's stomach churned. Yes, Misty was crazy and an intruder, but she'd told Micah she loved him and he'd brushed it off coldly. And she knew that he probably wouldn't accept her declaration any better.

His features were cold, tight, as he stalked across the bedroom, scooping up the woman's discarded clothes. He tossed them at her and Naked Misty's pout deepened.

"You're mean."

"Damn straight." He stood beside the bed, legs braced, arms folded across his broad chest, and gave Misty a look that singed even as it iced. "If you're not out of this house in two minutes flat, I'll have you arrested."

"But—"

"If you ever come back," he added, "I'll have you arrested."

Naked Misty was pulling on a shirt as quickly as she could, thankfully tucking away those humongous breasts. "I only wanted to tell you how I feel. I do *love* you."

Kelly was watching now and saw the miserable resignation on Micah's face, and she didn't know how to help. She felt sorry for Misty, but she felt sorrier for herself. Loving Micah was hard. Knowing he wouldn't want her to was even harder.

"You don't even know me." He moved out of the woman's way when she leaped out of the bed and dragged her jeans on. Once she was dressed, Micah gave her enough time to scoop up her shoes and grab her purse from a chair. Then he took her by the arm and steered her out of the room.

Kelly heard them taking the stairs, but she didn't wait for Micah to come back. The only way to get a handle on the strangest situation she'd ever been in was to return things to normal. She immediately began stripping the bed. When Micah returned, he helped her take the sheets and duvet off and put on fresh sheets. Through it all he was silent, but the expression on his face told Kelly he wasn't happy.

"Did Misty get away all right?"

"Yeah." He huffed out a breath. "What the hell kind of name is Misty?" He smoothed the sheet, still avoiding her gaze. Well, Kelly wanted things back to normal between them, too.

"This wasn't your fault, Micah." She pulled the top sheet taut and folded the top back.

"She only came here because of me," he said, reaching for a replacement duvet, this one brick red, and flipping it out to cover the mattress.

"Still doesn't make it your fault." Kelly stacked pillows in fresh cases against the headboard. "How did she even find you?"

"Easy enough." Scowling, he too tossed a few pillows onto the bed. "Like I told you. Social media is everywhere. Someone in Banner probably put it out on Facebook or Twitter that I was here. That's enough to get every nut in the world moving." Shaking his head, he smoothed wrinkles that weren't there. "She shows up in town, talks to a few people, finds out where I am and bingo. Naked in my bed."

That was just beyond creepy. Living your life knowing there were thousands of would-be stalkers out there, ready to hunt you down and barge into your life? Kelly shuddered. "I don't know how you deal with this stuff all the time."

"It's why I don't stay anywhere for very long," he said, walking around the end of the bed to come to her side. "And now that one has found me, others will be coming too. I can't stay, Kelly."

Panic blossomed in the center of her chest and sent out tendrils of ice that wrapped around her heart and squeezed. This was what she'd been feeling since their holiday in California. If Naked Misty hadn't shown up, it would have been something else. For whatever reason, Micah wanted to get away from Banner. From Kelly. "But…you haven't finished your book yet."

"I'm close though," he said. "I can finish it somewhere else."

She was losing him. Standing right in front of him and

he was slipping away. "Why should you have to move out because of a crazy person?"

He sighed, dropped both hands onto her shoulders and met her eyes squarely. "It's not just her. Things have gotten…complicated between us, and I think it'd be easier if I left early."

"Easier? On who?"

"On both of us," he said, and stepped back. "Better to stop this before things get more tangled up."

But she wanted those three months. She wanted Micah here for the first snow, for Christmas. For New Year's Eve. She wanted him here *always*.

"Micah—" She broke off because anything she said now would sound like begging him to stay and she couldn't bring herself to do it. Couldn't make herself say *I love you*, either. He wouldn't believe her any more than he had Misty. Or, worse, he *would* believe her and feel sorry for her, and she refused to put herself in the position of having to accept either reaction.

"It's the best way, Kelly." His gaze locked with hers, and though she tried to read what he was feeling, thinking, it was as if he'd erected a barrier across his eyes to keep her out.

"Halloween's in a few days," he said. "I'll stay for that, okay? I'd like to see the kids go through that maze after spending so much time building the damn thing…"

A few days. That was all she had with him. So she'd take it and never let him know what it cost her to stay quiet. To let him go without asking him to stay.

"I'd like that, too," she said, and forced a smile that felt brittle and cold. "Where will you go?"

"I don't know," he admitted, stuffing his hands into his

jeans pockets. "There's a hotel in Hawaii I like. Maybe I'll go there for a few months."

"Hawaii." Well, that couldn't be farther from Utah, could it? He was so anxious to be apart from her, he was sticking an ocean between them. Couldn't be clearer than that. "Okay, then."

He reached for her again but let his hand fall before he touched her, and that, Kelly thought, was so sad it nearly broke her heart.

"It's best this way, Kelly."

"Probably," she said, agreeing with him if only to see a flicker of surprise flash across his face. "Don't worry about me, Micah. I was good before you got here and I'll be fine when you leave." She wondered idly if her tongue would simply rot and fall out of her head on the strength of those lies. She picked up the dirty sheets and the duvet and held them to her like a shield. "I'll just go start the washing."

Kelly felt his gaze on her as she left the room, so she didn't look back. There was only so much she was willing to put herself through.

The morning of Halloween, Kelly had the black lights up and ready, the CD of haunted house noises—growls, moans, chains rattling and a great witch's cackle—loaded up and a mountain of candy for all of the trick-or-treaters.

She also had the same unhappy stomach she'd been dealing with for days. She wasn't worse, but she wasn't getting better, either. Which was why she'd made a quick trip to the drugstore. Not being a complete idiot, she didn't go to the mom-and-pop shop in Banner, instead driving down to Ogden to shop anonymously. One thing Kelly didn't need was the gossips in town speculating on if she was pregnant or not before she knew herself. At that thought, her stomach did another quick spin.

Micah was in his office typing away—pretty much where he'd been since Naked Misty had crashed into their lives uninvited, precipitating his announcement that he was leaving early.

The only time Kelly saw him lately was at night in bed. And though he might be trying to keep distance between them during the day, in the darkness Micah turned to her. Sex was just as staggering, but shadowed now with a thread of sorrow that neither of them wanted to talk about.

Kelly wanted to be with him as much as she could, but at the same time, whenever they came together, another tiny piece of her heart broke off and shattered at her feet. Seconds, minutes, hours were ticking away. All of her life she'd loved Halloween, and now for the first time, she hated it. Because he'd be leaving in the morning and Kelly was already dreading it.

She looked into the mirror over the bathroom sink and saw the misery in her own eyes. Her face was paler than usual, her freckles standing out like gold dust on vanilla ice cream. Kelly lifted her fingers to touch the cold surface of Micah's emerald as it shone brightly in the overhead light.

The tick of her kitchen timer sounded like a tiny heartbeat in the bathroom. *Tiny heartbeat.* Was it possible? Was she pregnant? And if she was, what then? When the buzzer sounded, letting her know the three minutes were up, Kelly shut down the timer, picked up the early-pregnancy-test stick and held her breath, still unsure what she was hoping for.

*"A plus sign."* She released that breath and giddily took

another one. "Plus sign means *pregnant*." She laughed and suddenly she knew exactly how she felt about this. Kelly grinned at her reflection. All of her doubts and worries disappeared, washed away by a wave of pure joy. "You don't have the flu. You have a *baby. Micah's baby.*"

She couldn't stop smiling. The woman in the mirror looked like a fool, standing there with that wide grin on her face, but Kelly didn't mind. This was…amazing. The most amazing thing that had ever happened to her. When Sean died, Kelly had never intended to remarry, so she'd had to accept that she'd never have children. And that was painful.

Then along came Micah, who swept her off her feet and into a tangle of emotions that had left her reeling right from the first time he'd kissed her. The misery of the last few days, pretending she was all right with him leaving just slid off her shoulders. He was leaving, but he had also given her a gift. A wonderful gift. When Micah was gone, she'd still have a part of him with her. Always. She wouldn't be alone. She'd have her child and the memories of the man who'd given that child to her.

"I have to tell him," she said aloud, and looked down at the pregnancy test stick again as if to reassure herself that this was really happening. *It was.* Even though Micah was leaving, he had a right to know about his child. Her feelings were her own, but this baby, they shared.

Still smiling, she laid one hand over her belly in a protective gesture. "We'll be okay, you know. Just you and me, we'll be good."

Steeling herself, she nodded at her reflection, feeling new strength and determination fill her. When Micah left, her heart would be crushed. But she would have her baby to look after now and that was enough to keep her strong. "I'll tell him tonight. When Halloween's over. I'll tell him. And then I'll let him go."

Halloween was a rush of noise, laughter, shrieks and a seemingly never-ending stream of children. Micah had never done Halloween as a foster kid. And as an adult, he'd kept his distance from kids on general principle, so this holiday had never made much of an impact on him. Until celebrating it with Kelly.

Up and down the block, porch lights were on and pumpkins glowed. Even the two nosy sisters, Margie and Sally, were across the street sitting on their front porch. They were bundled up against the cold and sipping tea, but they clearly wanted to watch all the kids.

The pumpkins Micah had taken Kelly to buy on their first ride together were carved into faces and shining with glow sticks inside them. Orange lights were stretched out along the porch railing. Black crepe paper fluttered from the gingerbread trim on the house and twisted in the wind. Polyester spiderwebs were strung out everywhere, and ghosts were suspended from the big oak tree out front.

Kelly was dressed up, of course, as her idea of a farmer, in overalls, a long-sleeved plaid shirt and work boots. Her hair was in pigtails and the emerald peeked out from behind the collar of her shirt. From the porch Micah handed out candy to those who made it through the haunted maze. Kelly had stationed herself in front of the maze to walk the little kids through personally so they wouldn't be scared. Cries of "Trick or treat!" rang out up and down the block. Parents kept stopping to congratulate him on his engagement, and Micah had to go along with the lies because he'd promised.

He wondered, though, what all of these people would think of him tomorrow when he left town, supposedly walking out on Kelly? He frowned. Good thing he didn't care.

Passing out candy like it was about to be banned, Micah glanced around the yard and knew he was right to leave early. This wasn't his home. The sooner he got to a nice anonymous hotel the better. For everyone. Hell, he was handing out *candy*. He was carving pumpkins, for God's sake. Too much was changing and he didn't like it.

Even the tone of the book he'd been working on had changed. As if Kelly and what he'd found here with her had invaded even his fictional world. His heroine was now stronger, sexier, funnier than before. She stood up for herself and drove the hero as crazy as Kelly made Micah. Life was definitely imitating art. Or more the other way around.

"Micah!" A small hand tugged at the hem of Micah's coat, splintering his thoughts, which was just as well, since he had at least three hundred pounds of candy to give out.

Jacob, dressed like a lion, stared up at him. His lion's mane was yellow yarn and his nose had been colored black to match the whiskers drawn across his cheeks. "Are you scared cuz I'm a lion?"

"You bet." No point in dampening the excitement in the boy's eyes just because Micah was in a crap mood. "You make a good one."

"I can roar."

"I believe you."

"And you can come see my pumpkin all lit up, can't you? I put a happy face on it, but Daddy cut it cuz I'm too little to hold the knife."

"I will later," Micah said, wondering how he and this little boy had become friends. "Don't you have to go with your brothers to get more candy?"

"Yeah, and I can have lots my dad says even though Mommy says no cuz daddies are the boss when Mom's not looking my dad says and Mommy laughed at him but said okay."

Micah blinked. That was a lot of words for one sentence. He wondered what the kid would be like next year. Or the year after. The kid would grow up in this town, play football, fall in love, get married and start the whole cycle over again. But Micah wouldn't be there to see any of it. Soon Jacob would forget all about a friend named Micah. And wasn't that irritating? "No, it's not."

"What?"

He looked down at the tiny lion. "Nothing, Jacob. Go on. Find your brothers. Have fun."

"Okay!"

As he ran off, Micah looked around and realized that he didn't belong there. He wasn't a part of this town. He could pretend to be. But the truth was he didn't belong anywhere and that's how he liked it. Who the hell else could just pick up and take off for Hawaii at a moment's notice? He was damn lucky living just the way he wanted to, answering to no one. He liked his life just fine and it was time to get back to it.

Several minutes later, he saw Jacob's parents rush up to Kelly, talking fast, looking all around frantically. Something was wrong. Micah left the candy bowl on the porch and took the steps down through the crowd. "What's going on?"

Kelly looked at him, worry etched into her features. "Jacob's missing."

He snorted. "No, he's not. He was just here a few minutes ago."

Jacob's mother, Nora, shook her head. "Jonas saw Jacob run into the woods. He was following a deer and Jonas ran to get us instead of going in after him."

"It was the right thing to do," her husband said. "Or they'd both be lost. You stay here, Nora, in case he finds his way out on his own. I've got my cell. Call me if you see him." Then he looked at Kelly, Micah and a few of the other adults. "If we split up, we should be able to find him fast."

Kelly pulled her cell phone out of her overalls, hit the flashlight app and looked up at Micah. "He's only three."

Micah was already headed to the woods, fighting a hard, cold knot that had settled in his gut. "We'll find him."

The woods were thick and dark and filled with the kind of shadows that lived in Micah's imagination. It was the perfect setting for murder. Wisps of fog, moonlight trickling through bare branches of trees, the rustle of dead leaves on the ground and the quick, scuttling noise of something rushing through them. It was as if he'd written the scene himself. But it wasn't so good for a lost little boy. They moved as quickly as they could, their flashlights bobbing and dancing in the darkness. Roots jutted from the ground and Kelly tripped more than once as they hurried through the trees.

Kelly called for Jacob over and over, but there was no answer. The flashlight beams looked eerie, shining past the skeletons of trees to get lost in the pines. *Where the hell was he? He hadn't had enough time to go far.* Micah fought down his own sense of frustration and worry, but they came rushing back up. Anything could happen to a kid that size. His writer's mind listed every possibility and each was worse than the last.

He shouldn't have let the kid wander off to find his brothers alone.

"God," Kelly murmured, turning in a slow circle. "Where is he?"

"Hiding? Chasing the deer?" Micah strained his eyes, looking from right to left. "Who the hell knows?"

From a distance came the calls of the others searching for the little boy, and their flashlights looked like ghosts moving through the shadows. Micah had to wonder why Jacob wasn't answering. Was he hurt? God. Unconscious? In the next instant, Micah thought he heard something so he pulled Kelly to a stop.

"Listen. There it is again." He whipped his head around. "Over there."

"Jacob?" Micah shouted and this time he was sure he heard the little boy yell, "I'm lost."

"Thank God." Kelly ran right behind him and in seconds they'd found him. Jacob was scared and cold and his sneaker was caught under a tree root.

"The deer ran away," he said as if that explained everything.

Micah's heart squeezed painfully. "The deer doesn't matter. You okay, buddy? Are you hurt?"

"No," he said, "I'm stuck. And I'm cold. And I spilled my candy."

Kelly's flashlight caught his overturned pumpkin basket with the candy bars scattered around it. She quickly scooped them all up.

"See? Kelly's got your stuff and we can fix the rest," Micah said. "Kelly, call Jacob's dad. Tell him he's okay."

"Already on it," she said, and he heard her talking.

"Am I in trouble?" Jacob rubbed his eyes, smearing his whiskers.

Once he freed the boy's foot, Micah picked him up. "I don't think so. Your parents are probably going to be too happy to see you to be mad."

"Okay, good. I still need to get more candy." Jacob wrapped his arms around Micah's neck. "When we get back you wanna see my pumpkin?"

Kelly laughed. Micah caught her eye and grinned. Kids were damn resilient. More so than the adults they scared the life out of. He took a breath and slowly released it. With the boy's arms around his shoulders and Kelly smiling at him, Micah knew he'd become too attached. Not just to Kelly, but to this place. Even this little boy.

And as they left the shadows and stepped into the light again, Micah knew he'd stayed too long. He had to leave. While he still could.

A part of Kelly wanted to do just what he was sure she would. Cry, ask him to stay. But none of that would help. Just as she'd told Terry, if she had to force him to be with her, then what they had wasn't worth having.

She wouldn't tell him she loved him. He should know that already from the way they were together—and if he didn't, it was because he didn't *want* to know. So Kelly would keep her feelings to herself and remain perfectly rational.

Too bad it did nothing for the hole opening up in the center of her chest.

"I called for the jet," Micah said, stuffing his folded clothes into a huge black duffel. His suits were already in a garment bag laid out on the bed. Their bed.

"So you'll be in Hawaii late tonight."

"Or early in the morning, yeah." He zipped the bag closed, straightened up and faced her. His features were unreadable, his eyes shadowed. "Look, I know I said I was leaving tomorrow, but there's no reason to wait and I thought it would be easier this way."

Nothing about this was easy, but Kelly smiled. She would get through this. "Did you get everything?"

He glanced around the room, "Yeah. I did. Kelly..."

God, she didn't want him to say he was sorry. Didn't want to see sympathy in his eyes or hear it in his voice. She cut him off with the one sure way she knew to make him stop talking. "Before you go, I've got something you need to see."

His eyes narrowed on her suspiciously. "What is it?"

Kelly took a breath, pulled the test stick from her pocket and handed it to him. Still confused, he stared at her for another second or two, then his gaze dropped to the stick. "Is this—" He looked into her eyes. "You're pregnant?"

"I am. Thought I was getting sick, but no."

"We used protection."

"Apparently latex just isn't what it used to be." It was hard to smile, but she did it. Hard to keep her spirits up, but she was determined. Kelly took a step toward him. "Micah, I just thought you had a right to know about the baby. I—"

"How long have you known?"

"Since this morning."

"And you waited until I'm all packed and ready to go before you drop it on me?"

"Well," she said, her temper beginning to rise, "I didn't know you were leaving tonight, did I? Sprung that one on me."

"What's that supposed to mean?"

"Oh, come on, Micah." Her vow to remain rational was slowly unraveling. But then, she told herself, temper wasn't pitiful. "You know exactly what I mean. You wanted to catch me off guard so I wouldn't have time to plead with you not to go."

He stiffened. "That's not—"

"Relax. I'm not asking you to stay, Micah. Go ahead. Leave. I know you have to, or at least that you think you have to, which pretty much amounts to the same thing anyway. So go. I'm fine."

"You're pregnant," he reminded her.

Kelly laid both hands on her belly and for the first time that night gave him a real smile. "And will be, whether you're here or not. I'm *happy* about the baby. This is a gift, Micah. The best one you could have given me."

"A gift." He shook his head and paced the room, occasionally glancing down at the stick he still held. "Happy. My God, you and this place…"

"What're you talking about?" Now it was her turn to be confused, but she didn't like the cornered anger snapping in his eyes.

He shoved one hand through his hair. "You don't even see it, do you?" Muttering now, he said, "I told myself earlier that I didn't belong here and I know why. But you just don't get it."

"I don't appreciate being talked down to," Kelly snapped. "So if you've got something to say, just say it."

"You're pregnant and you're *happy* about it, even though I'm walking out and leaving you alone to deal with it."

"That's a bad thing? Micah—"

"You live in a land of kids and dogs." He choked out

a short laugh and shook his head as if even he couldn't believe all of this. "You paint pictures on windows, carve pumpkins." He threw up his hands. "You have nosy neighbors, deer in your garden and ghosts hanging from your tree, and none of that has anything to do with the real world. With the world I live in."

He was simmering. She could see frustration and anger rippling off him in waves and Kelly responded to it. If he was leaving, let them at least have truth between them when he did.

"Which world is that, Micah?" When he didn't speak, she prompted, "Go ahead. You're clearly on a roll. Tell me all about how little I know about reality."

He laughed, but there was no humor in the sound. Tossing the test stick onto the bed, he stalked to her side. "You want reality?" He looked down into her eyes and said, "I grew up in foster homes. My mother walked out when I was six and I never saw her again. I didn't have a damn friend until I met Sam in the navy, because I never stayed anywhere long enough to make one." His gaze bored into hers. "My world is hard and cruel. I don't have the slightest clue how to live in a land where everything is rosy all the damn time."

He was breathing fast, his eyes flashing, but he had nothing on Kelly. She could feel her temper building inside her like a cresting wave, and like a surfer at the beach, she jumped on board and rode it.

"Rosy?" Insult stained her tone as she poked him in the chest with her index finger. "You think my world is some cozy little space? That my life is perfect? My parents died when I was little and I came here to live when I was twelve. Then my grandfather died. My *husband* died. And my best friend's husband is in danger every day he's deployed."

He swiped one hand across his face. "God, Kelly…"

"Not finished," she said, tipping her head back to glare at him. "Life happens, Micah. Even in *rosy* little towns. People die. Three-year-olds get lost in the woods. And men who don't know any better walk away."

His jaw was tight and turmoil churned in his eyes. "Damn it, Kelly, I wasn't thinking."

She heard the contrition in his voice, but she couldn't let go of her anger. If she did, the pain would slide in and that might just finish her off. Thank God she hadn't told him she loved him—that would have been the capper to this whole mess.

"You're the one who doesn't get it, Micah," she said. "Bad things happen. You just have to keep going."

"Or you stop," he countered. "And back away." Micah shook his head. "I don't know how to do this, Kelly. You. This town. A *baby*, for God's sake. Trust me when I say I'm not the guy you think I am."

"No, Micah," she said, feeling sorrow swallow the anger. "You're not the guy *you* think you are."

He snorted and shook his head. "Still surprising me." He walked to the bed, picked up his bags and stood there, staring at her. "Anything you need, call me. You or the baby. You've got my cell number."

"I do," she said, lifting her chin and meeting his gaze steadily. "But I won't need anything, Micah. I don't want anything from you." All she wanted was *him*. But she realized now she couldn't have him. Her heart was breaking and that empty place in her heart was spreading, opening like a black hole, devouring everything in its path.

She felt hollowed out, and looking at him now only made that worse. He was close enough to touch and so far away she couldn't reach him.

"Goodbye, Kelly," he said, and, carrying his bags, he walked past her.

She heard him on the stairs. Heard the front door open and then close, and he was gone.

Dropping to the end of the bed, Kelly looked around the empty room and listened to the silence.

# Ten

By the following afternoon, Kelly had most of the Halloween decorations down and stacked to be put away. This chore used to depress her, since the anticipation and fun of the holiday was over for another year. But today she already felt as low as she could go.

"I still can't believe he left, knowing you're pregnant."

Kelly sighed. She'd told her best friend the whole story and somehow felt better the more outraged Terry became. But it had been an hour and she was still furious. "Terry, he was always going to leave, remember?"

"Yeah, but *pregnant* changes things."

"No, it doesn't."

"Plus," Terry added, "I can't believe you're pregnant before me. Jimmy's got his work cut out for him when he gets home."

Kelly laughed as Terry had meant her to. What did

people without best friends do when the world exploded? Her mind wandered as she rolled up the orange twinkle lights from the porch and carefully stored them in a bag marked for Halloween.

She'd done a lot of thinking the night before—since God knows she hadn't gotten any sleep—and had come to the conclusion that she'd done the right thing. Kelly didn't want Micah to stay because of the baby. She wanted him to stay for *her*.

"If he had stayed because I'm pregnant," she told Terry, "sooner or later, he'd resent us both and *then* he'd leave." Shaking her head firmly, she said, "This way is better. Not great, but better."

"Okay, I get that, and I hate it when you're mature and I'm not," Terry said. "But I'd still feel better if Jimmy were here and I could tell him to go beat Micah up."

Kelly laughed, hugged her best friend and said, "It's the thought that counts."

Her cell phone rang and she cringed at the caller ID. Looking at Terry, she said, "It's Gran."

"Oh, boy." Shaking her head, Terry said, "Let's go inside. You can sit down and I'll make some tea."

As the phone continued to ring, Kelly mused, "It's a shame I can't have wine because, boy, after this conversation, I'm going to need some."

Kelly wasn't looking forward to breaking this news to her grandmother, but she might as well get it over with. She followed Terry into the house and answered the phone. "Hi, Gran."

"Sweetie, I found the prettiest wedding dress—it would be perfect on you. I'm going to send you the picture, okay, and I don't want to interfere, but—"

Kelly sat down at the table and winced at Terry, already moving around the kitchen. Bracing herself, she interrupted her grandmother's flow. "Gran, wait. I've got something to tell you."

"What is it, dear? Oh, hold on. Linda's here, I'm putting you on speaker."

Great. Kelly sighed and winced again. "Well, the good news is, I'm pregnant!"

Terry frowned at her and mouthed, *Chicken*, as she wandered the kitchen making tea. Kelly set the phone on the table, hit speaker and her grandmother's and Aunt Linda's voices spilled into the room.

"Oh, a baby!"

"That's so wonderful," Linda cooed. "You know my Debbie keeps telling me she's going to one of those sperm banks, but she hasn't done it yet. You should talk to her, Kelly."

Terry laughed and once again, Kelly felt bad for her cousin Debbie. First an engagement and now a baby. She was putting a lot of pressure on Debbie and Tara.

"Oh, Micah must be so excited," Gran said.

"Yeah," Terry threw in. "He's thrilled."

Kelly scowled at her. *Not helping.*

"That's the thing, Gran," Kelly said quickly. "The bad news is that Micah and I broke up."

*"What?"* Twin shrieks carried all the way from Florida, and Kelly had the distinct feeling she might have heard the two women without the phone.

Terry set out some cookies and brewed tea while Kelly went through the whole thing for the second time that day. A half hour later, Gran and Aunt Linda were both fuming.

"I'll get Big Eddie to go out there and give that boy a punch in the nose."

"Oh, for heaven's sake, Linda," Gran said. "Big Eddie's seventy-five years old."

"He's tough, though," Linda insisted. "Spry, too and I have reason to know."

"Spry or not, you can't ask the man to fly somewhere just to punch someone, no matter how badly he deserves it," Gran snapped.

Terry set cups of tea on the table, then gave two thumbs-ups in approval.

"No one needs to beat anybody up," Kelly said, sipping her fresh cup of tea. "I had no idea my family was so violent. Terry already offered to have Jimmy do the honors."

"Terry's a good girl, I always said so."

"Thanks, Gran," Terry called out.

"What are you going to do about all of this, Kelly?" Gran asked.

"I'm gonna have a baby," she said, then added quickly, "and I'm going to be fine, Gran. I don't want you rushing home to take care of me."

"She's got me right here," Terry said.

"This just doesn't seem right, though," Gran mumbled. "You shouldn't be alone."

Kelly ate a cookie and thought about another one.

"Get a clue, Bella," Linda told her. "The girl doesn't want you there hovering. She's got things to do, to think about, isn't that right, Kelly?"

If she'd been closer, Kelly would have kissed her aunt. "Thanks, Aunt Linda. Honest, Gran, I'm fine. Micah's doing what he has to do and so am I."

"I don't like it," her grandmother said, then sighed. "But you're a grown woman, Kelly, and I'll respect your decisions."

Terry's eyes went wide in surprise and Kelly stared at the phone, stunned. "Really?"

"You'll figure it out, honey," Gran said.

"You will," Linda added. "And if you need us for anything, you call and say so. A great-grandchild's something to celebrate, like I keep telling Debbie."

"This one's mine," Gran pointed out.

"Oh, you can share," Linda said. "I'll share when Debbie finally comes through."

Terry was laughing and Kelly almost cried. She'd been hit by a couple of huge emotional jolts in the last twenty-four hours, but the bottom line was that she had her family. She wasn't alone. She just didn't have Micah.

And that was going to hurt for a long time.

For a solid week, Micah holed up in his penthouse suite. He couldn't work. Couldn't sleep. Had no interest in eating. He lived on coffee and sandwiches from room service he forced down. A deep, simmering fury was his only companion and even at that, he knew it was useless. Hell, *he* was the one who left. Why was he so damn mad?

The second week gone was no better, though anger shifted to worry and that made him furious, too. He hadn't wanted any of this. Hadn't asked to care. Didn't want to wonder if Kelly was all right. If the baby was okay. And it was November and that meant snow for her, and he started thinking about her broken-down truck and her riding around in it, and that drove him even crazier.

Micah wasn't used to this. Once he moved on from a place, he wiped it from his mind as if it didn't even exist anymore. He was always about the next place. He didn't do the past. He moved around on his own and liked it.

He didn't *miss* people, so why the hell did he wake up every morning reaching for Kelly in that big empty bed?

"You Kelly Flynn?"

The burly man in a blue work shirt and khaki slacks held a clipboard and looked at her through a pair of black-framed glasses.

"Yes, I am. Who're you?"

"I'm Joe Hackett. I'm here to deliver your truck?"

"My what?" Kelly stepped onto the porch of the cottage and looked out at the driveway. Parked behind her old faithful truck was a brand-new one. November sunlight made the chrome sparkle against the deep glossy red paint. It was bigger than her old one, with a shorter bed but a longer cab with a back seat bench. It was shiny. And new. And beautiful. Kelly loved it. But it couldn't be hers. "There must be some mistake."

"No mistake, lady," Joe said. "Sign here and she's all yours. Paid for free and clear including tax and license."

She looked from the truck to the clipboard and saw her name and address on the delivery sheet. So not a mistake. Which could mean only one thing. Micah had sent it.

He'd been gone two weeks. The longest two weeks of her life. And, suddenly, here he was. Okay, not *him*, but his presence, definitely. Tears filled her eyes and she had to blink frantically to clear her vision. What was she supposed to think about this? He leaves but buys her a new truck? Why would he do it?

"Lady? Um, just sign here so we can get going?" He was giving her the nervous look most men wore around crying women.

"Right. Okay." She scrawled her name on the bottom line and took the keys Joe handed over. As he and another guy left in a compact car, Kelly walked to her new truck. She ran her hand across the gleaming paint, then opened the driver's-side door and got in. The interior sparkled just as brightly as the outside. Leather seats. Seat warmers. Backup camera. Four-wheel drive. She laughed sadly. The truck had so many extras it could probably drive itself.

"Micah, why?" She sat back and stared through the windshield at the Victorian. Her fingers traced across the surface of the emerald she still wore, and she wondered where he was now and if he missed her as much as she missed him.

Micah hated the hotel. He felt like a rat in a box.

The penthouse suite was huge, and still he felt claustrophobic. He couldn't just step outside and feel a cold fall breeze. No, he'd have to take an elevator down thirty floors and cross a lobby just to get to the damn parking lot.

He didn't keep the doors to the terrace open because they let in the muffled roar of the city far below. He'd gotten so used to the quiet at Kelly's place that the noise seemed intrusive rather than comforting.

Three weeks now since he'd left Kelly, and the anger, the worry, the outrage had all boiled down into a knot of guilt, which made him mad all over again.

What the hell did he have to feel guilty about? She'd known going in that he wasn't going to stay. And if she'd wanted him to stay why didn't she say so?

No. Not Kelly. *I'm fine. I have the baby. We don't need anything from you.*

"Perfect. She doesn't need me. I don't need her. Then we're both happy. *Right?*" Was she driving that new truck? Had it snowed yet? Had she gotten the plow blade attached to the new truck? Was she out plowing people's roads and drives? Was she doing it alone?

God, he hated this room.

Pregnant.

She was carrying *his* kid, and what the hell was he supposed to do about that? If she'd wanted his help, she would have said so. But she didn't beg him not to leave. Hell, she hadn't even watched him go. What the hell was that about? Did she just not give a damn?

Irritation spiking, he grabbed his cell phone, hit the speed dial and waited for Sam to answer.

"Hi, Micah. What's up?"

What *wasn't* up? Micah hadn't talked to Sam since leaving Utah mainly because he just hadn't wanted to talk to anyone, really. Now he'd been alone with his own thoughts for too long and needed…something. He pushed one hand through his hair, walked to the open terrace doors and stared out at the ocean. The last time he'd had an ocean view, he'd been on a different terrace. With Kelly. And *that* memory would kill him if he started thinking about it. So he didn't.

"Kelly's pregnant." He hadn't meant to just say it, but it was as if the words had been waiting for a chance to jump out.

"That's great. Congratulations, man."

He scowled. "Yeah, thanks I guess. Kelly told me about the baby the night I left."

"You left? Where the hell are you?"

"Hawaii." Paradise, his ass. There was too much sunshine here. People were too damn cheerful.

"Why?"

"Because it was time to go." Micah scrubbed one hand

across his jaw and remembered he hadn't shaved in a couple weeks. "I couldn't stay. Things were getting too—"

"Real?" Sam asked.

He frowned at the phone. "What's that supposed to mean?"

"It means that you've never lived an ordinary life, Micah. You went from your crap childhood to the navy to posh hotels."

Micah scowled into the wide mirror over the gas fireplace as he listened.

"You've never had a real woman, either. All those models and actresses? They weren't looking for anything more than you were—one night at a time." Sam paused. "Trust me when I say that has nothing to do with the real world."

God, hadn't he thrown practically the same accusation at Kelly that last night with her?

"What's your point?" God. *Points.* He rubbed his eyes tiredly. They felt like marbles in a bucket of sand.

"My point is—Kelly is *real.* What you had there mattered, Micah, whether you admit it or not, and I think it scared the crap out of you."

"I wasn't scared." He remembered telling little Jacob that everybody got scared sometimes. That included him, didn't it?

The realization was humbling.

"Sure you were," Sam said jovially. "Every guy is scared out of his mind when he meets the one woman who matters more than anything."

"I never said anything like that—"

"You didn't have to, Micah." He chuckled, which was damn irritating. "I've known you long enough to figure things out for myself. For example. When's the last time you left a hotel in the middle of a book?"

He blew out a breath. "Well…"

"Never, that's when," Sam told him. "You stay six months at every place you go. This time you bolt after three? Come on, Micah."

The man in the mirror looked confused. Worried. Was that it? Had he run from Kelly because she mattered? Because he was afraid? He turned away from the damn mirror because he couldn't stand to see the questions in his own eyes. "Look, I didn't call for advice. I just wanted you to know where I am."

"Great, but you get the advice anyway," Sam said. "Do yourself a favor and go back to Kelly. Throw yourself on her mercy and maybe she'll take your sorry ass back."

Micah glared at the room because it wasn't the Victorian. Because Kelly wasn't here with him. Because he was hundreds of miles away from her and he didn't know what she was doing. How she was feeling. "How the hell can I do that? What do I know about being somebody's father, for God's sake?"

"If nothing else," Sam said, "you know what *not* to do. And that's stay away from your own kid. You grew up without a father. That's what you want for your baby, too?"

Putting it like that gave Micah something to think about. He'd done to his kid exactly what his mother had done to him. "I'm no good at this stuff, Sam."

"Nobody is, Micah. We just figure it out as we go along."

"Well, that's comforting."

"Figure it out, Micah. Don't be an ass."

On that friendly piece of advice, Sam hung up, leaving Micah with too much to think about.

The first snow hit two days later, but it was a mild storm after warm days, so the snow wasn't sticking. Which meant Kelly didn't have to go out and clear any drives or private roads. Instead, she was cozy in the Victorian, enjoying the snap and hiss of the fireplace. She'd been staying in the cottage because she didn't want to torture herself with memories of Micah in the Victorian. But, with winter here, she wanted the fireplace, so she convinced herself that the only way to get past the pain of missing Micah was by facing it.

With a cup of tea, a book and the fire, the setting would have been perfect. If Micah were there.

The front door opened suddenly and Kelly's heart jolted. She jumped up, ran to the hall, and all of the air left her lungs as she stood there in shock staring at Micah. Snow dusted his shoulders and his hair. He dropped his duffel bag, slammed the front door and flipped the dead bolt. When he turned around and saw her, he scowled.

"Lock the damn door, Kelly. *Anybody* could just walk into the house."

She laughed shortly and seriously considered racing down the hall and throwing herself into his arms. It was only pride that kept her in place. "Anybody did."

"Very funny." Still scowling fiercely, he walked down the hall, took her arm and steered her into the living room.

"What're you doing, Micah?" She pulled her arm from his grip even though she wanted nothing more than to hold on to him. And she desperately wished she wasn't wearing her new flannel pajamas decorated with dancing pandas. "Why are you here?"

His gaze moved over her as if he were etching her image into his brain. Then he stepped back and stalked to the fireplace. Turning around to face her from a safe distance, he said, "You know, I thought I was doing the right thing."

"By leaving?"

"Yeah." He sighed heavily. Shaking his head, Micah stared down at the fire for a long minute before lifting his gaze to hers. "Kelly, I have no idea how to do *this*." He waved one hand to encompass the house, her, the baby and everything else that was so far out of his experience. "You know how I told you I was engaged once before? I said it didn't take?"

"Yes." She'd wondered about that woman in his past.

"I ended it because I didn't care enough. I figured I was incapable of caring enough," he ground out, and she could see that the words were costing him. "Then I met you."

Heat began to melt the ice that had been around her heart for weeks. Hope rose up in her chest, and Kelly clung to it but kept quiet, wanting him to go on. To say it all.

He threw his hands high, then snorted. "Hell, I've never known anyone like you. You made me nuts. Made me feel things I never have. Want things I never wanted."

"Thanks."

Micah laughed and shook his head. "See? Like that. You surprise me all the damn time, Kelly. I never know where I'm standing with you and, turns out, I like it."

"You do?"

"Gotta have it," he admitted, and swallowed hard. He

took a step toward her, then stopped. "The last three weeks I've been so bored I thought I was losing my mind. I was at a hotel I'd been in before and this time, I hated it. Hated that it was small and there was no damn yard with deer and kids running through it. Hated that it was so damn noisy—but the wrong kind of noise, you know?"

"No," she admitted, smiling. "What are you saying, Micah?"

"I'm saying—all I could think about was you. And the baby. And this place. But mostly *you.*"

Tears were coming and she couldn't stop them this time. Didn't even try. They rolled unheeded down her cheeks as Kelly kept her gaze fixed on the only man in the world for her.

"You love me," he said, pointing a finger at her.

"Do I?" she said, and her smile widened.

"Damn right you do." Micah started walking—well, *stalking* the perimeter of the room. "A woman like you… love shows. Not just the sex, though that was great, for sure."

"It was."

"But you were there. Every day. You laughed with me. You cooked with me." He glared at her. "Yet, when I tell you I'm leaving, you just say, have a nice trip and by the way I'm pregnant."

Kelly flushed. "Well, that's not exactly—"

"Basically," he snapped. "That was it. And I finally started wondering why you hadn't told me that you love me. Why didn't you use the baby as a lever to keep me here? Why didn't you beg me to stay?"

She stiffened and tried to look as dignified as possible in her panda pj's. "I don't beg."

"No," he said thoughtfully, his gaze locked with hers.

"You wouldn't. Just like you wouldn't coerce me to stay. You were way sneakier than that."

"Me?" Now Kelly laughed. "I am *not* sneaky."

"This time you were," he said, and walked across the room to her. "You let me go, knowing I'd be miserable without you. You didn't say you loved me because you knew I'd wonder about that. And you didn't tell me I loved you because you wanted me to figure it out for myself. You wanted me to be away long enough to realize I was being a damn fool."

"That was clever of me." Or would have been if she'd actually planned it. She swayed, bit her bottom lip and held her breath. "And did you? Figure it all out?"

"I'm here, aren't I?" He blew out a breath, grabbed her and pulled her in close to him. Wrapping his arms around her, he rested his chin on top of her head and whispered, "You feel so good. This—*us*—is so good. I love you, Kelly. Didn't know I *could* love. But maybe I was only waiting to find you."

"Oh, Micah…" She held on to him, nestled her head against his chest and listened to the steady beat of his heart. It was as if every one of her dreams was coming true. The last three weeks had been so painful. Now there was so much joy she felt as if she were overflowing. "I love you, too."

"I know."

She laughed and tipped her head back to stare at him. "Sure of yourself, are you?"

"I am now," he admitted. "And I'm sure about this, too. You're going to have to marry me for real. It's the only answer. I have to be here in this big old house with you. I need to be with you at Christmas. I have to help you run for mayor. And next year, Jacob and I will help

you plant the pumpkin patch. I want to meet Jimmy—
I think he and I can be friends when we bond over our
crazy women."

Kelly's heart was flying. "I'll have to give you a point
for that crazy proposal."

He grinned. "Not a proposal. Just an acceptance of
your earlier proposal. Remember?"

"You're right. So, no points."

"No more points at all," he said softly. "Say yes and
we *both* win."

Kelly laughed, delighted with him, with everything.
"Of course, yes."

"Good." He nodded as if checking things off a mental list. "That's settled. I've got to ride with you when
you start plowing and—" He stopped. "Did you like the
truck?"

She laughed again, a little wildly, but she didn't care.
"I love it, you crazy man."

"Huh. You plow snow, but I'm crazy." He shook his
head and stared down at her with hope and relief and *love*
shining in his eyes.

"I never should have left, Kelly," he whispered, "but
in a way I guess I had to, because I never learned how
to *stay.* But I want to stay now, Kelly. With you. With
our kids…"

"Kids?" she asked hopefully. "Plural?"

He grinned. "It's a big house. We should do our best
to fill it."

God, this was everything Kelly had ever wanted,
and more. The firelight threw dancing shadows across
Micah's face, making his eyes shine with hope and promise and love. "I love you so much, Micah. I'm so glad
you came home."

He cupped her face in his palms and kissed her tenderly. "The only home I ever want is wherever you are. For the first and last time in my life, I'm in love. And I never want to lose it."

"You won't," she promised. "*We* won't."

He blew out a breath and said, "Damn straight we won't. Now. For part two of my brilliant plan."

"You had a plan?"

"Still do and I think you'll like it," he said, sweeping her up in his arms, surprising a laugh out of her. He sat down in one of the overstuffed chairs and held her on his lap. He frowned at her pajamas. "What are those? Dogs?"

"Pandas."

"Sure. Why not?" Shaking his head, he said, "I'm thinking we hire a jet and fly to Florida tomorrow—"

"Tomorrow?"

"—pick up your grandmother and your aunt, and then all of us go to New York for a week. Maybe the Ritz-Carlton. I think they'd like that place."

*"What?"*

He shrugged. "I've never had a family before. I'd like to get to know them. Have them meet Sam and Jenny and the kids, because they're as close to family as I've ever known. And while we're there, your grandmother can help you pick out that ring we talked about."

"Oh, Micah!" Many more surprises and her head would simply spin right off her shoulders. She threw her arms around his neck and kissed him hard and fast. Then something occurred to her. "We'd better call first, though."

"Why?"

"I told Gran and Aunt Linda that we broke up and

they were arranging for one of the seniors to fly out and punch you in the nose."

"More surprises," Micah said, grinning. "I'll risk it if you will."

"Absolutely," she said.

"I love you, Kelly Flynn."

"I love you, Micah Hunter," she said, melting against him. As he bent his head to claim another kiss, Kelly whispered, "Welcome home."

\* \* \* \* \*

# COMING SOON!

We really hope you enjoyed reading this book.
If you're looking for more romance
be sure to head to the shops when
new books are available on

## Thursday 26th February

To see which titles are coming soon, please visit
**millsandboon.co.uk/nextmonth**

MILLS & BOON

# MILLS & BOON

## MODERN

# Power and Passion

Prepare to be swept off your feet by sophisticated, sexy and seductive heroes, in some of the world's most glamorous and romantic locations, where power and passion collide.

ght Modern stories published every month, find them all at:

## millsandboon.co.uk

# MILLS & BOON
# Love Always

Celebrate true love with tender stories of heartfelt romance, from the rush of falling in love to the joy a new baby can bring, and a focus on the emotional heart of a relationship.

Four Love Always stories published every month, find them a

**millsandboon.co.uk/LoveAlways**

# OUT NOW!

SECOND
*Chance*

3
BOOKS
IN ONE

- THEIR ENEMY SPARKS -

NAIMA
SIMONE

AMY
RUTTAN

STEFANIE
LONDON

Available at
millsandboon.co.uk

MILLS & BOON

# OUT NOW!

- THE SINFUL SLEUTHS CLUB -

## A TRAP
## FOR
## TWO

K.D.
RICHARDS

HEATHER
GRAHAM

Available at
millsandboon.co.uk

MILLS & BOON

# OUT NOW!

THE
**TYCOON'S**
**AFFAIR**
COLLECTION

# STEALING HIS HEART

USA TODAY BESTSELLING AUTHOR
## HEIDI RICE

Available at
millsandboon.co.uk

MILLS & BOON

# LET'S TALK
# *Romance*

For exclusive extracts, competitions and special offers, find us online:

- 🅕 MillsandBoon
- 𝕏 @MillsandBoon
- 📷 @MillsandBoonUK
- ♪ @MillsandBoonUK

Get in touch on 01413 063 232

For all the latest titles coming soon, visit
millsandboon.co.uk/nextmonth